To my husband, Peter, who
has such faith in me.

Prologue

Summer 1902 – Gilbert

Even this lowly bit of waste ground has took against him. Let go for a lifetime, baked by the summer heat, it's nigh on brick hard. But he daresn't go back for the pickaxe, not now – they'd want to know why.

Brambles tear at his skin, work their prickles in deep but he gives them no mind. Pain is the price of it, and 'tis nothing to the pain inside where she's been tore away, where he's all broke and bleeding. But their snaky roots are tough as old Harry. He uses the spade and his hurt and his hate and the ache in his head, to chop and prise, killing them, killing *him* for what he did...

He swipes at the sweat running into his eyes, as the black thunder clouds press down, squeezing the breath from the earth, leaving no breeze as respite.

The only sound is the jab, jab, jab of the fork. It's too hot even for the birds to sing and he can't hardly hear the river on the other side of the fence. No splash or ripple of ducks or boats. Water's down so low the barges hardly have passing room. He can smell it though. It's rank. And the gnats and flies down this end of the garden are bothersome. Buzzing, biting, like they know he shouldn't be doing this.

Don't think, just dig. Bend and dig. Get it over.

The crusty topsoil's giving at last, letting him deeper into the clay, and deeper still. Oh, my darling. This is the end for me, too, the very end.

1

What was that…? Someone there? His insides clump. His throat constricts. He straightens, cuffing the string of snot and sweat.

'Cheer up, young'un, it may never 'appen!'

Tears spring again to his eyes. You say! He could laugh if he wasn't dying inside. He drags the grief of what *has* happened back through his nose.

'Samuel?' he manages, casual like, while his heart's burning a hole in his chest. Damn, he'd thought they'd all knocked off next door. What if he spots the bundle behind the bush? What if he guesses?

There's a clank as a watering can is set down on paving and the old jaw-me-dead plonks his meaty forearms on the top of the fence, settling in for a chinwag.

'Doing for they brambles, eh? They do go deep. Got 'em over 'ere, an' all. Gonna try a drop o' that there weedkiller on ourn. Caustic. Save all that digging.'

A smile, a smile for God's sake. His face has forgotten how. Ye can do it. And think. He'll expect all the bushes cleared be morning.

'Mistress don't hold wi' poison, Samuel, and new trees to be planted.' He puts on her voice. '"Don't take them brambles all the way back, boy," says she. "Leave some to keep out trespassers."'

'Them swine…' The fat neck stretches with fellow feeling. 'Berberis, we got. Can't do no better than berberis. Keep an army out. Get they thorns in your backside, you'll know it. Burgle us blind else, they river trash.'

Blessed silence. He tries to breathe. It lasts all of ten seconds.

'Trees, eh? What ye got this time? Summat from China?'

He shrugs. 'Likely. Needs a big 'ole, that I do know, Samuel. She'll change her mind, like as not. Want it put up beside the house, next, or down by the rose garden, knowing her.' Oh God, his chin's trembling. Just don't. 'Well, best get on. Reckon there's a storm brewing…'

'Sooner you than me, young un.' He mops his red face with a

sorry-looking hanky. 'What a scorcher! Won't be getting much sleep the night, that I do know.'

He jerks his chin in unspoken agreement, continues digging. He won't sleep ever again.

All's quiet. Have 'e gone?

'Well, reckon I'll leave ye to it then, boy.'

At last. ''Night, Samuel,' he says hopefully.

'Best be off. She'll have us tea ready.'

He waits to hear the old boy trudging reluctantly up the path before unstopping his canteen and swallowing a mouthful of ale. Flat and tepid. But it's wet.

* * *

He'd known all his life she was the girl for him.

When he'd told Ma, years back, he were going to marry Nellie Redfern, she reckoned he were pulling her leg. 'What's that?' Then she'd tipped back her head, sweaty black hair sticking to her brow, and she'd laughed, showing all the gaps and the red of her mouth. She'd laughed like she'd never heard such a joke in all her born days, laughed 'til her ribs ached.

At the end she were lifting her specs and wiping away her tears, shaking her head all the while. 'Oh, Gil,' she said, still wheezing and coughing. 'Ye'll be the death o' me!'

'It's no joke, Ma.'

She moved the glasses down her nose, the better to study him. 'Marry a *Redfern*? Says who!'

'Says I. Says she an' all. I won't have another, Ma, nor her neither.'

'That'll be the day!'

'Just soon as we'm grown.'

'Listen to it, will ye…' she invited anyone within hearing, though they were alone in the steaming scullery. 'Wait 'til I tell your Pa. He'll die laughing.'

3

'I mean it, Ma!'

At that, the last trace of merriment slipped from her face. 'I mean it an' all, Gilbert Blackett,' her mouth now a tight knot of anger, her flinty eyes sparking. With hands that were still wet and wrinkled from rinsing she laid hold of him and shook him and shook him 'til his sight blurred and his nose ran. 'You get that dappy notion out your head right now, young Gil. Old Redfern'll have your guts for garters – mine and your Dad's, besides – he gets wind o' your nonsense. Nellie's outa your league, my lad, always was, always will be, you 'ear? Right? *Right?* she'd repeated. Another shake nearly separated his head from his spindly twelve-year-old neck and he'd had to nod compliance or risk losing it. She glared at him for a few moments longer, figuring whether her words had gone in, then released him and, turning, plunged her hands back into the blue rinse-water, pulled out a Sunday shirt, and wrung it like a chicken's neck. 'This time next year,' she advised him, slinging the white corkscrew into the bowl for the mangle, 'that young miss won' touch ye with a bargepole, mark my words.'

He did. He marked them, knowing they weren't true. From now on they'd have to be more careful, the two of them. There'd be no more reading books on the back step or kicking a ball around the yards. They'd have to become secretive and stealthy.

So, whenever they went up the market – Nellie and her maid, Maria – Nellie would give Maria the slip, soon as she could and meet him round the back of the newspaper stand, or at the tea stall, or in the General Store. And she'd tear into poor Maria when she found her, maybe an hour later.

'*You lost me!*' she'd protest, eyes flashing, 'I looked for you everywhere!'

'Oh, Miss Nellie, boot's on the other foot, an' you know it. You'll be the death o' me, your pa finds out what you two are up to.'

'Well, I won't tell him, if you won't.'

They'd take their time coming home from school or choir

4

practice, going hand-in-hand, the long way through the fields or the woods or by the reservoir, watching the hares leaping or the birds flocking and feeding, or picking buttercups.

It came to a head the time Gil's big brother, Wilf, found them together, learning some poem under the hay cart. Miss Prescott was testing them on it in the morning. And maybe Nellie thumped him when he got it wrong and maybe it developed into a tit-for-tat, a free-for-all, and maybe Nellie squealed and maybe she didn't, but Wilf chose to make a big thing of it. He dragged Gil out by his bare feet, with Nellie screaming at him to 'Let go, leave him alone, don't hit him, you bully!' But Wilf wouldn't stop and by the time they reached home, Gil had a bloody nose and a black eye and bruises all over, which Ma added to when she got to hear of it.

'Didn't I tell ye?' *(Smack!)* 'Didn't I say to leave that girl alone.' *(Slap! Thump!)* 'Damn ye, young Gil, it 'ad to be that one, didn't it? Your Dad'll lose his job, old Redfern gets wind of it.' *(Wallop!)* 'An' it'll be your fault, ye dirty little sod. Your fault, you 'ear, punching above ye weight!'

Nellie had run off in a state but that hadn't stopped her father belting her when he finally found her in the stables. And of course, it was all round the village quicker 'n spit – Nellie Redfern and young Gil Blackett, at it like rabbits.

Dad didn't lose his job, as it happened. The doctor was brought into it and he reckoned there was no harm done. Whatever had been going on – with hay in their hair and her skirts up to her bloomers – Wilf had got there in time. And they were only youngsters, when all was said and done, him just out of short britches and starting an apprenticeship, soon as like, up the river somewhere.

Next they knew she were being sent away to that posh school up Ipswich. Redfern put it about that it was all part of his plan. Daughters of businessmen had to learn French and drawing and how to waltz and how to sing and play the piano and how to act like a lady, in order to be a credit to their rich husbands. They wrote to each other but they didn't really need letters. They were connected by an invisible chain in their chests that broke last night, like a leg or an arm, and it hurt to hell and would never quite heal.

Nearly done, now, Nell. Just spreading the leftover dirt around and about, my love, so's no one knows you'm down there. Rain in the air. At last, eh? Garden's choking o' thirst. It'll help tamp it down, make it all of a piece. Before the brambles grow back over.

Oh, Nellie, love, ye don't deserve a burying under three foot of clay, down in some corner of Ardmore's estate without any marker, like some old cat. Ye don't deserve to die and I don't deserve to miss ye like I do. And only the thunder rolling about to mark your passing, and the wind getting up, scuffing the leaves, and clobbering the back fence, making it clatter... Sleep well.

One

1903

They heard the screams but took them for high spirits. 'Lord...' He winced as his ears rang. 'That girl and her shrieking! She could crack glass.' He regarded his tankard with a frown. It was still in one piece and he drained it. Setting it down on the rickety table he wiped the beer suds from his lips and returned to his drawing.

'It's all for show, Archie,' said Polly, marking her place in the book with an old negative. 'She doesn't want them knowing how tough she really is.' His mouth twisted in doubt. It was the toughness that was for show. Get past that and you'd find a soft centre.

'She's a bit young for all that shy-iking, isn't she?'

'Thirteen going on thirty.'

He frowned. 'Do you think she's all right? The boys aren't too boisterous for her?'

'Are you joking? If anyone's in danger it's certainly not your daughter. I'd be more concerned for Bertie and Sid. She could eat them alive.'

He still wasn't sure. Orphaned at an early age, Clara now lived in Camden with her grandparents, with Archie stepping in once or twice a week to give the old people a break. Today, he had invited the Reeves's three grandchildren along as company. It used to be the little 'copper-nob', Lilian Steggles, who went everywhere with them, but since she wasn't around… He sighed. How everyone missed the little sauce-box, that bright face, that tireless energy. Polly often accused him of being over-protective of his daughter but that just showed you – poor Lilian – something must have been said or not said to make her take off into the blue, like that. You couldn't be too careful.

Clara had long outgrown summer games of hide-and-seek and French cricket with him and Polly, and sketching and reading would only hold her attention for so long. She preferred to be larking about with youngsters her own age and the publican's progeny seemed to be at a loose end so … Bertha had been more than grateful. 'Don't get me started!' she'd groaned, her chins quivering. 'Running me ragged, they are! Like I don't 'ave enough to do wiv 'is lordship swanning off down his precious Palace all day, every day – *she* goes an' chooses now to go into labour! How am I expected to mind this lot and run the blooming pub all on me tod? Eh?' Nevertheless, she'd had time to sort out swimming costumes and towels for them all and make a dozen sandwiches.

They were safe enough, he knew, diving off the bank, slipping through the water as if they had fins and tails, in and out of the weeds and willow roots, keeping cool. They were all swimmers now, even young Sid, kicking up his feet and furiously paddling his arms. If he got into trouble Clara could save him.

Much as he loved doing so, it was thirsty work, just sitting here, drawing Polly's likeness, on the hottest day of the year so far. He'd taken off his collar and tie, rolled up his shirtsleeves and still his shirt was sticking to him. His pencil was slippery, his page curling at the corners, and his fingers were black where he'd smudged tones into her elfin bone structure and marked the criss-cross shadow of her straw hat where it fell across her face. He spat on his handkerchief and cleaned his hands of the worst of the graphite before picking up the pencil again and adding a few damp curling tendrils along her hairline, taking out bright highlights from her pearly-grey irises with his rubber. At least, they were pearly grey, now. They could change to turquoise or navy blue depending on her mood. 'That'll do,' he said, flipping his pad shut.

She read his mind. 'Another, Archie? No, no, I'll get these.' As her lacy sleeve emerged from her picnic bag with purse in hand, he slid off the bench, hooking up his empty tankard to take to the bar, pocketing Polly's proffered florin without argument. It did no good: she was earning, she insisted; she would always pay her way.

Her nodding bonnet alerted him, now, to a passing barge, painted in red, green and white: a beautiful thing, reflected in the water, making no sound as it slid past. He knew what she was suggesting but he'd drawn and painted so many of these working river vessels in his time, one missed sketch wouldn't kill him, and pencil and paper didn't really do them justice.

'Lovely day!' she called out, lifting her sunshade and raising the dregs of her port and lemon to the sweating bargee on the towpath opposite.

The man's grumbling 'All right for some!' was put on. He was happy enough. Jingling brasses and harness echoed cool and dank as the great horse plodded into the deep shadow of the railway bridge.

'Swop you, any day,' Archie offered from their side of the river. 'School holidays, eh?'

The bargee turned his head to see the children playing in the water and raised his chin in sympathy, his gesture implying *'rather-you-than-me-chum!'*

The barge was lying low in the water, weighed down by one bulky cargo under tarpaulins and another lounging in a chair on the deck: his wife wearing a man's trilby and squinting at a row of knitting. As they watched, a small dog, alerted by the children's shrieks, began barking and snarling and jumping frenziedly. Any minute now it would be up the side of the boat and joining them in the water. The woman grabbed its collar and then she, too, began shouting, growing redder in the face than her several pots of geraniums, leaning over the side and pointing at something with a knitting needle.

'What?' Archie yelled, screwing up his face and cupping his ear. He couldn't make out what she was saying over the dog's racket. A fuss about the children, was it? Oh, for heaven's sake, they had as much right in the water as the barge. These boat people thought they owned the river. Setting down his flagon, he flexed his fingers ready to defend his charges, if needs be, and crossed the landing stage to the water's edge. He wasn't one for bare-knuckle fighting – but he was no stranger to it. He and his friend, Stanley Beckett, had been known to go a couple of rounds at the gym.

Where were they, anyhow? He could hear their voices and their splashing but they weren't where he'd left them when he had come in to get changed and have a beer. Further along yet, past the willow tree. Damn and blast, he'd told them to stay this side of it.

The shrieking had altered in pitch. As he drew nearer, the cries that now reached him were tempered with nervous giggles. 'Go on then, I dare you!' and more screams split the air before Bertie's newly broken voice croaked, 'Mister Price, come quick!' Oh God, he thought, breaking into a run, was someone in trouble? He couldn't see them. He couldn't –

'Sid!' he yelled as he ran along the bank, 'Clara! Where the blue blazes are you?'

'Over here, Pops!'

So they were, waving skinny arms around a patch of reeds growing out of the water midstream, twenty yards away. As far as he could make out it was a poor excuse for an island, a ten foot sliver of silt thrown up by the passage of barges on either side, like earth thrown up by the plough, just wide enough to support a couple of coots' nests, a snaggle of weeds and an old tin can or two. Clinging to an overhanging branch, his boots sliding in the greasy mud, he counted two bare heads and two wearing those ghastly frilly mop hats. Blue-cold lips in bone-white faces gave the lie to eyes that were brimming with excitement and devilry. 'What are you playing at?' he barked, his relief hardening instantly to irritation. Blasted kids.

But their yelling contained a sense of urgency though he couldn't make out the words. They pointed at the rushes. What was it? What had they found? Squinting, he caught glimpses of what looked suspiciously like a small rotting carcase, something in which a buzz of bluebottles seemed very interested.

'Eh? What is it? *What!*' It was no good. With them all shouting at once, he only caught the stray word: '*dead … sick … drownded …*' but mostly '*Dead.*'

'One at a time, please. Clara, you tell me.'

'It's some old head, Pops!'

'Eeyagh!' someone else put in, expressively. 'An' there's all these flies!'

But he could see it now, half-hidden in the rushes. The skull of a large animal – or was it – was it *human*?

'Maudie found it, Mister Price! She was sick!'

'Damn near bust a gut, screaming!'

'Language, Bertie…'

'The rest of it's down on the bottom – Clarrie 'n' me went for a look-see. All these bones sticking up outa the mud, all green and slimy an' – '

'It ain't got no eyeballs, Mister Price,' young Sid said, with relish. 'Reckon the fishes ate 'em, pike or eels.'

'Rats, more like…' said Bertie, with adolescent wisdom. 'Or crows.'

'She nigh on drownded, Maudie did!' said his small brother, gleefully, 'and then she puked up in the water.'

'Shall I fetch it out, Mister Price – the skull?'

'Sid whacked it, Mister Price,' said Bertie, 'wiv a stick! An' its teef fell out!'

'I never! I just give it a poke.'

The little Reeves girl was snivelling now that an adult had arrived to witness her distress.

'Don't touch it, any of you! I want you all out of there, right now! You, too, Bertie. Now! Come on, hurry up.' Lord, the water

11

would be polluted. What if they caught cholera or typhoid or something? The smell alone was enough to make you gag. 'Give us your hand, Maudie. Up we come! Now, now, no need for tears. Clara's not crying, is she? You're not hurt, are you? Maudie? Here, blow your nose … Right, now you go and find Polly and let me deal with this. I'll have to fetch the police, I suppose.'

Lord, and this had been such a good idea, this swimming trip to mark the end of the holidays. A change from the baths and its saturating smell of chlorine. Poor kids. What a rotten memory to take back to school. *And what did you do in the holidays, Sid? I found a dead body in the river.* So long as they didn't have to illustrate it!

He pocketed his handkerchief, now unusable, and saw the child onto the path that led to Polly. But Clara was his real concern. She'd suffered enough fear and death in her young life. And she brooded. He studied her now as she trod water, waiting her turn to be hauled out. She was very pale; her lashes were wet and he suspected tears weren't far away. He hoped it wasn't damaging, this new encounter with horror, that it wouldn't cause her lasting problems. As he helped her up onto the muddy bank, he was aware of the swimwear dripping, sagging, moulding itself to the slight mounds of her chest, clinging to her waist, the skirt wrapping itself around her hips, her knees. Lord, when did this start happening? This lengthening of limbs, this shaping? With her hair up, bundled away inside her bathing cap he had an intimation of the woman she would become. He looked away, frowning. Hopefully, her grandmother was aware of this, all this change…

* * *

The children – heroes of the hour – shivered in their wet towels. The tale they told chilled the blood and turned the stomach – of stinking bones and matted hair, with worms and rotting flesh thrown in for good measure. With a proud flourish, the landlord of the Pride of Lea summoned the girl at the exchange on his new telephone and asked to be put through to the police station. By the time the children were dried and dressed, drinking tea with three sugars for shock, a cart was disgorging a gang of policemen who had arrived in a flurry of black uniforms and helmets and dust, their horses snorting and foam-flecked from the mad dash from Forest Road. Ahead of them all strode Detective Inspector Frank Tyrell, flicking smuts off his light summer civvies, and his assistant, DS Stanley Beckett, who stood apple-cheeked and beaming, in the sun, 'Well, look who it ain't!'

'Archie! Boyo! Might'a guessed you'd be in the thick of it. As if I ain't got enough to do, wivout bleeding skellingtons in the river! Oh, Miss Polly – begging yours – never saw you, ducks! What a turn-up, eh? 'Ere –,' he had a thought, 'you wouldn't have your camera on you? I might just ask you to do the honours on this one if you've got the stomach for it.'

Frank directed operations. Three constables were sent to rope off the scene and to halt oncoming river traffic – unsure yet what they were dealing with: an accidental drowning or something more sinister – while two more stripped off in the back room and put on diving suits. 'Oo-er!' murmured the onlookers, their eyes wide with astonishment as monsters clumped out of the pub in heavy boots, armed with spades and rakes, sieves and screw-on helmets. A skiff was commandeered for Polly and anyone requiring dry passage to the island, though it wasn't far: a couple of strokes and they were there. The divers simply jumped in backwards off the landing stage to sink in a flurry of bubbles. You could just see the tops of their helmets as they worked. Another boat was used to receive any nastiness that was dredged up. It was a slow business. The water grew murky and it was a wonder they could see anything down there at all. The rubber-necking pub clientele certainly couldn't. What's more, they were made to stand well away from the boats when, eventually, they tied up, to allow Tyrell and Beckett to sort through the muddy findings. Then the uniforms gently shepherded the children into the saloon bar, never mind their tender years. Their elders and betters, rudely ejected from their preferred watering hole, were compensated with glimpses of interesting wet sacks as they were loaded onto the police cart, the knobs and bulges providing food for speculation and fuel for nightmares.

Archie hoped that his ward was made of sterner stuff and that her deep frown, as she twisted her wet pigtail between her fingers and solemnly regarded the comings and goings through the pub window, was evidence of an academic interest only. Kidnapped at two, orphaned by five, she'd already had more trauma in her life than most adults ever knew.

Having had sole care of her after her mother, his darling wife, Lizzie died, Archie would never forget the little girl sobbing herself to sleep in his arms, and then waking and her eyes dulling as a new day of loss dawned. He recalled having to change her bed sheets constantly and trying to tempt her to eat – 'just a spoonful, lambkins.' He had devoted himself to her, swallowing his own tears and distracting her with books, making up stories, illustrating them with friendly creatures either drawn or made from the clay in Lizzie's pottery, nursing her back to something like normality. So it was that, each supporting the other, the child and the man had crawled out of that deepest pit of grief, Archie to find that months of inactivity had cleaned him out money-wise. For Clara's sake alone it was crucial that he stop painting obsessive images of her mother and paint art that sold. That, sadly, could only be accomplished without the constant demands and distraction of a clinging but adorable child. In Archie's eyes she had inherited the best qualities of both her parents: Lizzie's good looks and John's temperament – the old John, the one who had been Archie's best friend before laudanum stole him away. Even now, ten years after her father's death, a gesture would bring the man to life; a turn of her head, so like Lizzie's, would bring tears to his eyes. But needs must and, although it had broken his heart to let her go, he had seen Clara celebrate her fifth birthday in her grandparents' house, with a tea party attended by small schoolfriends bearing gifts; his mother-in-law had made a birthday cake and there were games of *Squeak Piggy Squeak* and *Blind Man's Buff*. Lizzie's father, Vic, a lecturer in fine arts at Camden College, soon realised that the little girl had the makings of an artist: her eye for detail, her clever fingers – she just needed direction. And Ivy Grant found in Clara a heaven-sent replacement for her daughter. Both spoiled her to death. (A kitten, dear? Of course. Dolls' house? No problem. Paper, paints, clay? Potter's wheel, kiln? An arm and a leg? Left or right?)

She attended school in Camden and, though the bond between them was as strong as ever, Archie saw her just twice a week during term time, if more frequently during the holidays. It was not enough but it gave him a chance to put money in the bank.

The divers went down one last time when the water had cleared a little, checking to see if there was anything they'd missed – stray bones or rings or teeth.

Meantime, in the saloon bar, Frank asked questions: who had seen what and where? Polly had her arms around Maud ready to give her a hug of encouragement when it was her turn to be interrogated.

'You never touched nothing?'

'Of course not,' said Polly on the child's behalf. 'They were frightened out of their wits, weren't you, Maud?' Wide-eyed, the ten-year-old nodded her assent.

Bertie could be relied upon to betray his brother. 'On'y whacked it wiv a stick, di'n't 'e?' he sighed, the older and more sensible sibling.

Hardly surprising, Archie pointed out – young Sid was squeamish. You hit out at things you didn't understand. Unlike Clara, he had never made friends with worms and snails, never drawn spiders or earwigs, never modelled beetles in clay or painted the fired pieces with glaze. For him, the sight of bluebottle maggots feasting on what had been a human face was just too much.

'Archie, mate, just pipe down, would you? Let the kids tell me in their own words. And Miss Polly – would you mind…?'

Oh, that was hard. So, the adults were forced to listen with buttoned lips as, between them, the children told the tale of a swimming spree that had ended horribly. Maudie had been intrigued by the promise of a coot's nest on that scrubby ribbon of land. She'd seen the mother bird hop out of the water with worms in her beak; she'd heard the cheeping of the chicks and had swum over for a better look. When something like blanket weed, all slick and slimy, wrapped around her legs and pulled her under she'd thought she was done for. The scream in her throat had been plugged with water and she might well have come to a sorry end if her kicking hadn't freed her. The clutching, clinging fronds had disintegrated on impact, proving to be the rotting cloth of a woman's dress. Panic impelled the child upwards, and she'd found herself breaking the surface, choking, spluttering, dragging air into her lungs, only to come face to face with a human skull in the last stages of decomposition, perched high, if not dry, and anchored by reeds growing through an eye socket. That was when she had brought up her cheese and pickle sandwiches. On hearing her screams, her playmates had swum over to *'Ave a look-see,'* raising the hullabaloo that had brought Archie running.

The police cart eventually headed back to town, taking every jot and tittle of evidence with them but the joy had gone out of the day. The children refused to go back into polluted water (despite Archie's assurances that Maudie's vomit had been washed down to the Thames by now). Instead, they hung around outside the pub, hot and irritable, while Archie and Polly picked over the bones, as it were, with the other customers.

What d'you reckon, was she a suicide? It had to be a woman, didn't it, with the skirts and the long hair?

Or had she fallen in the river by accident, drunk or mad? Had she missed her footing on a boat or slid down the slippery bank and, unable to swim, weighed down by her sodden clothes, had she drowned, drifting downriver towards the Pride of Lea where she'd become trapped in the rushes and roots of that small island?

'Nah.' Bertha's namesake, her pubescent grandson, suddenly appeared at Archie's side. ''Er ole man done 'er in, dinne?' he rasped. 'They 'ad a barney an' 'e done 'er in. Then 'e chucked 'er in the drink. Orf the railway bridge, I reckon.'

Privately, Archie thought Bertie was probably onto something but that he was relishing the situation a little too happily for his own good. Clara, sitting beside Polly to have her hair re-braided, was looking decidedly peaky. He hoped she hadn't swallowed any of the water. Changed out of her bathing costume into her dress and pinafore, her dark hair freed from that cap, she looked more like her old self, if a little tight-lipped. She'd get over it, he thought briskly – he just had to get her back home to food and normality.

They piled into the trap quietly, for once, and he geed up the mule. Half an hour across the marshes and they'd be home.

'Poor creature,' muttered Polly, her words juddering over the ruts.

'Pops,' Clara began, 'you don't think–?'

'Mmm?'

'You don't think it could be Lilian?'

Oh God. Is that what she'd been worrying about? He shook his head fiercely. 'No, never!'

Though now he came to think about it … No, of course not! Clara's friend, Lilian, the daughter of market-traders at the bottom of the High Street, had gone missing from home almost a month back. For the first time since the old Queen's passing the High Street had been silent and empty on a market day. Everyone in Walthamstow's famous mile, he and Polly included, had shut up shop that last Saturday in July and joined the long line of searchers sifting the forest floor, leaf by leaf, twig by twig, for clues. All to no avail.

The police had quizzed her parents, Izzy and Wilf Steggles, who could think of no earthly reason why Lilian would run off. She wanted for nothing; she loved school and had a string of good friends. She was as fit as a flea – well, she would be with all that swimming! She was all set to be an Olympics champion, didn't you know? Oh yes, Miss Smith, her coach, had said that the 1908 games would include ladies' swimming for the first time and their Lil would be in it! There'd been a bit of a bull and a cow, of course, between her and her old man but it hadn't meant nothing – they'd had set-tos before, plenty of them.

What was it about, the row?

Oh, just some girly silliness. Showing off, that's all it was. Getting uppity. Answering back. The officers nodded knowingly. They'd all had a taste of Lilian's high spirits. Pure swank – had to be. As if she really wanted to give up swimming – she was so good at it. Had they said she was going to be a contender in the next…? Oh, right. So, why'd she run off? Well, neither Wilf nor Izzy could make head or tail of it. See all her medals and cups on the sideboard! And sustificates – the drawer was full of 'em. She was going to make them so proud. So, when she'd flounced out of the house that night, they'd fully expected her to go around the block a few times and come back when she'd calmed down. 'I mean,' said Izzy, 'girls that age, they're always coming the old acid, ain't they?'

But she hadn't come back.

Archie rather suspected the girl had been lured away by a rival club or coach. Clara said there'd been some bad feeling between Lilian and Miss Smith, some sort of falling out, she thought. If Lilian was fed up with Smithy, she'd be open to offers. And Clara had said that Lil had behaved very oddly when she'd seen her last. Like she had secrets.

No, he wasn't too worried about little Miss Steggles. She had her head firmly screwed on – she'd probably struck a hard bargain with her new managers, and it was in their interest, of course, to keep her happy, well fed, well looked after. But her disappearance had hit his daughter hard. They'd been good friends.

He explained, without being too ghoulish he hoped, that Lilian had only been missing a few weeks and, if she had been killed – which was highly unlikely – her flesh wouldn't have deteriorated to that degree in such a short time. 'I mean, that body must've been in the water a long while – months and months.'

She sagged. 'I knew that really – I was just checking.' She frowned. 'I expect she's well away by now. Probably too busy to write…'

Clara did not share her adoptive father's theory about Lilian's disappearance. Her friend was true blue loyal, she insisted. Smithy may have been a hard taskmaster but she got results and Lil knew that. She would never have betrayed her no matter how hard-pressed she was. She had been relying on swimming as a means of escaping life on the market stall. If a falling out with Smithy had put paid to that, she might have seen running away to find employment as a cleaner, or a maid in some big house, as her only option. Clara hoped she would soon repent her hasty actions and come home, safe and sound.

'Let's hope so,' muttered Polly.

'Our Mum packs a bag for Bertie when 'e says 'e's leaving 'ome. Gives 'im a penny for the 'bus an' all.'

'Oh, Maudie…' It was a relief to laugh.

Only Clara didn't seem to find it funny. 'Will Uncle Frank find out what happened to her?'

'Who – Lilian?'

'No, the dead one.'

'Oh, bound to,' he said cheerfully.

'What will they do to her murderer?'

'String 'im up,' said Bertie.

'We don't know she was killed,' Polly reasoned. 'She might just have fallen in and drowned.'

'And nobody knew to this day,' said Bertie in a lugubrious voice, 'on'y the fishes see 'er moulderin' away…' He broke into a mournful song. *'The worms crawled in and the worms crawled out…'*

'Bertie, for the love of God!'

But Polly's plea came too late. The children seized on the gloom of the situation and wallowed in it, their faces closing like flowers at dusk. In vain, Archie and Polly tried to lift the mood, pointing to a dog chasing a rabbit, a cow in a field, chickens in the road, a cloud that looked like a castle. At the bottom of the High Street, a solution presented itself.

'Who's for a penn'orth o' chips, eh? Bertie? Sid?' Archie stopped the cart, jumped down and entered the crowded shop, returning with a fat newspaper parcel, reeking seductively of fat and vinegar. Nostrils flared and the pink tips of tongues appeared and somehow, despite their poor appetites and dark thoughts, the newspaper was empty, bar a smear of grease, by the time they reached home.

And, when Bertha appeared at the door of the public bar, shading her eyes against the sunset, Maudie was the first to jump down from the cart and barrel across the road into the plump apron, yelling, 'Nan, Nan, you'll never guess what!'

Two

Shadows at the top of the enormous canvas made for eye-strain and it was as hot as hell. Neither the much-vaunted electric lighting nor the gas backup was working yet and painting likenesses by naphtha flares was a nightmare. Trying to get your subjects looking natural, interacting normally was hard enough when all you had to work from were publicity photos; having to squint and blink away a mist of sweat made it doubly difficult. Like all the other workmen in Percy's Palace he had stripped off his shirt and was working barefoot. With a handkerchief knotted over his hair he could have been a day tripper on Southend beach, about to dip a toe into the muddy brine. He wished it were so – he'd rather be anywhere than this close to an ornate ceiling that seemed to melt and boil in the rising heat. This was no holiday. Even Michelangelo, painting the Sistine Chapel in Rome, was not so tormented. Not that Archie was on his back with wet plaster and paint dripping onto his face but, with the racket of hammering and sawing and the labourers' once-funny banter and bawdy songs in his ears, he was pushed to the limit.

He'd been up on the scaffolding since early morning, trying to catch something of Mickey Markov's smart-alecky manner while, at the same time, attempting to stave off his dummy's creepiness. The ventriloquist probably wouldn't have appreciated being relegated to the back row of a multiple portrait of his peers but he was unlikely ever to see it. Percy had sworn never to have him on the bill again. Clearly he'd been ill or three sheets to the wind, swearing at his wooden sidekick, accusing it of forcing him to do things against his will. *'You made me do it – you made me – you said!'* It wasn't funny and the audience began to fidget. And when Algie, too, began to hiccup and mumble, when eventually those mechanical lips ceased their clacking and the painted eyes slid hopelessly from side to side in their wooden sockets, the saloon bar audience had been merciless. Orange peel and messier missiles had landed on the stage and catcalls and whistles had accompanied rhythmic stamping. Percy Reeves, the owner, had brought the curtain down before things had got really out of hand, and wheeled the unhappy pair off the stage. Luckily a few decent acts followed – a barbershop quartet and some acrobats – or he would have had to give the patrons their money back.

A multitude of music hall stars in one painting was a mistake; Archie had known that even before he'd primed the thing. The Old Masters seemed to have managed composite portraits to everybody's satisfaction (Botticelli had even dared to paint himself among the infant Christ's adoring Magi and got away with it), but perhaps their sitters were happy simply to have their faces recorded for posterity. Variety artistes wanted more. They each wanted to be in the spotlight. But Percy wouldn't wear it. Veins had stood out on his greasy forehead, his eyes had flamed red and spittle flew as his blood vessels prepared to burst.

'Archie Price, you – you *dare…!* All these years you been givin' me grief. "*Oh Percy, Percy, oh don't forget you promised me…*"' But there the mimicry stopped and harsh scorn took over. 'The cream of British music hall, you said, all in the one place. Be a real winner, you said. Bring the customers pouring in, you said. What's changed your mind? You too big for us now you got paintings up London?'

That was uncalled for. Percy had been only too happy to squire Bertha around the Royal Academy preview, in her rabbit fur tippet and fake pearls, the two of them boasting to anyone who'd listen about the portraits he'd done of them, for free, that were now hanging in the bar alongside Bertha's angels and spiritualist texts. What about his babysitting the busy couple's grandchildren, taking them out on jollies with Clara? Didn't that count for anything? It wasn't his fault they'd come face to face with a corpse! He frowned reflectively and tried to mix a warmer black for the dummy's hair: something to alleviate the chill of that painted grin.

Bertha had no call to say what she had: *'Neglecting the kids whiles you and Polly goes off canoodling … Oh yeah, no need to tell me what you two was a-doing of.'*

It was all in her head. He counted himself lucky to have Polly around as his best friend, someone he trusted; someone he could confide in without fear of censure. But, sad to say, that was as far as it went.

'Don't! Don't!' she'd moaned, pushing him away, after that Christmas Eve party, when too much drink had clouded their judgement if not their senses and he'd finally got her into bed. She'd seemed as aroused as him, tearing the nightshirt from his back, kissing and biting, moaning with desire, digging her nails into his skin, winding her legs around him … But, suddenly, she'd stopped dead before extricating herself, a look of sheer misery on her face. 'I can't do this, Archie. I'm so sorry,' she said, dissolving into tears. He'd rolled away in confusion, attempting to get himself under control.

'It's not you, Archie, it's not!' she sobbed. 'I want to, I do, but I can't – can't let you in. I keep – keep seeing Fred, remembering how he – what he did to me – and I just feel – I just feel so dirty.'

'What! You mean, you think he might have passed on some disease?'

'No – that's not it. Oh, Archie, I'm so sorry!'

He'd thought she'd have got over her qualms years ago, but she clearly hadn't. 'God, Polly!' He gritted his teeth, for fear of saying something cruel, and she'd wept even harder, turning her head away. 'It's all right, sweetheart, it's all right, love,' he'd soothed, smearing her tears away, knowing it wasn't all right and that he felt like howling, a beaten dog.

She had been so wretched that night, crying, pulling at her hair, punching the pillows in sorrow and frustration, he had been afraid to leave her lest she really did herself harm. Rather than go back to his lodgings he had stayed in the chair at her bedside, holding her hands to stop her biting them, trying to soothe her, comfort her, like a parent with a sick child.

God, he hated her brother, not dead enough, clearly. Taken in off the streets by the Porters, before Polly was born, and adopted, he had never settled down to family life. He continued to obey his baser instincts and had used and abused his little sister again and again. For nearly twenty years until his death, she had been sex slave and skivvy to a warped, cruel man.

'I hate being like this, Archie, letting you down,' she'd said next morning when she awoke and found him there, still holding her hand, 'I've told you before, I'm damaged goods.'

'God, Polly, I'm more likely to have a disease than…'

'No, it's not that. I had Effie check me over, years ago, and there's nothing – nothing like that. I think what stops me from – you know – giving myself to you is some sort of hysteria.' She stroked his cheek, 'Much as I love you I'll never be the woman you want, never a wife, not a proper one. I couldn't give you children for a start. In all the years Fred did what he did I never fell pregnant so that tells you, doesn't it? Being used as a punchbag and a – and a *receptacle* doesn't do much for your insides, I suppose. He put paid to any hope there.' She gazed at him imploringly. 'Find someone else, Archie. I'll just make you miserable.'

'And I'll be miserable without you,' he'd replied. 'Marry me, Polly. We need each other. We do. And if you can't face intimacy, that's all right. Just so long as I can see you every day, talk to you, love you. There's more to life and love than sex. And I have Clara. I don't need any more children.'

'Kindly meant, but no, my boy, I won't marry you. We'll be

friends always, of course we will. But as for celibacy, good God, you'd shrivel up and die! You're a passionate man. You have sexual needs and dozens of adoring women just aching to get you into bed. Though be careful. You don't want to be cut down in your prime by … you know, the clap.'

'Poll-eeee!' he winced. In fact, as soon as he'd announced he was going to London to become an artist his father had warned him of the dangers of loose women and advised him to take precautions and have regular health checks. So far so good.

She grinned. 'As one friend to another,' she said.

'Is that what's stopping you?'

'It wouldn't, my love – I assure you. We could both rot together. Oh, don't look so sad. Come here.'

He held her tight, moving away when closeness threatened to betray him.

'Besides,' she said, surfacing, 'with the shop and my own bank account, I'll wager I'm happier than many a married woman. Just think, the minute I hitched up to you, what's mine would become yours.'

He was under no illusions about her independent spirit. It was part of her attraction. She'd given up her shop in Chelmsford in order to concentrate on the one across the road from him, and refused to employ a manager or even an assistant. And it was more than his life was worth to interfere or make suggestions. As he'd told her that Christmas morning, holding up his hands in defence, he didn't want any part of her shop, didn't have time for it and, as she'd probably noticed, he had no head for business. The shop would always be hers *and* any money she made. He would never take advantage of her no matter what the law said.

She simply raised an eyebrow. 'We'll see. Move now, Arch, I must get up and put the chicken in the oven. And you've your dad's painting to finish. You want it dry in time for his birthday, don't you? Ooh, my head. I'm never going to drink again! Happy Christmas, by the way!'

Sighing, he'd made his way through her studio, out of her shop and across the High Street to his own front door. The gulf between them was insurmountable, it seemed.

Her shop window was presently given over to photographs of women favouring the new looser, uncorseted style of dress. Dotted among her own informal studies of local women were more famous writers, poets and artists: people like Virginia Woolf and Vanessa Bell, May Morris, Isadora Duncan, and the actress Mrs Patrick Campbell. The centrepiece was an eye-catching, loose and silky cream outfit, strung with a sash bearing the motto *'Freedom from Tyranny'*. On a card leaning against a discarded corpse-like corset, she'd written, *'Ladies, why suffer to be beautiful? Ditch the whalebone and steel and breathe!'*

From behind his easel, he found it interesting to see who stopped to browse, who to nod their approval, and who to tut-tut and shake their heads. With his window open he caught outraged comments on the breeze: *'All very well for those bluestockings but I wouldn't feel right without my stays.' 'Votes for Women, indeed! I'm very happy as I am, thank you. Goodness, it would mean reading the newspapers and making laws. Don't know about you, Ethel, but I wouldn't want the responsibility!'* And he had to chuckle at, *'Talk about loose women! They should have my floppy bits!'*

Polly had no floppy bits, unlike some of his models, no discernible bulges, except where it mattered. She kept herself trim, cycling to local assignments and events, a man's peaked hat jammed on her head to keep out the sun, her camera in the basket in front, the tripod strapped to her back. If her assignments took her further afield she'd take the mule cart, which they shared, along with the cost of stabling Jessie down the road behind the Dolls' Hospital. He liked to watch her striding about the market with her shopping bags, her back straight and determined not to miss a bargain, to get to the shops while the buns were still hot, the fish still fresh. If she saw him, she'd call up, 'Shall I get you a paper? Want anything at the post office?'

She had such energy. Very often it was she who turned him out of doors, to play tennis, to take the train into town, to go for a walk in the forest. 'Come on, you old stick-in-the-mud. Leave that painting. You haven't been out for days!'

But regarding Bertha Reeves's longed-for 'hanky-panky', Polly's promise of *'We'll see,'* was the best she could do and on this he pinned his hopes.

As for the gossip ... 'Sticks and stones may break my bones, Archie, but Bertha's tittle-tattle is water off a duck's back.'

'Just hear us out, will you?' Archie had said in the face of Percy's temper.

Kitty Flanagan, singer and Archie's one-time model, had nodded thoughtfully when he'd first broached the idea, some years before, of a multiple portrait to grace the vestibule in Percy's new theatre. But, she had pointed out, while every 'turn' she could think of would want to be included in a mural of British music hall stars, there wasn't one who would thank him for being some blurry face in the back row. In fact, she'd said, after giving the matter a little more thought, she even doubted that they'd settle for being one of a crowd. Each, in his (or her) own eyes, was the star of the show and deserved a portrait on their own. 'No,' she said, 'you tell Reeves he'd do better with a row of signed photos.'

But Kitty's advice fell on deaf ears. Percy was obsessed with the idea that the first thing punters would see as they came into the theatre would be Archie's painting of show people, many of whom they'd seen treading the boards of the Horse and Groom up the road, and would, doubtless, pay to see here in the years to come. And who was Kitty Flanagan when she was at home? Just some fat ex-showgirl. Clearly she didn't know the value of diets or publicity. With his dream of a proper Palace of Varieties almost realised, Percy would not now be talked down. He *would* have his foyer painting and he *would* have it finished and framed before the opening in October. Never mind that some of it might still be tacky and that Archie would have to leave it unvarnished until it was properly dry the following summer. They'd put a guard round to stop people touching it.

So, it was with a heavy heart that Archie mounted the scaffolding each morning. He didn't need the extra work and it would do nothing to further his career. What he should have been doing was experimenting with new ideas, new methods, painting pictures to move people not just to impress them. He should be putting his energies into commissions that would trade off the acclaim he was receiving in the galleries rather than this bread and butter copying. But needs must. He'd promised Percy long ago that he would do it and he was a man of his word.

To protect the painting from airborne sawdust and grit, Percy had rigged up a screen of old sheets, shielding the artist from the sight if not the sound of the other trades. It was a sort of peace – just him and his scaffolding and his wall-mounted canvas (five yards by four) – though from time to time his concentration was shattered by a particularly loud bang or clang or a shout of pain as a marble slab landed on a foot, or a warning cry, 'Look out, below!'

What he had painted already, as a background, was an imaginary reception room beyond this mural, a *trompe l'oeil* of walls and ceilings, of chandeliers, windows and drapes. Crimson carpets and plush upholstery completed the set, the whole painted in perspective, of course, and in slightly out-of-focus, faded tones to give the effect of distance. Onto this background he had imposed the amorphous overall shape of his assembled artistes as though he were mapping a continent, a coastline. Negative space – it was the most important thing in a composition – outside the outlines of images, the 'empty' spaces between things, such as the triangle formed by an arm held akimbo, the shape between one head and the next, the space around a curtain. Having his boundaries mapped in he could then pat the positives into being. Now, fifty-six bland silhouettes were patched with light and shade as their individual bone structures dictated. The workmen, lifting the dustsheet at the end of the day to wish him goodnight, took delight in naming their favourites from the few clues Archie had given them. (*'That's gonna be Florrie Ford!'* and *'I'll bet a week's wages that there's Harry Champion.'*)

The next step was to define the depth of each shadow. Then, and only then, did he feel confident to paint in the features proper: the eyes, noses and mouths. So far he had completed seven of the nine artistes in the back row. Forty-*nine* faces to go.

Frowning, and without much thought, Archie added highlights to the dull and muddy eyes with which Algie fixed his public, to make them a touch more animate.

Oh, good God – he had brought the wretched thing to life!

The photograph he was working from was bad enough; in colour it was truly terrifying. The brown shaggy eyebrows, sardonically raised, those feverish red cheeks and that leering mechanical smile gave the dummy's face an evil, menacing look. In spite of the heat, he shivered. 'God, Markov,' he spoke to the painted ventriloquist before him, 'I can see why you drink, having to work with that – that thing…'

He felt for his rag to wipe away the mistake but saw it had fallen out of his belt. As he bent to pick it up, he became aware of a familiar figure staring up, foreshortened and appraising his work, thumb on his chin as he stroked his silky moustache.

'Aye, aye, boyo! Talking to yourself now, are you? Said it would send you doolally.'

Now what? It wasn't like Frank Tyrell to take time out from detective work to look in on a humble painter.

'How long you gonna be?'

'Another month or two, barring high days and holidays. Why?'

'Got a little job for you – take care of any spare time.'

His heart sank. He wanted to get on with this. He really didn't have time for 'little jobs' right now. 'Not urgent, I hope?'

'Maybe, maybe not.'

What did that mean? 'Just let me – kill off – this little chap.'

Quickly he painted out the highlights in Algernon's eyes. A dead look was better than that spark of life any day. Congratulating himself on rendering the damned thing harmless, he cleaned his brushes in thinner, dropped more oil of cloves onto the sponge in his palette box and closed the lid. There was no knowing how long Frank would keep him talking and he didn't want the paints drying out in this heat. He came down the ladder.

'What's up, Frank?'

The policeman looked to right and left, checking that they couldn't be overheard and lowered his voice. 'Get dressed, mate. If you'll come down the station, I'd like you to have another look at that skull you found. I've had a bit of a brainwave but it's a long shot and there ain't no knowing if you'll be up for it.'

What? Why? His curiosity piqued, Archie wiped his hands on trousers already paint-spotted and streaked and pulled on his shirt. Why did Frank want him on the case? He couldn't shed light on the killer.

'Not here, not here…' But even when they were alone, walking briskly along the street, Frank refused to enlighten him. Why so secretive?

'Down 'ere,' he said, opening a door onto dark steps leading to a closed room below.

'The morgue?'

Archie had been here before, making drawings and death masks of victims for police records, though more often, these days, they engaged photographers who would achieve, in a flash, what used to take him half an hour or more, more accurately, too, if open wounds were involved or if there was bruising to be analysed. But Tyrell insisted a camera wouldn't do in this case.

There was a rush of cold air as the door was opened. The subterranean room didn't boast the refrigeration of some of the hospital mortuaries, but the absence of sunlight slowed down decomposition by a week or two. It was cold enough, at any rate, for the police to keep their milk down here in hot weather, Archie noticed with a grimace, the jugs sealed with beaded lace doilies.

He fished out his handkerchief. Redolent of oil and turps though the rag was, it was preferable to the stench of rotting flesh, death and decay that met his nostrils.

'Jesus!'

There came the flare of a match and a hiss and pop as Frank lit the gas and Archie was able to see the source of the smell brightly illuminated by two, then three, then four gas lamps fixed at strategic intervals around the walls. The skeleton had been loosely reconstructed and laid out on a marble-topped table. Archie's mighty shiver had nothing to do with the chill, or the smell or even the flies that awoke with the light and flew in loops and excited spirals between the corpse and the dripping shreds of rotten rags spread out on a neighbouring slab to dry.

'Shut the door, Arch, there's a good chap – don't let the heat in.'

'Where's her foot?' The skeleton was complete apart from bones below the right ankle.

'You got me there. Could'a lost it when she was alive though the Doc thinks not. He reckons her other bones would've been put out, grown misshapen, like, if she'd had a walking stick or crutches. My guess is the rats've had it, or otters. Or p'raps it got caught up in the weeds and got left be'ind when the rest of her washed down on the current.'

Lord, Archie thought, only a year ago this, this *thing* had been flesh and blood, walking about on two strong feet; she'd been a living, breathing woman with no more thought of dying than him. And now look – a pile of bones on a marble slab, poor soul, her flesh fattening the fish in the River Lea. He must remember to avoid locally sourced trout and eels from now on.

'Do we – do *you* know who she is?'

'No idea, and that's where you come in.'

'Me?'

'Mmm,' the policeman stroked his moustache flat over his long

31

upper lip, studying the artist with a brown gaze. 'You done bones an' muscles an' that when you was at art school, didn't you?'

'Anatomy? Well, we didn't cut up bodies like doctors do but yes, we needed to know what went where. But we were taught from diagrams, mostly – 'muscle maps' they called them. There was a real skeleton they wheeled out from time to time but mostly we learned from observation of live models – hundreds and hundreds of sketches until we knew exactly how the limbs moved, how the muscles expanded and contracted...' Reaching over, he patted the policeman's rounded paunch. 'How they deteriorated with age and neglect!'

'All right, all right ... less of your sauce.' Frank frowned, his wrinkles catching the light, ploughing furrows through an earthy face, setting his moustache bristling. 'So, you couldn't put a face to this young lady?'

'How do you suggest I go about it, Frank?' he smiled, his head aslant.

'Well, there's the skull. If you could give us some idea what she looked like before she went in the drink, we'd have something to go on, find out who the devil she is for starters.'

'Tell me you're joking! I've never done anything like that in my life and I don't know anybody who has.'

'So, now's your chance to try, boyo. Be the first, a pioneer, like. You've drawn enough likenesses in your time – you must have some idea. I don't expect you to get it exact,' he wheedled, 'just enough so's we can get a poster up – jog a few memories. Someone might even recognise her, put us in touch with her loved ones, like – her mum and dad, kids, mates...' He paused, looked up at his friend, his eyes narrowing as he read his mind. 'And before you ask, it ain't young Lil Steggles – wrong age, wrong everything.'

He knew that, of course he did, but he still couldn't help relief sagging his shoulders. Perhaps, just for a moment there, he'd thought – who knows what he'd thought? But the two girls – Lilian and this one – weren't that different. They both had wide-set eye sockets, a fine jaw and firm chin, but then he supposed there were dozens of girls with those attributes. And then there were the teeth. Lilian had the missing molars and cavities of the confirmed sweet-eater. This girl's teeth were sound.

But still he felt dismay. What Frank was asking was well-nigh impossible. Bones were only the framework, the underpinning. This girl's facial features had been composed of cartilage, gristle and fat, sinew, muscle, blood and skin, and shaped by any number of factors, some inherited, some forged by life itself. Were her cheeks hollow with hunger, her eyes deep set or protruding? Were they shadowed from lack of sleep or illness? Was her nose pinched, her mouth grown mean with the stresses and strains of hard manual work? Or, did she 'sit on a cushion and sew a fine seam and feed upon strawberries, sugar and cream?' Did she wear spectacles? Who could tell? he asked the policeman.

'There might be something you get right,' argued Frank, 'something that rings a bell with someone. At least 'ave a go, Arch,' he begged. 'Girls, besides Lilian, are going missing, all over – their families are sick with worry. One of their daughters could be Jane Doe 'ere, but we'll never know if you don't put a face to her. And her people would rather know than not, I'm sure. I mean, wouldn't you?'

'I would.' He blew out his breath, frowning. God, if Clara ever went missing he'd be out of his mind with worry.

He gave in with a sigh. 'I'm not promising anything, mind.'

'I mean, as and when, boyo. I know you're tied up with Percy's painting but like, whenever you feel like a break from his old *Aunty Alice* you could pop round here, do a bit of drawring. See where we get to.'

Aunty Alice? Did he know any old -? Tch, not for the first time he'd been fooled by Cockney rhyming slang. *Percy's Palace,* he meant. Oh God, he had so much work on – three paintings on the go – the mural and a couple of urgent commissions, not to mention all his social engagements: gallery previews he simply couldn't get out of, that piece for the *Art Magazine*. Plus, he'd said he'd take Clara and Polly to see *Floradora*. And when was he going to fit in that trip to the seaside he'd promised them? He supposed he could miss the match on Saturday and cancel the billiards – and the *Whist* drive. Lord, at this rate he'd be lucky to squeeze in a pint before bedtime.

But, think of this young lady's family desperate for news…

It was a gloomy prospect, being stuck down here in the chilly bowels of the police station, with the flies and the stench, attempting to fit a face to the skull of a dead woman.

'We can help you out a bit.' The policeman referred to his notes. 'Female decedent, of course: a *Jane* Doe, not John. You can tell from the bones, the ribs and the, er, pelvis.' He indicated the skeleton on the slab, wafting his fingers vaguely in *that* direction. 'And the small skull, of course – a man's being larger on account of his superior brain.'

'On account of *what…?*'

'What?'

'*Superior..?*'

'Bigger, then – you'd go along with that – our heads are generally bigger. To house more brain.'

'Frank! Our heads are bigger to balance our *height!* Men are mostly taller than women. Our feet and hands are bigger, too, generally,' he added, raising an eyebrow. 'That other nonsense went out with the ark. Women's brains are no different from ours. Smaller maybe, but perfectly formed and just as intelligent, sometimes more so. You'd better not let Polly catch you spouting such tommyrot – she'd have your liver on toast.'

'Any old 'ow,' Frank shrugged, choosing to ignore the image of an irate photographer brandishing a toasting fork, 'there was a skirt – not much left of it now but we know it was once good quality linen – summer wear – machine-stitched with a Gamages label. Might be a clue to her shopping habits or she could'a got it off a second-hand rail down the market. Maybe not even our market –

she could'a floated downriver from a county away or more, on the current, like. We're asking round, o' course, see if anyone remembers selling a Gamages skirt off their stall but so far, nothing. There wasn't no shoes nor stockings, though the divers searched long an' 'ard. So, did she lose 'em on 'er travels, along with her foot, or was she one of the barefoot poor? See her toes are small and straight, no deformities, so if she was a lady, she was a sensible one – didn't cram her feet into shoes that was too small.'

His pencil moved down the page to the next point. 'Wiv regard to her, hrrm, her undergarments, didn't look like she wore no stays. I mean, any whalebone or wire or whatever they use would probably still be in evidence though any cotton would've perished.' Archie nodded, remembering Polly's shop window. Stays were out! This was a modern miss. 'Top to toe,' Tyrell went on, 'we reckon her to've been five foot three or four. The skirt label said a twenty-three-inch waist – she'd a been a trim little lady. No excess fat, like.' He opened a drawer beside him and took out a wad of some felted material. 'Hair, Arch,' he said, unwinding a ropey length.

Archie gagged. A skull was one thing, hair another. Too, too real. The girl's hair must have come away when her scalp rotted.

'It was all tangled up in the reeds fastening her head to the island.' How had Archie missed that? 'It come away as we moved her, like.' Archie swallowed bile. 'Now, as you can see it's pretty long. What – two, three feet would you say? Untrimmed and naturally chestnut in colour. Usual combs and 'airpins still attached.'

'Let's see them.'

The inspector opened an envelope and tipped out an array of pins and grips and two curved metal combs studded with stones of some sort.

'They real?'

''Fraid not, on'y rhinestones. Real diamonds would've helped place her, like.' Tyrell gestured him to come nearer. 'Now her teeth are interesting. We glued 'em all back in and there's just the one molar missing. It might still be at the bottom of the river or in the belly of a fish or a dentist might've took it out or, you know, some charmer might have knocked it out. There's still a bit of serration on the incisors so she's youngish. Touch of decay at the back 'ere but either it never bothered her or she couldn't afford no dentists – otherwise, I'd say she had a good set a choppers.'

'See, Frank,' he said, with a frown, 'I don't know that any of this stuff is going to help me get her likeness. You say she shopped at Gamages? That won't give her a double chin, will it, or cauliflower ears? So, she wore sensible shoes and rhinestones in her haircombs?' He rocked his head from side to side. 'None of that helps define the shape of her nose or the thickness of her eyebrows. Sorry but all that's neither here nor there, really.'

'Oh,' the detective looked disappointed. 'I thought it might help you get some idea of her standing like, whether she's moneyed or poor, clever or not.'

'Well, that's for you to find out. I'm not sure class and breeding show in a person's face anyway. In their teeth, maybe – but even rich people can have terrible teeth and we both know folk without a pot to piss in, who clean their teeth regularly with soot or salt. It probably helps if you can't afford sweets and cigarettes. No, I think it'd be more helpful if you could give me some idea of her age.'

Tyrell stroked his moustache. 'She was a properly formed woman, bone-wise. And I said about the teeth, didn't I? Well into her teens when she went in the drink, sometime last year, the doctor thinks. The dress was a summer one.'

'From Gamages – yeah, you said.'

'Oh, and Doc reckons she was dead when she went in. Still,' he said archly, 'I don't suppose you'd be interested in the cause of death…'

'Tch.' Clearly Tyrell was feeling rattled. 'Go on then.'

'One of the hyoid bones was fractured.' He consulted his notes. 'The left cornu or horn. Because there's three, see, joined together usually. And they got separated somehow.'

Archie professed ignorance. Hyoid bones? No bells rang.

'No,' his friend conceded, 'I never knew either 'til the Doc showed me. It's this one, here.' It had been placed high up in the throat area, a delicate horseshoe-shaped bone, splintered almost in two, putting Archie in mind of a snapped chicken wishbone, though this break had brought no one any luck. 'See how they come apart? Now we have to ask ourselves whether these 'ere bones was separated in the act of strangulation or fell apart as the flesh rotted, to be eaten by fishes and was then cracked, somehow.'

'The doctor tell you this?'

'He did, as a matter of fact.'

'Hmm,' he frowned. 'Doubt any fish can crack a neck-bone, Frank, but strong hands can. Or a rope.'

'What, like she hung herself and then jumped in the river?'

'Mmm,' he paused, allowing the detective his moment to shine, 'probably not.'

'Hands or rope, Archie, she never did this to herself. Deduction, my dear Watson … we're looking for a murderer, son.'

Archie nodded agreement.

As he jotted down everything Frank was able to tell him, Archie found himself warming to this poor girl, small-boned, with what must have been conker-coloured hair before it faded. Someone may have knocked her about, punched her tooth out, but finally strangled or hung her and disposed of the body in the River Lea. Was she a runaway who had fallen in with a bad lot, or was she unlucky in her choice of lovers? Or what?

Three

He stared mournfully at the skull as it nestled, like an artfully arranged still life, between a corner of fresh white bread – over which it cast an unappetising shadow – and a glass of ale whose dancing lights lent the white bone amber dappling. The sun was still fierce, even strained through the gauze of teatime smoke. Half past five in the High Street was marked by the lighting of fires, even in the heat of summer. Homecoming husbands demanded a kettle of hot water to wash off the dirt of toil and a hot meal to bring them back to life.

These long hot days Archie was apt to skimp meals, just grabbing a saveloy or a pie from a local shop on the way home from the Palace, picking up a bit of salad from Bob's greengrocery downstairs, and making do with that. The alternative was to spend valuable painting time lighting fires, preparing vegetables, cooking and washing up. If it wasn't too late and he had the energy he might pick up where he'd left off on whatever canvas he had on his easel. He couldn't waste good painting light. Not tonight, though.

True to his word, after Polly had taken a dozen photographs of the complete skeleton and close-ups of the fast-decomposing face, Frank Tyrell had had the skull boiled and cleaned up. All brain tissue and other fleshy matter had been removed and the bones given a good scrub. He'd brought it round earlier on, breathless and eager, expecting Archie to drop everything, start sketching and solve the mystery straightaway. No such luck, Archie had told him testily, continuing to wash his brushes. It wouldn't be that easy. Come back in a week or two.

Poor bones, he thought now, as he pushed the remains of his scratch meal aside and took up paper and a pencil; what can you tell me, eh? Did these teeth get to crunch the crackling from a pork joint, bite cleanly into crisp apples? Or were others' leavings the best you could hope for? Were you admired for your dazzling smile, your clear skin, your flashing eyes? Or did you cram an old hat over your dirty hair and scuttle about in the shadows in rags? Rich or poor? Rosy or pale? What were you? A fine lady, a washerwoman, a doxy? Married, single? *Who* were you?

His pages quickly filled with drawings of jawbones, cheekbones, eye sockets and nasal cavities, flickering in the lamplight, but no nearer being fleshed out.

Midnight found him still at it, outlining another skull and mapping in the exact shapes of the facial cavities, constantly checking measurements with ruler and callipers, prodding his own face and asking himself how big, how wide, how thick, how long? There really was no knowing, no clues. How big was her eyeball? How much of the eye socket did it occupy? How deeply was it set? Was her nose longer or shorter than average; was it straight and thin, aquiline, or snub? Were the ears large or small, lying flat against the sides of the skull or protruding from it? Was the mouth wide and generous, revealing a complete set of teeth in a smile or were the lips thin and mean? There were just too many variables.

How would he know when it was right?

Perhaps if he had some other frame of reference – photographs, for instance, of all the young women who'd gone missing from their homes since last summer – he could begin a process of elimination. What if he were to start from there?

With that thought in mind he went to bed to dream that the face to fit the bones was a wooden one with painted eyes and thick eyebrows lifted on a comic slant, wooden lips that opened and shut with a clatter, opened and shut as slimy weeds wafted on the current of a river current and fish swam in and out. He awoke in a sweat.

Clara's smile was a little unsteady. 'Lordy...' she breathed. 'She's changed.' She felt for her plait and stroked its wispy end, backwards and forwards across her upper lip. It had been her comfort since early childhood. Some children bit their nails, some sucked their thumb; Clara used her braid like a paint brush.

'*"Lordy, Miss Clara!"*' A male voice twitted in mimicry and Clara poked out her tongue at young Henry Waddington, a first-year student at her grandfather's School of Art.

'Where'd you get it, Mister Price?' enquired another of the Grants' dinner guests.

'You turned bodysnatcher now, Arch?'

He told them where the skull had come from and of Clara's part in finding it, and explained that he was now tasked, by the police, with coming up with a face to match the bones. 'She was probably something of a beauty with those high cheekbones and those big eye sockets.'

Clara swung her plait behind her with a swish of the head and examined the skull carefully. 'Guess she was kinda cute.'

'Cute!' guffawed Henry, 'what sort of a word is that?' Eighteen years old and the *enfant terrible* of the Camden art scene, already he was daubing canvases in the strong colours and flatness of the post-Impressionists. He admired Paul Gauguin, who'd died that June, and his so-called 'Synthetism'. Like the Frenchman he believed that painting, like music, should be able to move the viewer emotionally. Archie thought he was an insufferable prig.

'Blame my son-in-law.' Vic turned in his chair to wag at Archie with a bent, arthritic forefinger. 'If you will keep giving her these American books, Arch ... Mark Twain and the like. It's all we hear these days – *Lordy* and *Glory be* and, what's the other one? *Jeepers,* that's it.' He mocked her, '*Jeepers, Granpappy, you're awfu' particular!*'

'Granpappy!' Archie choked on his beer.

Ivy chuckled. 'I like it. I think that's what I'll call you from now on.'

'Particular goes with the job, eh, Vic?' It was his turn to mimic now. *'– Paint what you can see, my boy! Look, look and look again! Perspective, proportion, tones – get them right and you're halfway there!'* Vic shrugged, recognising his own mantra. Henry was shaking his head sadly. To him, Vic's ideals were old hat and passé.

'I'm glad you're enjoying the books, Clara.'

The girl was too busy to answer him, turning the skull in a sunbeam from the long window, seeming to study the light and shadow flickering across the undulating bone. Then she gazed steadily into the empty eye sockets as if to read the mind within.

'Who did this to you, honey?' she murmured.

Archie sensed she was showing off to the young men – he hadn't noticed any Americanisms last week in Walthamstow. Maudie and her brothers would have taken the rise out of her. Her Camden audience seemed enraptured, however, gazing at the girl with shining eyes. Was this bravado – this show of having no horror of dead things? Or, if it were real, was it something he should be pleased about? He sometimes didn't know what to make of her. On the other hand, he liked that she recognised the humanity that had once inhabited the bones. 'She's Jane Doe,' he told her.

'How come you know her name?'

'It's what the police call any dead female body they can't identify. Just for convenience really. Men are called John. John Doe.'

'Oh, I see. Pleased to meet you, Jane,' she addressed the skull with a smile. 'Oh,' she said, then, as if in reply to something it had said to her, 'don't worry…' Her smile faded and a small pucker of concern clouded her brow. 'It's only for now, until they find out who you really are.'

Such a child still, despite appearances; she could have been playing with her dolls.

'Archie, I don't think…' Vic was frowning and shaking his head.

'What? Oh Vic, she's fine with it…'

Ivy was trying to get her son-in-law to read the message in her eyes. What? She was frowning and wagging her head meaningfully in Clara's direction. What was it? Suddenly it dawned on him that she was mouthing Lizzie's name. Of course, her mother would be in a similar state by now. Both her parents would be. Damn, what an ass he was. 'Oh God,' he blurted, snatching the grisly thing from the girl's startled grasp. 'Sorry, sorry, sorry!'

'It's too much at the dinner table, Archie.'

'Yes, yes, Ivy, of course. Stupid of me.' How could he have been so thoughtless? Clara could be expected to gnaw happily on chicken bones but human remains and a young orphan did not go together well. 'Let's put it on the mantelpiece for now.' He covered it with his napkin. Out of sight and, hopefully, out of mind.

It was always hard to know how to play it. He didn't want to be over-protective – he was delighted the girl showed none of the squeamishness some of her sex affected in order to appear delicate and weak to men, in need of their protection – but neither did he want her to grow up hard and unfeeling. 'So – you like your Mark Twain?' he asked.

'We all do,' Vic answered for the girl, who was now staring into space, a quizzical look on her face as her mind travelled to some other place. '*Tom Sawyer's* a real favourite.'

'Oh, good. You must tell Polly. She's read all the books.'

On cue, Polly popped her flaxen head round the door, claiming everyone's attention. 'Did I hear my name? What have I done?' As she came into the crowded dining room, bearing two steaming roast chickens on a platter, several voices strove to enlighten her. She set the dish down in front of their host and, weaving her way around the chairs at the huge square table, she responded, 'Mark Twain? Oh absolutely – a brilliant writer!' all the while pulling pins from her hat, her Sunday best. An over-large black concoction set off with parallel birds' wings, it was removed at last and the pins stuck back so that Ivy could bear it away to safety.

Polly was a popular guest – with Ivy because she did what she could in the kitchen and never came empty-handed (today she had brought enough apple pie to feed an army) – and, also, with Vic and his entourage. Although she didn't paint or sculpt and had never had an art lesson in her life, they recognised her talent for eloquent photographic portraits and compositions. In fact, attempts had been made to reproduce her work in paint but never as successfully. She sat down next to Clara and waited for Ivy to return.

'Oh, do start, please!' exclaimed their hostess, retaking her seat. 'It'll get cold and spoil. Help yourselves, everyone. Vic, will you carve? Potatoes, Roger? Oh, no, no Vic, Henry doesn't like the dark meat, do you, Henry? Julian would you pass the red cabbage, please? Just the way you like it, Archie, with vinegar, onions and apples.'

'Red cabbage!' cried Waddington, loudly and unnecessarily, 'Ugh. Horrid stuff!' Archie gave him a reproving glance. Genius he may be, but he could do with learning some bloody manners.

Clara hadn't even noticed his outburst. She seemed preoccupied and Polly had to ask her twice whether she could help her to carrots.

'Are you feeling quite well, Clara?'

'Sorry? Oh, um, yeah. Fine, thanks.'

Polly realised the girl was gazing at the mantelpiece, her dark eyes shadowed in thought. 'What if…?' she began and bit her lip.

Puzzled, Polly followed Clara's gaze and her eyes filled with horror. 'Oh, Archie, you didn't bring the wretched thing here! I thought we agreed…'

Clara was speaking – 'It's not the same as doing a portrait, is it, Pops? I mean you've no sitter, no photograph, nothing. How can you be sure anything you draw is the truth?'

Wonderful girl! So, her reverie had had nothing to do with gloomy or ghoulish thoughts just with the practicalities of giving the skull a face.

'When someone recognises her,' he said. She nodded and thoughtfully speared a slice of carrot.

Jaws slowed and stilled as the company followed her gaze, eyes narrowing as each envisioned a face beneath the napkin.

'Any idea how old she was?' someone asked.

He told them what he could about her age – sixteen or seventeen – height and build, about her hair colour, her style of dress. 'What we don't know is what she looked like from the neck up.'

'Well, you're not going to get her down to her dimples or her long fluttering eyelashes but you've got the basics,' said Vic, who had put down his fork to consider the problem. 'Some of the features you'll be able to *place* correctly – they'll be dictated by the eye sockets, cheekbones, jawline – and the teeth, of course – but as for the size and shape…' His old apple cheeks wrinkled in doubt. 'And the nose and ears, the lips?' He shrugged. 'Anybody's guess. I can't see you achieving a perfect likeness with just bones as reference. As you say, the best you can hope for is that something about your picture triggers a memory in somebody with a missing daughter or wife or sister.'

Suggestions came thick and fast. Had he tried covering the skull in ink or paint and printing from it? Using that print as a guide? Or tracing over a photo? What about using a grid? Papier mâché? As fast as a suggestion was put up it was knocked down. Printing ink would damage the skull, which the family might want to bury eventually. Archie said he had traced any number of faces over photographs of the skull that Polly had taken for him. All of them had become different people, mostly feminine but some quite androgynous. As for using papier mâché, you'd get some sort of face, one supposed, but the chances of it being a true likeness were a million to one. And how would you know, anyway?

'Archie's problem is himself,' Roger Gresham pointed out. Gresham had been a student at the same time as Archie and was now a Fine Arts tutor in his own right. He knew his friend to be a perfectionist, he said, and Archie's lips muscled, in rueful agreement. He was never going to be satisfied with an approximation. 'For him it's got to be a true likeness, or why bother?' Roger went on. 'Not a millimetre or a brushstroke out. Have you ever known him not to get a likeness? I don't know how he does it. He probably came out of the womb with the gift of judging size and proportion, by eye alone, embedded in his brain. I mean he could draw any one of us accurately, from memory, and probably has, without recourse to measuring tools, but as Clara says – his task is to add flesh to a skull without any other clues. And, for him, it must be precisely the right amount of flesh, no more, no less. That's what's bothering him.'

The way Clara pursed her lips was so like her mother, cupping her chin, her head aslant. She still had some growing to do, Archie was pleased to observe, but she was promising to take after Lizzie in looks, too. And her mind – her *mind* – was even more beautiful. The breadth of her imagination! No wonder Henry Waddington was gazing at her, entranced. When he caught Archie looking at him, he averted his eyes quickly. So he should, Archie thought: she was far too young for him. Luckily, Clara seemed to have only contempt for him.

She frowned as she gathered her thoughts and her plait, running her fingers over the shiny knobs of black braid. It now became an aid to concentration. 'No,' she said slowly, 'you mustn't damage the skull with paint or ink or papier mâché but you could take a *mould* from it, cast it in plaster and work from that – more than one cast if you wanted. Then...' she paused, her eyes narrowing on her vision, 'you could – or I could, if you tell me what to do – make all the meat that lies under the skin, the smile muscles and the fatty bits and whatnot, out of clay! You could stick them on to the cast where they should go – and then you could cover the lot with more clay for the skin. I guess it would have to be very thinly rolled-out clay, difficult to handle but not impossible. Or simply paint it on with a thickish slip. Yes, that's probably best. Gosh oh, gee, Pops, that's the answer! Jane Doe in three dimensions!'

'*Clarrie…*' said Archie, in awe. She dazzled him. What she suggested must be possible with a proper knowledge of what went under the skin.

'Damn fiddly, though,' said Gresham.

'But possible,' said Archie, with mounting conviction. 'Perfectly possible.'

Vic sucked his cheeks. 'I'm not happy about you working with that skull, Claribelle.'

'*What!*' There was a chorus of disbelief.

'Well,' the old man sighed and cleared his throat, 'I don't want you having bad dreams or being worried by dark thoughts.'

'What's wrong with a few dark thoughts, Granddad? They're allowed. Edgar Allan Poe had them all the time.'

'And drove himself mad, in the end,' observed one of the dinner guests.

'Unproven,' said another.

'Edgar Allan Poe! You're not reading that drivel, are you?' demanded Henry Waddington.

'What's wrong with it?'

'Lordy, Miss Clara, it's entirely unsuitable!'

Archie thought so, too, but Clara was a free spirit, which was good, generally, and if she had read Poe to no ill effect, well… 'I don't think you need worry about Clarrie, Henry,' he said. 'She's a sensible girl. When we fished that skull out of the river it was in a far worse state than it is now and she took that in her stride. You haven't had any nightmares since, have you, Clarrie?'

She shook her head firmly. 'The one to be scared of is the man who killed her, not the poor dead woman.'

'Goodness me, yes,' said someone. 'There's a murderer out there somewhere just waiting for his next victim.'

'Woo-hoo-hoo!' went Henry Waddington, making an ugly face and clawing his fingers. There was something not quite right about that boy.

'Henry!' scolded Clara. 'Grow up, for goodness' sake!'

What had Polly said? *'Thirteen going on thirty.'* A smile started to stretch his mouth but suddenly froze. Thirteen was the age of Gauguin's Tahitian bride and he a middle-aged man with a wife and family at home in England. Monsters like that could be preying on the young girls of Walthamstow. The missing ones. Even Clara could be in danger. Feeling unaccountably testy he shot Henry a withering look, to the boy's obvious delight.

'So – when do we get started, Pops?'

'Your granddad doesn't want you to do it, Clarrie,' he snapped. God, he'd like to punch the lights out of Henry bloody Waddington.

Oblivious to his mood Clara went blithely on, ''Course you do, don't you, Granpappy? Ain't nobody else with the know-how, just li'l ole me.' Then the façade fell away and she became serious. 'No, it stands to reason; I have the tools, the clay and the time until I go back to school next Monday. It'll be a lovely way to end the holidays.'

Vic sighed in defeat and turned to Archie. 'Guess I'd just better shut up. Do you have everything you need, son, anatomical maps and suchlike, callipers, measuring tapes and so on?'

Glad to have something else to think about beside Waddington's possible designs on his daughter, Archie replied, 'I think so, Vic – I dug out my old books when I thought I was going to have to draw the thing freehand – but I'd welcome any help you can give me.' He frowned now, at the enormity of the task before him. 'I have worked in clay before, of course. I used to help Lizzie out with big orders for her art deco tiles, but I can't claim any real affinity with the material. Clarrie's the one with the magic touch.'

'If you need any help…' Henry Waddington was trying to muscle in on the act.

'No thanks.' Clara's put down was short and final. 'We don't want Jane Doe looking like some Peruvian tribal mask.' She was referring to Waddington's taking up Gauguin's search for the primitive.

'I think you'll find, Henry, that Clarrie's quite capable. You only have to look around…'

Every horizontal space in the room, between the framed photographs and vases, was home to Clara's pots and models. There were people, animals and really quite abstract pieces based on bones and rocks. The most recent study, a life-size bust of himself, was impressive – it might well have been a submission by a much older student for a degree show. Not that she had flattered him. The terracotta eyes were challenging, glaring out from under a deep frown; the long nose looked particularly arrogant and the lips were parted, mid-sentence, probably talking rot, as usual. You could just see teeth and a bit of tongue. But it was the wild, unruly hair that got him. There was movement in it; it was just about to flop into his eyes, as his facsimile raised its square chin to make a point. She saw him for what he was, and that was good.

'I'm going to be the assistant here but neither of us has a detailed knowledge of facial musculature,' he pointed out. 'My own anatomy classes were a long time ago and I doubt Clara's ever had one. She models her clay on what she can see, not what lies beneath. In the same way, I suppose, as I paint a face according to how the light falls on it. That's not going to be enough in this case.'

'If I can help…' Henry repeated. They ignored him.

'Well, of course,' said Ivy, passing Archie a tureen of cauliflower cheese. 'We can't all be Leonardos.'

'Thanks, Mother-in-law.'

'Effie's the one!' Polly's eyes widened. 'All the dissection she's done, she'll know exactly what goes where and how it adds up to flesh.'

Their friend Effie, of course! Now she was Doctor Effie. He cast his mind back to when he had last seen the girl, mounting the steps of the podium at the Royal Free Hospital, a diminutive figure wearing something silky and grey under her black graduate gown, eager to receive her scroll from the hands of Elizabeth Garrett Anderson herself. He reached for his beer and took a long draught, remembering the enormous hat she had donned in place of the mortar board at the Albany restaurant, afterwards, the hat all that could be seen of her, for a while, among the crowd of attentive young men. Douglas McKay, down in London with his wife for the ceremony, had voiced their reluctance at having to return home, leaving their girl to fend off the perils of the metropolis alone. As a junior doctor she would have to work and live at least two more years in the hospital and any entanglements of the heart had to be avoided or she would never complete her training.

'You'll keep an eye on her, won't you, Archie?'

'Gladly!' he'd said, meaning it but, somehow, what with the vestibule painting, the discovery of the skull, and the young doctor's unsocial working hours, he had failed to look in on her in the four weeks (or was it five or six?) that had elapsed since her graduation.

If he sent a note to her room at the nurses' home, asking if he might call on her and take her out to tea, it would be a chance to keep his promise to her father. He would explain the challenge Frank Tyrell had set him and, hopefully, persuade Effie to pop over to supervise the anatomical correctness of their project.

Clara piped up, 'So if you leave the skull with me, Pops, I'll make a mould tonight and a cast tomorrow, maybe two – and they should be dry enough to use by the end of the week. Then we can get started, eh?'

Vic rolled his eyes heavenwards in a vain appeal to the gods for help. 'You may as well come over next Saturday,' he said. 'In the meantime, I'll rig up some sort of infrastructure to hold the skull in place while you work. You'll need a neck, of course – without a neck to hold it straight it'll be difficult to manage…'

Now it was the old man's turn to gaze at the mantelpiece while he worked on a plan and when, towards the end of the meal, the conversation veered, as it was bound to, into the realms of each artist's personal sales and successes, their host began fidgeting, his eyes straying constantly to the covered skull over the fire.

Polly whispered, 'He wants to get on with it, doesn't he?'

Clara nodded. 'And he will, just as soon as the last person leaves, down to the clay-room, lickety-split. Me, too, tomorrow not being a school day.'

'*Lickety-split?* Uncle Remus?' guessed Polly.

'*Brer Rabbit and the Tar Baby,*' Clara confirmed.

Four

He was used to taking the mule trap to Camden on a Sunday. How difficult could it be, he wondered, to go the extra mile or two to Hampstead on a Monday morning?

Well-nigh bloody impossible! The mixture of petrol-driven cars, trams, bicycles, tricycles, horse-drawn everything else and policemen directing traffic at the crossroads made for complete and utter chaos! He started out from Walthamstow at seven, hoping to catch Effie coming off a night shift, and didn't arrive at the entrance to Hampstead Hospital until gone ten, when the young doctor had returned home to bed, not to be disturbed.

He hung about in the entrance hall of her lodgings until the caretaker told him, politely, to move. The young ladies were not permitted gentlemen callers. He'd no idea when she'd wake up, he said, probably not until late afternoon. He agreed to give her a note.

He couldn't face the return journey so soon, if at all. Jesus. And the poor mule, so docile, so patient! She must be exhausted. He drove up to the Heath where there was a horse trough, unhitched Jessie from the trap, and let her drink her fill. Then he led her to a wooden bench overlooking the grassy slopes and hitched her beside him to graze while he pulled out his sketchbook. However long it took, Doctor Effie … he wasn't going to let Clara down.

He couldn't help wondering what she looked like asleep in her darkened room. Did she wear some sort of eye-covering to keep out the light? A mask? Did she have an alarm clock? What did she wear in bed on a hot day, with the sun beating against the walls and windows of her room? Did she kick off the bed clothes, pull up her shift, allow a flow of air to cool her inner thighs?

His drawing became more and more erotic but he saw naked females every day in his life classes and what he drew now was purely academic. Polly had, more or less, encouraged him to form other romantic attachments, but he felt no inclination to profligacy. He had plenty of lady friends but the thought of getting into bed with any of them left him cold. He loved Polly and, besides, he had a daughter who would be devastated to learn that he had been unfaithful to her mother. But, on the other hand… He frowned.

There was that young woman, Sophie Hudson, who had come knocking on his door the other day, with a portfolio tucked under her arm, dimpling prettily and asking for lessons.

'I'm sorry, my dear,' he'd had to say, 'I don't take students.'

By God, she was gorgeous, with masses of dark curly hair, much of which had escaped her ridiculous hat, and the biggest brown eyes that brimmed with disappointment. She was young – he could give her a good ten years, he thought – and curvy; her bodice was stretched to bursting. What was he supposed to do?

'Show me your work, anyway,' he'd said, there on the doorstep, gallantly resisting an urgent desire to invite her in.

They were nearly all watercolours. Dainty flowers and landscapes. Village streets, forest scenes, well executed and worthy but he'd seen hundreds like them. Some pen-and-wash still lifes were slightly more interesting, with unusual subjects: engineering tools and machine interiors. Her pencil and charcoal life drawings and portraits showed some skill but – he sifted through them again – they were all so ladylike, so prim and proper. She was a good draftswoman but lacked any passion or narrative. Very nice, he said. Had she thought of illustrating?

'That's not what I want,' she said, stamping her foot. 'I want to be a painter!' He'd raised his eyebrows and she'd pouted and lowered her eyes, her lashes sweeping her cheeks becomingly. 'I've been to the galleries, seen all the modern stuff, the Impressionists and Post-Impressionists, Fauvists, Colourists ... I know I should be experimenting, too – trying to engage the intellect as well as the eye – but I – I'm not brave enough. I hang onto the safety of rules. Now you – you paint in a fresh, modern way – your paintings of gypsies are wild – you achieve a difference without resorting to Cezanne's distortion of perspective or Van Gogh's heavy-handedness. As for your portraits...' She was lost for words. 'The one of your mother hanging in the Academy ... oh, it's exquisite.'

Archie lapped it up. He knew he should take this flattery with a pinch of salt, but it was very pleasant, standing here in the late August sunshine, listening to this lovely girl.

'Which is why I've come to you. I – I need a teacher and I'm sure you're the one to take me forward.' Again, that lovely sweep of eyelashes against her rounded cheeks. She explained how she'd left school with a higher Art Certificate and had started her working career as a pupil-teacher at the new girls' school up the road. She was now twenty-six years old and an established member of staff, earning a salary, teaching her pupils what she'd been taught, how to be little conformists, how not to rock the boat, when in her heart of hearts she knew that the future in art was all about throwing caution to the wind, trying out new ideas.

'Well, just go ahead and do it. Forget the rules. Let yourself go.'

'I've tried and I can't!' She gazed at him piteously, 'I need to be shown how!' She looked down, biting her luscious lower lip. 'Could you, perhaps, teach me, you know ... to paint like you?' and, raising her eyes to meet his, smiled shyly, slyly. 'I could come to you after school and at weekends and holidays ... I would pay you.'

Irresistible! What's more, he thought quickly, as his student she could help him finish Percy's painting. Most famous artists with large studios and several works on the go, assigned students specialising in skin tones, perhaps, or vegetation, to do the mundane or repetitive areas of the piece, while they, the masters saved the juicy bits for themselves. But did he have the time or the patience for teaching? Could he, seriously, let some hare-brained amateur loose on Percy's beloved painting? He'd be forever up and down ladders correcting her mistakes! Students were more trouble than they were worth. But she had such winning ways…

He'd capitulated. 'Well, my dear, I'm just off to work now. If you'd care to accompany me down to the Palace I can show you what I'm about.'

The note that he'd left with the janitor suggested Effie meet him in the tea shop he had passed down the road, at five. Meanwhile, he drew until hunger gnawed at his innards and he had to go in search of food. Luckily, a motley collection of vendors and peddlers hung around the hospital gates providing food for visitors, staff or indeed, anyone, like him, just passing. He bought a hot potato from a chap tending a roasting contraption with hot coals beneath and a chimney to take out the steam. He bought piping hot coffee from a wheeled stall. And a peddler was selling freshly made ginger cakes from a tray round his neck. He bought three, two for him and one for the little old lady, a Mrs Mimms, who had been minding his seat and Jessie while he was gone. She was still there, thank goodness, and so was Jessie. In return, he was to mind her dog for an hour. The dog's name was Toby.

'Like Punch and Judy's little dog,' she'd enlightened him earlier. 'He's all the world to me, now my husband's gone. We go everywhere together. Unfortunately, they won't let him into the hospital, and I can't leave him tied up on the railings for an hour, he pines so.' Archie listened to the entire story of how her dear sister had fallen down the stairs, last Thursday, in their little cottage in Gospel Oak and broken her hip. 'She'll be in for weeks, they tell me.'

The dog, a little brown and white terrier, whinged a little as she toddled off (after feeding him her cake), and then settled down resignedly under the bench, to wait. He'd obviously done this before. At three, Mrs Mimms returned to collect her dog, to tell him all about her sister's condition and to thank him effusively, offering him a peppermint for his trouble.

'And what have you drawn, dear boy?'

Oh dear. Archie took out his sketchbook to find something suitable to show her. Thankfully there were rabbits, magpies and trees, nursemaids wheeling perambulators, and herself, drawn from memory and Toby, from life. He ripped out the page and gave it to her.

'Dear boy!' She was overwhelmed.

When she'd gone he flipped through the rest of his day's work: lady school teachers in various stages of undress, slim lady doctors, their arms thrown about in sleep, buxom actresses blowing kisses to their audience, but most of all, there was Polly. Sitting, standing, behind a camera, behind her counter, driving the mule trap, asleep, awake, smiling, frowning, he'd filled page after page with her. Beloved, unattainable Polly. Lord help him, anyone who didn't know him would think he was obsessed. Or desperate. Damn. He wiped away the sweat stinging his eyes and snapped the sketchbook shut.

At a quarter to six he was trying to make up his mind whether to leave the tea shop or order another pot of tea when the door swung open and Effie stepped into the dim and fragrant interior.

'Archie!' she beamed. 'What a treat!' He might have said the same.

She was looking crisp in a striped blouse with leg o' mutton sleeves, a navy-blue skirt with a trailing hem and a wide-brimmed creation of the same colour on her blonde hair. Lovely.

He jumped to his feet and stood to steady her chair as she sat down, catching the waitress's eye as he did so.

They placed an order for tea and buttered buns and she leaned on her elbows to regard him with a mixture of affection and amusement. 'Dear Archie…'

55

'Sorry, I meant to come by before but…'

'You've been sketching.'

'Eh?'

'Smudges.' She touched his face with warm fingers. 'Here and here and here.' She produced a clean white scrap of a handkerchief. 'Spit,' she commanded.

'Effie!'

'Just keep still.' He let her clean him up, feeling like a grubby-kneed schoolboy about to meet his maiden aunt.

'Sorry,' he said.

'Oh, for goodness' sake, don't apologise. We're friends, aren't we? There now, that's better.' Her hanky was filthy. 'Glad I could help. So – are you going to show me what you've drawn?'

'Good God, no!'

'That bad, are they?' And thankfully, she didn't pursue it. 'Now I can't stop very long, I'm afraid. I need to get back for ward rounds. But what about you? Polly says you've started your mural at long last…'

They chatted about the Palace Theatre which would soon be up and running and, when a pot of tea and two rounds of toasted buns duly arrived, the butter melting nicely into the spicy sweetness, he suddenly realised he was starving. He poured.

'Should be a wonderful line-up for the opening. The last Saturday in October – put it in your diary. Percy's signed up some big names already: Marie Lloyd, Lottie Collins, and a couple of speciality acts. What's more he's offered me free tickets!'

He looked up. Her cheeks were pink, her lips shiny with butter and dotted with crumbs, her eyes were alight and, despite her cleverness and her veneer of sophistication, she put down the teacake and clapped her hands like an excited six-year-old.

'Oh, how exciting!' He watched, fascinated, as her joyful expression slipped and became more calculating. 'Who else is going?'

'Well, Polly and Bart, of course, and maybe Clara and the old couple…' For a split second he thought of including Sophie Hudson, his student, but she wouldn't fit in, somehow.

'Lovely!' Effie took another bite of bun, chewed thoughtfully, swallowed and said, 'Gosh, I am looking forward to this. I haven't seen anyone or been anywhere, outside the hospital, for weeks. Polly writes, and Bart – about what's going on in Chelmsford – and I get the odd little drawing from you, and letters from home but otherwise I work, eat, study and sleep, work, eat, study and…'

'And there was I thinking you were out on the town every night.'

'Archie, I saw Beethoven's Fifth at the Queen's Hall last month with Polly, and that's the sum total of my gadding about.'

'So, you do get out sometimes?'

'I could probably get them to change my rota, if you were to ask me well in advance,' she said, cocking her head.

'What are you doing this weekend?' he asked. Quickly he explained what he had in mind. 'It has to be Saturday or Sunday as Clara goes back to school next Monday.'

'Archie Price! Is that the best you can do? An invitation to watch you and your little girl making mud pies? Oh, don't look like that – I'm joking. Of course, I'll come. I'm on call on Saturday night but I'm free all day. Just so long as I can get back by seven.'

He, too, had plans for Saturday evening – the Old Bedford music hall, around the corner from the Grants. Sophie would meet him there.

Frank Tyrell beamed at him. 'You'll be pleased to know Miss Doe's been reunited with her toes.' He smirked at his cleverness, having rehearsed for the last ten minutes. But Archie didn't get it. Head in the clouds – still thinking of his painting, or some woman, more like. He gave up. 'The missing foot, boyo – Broxbourne had it, what's left of it.'

'Really?' That got through. 'Broxbourne? But that's miles away. How did they manage to..? It wasn't in the river, was it?'

'No – funny thing – it was in the garden of one o' them big houses up there.' He referred to his file. 'Place called *High Chimleys,* family be the name of Bellingham. A gardener found a mess of bones under a bush he was trimming, thought it was some animal remains, but Bellingham's a coroner and he knew, straightaway, they was 'uman – took 'em to the police. What they call them foot bones, Arch? You'd know. Marsupials?'

'Metatarsals.'

'Right. Any old how, they was a bit chewed up, some of them. Broxbourne are thinking foxes. They've dug up the grounds, looking for the rest of the body. No luck, though. Not even a wishbone.'

He could see Archie puzzling over that one. How could the foot have separated from the rest of the body? 'It is *her* foot, I suppose?' he said. 'I mean, the foxes – if it was foxes – might have dug up a grave in some local churchyard … Or dogs?'

'That's what they thought, an' all, but there wasn't no disturbed graves in the graveyard or nothing. Broxbourne were stumped 'til they heard about our find. And, as it happens, all the bones they collected was an exact match for our little lady.'

'So where is this *High Chimneys* place?'

'I'll get the map.'

Together they traced the blue River Lea as it wriggled through the valley, with Tyrell pointing out the landmarks: Enfield, Edmonton, Tottenham with a view through to Alexandra Palace, then Hackney, Bow, all the way to the metropolis. And, on the opposite bank, Waltham Abbey, Chingford and Walthamstow, Leyton, Stratford, West Ham…

'But the foot was found where?'

'Way back here – that's Broxbourne, see? Up in Hertfordshire.' The forefingers of his two hands were about a foot apart. 'And this 'ere's the Pride of Lea.' He stabbed his finger at the spot, way, way downriver in Essex, where the children had found the body. 'Miles away, see?'

'The foot couldn't have been taken *up*-river somehow?'

'Against the flow, Arch? Unless an animal, an otter or something, swam miles upstream with it, and then left it on the bank for the foxes to find. Not very likely.'

'What if the murderer killed the girl in Broxbourne, started chopping up the body to dispose of it, and then thought better of it once he'd cut off the foot, and simply chucked the rest of her in the river, where she was carried downstream to the Pride of Lea?'

'Nah. The marks ain't straight like they would be if they was cut by a chopper or saw, just gnawed and jagged like an animal's bite marks. So, I'm guessing the foot come off *in the water* when the body rotted. Could'a been caught in the paddle of a steamer or something and been carried upstream that way. The foxes must've found it on the bank at Broxbourne and carried it away.'

'A rotten foot?'

'Well, yeah.'

'Foxes like fresh meat, Frank.'

He combed his silky moustache with two fingers of his left hand while he searched the ceiling. 'Yeah. 'Course. Think again, Frank, eh?'

Saturday was Polly's busiest day, with late-summer weddings to photograph and fetes and tennis matches and bicycle races. She shut the shop and set off with the mule trap, leaving Archie to take the 'bus to Camden.

Effie and Clara barely looked up as he came upon them bent over the worktable in the clay room: dark schoolgirl plaits and a blonde whose braids were wound round her ears somehow, like the headphones for a crystal set. They were examining the plaster skull which Clara had cast in three parts and glued together. Vic had fashioned a stand for it from an old camera tripod of Polly's which he had secured to a base of thick plywood. A length of piping and a couple of bolts joined the inside of the plaster skull to the stand.

'He's thought of everything, your granddad,' Effie said to Clara. 'See, Archie, he's made a neck out of chicken wire, for you to build on. Unfortunately, my diagram doesn't include the neck. But a neck is a neck is a neck. You've painted scores of them. I'm sure you could come up with something.'

'I'll copy yours if I get stuck,' he joked.

'Mid to late teens, you said. You'd do better to copy Clara's.'

Lord, yes, he thought with a start. Clara was about the right age. Well, nearly. Give her a year or two. In fact, most of the girls on the Missing List were mid to late teens. And Clara looked older than her years. The thought made him catch his breath.

'It's all right, Pops,' she said, reading his anxious frown correctly. 'They've dinned it into us at school about not speaking to strange men, about going about in pairs, and Nana never stops going on about 'nasty men' trying to pick up girls on their own. She reckons I should stab them with a hat pin, scream loudly, pick up my skirts and run like hell.'

'Absolutely.' He forced himself to make light of it. 'It's not a time to be ladylike.' So, she'd been warned. She knew the dangers. Even so it was a while before he could focus on a large diagram of facial musculature that lay beside the skull and a pair of globular eyeballs that goggled up at them, unsettling with their unrelieved whites. Effie had brought them, too, having raided the prosthetics cupboard in the burns unit, she said.

'I couldn't decide which colour to bring. You said her hair was auburn, Archie – like yours – so in the end I brought this whisky colour.'

Archie blinked. Whisky? Should he be flattered?

Clara was wrinkling her nose. 'Funny,' she said, 'I see her with blue eyes.'

'Really?'

'Yes. My friend, Lilian, she went missing recently – her people have the sweet stall in the High Street – she has redder hair than Pops, carroty, you might say, and really zingy blue eyes.'

Lilian, again. Her friend was really preying on her mind, thought Archie. And *zingy*? Was that even English? These Yanks had a lot to answer for. 'Redheads have green eyes, brown eyes, blue eyes, all sorts,' he said. (Please God, let Lilian turn up soon so that Clara can stop worrying.)

'Just saying…'

In any case, he pointed out, the modelled head would be the basis of an etching, a poster, printed in black ink, like the one they'd done for Lilian, so it didn't really matter whether her eyes were light or dark.

'Effie,' he said, *sotto voce,* 'Polly took some photos of the decomposing head at the crime scene before they cleaned it up. I, em, I don't know – I mean – is your stomach strong enough? They might give you some idea.'

'Ri – i – ght.' and she leafed through the photographs without so much as a grimace. 'Now these are useful, Archie. In fact, you can see, here and here,' she pointed to rotting areas that had once been a chin and a ravaged cheek. 'No, not there, that's a maggot. Just there – see – there's very little build-up of fat deposits. I'm thinking she'd have been quite a bony little thing, delicate, you know, and thin-skinned. See, that vein shows through the skin just here!'

'But wouldn't she have slimmed down, anyway, the longer she was dead?'

'Uh? Oh, Clara…' She'd been listening! 'Well, that's a good point.' Effie put on a smile and turned to the girl. 'But no. You need energy to burn up fat stored in your body, and once your heart stops beating your bodily functions stop, too. The fat stays where it is. And rots,' she added.

'But she wouldn't be eating, either. She'd starve, in fact. Get thinner.'

Effie frowned. 'It doesn't work like that, dear. Everything stops when you die. Your body doesn't need food anymore. It doesn't feel hunger. It doesn't starve and waste away. The only way it loses weight is by decomposition – rotting, decay…' she explained. 'Take it from me, this young lady, here, is probably not dissimilar in build to Polly.'

And Polly was elfin – you'd imagine her blowing away like gossamer, if you didn't know her better. Tough as old boots, that was Poll, with an iron will. Even thinking of her caused a twitch in his nerve endings.

He concerned himself with returning the photographs to his bag. When he came back his daughter was wedging a great lump of white clay, throwing it on the table, punching it, kneading it. 'Porcelain,' she explained to Effie. 'It's finer and ideal for detailing. And all this banging and punching is called wedging. It's to get rid of any air bubbles that would explode in the kiln. Not that we need to fire it, eh, Pops? It's not going to be permanent, is it, if you only need it for a picture? But we will be layering and that'll trap the air, too, you see. Once the skin's on, any air bubbles could still burst and leave her looking like she's had the pox – all clay blisters and scars.'

The adults blinked.

'Though I suppose she might have had, and we'd never know,' Clara went on, blithely. 'I've got loads of scars from when I had it a couple of years ago – one here,' she pointed to a place under her eye, 'one on my chest...'

'Oh, *chicken* pox!' Archie breathed with relief. 'I thought you meant ... er ...'

'Small pox,' Effie put in smoothly. 'Shall we make a start?'

Clara began by attaching clay to the inside of the plaster cast behind the eye sockets to take the prosthetic eyeballs, the irises centred and slightly tilted in line with a ruler held between the eyebrow and cheekbone as the doctor indicated. They immediately brought the skull to life, too much so.

'Oh Lord,' he said. 'Hurry up and give her eyelids, Clara, do. She looks ghastly.'

Clara obliged and soon, framed in clay, the eyes, though lashless, lost some of their unnerving glare. Then the crafting began in earnest. Under Effie's direction, what Clara made Archie copied, measuring the thickness carefully so that they produced symmetrical muscles, ligaments, fat deposits, nerves and glands.

Archie placed his pieces on the right side of the skull, Clara on the left, both attaching them with slip and building up from the plaster cast, using a crochet hook to lift and place the delicate blood vessels, and a fine-toothed steel nitcomb and tweezers to striate the musculature. Archie had sole charge of the nose.

'You're guessing, right?' asked Effie.

He shrugged as he flared the nostrils. 'Well, we know she's Caucasian from the hair. I'm letting the nasal bones guide me. The nose cavities of the skull are quite narrow and go deep but the bridge itself is high. If the cartilage followed that plane exactly the nose would be overly prominent and the cavities shallower.' He paused. 'I think,' he added, crossing his fingers. 'Anyway, I quite fancy Roman noses. Delicate ones, like Polly's. As for the length, some noses are longer, some shorter,' he told them, 'but from the photos, it looks as though hers was about average.'

'I remember. And her nose was a bit narrower here. Like this.' She pinched the tip of the clay nose, very slightly and smoothed it round. 'It fell off when Sid whacked it.'

Archie swallowed. Right.

'Any clues as to the ears?' While Archie had been making the nose, his daughter had been fashioning a pair of ears from twin lumps of clay. 'She didn't have any left when we found her.'

'I – I think those are probably about right.'

'Good.' She laid wet cloths over them to stop them drying out. 'I tried to copy Effie's but they're mostly covered with her hair.'

'Did you? I didn't feel a thing,' she joked. Archie smiled grimly. It was hard to make light of this job. 'You never know,' the young doctor went on, 'your Jane Doe might have had her hair styled in the same way as me.'

'That's the fashion, is it?'

'Pops, don't you know anything?'

Under Effie's supervision, with frequent references to the diagram, they rolled out a thin, and then thinner still, band of muscle for the forehead, stuck it on and gently combed it up and

63

over Jane's forehead, like some water-driven blanket weed. In the minds of each of her creators were her last moments, when this muscle would have moved the skin to register fear and horror as she faced her killer.

Twin temporalis muscles followed, on either side of the skull, their ridges fanning out from just above the cheekbone to the top of the skull, thinning with combing and separating to infinitesimal tendrils as they crept over the top of the skull. They did one each as Effie voiced concern that the face might become too symmetrical.

'Good, that's very good,' she said. 'She's beginning to take shape already. I'd better take a photo, what do you think? Polly did show me how to work this camera but I … oh thanks, Archie, this button here?'

Eventually the skull had all but disappeared under layers of white clay that recreated, as nearly as possible, the flesh that was now silt at the bottom of the river. Muscles circled the eyes, straddled the lids, flowed down the sides of the nose and around the mouth, in striated bands and snakes and blobs. With glands and ligaments, they criss-crossed and shaped the cheeks and bound the jaw and chin, like bandages on a war victim. At last they were ready to attach some lips.

'This is the difficult bit. Pops always says if you get a person's mouth right you get their likeness.'

'I thought it was the eyes, the windows of the soul,' said Effie.

'Mouths,' said the Prices together.

'But we may never know what Jane Doe's mouth was like.'

'Well…' said Archie, 'the size of the mouth is dictated by the position of the eyes. See? If you drop imaginary lines from her pupils to her teeth, her mouth will fit snugly inside them. From there to there. That's our parameter. And the top lip is usually fuller than the lower lip, and there's always a slight overbite. Now Jane Doe's teeth are very good, so the chances are her mouth was well proportioned, too. Right, Clara. Your turn to be creative.'

'Holy Moley!' Her rictal grin was a match for any skull. 'If I get it wrong, I'll mess up the whole project.'

'Just a minute.' He took an ancient mirror from the wall, cleaned off spots of clay and mildew and propped it in front of her. 'Use yourself as a model, Clara. It's the best you can do.'

Sighing, she got to work, rolling two cushions of clay between her fingers, that she angled over the teeth, shaping them with a palette knife and an orange stick. 'Don't look at me,' she said, waving them both away. 'And don't blame me if it all goes horribly wrong.'

He put the kettle on, and by the time the tea was made and drunk it was done. It wasn't an exact copy of her own mouth but it looked perfectly real.

All that remained was to draw together the chicken wire protruding from the hole and fashion the neck, layering on the long muscles that Effie said were there, too.

'Now I really have to go,' she announced, ducking to look in the mirror over Clara's shoulder. She squared her hat and stuck it with pins.

'What, *now?*' wailed Clara. 'But we're just about to put on her skin! It's the best bit!'

'I can tell what she's going to look like already.'

'You can't,' the girl insisted. 'Beauty is skin deep.'

Effie shrugged. 'You don't need me anymore and the hospital does.'

Archie pleaded, 'Really, Effie, it shouldn't take too long.'

But she wouldn't be persuaded and as the door closed behind her, stepfather and daughter gazed at each other, utterly floored. How could you deny yourself the fruits of your labour? The whole point of the exercise? Ah well, it took all sorts…

'You know what?' said Clara, after some thought. 'Rather than painting on the slip, I'm going to dip it, like a glaze. I think brushing it on might damage what we've done.'

He could see that. The result would be uniform and smooth

and any hollows and crevices would be evened out. 'But what about the eyes?'

'We can scrape them clean afterwards … if we want.'

She mixed a quantity of clay and water in a bucket.

'Ready?'

Archie's fingers were long enough to hold the fleshed-out skull, upside down, thumbs on the edge of the neck, middle fingers on the cranium, and immerse it in the creamy liquid.

'Out, now!'

After a few minutes they gave it a second dipping: dermis and epidermis.

'Oh my!'

'Hello, Jane Doe! I'd say you were almost perfect.'

While Archie washed his hands, Clara cleaned the eyeballs, then shook out her arms, preparing for the finishing touches.

The eyebrows followed the brow line perfectly, tiny hairs of clay fastened into the damp slip. The eyelashes performed their miracle and, once the ears were in place, they both stood back to appraise the look of the thing. Lord, he thought, Clara was truly talented. She had breathed life into it.

Into *her*. She was real. Her eyes seemed to sparkle. Despite her baldness, this was a girl you could believe might still breathe, laugh, speak. They left her to dry.

More life in the sculpture, he thought, than in Sophie, whom he took to the Hackney Empire that night. She found the music hall 'vulgar'. They nudged and winked in Mozart's operas, she said, and that was bad enough but this… This! She sat, wincing, in the best seats he could afford, tut-tutting and turning away in the cancan, at the splits. She said Marie Lloyd's 'A Little of What You Fancy' was insulting to womankind. As for the comedians with their innuendoes and *doubles entendres* – they should be ashamed.

Good God, he thought, this was a new way of looking at his favourite form of entertainment. Polly was a suffragist, too, and she was a regular at the Horse and Groom's saloon bar entertainment. Effie, as well. No, despite her dimples and her flattery, Miss Hudson had a fatal flaw, and that was prudery. Maybe snobbery was another. Only tonight Clara had warned him against her.

'Can I come?' she'd asked when he'd said he was going to the Empire and he'd had to explain that he was taking his new student, a Miss Hudson.

A look of sheer horror had transformed her happy face. 'Miss Hudson!' she'd cried. 'But you can't!'

A 'gold-digger' she'd called her. Apparently Lilian had told her that Sophie was out to get him. Lilian knew her from school and had taken a dislike to her. 'She's only after what she can get out of you, Pops – what you can teach her about painting and your money. She'll get you to marry her and then she'll bleed you dry! You must drop her straightaway. Oh, please don't go out with her tonight! Please!'

He'd never thought of Lilian as a particularly good judge of character, but maybe she knew something he didn't. Pity she wasn't around to ask. Anyway, he had no intention of getting tied up with Sophie, no intention at all – just that the girl happened to let slip that she had never been to the music hall and he'd offered to take her. It was too late now to put her off.

In any case, she was a great help with Percy's picture. Percy had put back the grand opening to Christmas, now. With a bit of luck, between them, they'd have it finished by then.

In the days following, when the bust was dry, Archie painted it with egg tempera – gently blending the colours with his fingers for a more natural-looking finish than oils. Finally, Clara lowered Jane Doe's crowning glory, a flowing chestnut-coloured wig, into place and, after half an hour of plaiting and gently pinning, she had created the modern style that Effie wore, showing the lower half of the dead girl's lovely ears.

Father and daughter solemnly shook hands.

'So *that's* who she is. Thank you, Clara, she's ready for her photograph now.'

'No, thank *you,* Pops.'

'I'll tell Tyrell he can have his poster tomorrow.'

'And take the skull back, please. I'd rather not think of what we look like underneath our skins. And Jane's so pretty, now. I'm happy to make up stories about her, like you do with a doll, I suppose, when you're little. I can see her dancing, or riding a horse, or kissing some handsome prince.'

Five

Clara loved the fact that she'd been able to help Archie reconstruct the dead girl's face. She so wanted to help her 'father' solve this mystery. Because Pops was her real father – she was convinced. He'd told her he had loved her mother since they were college students together, and she, him. Perhaps Lizzie had gotten pregnant and had told him? Who knew? Perhaps he'd informed her he couldn't make her an offer of marriage with holes in his pockets. Or perhaps she'd turned him down. Whatever – Lizzie had married his friend, John, who was madly in love with her and was already making a name for himself with his decorative wall tiles. And Clara was born. She took after her mother in looks, otherwise, she was sure she'd have had hair with russet tints like his and been big-boned. She couldn't bear to think of being sired by surly old John Kington, the laudanum addict, who had allowed a thief to kidnap her and only come to her rescue when Archie had sobered him up and forced him to go looking for her.

Although she had been only a toddler when it happened, it was burnt into her brain. Even now, in the middle of the night, she'd sometimes wake with a howl of 'Ma-a-ma!' having seen a flash of that terrible separation in a dream. Lizzie would be standing there helpless, reaching for her baby, her face a twisted scream of despair. 'Clara!'

Then she would always remember seeing her upside-down mother disappearing into jiggering nothingness as she, slung across

Mad Tommo Hegarty's saddle, had jounced and jiggled against the horse's warm flank, seeing, when she lifted her head to scream and kick, the road a blur under the horse's hooves. Otherwise her runny nose was either jammed up against her captor's thigh, or was being slapped by the reins and the horse's flying slaver. They'd ridden like that all the way to the smelliest, dingiest part of London. And then there was that dark hayloft, redolent of fish glue, middens, sweat and dirt. She recalled children's voices down below but she hadn't been able to cry out to them for the rag tied over her mouth. Apparently Papa had been killed trying to rescue her. But she didn't remember that happening. All she could recall was black misery and the man's face, dirt-streaked and desperate, his sneaky brown eyes and snarling mouth – *'Shut the fuck up, brat!'* He'd smacked her around the head, making bright zigzags of the dark walls. And he'd shaken her to make her stop crying, thrown her into a corner, smacked her again. She'd soon learned to cry silently, but it had been hard, so very hard.

At last, at last, somehow she had been returned to Mama, put back into those fierce arms, held tight, smothered with kisses and quieted, rocked at last to sleep. When she'd woken up she'd been clean, dry and warm, her tormentor was gone, and the man she'd called Papa was gone, too. Forever. Only Mama and Pops remained, and between them, they tried to make up for that dark, painful time, loving her, sharing in her play and learning, making her feel an equal part of their married bliss, believe that what she said and did had worth. They'd succeeded in burying the horrors, limiting the damage. And then, just when things were sailing along nicely, Mama had died, too, in a bloody bed, along with Clara's new baby sister.

There followed a terrible time, when both Pops and she were sinking beneath a tidal wave of grief. Nana Grant and Granddad, over from Camden and trying to help, wanted to take her away with them, since, they said, it wasn't right that a man, unrelated to her, should have guardianship of a girl-child. 'Over my dead body,' he'd cried. 'She's mine by law. Lizzie expected me to look after her and look after her I will.' He'd tried to put on a brave smile because Mama would have wanted them to be happy, he said, but his eyes weren't in it, and every night she was woken up by these horrible sounds that men make when they cry. Then came the time he'd told her it made him sad to be around the things that reminded him so much of Mama and would she mind very much if he sold The Pottery? They moved to the room above the greengrocer's that he called his studio because of the big windows and the fanlight that made it easier to see what he was painting. Sadly, all his pictures were of Mama and he wouldn't let anyone buy them. They grew poorer and poorer living on the vegetables Mister Bob, from downstairs, gave them. Granny Price and Grandpa came over from Wales – they'd had a letter from the Camden grandparents saying all was not well – and they gave Pops such a talking to, mostly, she remembered, about the state of her shoes, which pinched and let in water. Grandpa took her down the High Street to the Shoe Emporium and bought her some lovely button-up boots and a hot pie and mash, with peas, while Granny stayed behind to 'talk some sense' into Pops. Despite her protests, Clara had to go back with them to Wales for the summer, while Pops got down to some serious painting. In his letters, which Granny read to her, he said she was never to forget that he was and would always be, 'her own loving Pops,' but there were going to have to be changes. She could choose to stay in Wales or live with the Grants in Camden – her father's people, the Kingtons, didn't come into it, not that she would have wanted to go to Ireland to live. Anyway, it was up to her. But if she lived in Wales he couldn't get to see her very often. In Camden, she would sleep in Mama's old truckle bed and Nana and Granddad would love her and look after her, though she'd still be his girl and he'd see her at weekends because she'd have to go to school during the week. After school, he said, she'd be able to paint and make her clay models and Granddad Grant would teach her, because that's what Granddad did. He'd taught Mama and he'd

71

taught Pops. That decided her. Sometimes, in the school holidays, he said, and other times, she would come and stay with him, but in the meantime he simply had to knuckle down to it and make some money.

And that was what happened. She loved school, loved her grandparents and had everything she could possibly want: holidays on the Welsh coast, where Pops taught her to swim, and a busy, bohemian home in Camden, chock-full of artefacts, where interesting people dropped in and out, including Pops on Sundays. And, just recently, now she was old enough, she caught the tram outside school on Wednesday afternoons and came over to Walthamstow to hone her swimming skills at the municipal baths, just down the road from Pops's place. There was always room for improvement, he said, and it was important to learn to dive and life-save and to do other strokes than doggy-paddle. He wouldn't let her travel back on her own at night, of course, but would either take her home in the mule trap, or she would stop over, sleeping on her own little camp bed that he kept under his big one. The only trouble with that was they had to get up early the next day so he could drive her to school. But it was quite exciting, tearing through the streets, chewing on a bacon sandwich, with the wind in her hair, holding on for dear life, usually arriving just in time to hear the handbell summoning the girls in from the playground. Only once were they late, when the river flooded St Pancras Way, and Pops got a ticking off from the headmistress.

She loved this project of theirs, putting a face to a skull. She loved that he relied on her skills. In the few years she'd had with her, Mama had taught her everything she knew: how to have respect for the material, how to prepare it, work it, how to get the best out of it. Clay modelling was something she'd always done as far back as she could remember.

And somehow she felt she knew this face with its sprinkling of freckles that Pops had dotted on at the last minute. Very attractive, he said. He only said that because he had freckles, too. Not as many as Lilian Steggles though. Lilian was her friend from swimming. She looked like her Mum had shaken the spice jar over her. Some of the boys down the market called her Lilian Freggles.

Progressing quickly from widths to lengths to half-miles, Clara had become a strong swimmer, thanks to Miss Smith's coaching and, last year, had found herself in the diving queue behind the famous Lilian, who won all the races. To Clara's surprise, the girl was shivering on the springboard, quite unable to take the plunge. 'I c-ca-a-n't!' she'd wailed.

'Come on, Lil, you're holding everybody up! Take the ruddy dive!' Miss Smith's swear word echoed round and round the vast pool, raising goose pimples and eyebrows. Miss Smith, with her modern square-cut hair, in her culottes and plimsolls, was a tartar. (That's what Pops called her, trying not to smile, which immediately made Clara think there was something odd about her coach, but he simply shook his head and said, 'She's a good teacher, never mind her little ways.') Unfortunately, there weren't any other female instructors to be had and, as it wasn't 'done' for men to teach girls swimming, exposing them to 'arms and charms,' as Pops put it, brusque 'Smithy', as she preferred to be called – had to do. Lilian was the star swimmer, Miss Smith's favourite, and Clara had seen her do a perfect swallow dive just ten minutes before, but now the coach wanted her to do some sort of backward flip and she couldn't. Someone in the boys' class, earlier in the year, had misjudged where the edge of the springboard was, and cracked his chin. He'd nearly drowned and had to be taken to hospital. He wasn't right yet. Clara, waiting at the top of the ladder, saw Lilian's body droop in defeat.

'Come on, come on! Bouncy, bouncy, that's the way. Trust me, Lil, you *will* land on the same spot. One and two and – oh Christ!' She threw up her hands as Lilian stopped dead. 'Don't look down! Come *on!* Shut your eyes and go! One and two and – oh, get off that ruddy board – we haven't got all ruddy night!'

Clara had felt Lilian's fear through the soles of her feet as the board quaked with the girl's nerves. They were catching. This was to have been Clara's very first high dive, a simple forward-facing affair, and she'd had to summon all her courage to get this far – it was miles down – but now her resolve was fading. She couldn't retreat. There was a long queue behind her.

In the end, in her one and only act of kindness, Miss Smith had made them all come down off the ladder so Lilian could crawl back along the springboard to safety, her face drained of ought but freckles, her blue eyes big and wet.

'What we gonna do with you, Lil, eh? Eh? I don't have time for ruddy histrionics,' the instructor maintained, 'I've got a class to run. You'd best go and practise on the low board. No, you can't go and get changed. You stop there with her, Clara Price. You can practise dives together. Won't do *you* any harm – might even cure you of bellyflops.' So, the girls had spent the rest of the time doing simple standing dives, urging each other on and cheering when they each hit the water cleanly.

Chatting through the wall of adjoining cubicles afterwards, Clara had been surprised to learn that Lilian was the daughter of the Steggleses, who owned the sweet stall where Clara bought toffee apples.

'It's a family business,' she revealed in response to Clara's probing. 'Nan and Auntie Vi make the sweets and Mum and Dad sell 'em. Me and me brothers help out when there ain't no school.'

'It's a wonder you're so slim.' Lilian, two years older than Clara, was streamlined.

'Eh?'

'I'd be a right roly-poly with free sweets all day long.'

'No, I lay off sweets,' she said. 'I have to. Smithy says I gotta watch me weight.'

'She tells you what to *eat?*' Clara was incredulous.

'Not here.' Cubicles had ears, they both knew that. 'Tell you after.'

Aged twelve by then, Clara didn't need Pops to collect her from the pool. She could easily walk to his studio and enjoyed telling him of her progress over tea. She thought of asking Lilian home with her now, but, with only the one big room, half of which was her stepfather's studio, there was nowhere private to talk and Lilian might be shy, with him putting in his twopenn'orth of wisdom. Try and stop him! So, when they met in the entrance hall, swimming rolls under their arms, long hair twisted into dripping wet knots, she suggested going across the road for a Horlicks.

The place was steamy and crowded with their swimming class, now at liberty and shrieking and giggling as girls do. Spotting a couple of older women beating a hasty retreat, Clara and Lilian were able to slide into their warm seats and talk without being overheard. Though they both sipped their drinks with relish, acquiring milky moustaches that they licked off, Clara noticed that Lilian refused sugar when she passed her the bowl.

'See, I try and think of sugar as poison – like I don't dare touch it.'

'Really? Poison?' Clara couldn't imagine a world without sugar. She could live without sweets, she supposed, at a pinch, but Nana's apple pie and her spicy fruit cake made life in Camden worth living.

'Stuffed meself when I was a littl'un,' Lilian confessed. 'Jujubes, jelly babies, dolly mixtures, you name it. I was a right little porker. Mum said it was puppy fat and I'd lose it as I got older but I didn't. I just got fatter and fatter. I mean you try living in a house where there's toffee boiling on the stove all day, every day, and bullseyes setting in trays, and wine gums and jelly babies and chocolate everywhere you look. I mean just the smell of it was enough to put the pounds on. I couldn't wait to get home from school to fill me face. I hated school. I got bullied and called names – Lardy-Lil was their favourite – and it wasn't much different when I went to the 'big' school, up the road. I was so unhappy, Clara. I mean I couldn't have joined in their games if they'd asked me – and they didn't – it made me puff just to tie me shoelaces. Anyhow, one day I overheard Miss Hudson, the art teacher, asking our form mistress about the fat, ginger girl sitting alone at the back of the class and me ears pricked up. 'Ostracism is so cruel,' she said. 'But she's an obvious target. The size of her! And really, someone, with a kind heart, ought to tell her that she smells.'

'Lilian! Oh, you poor thing!' Clara's eyes filled with tears.

'Oh, Clara, you don't know the half of it.' She swallowed. 'See, I never knew that I – that I was, you know – whiffy. It weren't that I didn't wash – I did – I do – I have a bath every Friday night!' Clara nodded. She did, too, as did everyone she knew. Friday night was bath night, worldwide – everyone spent Friday night in front of the fire, drying their hair. 'But, being blubbery,' she went on, frowning with the effort of complete honesty, 'the slightest effort brought me out in a sweat, you know?' Clara didn't know but she nodded encouragement. 'And her saying that, I mean it really hit home. She's really pretty, Miss Hudson is, and *she* smells lovely – Devon Violets, I reckon. I, well, I had a bit of a crush, you know? I couldn't bear to have her turning up her nose at me. So, I decided then and there, no more sweets. I mean it wouldn't kill me. It was just a habit, like biting your nails. Once you make up your mind to it you can just stop and pretty soon it becomes natural.'

'Gosh!' Clara knew all about bad habits and how hard they were to break. No 'just' about it. She'd tried everything to stop brushing her top lip with her hair. It helped focus her mind and it was calming somehow. She could almost hear her mother's voice, saying, 'There, there.'

'Well,' said Lilian, 'Mum was a bit put out when I wouldn't eat me puddings and pies. But when I started losing weight and she knew I felt better for it she stopped nagging. Then I saw these swimming classes Smithy was running so I joined up. I mean even roly-poly people can swim. And I started to shape up. I mean that was two or three years ago and I'm still doing all right. I can do my stint of stirring the boiling sugar and setting and pulling and rolling the sweets and that without having to try them out, like.'

'Do you still fancy them though?'

'No,' she said firmly. 'I keep telling myself they're bad, bad, bad and I'm beginning to believe it.'

'And do you still have a crush on Miss Hudson?'

'No way!'

They'd continued to be friends, corresponding by post and meeting up on Wednesdays and some weekends when Clara came to stay with Archie. They told each other everything. Or, at least, Clara did. This last year, Lilian hadn't been quite so open. She seemed moody and secretive, staring off into space, jumping when Clara spoke to her. She said it was school. She said she was beginning to think it was a waste of time, her trying to get good results. 'What's the point? I ain't clever like you. If I don't make it in swimming I'm going to finish up on the stall and that's all there is to it.'

Was it that loss of hope that had dulled her eyes sometimes, that gave her dark shadows under them and made her look away as though she didn't want you reading her thoughts? Polly said girls Lilian's age got moody from time to time. It was part of growing up and she didn't mean anything by it.

When summer came you could sometimes jolly her out of these 'sulks' with walks in the forest, games of tennis or a picnic in the park but on rainy days Clara often caught her slumped in a corner, brooding.

The last time Clara had seen her friend had been a month or two back and that was when she'd warned her about the 'gold-digger'. They'd been standing in yet another queue, this time for the magic lantern show at the Town Hall to which Lilian's Auntie Vi was treating them. Lilian – this was one of her sunnier days – had been eager to tell Clara that the lovely Miss Hudson had been asking after her.

'Me? But she doesn't know me from Adam.'

'She stopped us in the school corridor, yesterday. Blimey, I couldn't hardly breathe, Clara. Turns out she was at the gala, last week, and she saw *you,* she said, winning your races. When she saw we was mates, she thought she'd have a word. Not about you so much as your old man…'

'Pops?' Now this was really puzzling.

'Said she admired a man who wore his heart on his sleeve.'

'Eh?'

'He'd come to support you and support you he would, never mind what people thought.'

Clara laughed. 'He *was* loud! I could hear him over the din of everyone else and the water and everything!'

'Yeah, he even drowned out my mum and that takes some doing. Mind you, there's not that many dads would take time off work to watch *girls* swim, even if they could, and most of the mums was too proper to shout the odds. Made me laugh when you made up that half-length in the relay and your old man was hopping around like a frog – thought he was going to jump in himself. Anyway, Miss Hudson said he must think the world of you.'

'Feeling's mutual.'

'Yeah, I said you was close. Well, someone must've told her he was Archie Price, the painter, and she said she knew his stuff, seen it in magazines and galleries and that, and she liked his style. Be honest, I reckon that's the real reason she come to the gala, so's she could give him the once over. I mean she ain't never set foot in the baths before.' Her lip curled. 'She don't like sweaty girls.'

Clara smiled ruefully and squeezed her friend's arm. It still rankled, then, that remark Lilian had overheard.

'What she wanted to know was, would he come up the school and give a talk to her girls, like, maybe give them a demo? I mean, how am I supposed to know? I said he might if they paid him. And she said she was hoping, now he was on the up, he'd do it for nothing. He mustn't be short of a bob or two, she said. I mean she was fishing. I said I didn't think he was that well off, living over the greengrocer's shop.'

Clara frowned. 'I wonder which paintings she's seen. I bet she's been to the RA and seen his portrait of Granny Price. It really is special. She wants it back when the Summer exhibition ends but I'm going to ask her if I can borrow it for a while.'

'That the one in Wales? You like her best, don't you?'

'Yeah, but don't tell Pops. He says I shouldn't have favourites, not when the Grants have given me a home.'

'What about your real dad's mum and dad?'

'Never see them, Lil.'

That was when Auntie Vi, who had been chatting to Charlotte, off the bric-a-brac stall, suddenly poked her fat face between their shoulders. 'Ain't that your gorgeous George, Lil?' Clara looked across the road to the tall boy, with his black curly hair and nice teeth. 'He's waving, Lil. Lil, look – over there!' But Lilian had blushed deepest red and turned her head away. 'What, ain't you speaking to 'im no more? Lovers' tiff, eh?' she chortled.

Clara was surprised, remembering how, not so long ago, Lilian had made her walk backwards and forwards past George's house and report on what was happening in his front parlour.

'Lil?'

Lilian made a face and mouthed, *Leave it, Clara. Not now.'*

Oh dear.

'Gawd, Lil, you're a right little sourpuss these days,' went Auntie Vi. 'I thought this afternoon might take you out of yourself but it don't seem to be working.'

Lilian chose to ignore her. 'I think she was angling for an introduction.' Clara frowned, having lost the thread. 'Miss Hudson,' Lilian reminded her. 'I reckon she's got her eye on your old man.' She lowered her voice dramatically. 'Like she's after his money, I reckon. You know, seeing as he's a widower an' that.'

'You told her that?'

'Had to, she asked if your mum was an artist, too.' She paused. 'What was I to say? 'Cause he is nice looking, for a dad.'

'Who's this, Lil? Clara's dad?' Auntie Vi was earwigging. 'Yeah, he's a bit of all right, he is!'

'Telling me, ducks,' put in Charlotte, who had once posed for Pops. 'All the girls down the market fancy him,'

They fell out of earshot as the queue moved up and Clara muttered. 'There's only one woman stands a chance with Pops and that's Polly. Your teacher will have her work cut out getting past her. And he's got no money – so she's out of luck there. I know he gives a lot to charity, Women's Suffrage and that, but he has to take on work for the police and sketch at the courts of justice to make ends meet.'

'I'll tell her.'

'And I'll tell him to watch out for a nasty little gold-digger called Hudson. Blooming cheek!' By now they'd reached the Town Hall steps. 'Nearly there. Oh, look, there's Smithy just going in the door with two old dears – must be her mum and dad.'

'Never! Oh Christ, don't let her see me, Clara.' Lilian pulled her shawl over her red hair and tried to make herself smaller.

Clara was puzzled. *She* didn't like Miss Smith, found her quite creepy. That time she'd put her arm round her and squeezed her, she'd squealed and wriggled away. 'Please don't do that!' she'd said at the top of her voice.

'Don't let anyone touch you in any way you don't want them to,' Archie had told her. 'Not doctors, not family, no one at all. No one else has any right to touch you unless you give them permission.'

Since then Smithy had steered well clear of her.

'I thought you liked her,' she said to Lilian.

'Whatever gave you that idea?'

Clara blinked. She'd always assumed – because Lilian treated her more like an aunty than a swimming coach, because she was the star pupil and Smithy wanted her to go far in the sport – that she was all right with the patting and cuddling that went on. But now it was clear, from her expression of sheer revulsion, from the fact that she was trying to hide from the woman, that she didn't like her at all.

In fact, even before the lights went down Lilian was complaining of a headache. She didn't look well, to be honest. Her freckles were dark against her whiter than white skin and there were drops of sweat on her forehead.

'What's up, Lil?'

Her friend was looking along the rows, twisting round. 'Where is she? Does she know we're here?'

''Ere, Lil,' said Aunty Vi, rattling a paper bag of chocolate toffees, ''ave a sweetie, go on. I 'spect you're just 'ungry.' And, lo and behold, Lilian took one and another and another.

She'll regret that, Clara remembered thinking at the time, and, indeed, soon afterwards, Lilian had to run outside to throw up and Clara had had to take her home and miss the rest of the show.

Then she'd run away and Clara had never had a chance to invite her to the swimming spree over at the Pride of Lea, planned for two Sundays' time. Just as well, perhaps – given her delicate stomach, Lil would never have been able to stomach a rotting skull.

Six

July 1903

A little of what you fancy does you good, Marie Lloyd would sing with a sly wink, a bump and a grind. But the trouble with just a little was that it made you want more. Lilian's mouth had filled with the sweet caramel flavour and then the chocolate had seeped through the melted toffee and she could have fainted with joy. Or misery. Or guilt. She couldn't stop. Four years' self-denial was going down the drain.

'I'll suck it slow, make it last...' she promised herself.

But she found herself eating another and then another, until she was cramming them down so fast she could hardly wait to swallow the last one before the next was in her mouth.

She had to get out of there. Away from temptation.

It was all Smithy's fault, giving her the jitters, making her panic, making her skin crawl. She couldn't breathe, let alone resist the temptation of sweets. Bugger Aunty Vi.

The magic lantern show went on, oblivious to her distress, photographs projected onto the screen showing the wonders of the world. She tried to take an interest in the pyramids and pigmies, the Zulus and Eskimos, the strange men with bones through their noses, and those others with earlobes down past their shoulders. There were giraffe-necked women, with a dozen rings round their necks and others with saucers in their lips. None with freckles and ginger hair.

'You're a curiosity, my girl,' she'd said, as she'd held her and touched her in places that made her stiffen with shock. *'Freckles everywhere like seedy bread. Do they go inside, as well, I wonder?'*

She couldn't push her away and beg her to stop. Dad always said she had to pay heed to Miss Smith. She was her lifeline, her one hope. She was the only one who was going to make her a champion. She was Lilian's ticket away from the sweet stall.

There were freaks on the screen now: Siamese Twins, tiny General Tom Thumb, a bearded lady, a tattooed man, the tallest man in the world – and there silhouetted against the light was her own personal monster, her long nose – that had poked into all Lilian's hidden places – profiled as she turned to speak to her mum.

The problem was Lilian's response. What she should have said was, 'No!' and legged it. But her body had betrayed her, had responded by wanting more; she'd grown hot and eager and Smithy had smiled a wicked smile, and obliged her. It was wrong, so wrong. God would punish her, sure as sure. But she couldn't help herself, and Smithy had sent her whirling down to hell, like the devil she was. She'd said, 'You're mine, now, girly, all mine.'

She'd never go to heaven now. She was so ashamed, so dirty, so defiled, she wanted to run away and hide. Peel away her skin with its wicked nerves and freckles and burn it. There was Smithy now, acting so charming, so warm and caring of her old mum and dad and they had no idea – how could they possibly imagine – the disgusting things their daughter had done to her young charge? If Lilian said anything they'd reckon she was a loony and put her away – *her*, not Smithy – like that housemaid down Coppermill Lane, who complained to her mistress about the master touching her up. She had unnatural obsessions, they said, and men in white coats had come and shut her up in the loony bin.

Oh God. She'd stuffed herself with Aunty Vi's caramel and chocolate to make it better. It didn't, of course. Nothing would. And now, to make things even worse, she'd broken her four-year fast. What could she do? What could she *do?*

Rushing from the hall, treading on toes, scattering programmes and drinks, out, out into the night, she couldn't wait to stick her fingers down her throat. Clara, dear soul, had followed her out, just in time to hold back her hair ready for the second bout of heaving and retching up brown slime.

When it was over and she was all teary and shaky, Clara had lent her a hanky to wipe her face. Lil couldn't hardly look at her friend, so good and innocent and herself so foul. She'd refused to go back inside and they'd gone home, the two of them, leaving Auntie Vi goggling at the screen. Now all she wanted was to be left alone, but Clara was all for fetching Mum.

'Don't!' she'd begged. 'She can't leave the stall on a Saturday. And I'll be all right after a kip.' But, as soon as her friend had left, she had gone down to the cookhouse where Auntie Vi had left all the sweets out on racks to cool and stuffed herself silly.

In her head, she could hear Smithy saying, in her nasty way so that everyone could hear, 'Been in the trough again, piggy? Jesus, look at you! You're swimming the mile, Lil, not the ruddy Channel. You don't need ruddy blubber!'

She took another caramel to drown out her voice and another to wipe out the memory of those hands on her. And another for the – oh dear God, she had to stop! Mum and Dad would notice half a tray of chocolate caramels missing and that would be another hiding. What could she say? Mice? Rats? Plead ignorance? Or perhaps she should eat them all, wash the tray up, put it away and rearrange the other trays to cover the space. Then Auntie Vi would get the blame for forgetting to do a tray of chocolate caramels. She'd believe them. Her memory wasn't what it was, poor old cow!

Seven

Polly's brow had puckered when he brought the porcelain head into the shop for her to photograph. 'So that's her, is it?' she'd said. 'Pretty girl.' Twin lines formed between her brows. 'You sure she's not local? I feel I know her from somewhere.'

'Really? You've spoken to her?'

'I'm almost sure…' Her frown deepened. 'I'm wondering where – she may have been a customer.'

'Polly, that would be so helpful…'

'Wait. Let me look.' She pulled a heavy ledger towards her and opened it at the beginning. 'Given that she was in the water for months it won't be recent, will it? Perhaps if I see her name I'll know…'

One by one the handwritten pages furled and flattened as she smoothed them and ran her finger down through the columns of names, addresses and payments. Archie held his breath, then let it out. This was going to take a long time. Never one to waste an opportunity he got out his sketchbook. He liked watching her working.

'No,' she said, at last, looking up, her mouth a thin line of regret. 'Sorry, I can't find her. I've gone back three years. Pity, because if I had taken her photograph I would have an address for her as well as a name, and copies of any studies I'd taken of her. But it was always an outside chance, wasn't it?'

'Never mind, you've done your best.'

'But I'm sure I've seen her before…' Her brow puckered with

the effort of remembering. 'It – it may not have been in the shop now I come to think of it. A meeting, maybe..?'

'Votes for Women?'

'Probably.'

'Was she a speaker or someone in the audience?'

She had no idea. 'It was a long time ago, Archie, last summer, I think.'

The Old Meeting House was a sea of hats: from ripples to cresting waves, with turbans and toques bobbing along, and Polly's straw fancy didn't look wildly out of place. There were one or two toddlers and babes in arms, but generally any children not in school had been parked with nursery maids or female relatives for an hour or two, leaving their mothers free to meet and mingle, laugh and chat and cool themselves with fans or leaflets.

'Hello, young Polly!' An elderly woman coming up the aisle stopped to talk. 'Your doctor friend not with you today?'

'Up to her ears in work, I'm afraid.'

'And you've brought your young man, I see.'

'Ah, no.' She was quick to deny it. Too quick, thought Archie. 'This is my good friend Archie Price.'

He forced his mouth to stretch into a smile.

'You're the artist, aren't you?' For some reason, the woman was bristling with hostility. 'Last time you were here you were engrossed in your sketching – everyone and her grandmother, it seemed to me. You'll forgive me if I don't sit next to you, I find it most distracting.'

'Oh, I do beg your pardon.' He was taken aback. 'It's something I do for the newspapers,' he explained.

'I'd have thought photographs were the thing these days.' She was clearly trying to ruffle his feathers. 'Tell me,' she went on, her eyes glinting with malice beneath fleshy folds of skin, 'is that the only reason you come to these meetings? I wouldn't have thought it possible to listen to the speeches at the same time.'

'Not only listen,' remarked Polly, coldly, taking his arm protectively, 'he can quote them word for word, weeks afterwards. And argue for and against.'

'I'm not the enemy, madam,' Archie felt constrained to say. 'I'm all for equality. Many men are.' Without altering her expression, the woman inclined her head and sat down stiffly. 'Dear me,' he said as they made their way to the back of the hall. 'What's got her goat?'

'She's bitter,' said Polly. 'It's not just you, Archie, it's *all* men, starting with her father, probably, then her uncles and brothers, then her husband and sons, even the man next door, treating her like dirt on their shoes. She's knows now it's a con trick and she's been had. Meetings like this offer her hope and here's a young waster, she thinks, with nothing better to do than draw pictures, making light of the whole business.'

'Oh, bugger,' he said, turning to go back and make peace with the woman.

'Leave it, Arch. I doubt you'll change her mind, she's that prejudiced. Come on, there's a couple of seats in the back row. We want to be first out at the end.'

'Tch – that troublemaker's here again,' observed the woman next to Archie, lowering her chin in the direction of a bowler-hatted gent further down the hall. 'He only comes to heckle and boo. I'm surprised they let him in after last time.'

'He's worried,' said Polly from the aisle seat. 'He can see the day coming when his wife goes out to work and he has to do the chores on the maid's day off.'

The woman laughed sourly. 'That'll be the day! If my hubby is anything to go by, it won't enter his mind. When I get back of a morning from scrubbing milady's steps it's all there waiting for me. Kids screaming to be fed, beds not made, pots and pans in the sink from the night before, and 'im with his head stuck in the runners and riders.' She elbowed Archie. 'What about you, young man? Can you iron a shirt?'

'Archie has always fended for himself. He can cook, too.'

'Oh my, you've struck gold there, love!' said the woman.

'He's not…'

Archie broke in. 'Is it true they're planning to ban men from meetings altogether?'

'Never! Where d'you hear that, darlin'?'

''Bout time an' all!' offered a woman in front of them.

'Oh yes,' said someone else, 'Mrs P's got all these big ideas…'

'It was in the paper, yesterday,' Polly informed them. 'She reckons the Society has to change radically if we're to achieve anything at all.'

Her words fell on deaf ears as the row of chairs on the platform began to fill. The audience leaned forward to compete in naming the wives of local worthies, for the most part, though Archie recognised the matron of Connaught Hospital, a professional and taxpayer in her own right.

Polly, too, was on tiptoe. 'No Mrs Pankhurst this time,' she announced.

'Ssshh!' hissed a dozen voices. The fur-wrapped woman at the lectern was introducing the first speaker who went on to tell a tale of unfairness, of a dear father who had died, leaving his entire estate to a distant cousin, the only man left in the family. She had been forced to leave home and seek work as a governess in order to survive. She sat down to sympathetic clapping. Three more women stood up with their own tales of injustice, of hardship, or ill treatment by their husbands, and then it was the turn of Mrs Mildred Brett.

Rapturous applause greeted her. The camera flashed and the renowned Secretary of the National Union was recorded for posterity.

'She's good!' Polly was whispering now as the applause died away. 'Effie and I saw her in Hampstead.'

The visitor, a slim young woman, smartly dressed, held up pale leather-clad hands, both to acknowledge the greeting and to hush her audience.

'Look at you all!' she enthused. 'The hall is packed! Look what you have achieved, you women of Walthamstow, just by attending this meeting in the face of male opposition! Wonderful. Well done, all of you.'

While they were still basking in a glow of self-congratulation she went on to tell them that although they were pivotal within the home, men had all the rights, women none. They were chattels. All that they were, all that they had, became the property of their husbands on marriage. Like some old oak dresser, they had no voice; they could be used, kicked, broken or thrown out, with no recourse whatsoever.

So far, she'd said nothing they didn't already know.

'So yes, we want the vote – we want Parliament to recognise that we are intelligent, rational human beings, with rights, just like our husbands. Why not? We come from the same stock as our fathers and brothers. We are not inferior to them just because we are female. We should not be denied the vote because of biology.

'But there is so much more to our great movement than simply getting the vote. We are *demonstrating* women's solidarity, we are making it plain to all that we can work and fight together, write and speak from our own experience, not just on the vote but on sexual, social and vocational freedoms, like fair pay and reproductive rights. Being denied a say in such matters is an insult to women and to humanity. Using the vote is almost beside the point compared to what it will mean for women to *have* the vote, to not be mere extensions of our husbands.'

A cheer went up. A flutter of pale leather-clad fingers quelled it.

'So far, ladies, we have campaigned peacefully; led by Millicent Fawcett the NUWSS has held meetings and rallies; we have marched, printed pamphlets, we have drawn up petitions, we have lobbied our MPs, all in the belief that if our organisation was seen to be intelligent, polite and law-abiding then we would *prove* ourselves responsible enough to participate fully in politics. We have had the support of some members of Parliament but all private members' bills have failed. Good behaviour has failed. Peaceful means have failed. *What can we do?*'

Everyone held their breath. Archie stopped drawing. What was she suggesting?

'Ladies, I believe our tactics will have to change. Just like our men before us we have no choice but to resort to more violent means to get ourselves noticed, make our voices heard. They were not well behaved, why should we be any different?'

All around the hall, eyes blinked, faces were touched by fear, by possibility. The camera flashed again. Voices protested. Questions flew backwards and forwards. Violence? But they were women. And wasn't that the point? Could they? Fight authority? Fight the police? Face imprisonment?

Oh yes, Mrs Brett said they could and, indeed, they must. They had to be a thorn in the side of Parliament, one it could not ignore. They had to be brave. They had to be noticed.

'In addition, ladies, we must recognise that we cannot do this alone. We are but a small part of womanhood. We must extend our ranks to include women from all walks of life. It is my belief that we cannot win without them.'

The air moved with a general intake of breath. Veiled looks were cast at the women occupying benches at the back of the hall. Women like *them*, did she mean? Working women? The wives of common labourers? Servants? Worse? Goodness – she was proposing that they rubbed shoulders with the hoi polloi! Journalists' heads were down, scribbling now, for all they were worth, as more indignant questions were lobbed and returned.

'I leave you to think over what I have said. I think you will come to see that this is the way to go, the *only* way to go. We have no choice.'

'Well!' A man's harsh voice broke in on the thoughtful silence that followed her words. 'You have written your own epitaph, Mrs Brett. I need say no more. You have doomed this cause of yours to failure.'

'Come on, Arch!' Polly grabbed his arm and propelled him from the hall. He stumbled behind her, at a loss. They were heading in the wrong direction if she wanted to take a close-up of the speaker. She thrust a photo under his nose and he gave a start.

Oh yes, of course, this was their main reason for being here. It was a long shot but Polly had thought this was a meeting their murder victim might have attended had she lived. Someone here might remember her, know who she was. They took up positions either side of the main exit.

No one in the flood from the hall was unaffected by the speeches. Some were arguing heatedly, some were consumed by anxiety, some were wreathed in smiles, so excited they were hardly able to connect with what they were being asked by the tall man and his petite lady friend, as they thrust photographs under their noses.

'Sorry, what? Do I recognise this woman? Should I? Who is she?'

Those from the back of the hall pushed by them. There were last-minute errands to run, children to collect from school, meals to cook – they really couldn't stop. As the body of the hall emerged, some paused for longer, gradually bringing their minds to bear on what was being asked. They'd like to be helpful but, though she seemed familiar they couldn't place her. One or two claimed to have seen her at past suffragist meetings. 'Not lately, though. Not for a long time.'

'I don't think it was here,' said one. 'Maybe London? It's what I told the gentleman who was here before asking after her.'

'What gentleman was that?' Polly asked sharply.

'You've got me there, I'm afraid. Well-turned-out sort of chap, looked like he might have money. He had a photograph of this same young lady, his daughter, I think it was. Like you, he wanted to know if anyone here had seen her. I believe she'd run away from school or something…'

'Are you in a hurry to get away?' Archie asked. 'If not, I wonder if you'd mind helping me reconstruct a picture of this chap.'

'If I can…'

He left Polly to continue quizzing the exiting crowd while he quickly sketched a portly, moustachioed gentleman from the woman's description. Finished, he looked up to find Polly talking earnestly to an elderly couple who remembered the girl herself. 'I never forget a pretty face,' the gentleman told Archie as he joined them.

'Pleasant young woman wasn't she, John?' said his wife. 'Very well spoken, nicely dressed. Educated, I'd say. She showed us to a seat in the front row, on account of John's hearing. It wasn't here though, John. Now where was it?'

'Eh?' He produced an ear trumpet and she repeated what she'd said, slowly and clearly. 'Ah! You see, we've been to so many of these meetings,' he explained to Archie, 'here, there and everywhere. Our daughter, Emily, is a keen worker for women's rights,' he said with a touch of pride. 'You may have heard her speak – Emily Perkins?'

Eventually they agreed that it might have been Tottenham where they'd met the girl, the Guild Hall being one of the places Emily attended regularly and they remembered the same young woman coming up, afterwards, to congratulate Emily on her speech. Polly was frowning hard, her mouth like an o. Archie, too, was excited. They might be getting somewhere.

'Yes, it was definitely Tottenham, Birdie,' Mr Perkins said. He could even remember the date: the nineteenth of June. They were travelling back to Hackney that night to celebrate his birthday the next day, with a trip to the Empire.

'Don't you remember how hot it had been that month, how glad we were when it did eventually rain? The garden was so dry, you know,' he said, in an aside to Polly, who merely blinked. 'We read in the paper that the hall we had been sitting in only five days before, fanning ourselves just like tonight, was flooded out in that terrible storm?'

Birdie looked blank.

'Yes, you do, dear – and you talked about crowds and panic and how we wouldn't have stood a chance – and how lucky we were that it was my birthday, otherwise we might not have come home when we did…'

She remembered. They all did. Tottenham, like many towns in the floodplain of the River Lea, had been under water for days, following the rain. Camden had flooded and the Walthamstow marshes were awash. People lost their homes, cattle died and ploughs and carts were lost.

So, Jane Doe had been alive on the nineteenth of June? The floods must have come on the twenty-fourth of June. He'd better look that up, check…

'And she was there, this girl, in the Tottenham Guild Hall, before the flood?'

They nodded.

'Don't think we caught her name, though, did we, John?'

'Emily might know. She's speaking up north today – we came to take notes for her. Leave me your card, young man, and I'll get back to you if she comes up with anything useful.'

'Do you need the young lady urgently? I don't know when we'll see Emily next.'

Archie explained that they believed the girl to have been a murder victim. The police needed to find out who she was so they could inform her next of kin.

'Murdered! Oh, that's terrible! Oh, the poor young woman! Was it because of her politics, do you think? If I've told Emily once, I've told her a thousand times, "You'll make enemies, my girl. You must be so careful." And this young lady was so nicely spoken, too.'

Eight

Archie returned the skull to the police station, together with the reconstructed head, Polly's photo of it, the sketch of the portly gentleman believed to be the girl's father and news of Jane Doe's last known whereabouts.

'Blimey, mate, you have been busy. Who done the 'ead?' He told him. 'Gawd, she's a chip off the old block, your Clara, and no mistake.' Archie raised an eyebrow. 'Oh, of course, em, I mean, like, her old man – her real dad, that is, that *was*—' Digging himself quickly out of a deepening hole, he cleared his throat noisily. 'Last seen Tottenham, you say? The Guild Hall? Five days before last year's floods? What's that, the nineteenth?'

'Show us that picture again, Arch – the bloke asking about his missing girl.' DS Beckett stared hard at the drawing. 'He come in 'ere, asking about her, I'm sure.' Narrowing his eyes and mouth to aid his thinking, he went over to the wooden cabinet, pulled out a drawer, riffled through for the relevant file and took out some papers. 'Here we are,' he said, smoothing out a document on the counter and moving a thick forefinger from where the date was written as June 20th 1902, along the salient sentences. He read aloud, '*Reported missing by one Elias Redfern, of Headley House, Tottenham…*' and followed his finger along the lines. 'Looks like he done the rounds. Started out at Tottenham Green police station, worked his way down, Wanstead, Stratford, Leyton, then here.' He paused, widening his eyes, and his next words throbbed with excitement. 'It says here, gents, the daughter was a *"Miss Eleanor Mary Redfern, aged seventeen years. Last seen, the morning of Sunday, the thirteenth of June, nineteen-ought-two at Miss Stevens' Academy for Young Ladies, Ipswich."* She was a school runaway!'

He looked up, his face closing as the import struck him. A young married man in his late twenties, Stanley Beckett was already father to five, and Archie could well understand the look of utter bewilderment on his face. 'Would you believe her old man didn't report her missing 'til a week later, the what – the twentieth, the day after that women's meeting in Tottenham? What's going on here? I mean, the Guild Hall's only round the corner from the flaming police station – she was practically on their doorstep!'

'Perhaps she got within spitting distance and thought better of it.'

'See who it is, though, boyo?' Tyrell was leaning over Beckett's shoulder. 'Elias Redfern owns a stretch of land over Tottenham way – big vegetable grower, glasshouses far as the eye can see. Made of money. You must've seen his big red fern leaf on the side of carts delivering stuff to your Bob Cheshire, Arch. He's cornered the market round here. She was an heiress, that young girl. Guess he was keeping schtum, 'case some villain had took her and wanted a ransom. She'd fetch a fortune.'

'Seventeen, though?' mused Beckett. 'Round about the age girls like her 'come out', innit? Go up the Palace to be presented at Court? Redfern would of been thinking about marrying her off, most likely to someone who could do him a bit of good. He wouldn't want a little thing like her going missing to gum up the works. He'd keep it to himself, long as he could.'

'You reckon?'

Archie said, 'Whose land was it they found the foot bones on?'

'Not Redfern's,' said Tyrell, reading his mind.

'Does he live anywhere near there, though?'

'No, he's got a big house adjoining his glasshouses. I showed you where them marsupials was found, over Broxbourne way. That's bloody miles upriver from Redfern's. Here, let's see your photo again, Arch. It's a sight clearer than this one on file.' He adjusted his reading glasses. 'She was a lot younger when he had that one took – early teens, I'd say. But it's her, all right. Young Clara's got her off to a T. Good job – tell her. Spot on.'

'And that drawing you done of the dad is very like,' said Beckett.

'Redfern…' Archie murmured, committing the name to memory. 'And now, I suppose, you have to go and tell the poor man that his daughter is dead and we've only the bones to give him for burial.'

'Strictly speaking, that's Tottenham's job, mate. That's where he's resident.'

Archie was shocked. 'I call that passing the buck, Frank.'

'Yeah, you're right. We best go and get it over with.'

'We?'

'Yeah, you can come an' all, seeing as you're keen. You can bring that head along with you: he might like it to remember her by, as a keepsake, like.'

'But the skull's still in it, Guv,' said Beckett. 'That ain't nice!'

'Keep up, Stan. It's a plaster cast, innit? This *here's* the skull.' He reached down under the counter and produced the grinning bones.

'I hardly think her father will want…' Archie began.

'What else you gonna do with it? Put it on your mantelpiece?'

They were kept waiting on beautifully carved wooden chairs while Elias Redfern finished a telephone conversation in another room. They could hear him shouting at some underling. *'Time? Time? Do you think I don't know that? Mmm? Time is what we don't have in this business! A day, an hour, too late and that's hundreds of pounds you can kiss goodbye … Yes – yes … I should think so, too … Well, make sure you do! Mmm? Otherwise it's coming out of your pocket!'* The earpiece slammed onto the upright and there was a moment's heavy silence. Then a drawer opened and shut with a bang. A few moments more and the door swung open to reveal a well-built gentleman in waistcoat and shirtsleeves, with a high colour and a red silk cravat at his throat. He mopped his brow with his handkerchief and settled a pince-nez on his nose, in order to glare at them.

'Pah! Middlemen!' he huffed. 'And you, gentlemen – from your faces I gather you've come to add to my troubles…'

'These are police detectives, Mister Redfern,' said the manservant who had shown them in and who now, discreetly, closed the door to the office and withdrew.

They introduced themselves.

'Police?' he said lightly. 'Oh dear, what have I done wrong now?'

When they suggested he might prefer to sit down his expression changed from one of derision to distress. 'Oh! Oh, my God!' he cried, 'you've found her, haven't you?' He sat down heavily and, burying his face in his hands, commenced rocking from side to side, uttering little cries, 'Oh no! Oh no, no, no, no, no…!'

Archie looked hard at Tyrell whose eyebrows moved a fraction to show he'd understood. When a policeman asked you to sit down it usually meant bad news, any bad news. It could have meant they'd found Eleanor and she didn't want to come home or couldn't. It didn't necessarily mean that the girl was dead. Most parents would hold onto hope, he thought.

At last the man recovered enough to raise his eyes, though keeping them screened with one hand while he pulled his handkerchief from his pocket and blew his nose, loudly. After a moment or two he was able to address them, albeit rudely. 'You took your time, didn't you? I've been expecting you every day for over a year.'

Archie bristled; Frank merely nodded. 'July,' he said, grimly, and Archie realised that the detective was holding back information, waiting for Redfern to put a foot wrong. 'We've only just identified her as your daughter.'

'July? Mmm?' He seemed to be searching their faces for clues. 'You found her in July? Over a year ago! Why wasn't I told?'

'*This* July.'

'You've only just found her? Good God, what've you been playing at?'

Not, where has she been all this time, or even, can I see her? Archie thought.

Tyrell broke it to him, then, that she was indeed, dead. 'There's strong evidence to suggest that your daughter was murdered but—'

'Murdered?' My lovely girl? Oh my God – have you got him?'

Not *how* was she murdered? Or when, where or why?

Only when they told him her remains had washed up in the middle of the River Lea near the Walthamstow marshes did he appear genuinely puzzled and surprised.

'*Walthamstow?*' He said it as though it was the last place on earth. The pits. 'How the devil did she end up there?'

'We think she may have been swept down the river from Broxbourne. There's evidence to suggest she spent some time there.' Her foot stayed longer, thought Archie.

'Broxbourne, eh? What, so someone killed her up there and dumped her body in the river and it was carried downstream?'

'It's a possibility.'

'Well, how else did she get there?'

'She might have committed suicide or drowned by accident.'

Ah, so Tyrell wasn't going to mention the hyoid bone and its fracture? Archie thought he knew why.

'Yes, of course,' the girl's father nodded sagely. 'But Broxbourne of all places? What was she doing there, I wonder? Broxbourne?' he mused, stroking his chin, squinting at the ceiling. 'We don't know anyone in Broxbourne. Well, I certainly don't.'

'She may just have been passing through.'

'It rings a bell, though…' He pressed his lips together.

'Yes?'

'No, I –,' he hesitated. 'Well –,' he began and changed his mind. 'No, nothing.' He breathed deeply and adjusted his pince-nez. 'You see, I suppose she might conceivably have known someone who lived there, worked there. It's just speculation though.'

'Mister Redfern, if you can think of anything that might have a bearing on the case you should tell us.'

'Well, there was a young gardener chappie left the estate, a year or two ago to take up an apprenticeship in Broxbourne.'

'What was his name, do you remember?'

'Blackett. Gilbert. His father works for me. But there's no way my Eleanor would have had anything to say to the likes of – no, it's unthinkable. No, she was on her way home. She'd run away from school, you see. Yes, she'd have headed straight home to me, and, as she was passing through Broxbourne, some bastard—, ' but his lip crumpled and he couldn't go on.

'*You* didn't see her at all?'

'No.' He swallowed and wiped the corner of his eye. 'She didn't make it this far.'

Tyrell's moustache trembled as he firmed his lips over his teeth. It was all Archie could do not to shout out, *But she did! She made it as far as the Guild Hall!* What's more, he thought, neither Birdie nor her husband had thought her appearance worthy of comment. Nicely dressed, they'd said. If she had been roaming round the countryside for a week or more, finding her way home, she'd have been bedraggled, to say the least. But when Mr and Mrs Perkins saw her she wasn't wearing a ragged school uniform; she may even have been wearing that Gamages outfit. She must have come home and changed, had a wash, at least, tidied her hair. Why hadn't her father seen her? Had he been working or out socialising? In which case, why hadn't she stayed to see him?

'Was she unhappy at school, d'you know? Was she worried about something – exams – bullying?'

'Well, of course, she was worried about *something*!' he snapped. 'You don't run away from school for nothing. But that's the puzzling thing. She was a popular girl and she wasn't in trouble at school – they were perfectly satisfied with her work. The only thing they were concerned about was her meddling in politics, attaching herself to silly causes, you know.'

'Causes?'

'The women's thing – that wretched Pankhurst woman, filling girls' heads with nonsense. Pah! Can you see it happening? Mmm? Women having a hand in running the country? They wouldn't have a clue. Dear God, they can only just about manage to look after themselves, most of them. They need a man to guide them, advise them, protect them. It's clearly states in the Bible, *'Man-is-the-head-of-the-woman!'* and he beat his hand in his palm in time with the words. 'What they're asking for is *unnatural!* It's against the teaching of Christ.'

'Paul.' Archie couldn't help himself.

'Eh?'

'It was St Paul who didn't like women. Christ had little to say on the matter.'

'What!' Words failed him. He shook his head and growled.

Archie saw that Tyrell was also scowling at him and he shrugged. Well, these two were in for a shock if the suffragists had their way. No more peaceful demonstrations. Women were determined to get their demands met, by hook or by crook. They were going to use violent and aggressive means, if necessary.

Tyrell tried another tack. 'There were no men in her life, no one you could think of who would, em…'

'Who would murder her? Of course not. She was seventeen, at a well-run establishment for ladies. A seminary. Where would she meet men? She wasn't due to "come out" until this year. No, it must have been some lowlife who chanced on her. Mmm? Running away from school, traipsing through woods and fields, she was easy prey for some thug. She brought it on herself, poor silly girl. Oh, Eleanor. Oh, it doesn't bear thinking of.'

Tyrell looked up from notes he was making. 'Would she have had money on her? Jewellery? Something worth stealing?'

'I doubt it. She had an allowance but the school looked after all the monies. But she was young, sweet and pretty, let's say. And on foot? Easy game!'

'We don't know she was on foot. She might have got a lift on a cart, or used public transport, hired a hansom.'

(Of course, Archie told himself, a lift would account for her neat appearance at the Guild Hall. She needn't have come home to change, after all. But why didn't she come home? Why come all the way from Ipswich just for a suffragist meeting – it didn't make sense.)

'We shouldn't jump to conclusions, Mister Redfern,' Tyrell was saying. 'And, by the way, there's nothing to indicate she was, um, sexually assaulted.'

'Nothing at all? No, erm … nothing out of the ordinary?' He seemed more puzzled than relieved.

'There was no evidence of anything like that.' Archie glanced across at his friend. Tyrell was sticking to his guns, then – he wasn't about to tell Redfern of Eleanor's condition when she was found.

'Oh.' The man sank back in his chair, frowning. That wasn't what he'd expected to hear.

Tyrell cleared his throat. 'When she came home for the holidays, how did she usually spend her time?'

'Did she have friends?' said Archie.

'Sorry? What? Oh, friends. Local girls, you mean? Yes, there was the vicar's daughter, Mavis. She played tennis with her and the girls from the manse up the road. Went riding with them. Boating, hiking. Mmm? The local schoolmistress came to tea from time to time – a Miss Prescott – and I believe they went to talks and concerts and, um, women's meetings. But she didn't socialise with the riff-raff from the village, if that's what you were getting at.'

'And that was her choice or yours?'

'She knew it would have displeased me.'

'Did she, did she see much of *you* in the holidays? I mean did you do things together?'

'My God, man, I have a business to run. I can't let go of the reins for an instant. She understood that. No, I saw her in the evenings at dinner, that's if I wasn't at my club, or, more likely, in my London office. A few precious moments let's say. I – I –' Redfern's voice caught, 'Oh, Eleanor. I had such hopes for her, you know.'

'Would you mind telling us about those hopes? They could have a bearing on what happened to her.'

'In what way?' He looked from one to the other. 'Oh well, I suppose it won't hurt to tell you now – there were plans afoot for her to marry Ephraim Mortimer – the railway owner? Mmm? It would have been a union beneficial to all. I mean all of *England*. I have a dream, you see, of providing the country with fresh vegetables all year round. I mean really fresh: picked one day, in the shops the next. And not just in London. I want to extend my market to the Midlands, the north of England, Wales. Mmm? River transport is fine in so far as it goes but far too slow for my needs. Trains are the answer. But the costs, you see, would be prohibitive and I'd have to pass them on to the customers.'

'Unless,' suggested Frank, 'you could cut a deal with the railway owner.'

'A merger,' murmured Archie.

'Exactly so.'

'Did your daughter know about your plans?'

'We'd only just held preliminary talks, Mortimer and me. I intended telling her when she came home for the summer last year. But, of course, she – she never came.' And he wiped away another tear.

'You never give him that pottery 'ead,' Tyrell commented, on the long drive back to Walthamstow.

'Funny that.' Archie wrinkled his nose as though at a nasty smell. 'No, he'll never get his hands on it, if I have anything to do with it. He'd put it out to the highest bidder, mercenary bugger. Anyway, it isn't mine to give. Clara has to say what happens to it.'

They drove on in silence for a bit. With a father like that, thought Archie, Eleanor was probably better off out of it. How would she, a committed suffragist, have felt about being a pawn in her father's game? Ephraim Mortimer must be at least twenty years older than his blushing bride would have been. If she *had* known about it – and they only had Redfern's word for it that she didn't – she might well have had cause to hang herself. That fractured hyoid bone could have been caused by the jolt of a rope. He put it to Tyrell, who nodded agreement and took his pipe from his mouth.

'Occurred to me, an' all,' he said, thoughtfully. 'And someone, finding her dead and not wanting to incriminate himself, might have took her body down and chucked her in the drink. Wash away any evidence. All conjecture, of course. No, Arch, we still got a long way to go. But we'll get there, mark my words.' He turned his pipe stem to Archie to make his point. 'I don't think Mister Elias Redfern has told us everything, by a long chalk.'

'I'm sure of it,' said Archie. 'I'm not convinced she didn't call in to Headley House on the way to Broxbourne, for a wash and brush up. By the time she got to the Guild Hall she was a nice, clean, respectably dressed young lady, not a scruffy schoolgirl. Surely, even if he wasn't there to see her, he'd have known of her visit from the household staff.'

'Mmm, so why's he lying? Is he protecting someone else, I wonder? 'Cause he's ruled himself out of any list of murder suspects, Arch. No way would he have wanted his girl dead. She was his meal ticket.'

'But he still hasn't asked to see the body. He hasn't asked any of the usual questions, in fact, it's almost as though he knows the answers already.'

Back at the section house, Tyrell began typing up Redfern's statement from their notes and, after downing a welcome cup of tea – they hadn't been offered any refreshment at Redfern's – Archie prepared to leave.

'Arch – before you go…'

'Yes?'

'Now I wonder – I'll be a bit tied up with this tonight – can you maybe help us out, again?' He took some typewritten notes from another folder on his desk. 'See this 'ere, this is another missing girl. Like 'buses, ain't they? Eleanor, Lilian, all coming along at once. Might be connected, I dunno. Now we ain't got no photos of this one and I'll tell you for why. Her old man's a quack healer. Laying on of 'ands and that. He reckons taking photos is dangerous, right? Like photos steal a person's soul or some such guff. Girl's name is Meredith, Augustine Meredith – fifteen years old she'll be now, if she's still alive. Been gone a week or so. They call her 'Gussie', her mum and dad – and they live up in them big houses in the Drive. Funny couple, like I said. Any old how, you'll see what I mean when you go up there.'

'Me?'

'Ain't you been listening? I said we ain't got no photo. See, you're the on'y one can put a face to 'er. Talk to the Merediths. Find out what she looked like and do us one of your drawings.'

The Drive was posh. An L-shaped avenue at the top of Church Hill, it was distinguished by the *'Private Road'* notice and a heavy iron chain looped across its leafy entrance, which the visitor was required to unfasten before passing through, and then replace. It was one of the few roads in Walthamstow that had not been recently paved, presumably at the behest of the residents. Over the summer, tufts of grass, now wisps of hay had grown between parallel wheel ruts. When it rained, horses and their vehicles, ferrying the gentry to and from their front doors, or transporting servants or tradesmen to the backs of the mansions, would churn the ancient leaf litter to a muddy soup, making walking or cycling unthinkable except in waders and overshoes. However, the cool shade afforded by the tall young plane trees on this sunny Saturday was pleasant and, from this distance, you could not hear the market traders promoting their wares at the bottom end of the hill, just the benign clunk of tennis balls in the courts over the way and the twittering of sparrows among the leaves. Here were no unpleasant smells, no common people or drains, no tanneries or second-hand stalls. No industry, no commerce, no poverty. Just fragrant, sun-dried leaves underfoot, freshly clipped privet hedges and Brasso polish on the letterboxes.

He found it, at last, the shiny plate announcing that *Thos. Meredith, Faith Healer* resided within. He stepped down from the cart, hitched the mule to some railings guarding a semi-basement, and ran up the steps to the front door.

A skinny housemaid eventually answered the clanging of the doorbell.

'Good afternoon. Might I speak to one of the Merediths, please?'

'The doctor?'

'Or his wife...'

'New patient, is it?' Her voice had an Irish lilt.

'No, no, this is about another matter entirely.'

'Tradesmen round the side.'

'Look, this is a police matter. If you wouldn't mind giving him my card...'

The girl was gone for a matter of seconds, it seemed, before her master burst into the entrance hall, one eyeglass flashing strangely in the light from the door. 'Police? Police? Have you found her, then?'

'I'm afraid not.'

He wilted visibly, and his 'Oh,' of disappointment was like a final expiration. 'So...' he took a deep breath, pulling himself together, and squared his shoulders. 'What is it, then?'

Having verified that the family had no photograph of the missing Augustine, Archie explained that he had come to draw a likeness of the girl at her parents' dictation in order that the police might have something to go on.

Mr Meredith frowned over his monocle and jutted out a doubtful lower lip. 'Hmm...' he said, scratching his head, 'A drawing, eh?' Pondering, he pulled at his curly white side whiskers. If anyone ever needed a Father Christmas at a children's party, thought Archie, this man would be their first choice. Presumably his blue eyes twinkled in the right circumstances. These were not they, though.

'Any port in a storm, I suppose,' he said, his voice heavy with despair. Turning from Archie he gathered his strength to yell at the door, 'Bell-a! Can you come, my love? Front parlour!'

Turning back to Archie he said that Augustine, a lively if home-loving child, had a good attitude to work in her school down the road and plenty of friends. She was in the school netball team and she played the piano. That was something he missed, hearing her tinkling away. Gilbert and Sullivan were her favourites. She and her mother played duets. He started to sing, 'A wand'ring minstrel…' but choked on the words, and squeezed his eyes shut over unmanly tears. His pale lashes were wet when he searched Archie's face, as if he might have answers. She had no reason to run off, he said through gritted teeth, none whatsoever. She must have been lured away or abducted by wicked men.

Mrs Meredith came scurrying from somewhere at the back of the house, eyes alight with hope and wringing her hands. 'You've found our Gussie? Where is she?'

The light went out when she saw her husband sadly shaking his head. Poor mother, thought Archie, poor father. They must both be trying hard to hold the pieces of their hearts together over a gaping hole where their child should have been. The pain must have been excruciating.

Neither of the Merediths was convinced that constructing a likeness of their poor dear child from memory was any better for Gussie's soul than photography but they were desperate and, if it would help get her back … Perhaps a drawing wasn't quite the same as a photograph. When it came down to it.

As it happened, they were quite unable to agree on the face that had shared their home for some fifteen years.

Was their daughter's nose perfectly straight or, as her father suggested, was it ever so slightly hooked, like his, and slightly longer? Were her front teeth crooked or, as Mrs Meredith insisted, were they perfectly graduated little pearls? And her hair – was it golden, as her mother described it or auburn, like her paternal grandmother's?

'Oh, not at all like your mother's, Thomas. Bessie was quite carroty!'

Perhaps parents, seeing their child changing minute by minute, week by week, year by year, didn't quite notice the latest manifestation of her nose or teeth or hair. She was just their beloved girl, an extension of themselves, the same then, now and always. Archie told them that hair colour didn't really matter as he only had a graphite pencil. He would give it a slight tonal quality however, to show that it wasn't flaxen or brunette.

Eventually, he was able to draw up a likeness on which they both agreed, and so like their memory of the missing girl that Mrs Meredith was unable to contain her tears.

'Oh, Mister Price you have her. The laughter in her eyes. One could almost believe she could speak from the page and tell us where she is, who has taken her…'

'May we keep it?'

'I'll make a copy,' he said, explaining that the police would need the original in their search. He flipped over to a clean page.

'It'll be something to remember her by,' Mrs Meredith observed quietly.

Archie looked up in surprise. Why were these parents so sure their children were gone forever? 'She'll turn up, I'm sure. You mustn't give up hope.'

'What if she went willingly?' said Meredith, with a heavy sigh. 'What if she ran away from us? She wanted so much to be *modern*, like her friends. We are a bit, I suppose, old and fuddy-duddy. She didn't always agree with us on matters of – of faith.'

Mrs Meredith's lip trembled and she dabbed at her wet eyes with her handkerchief. 'I'm sure she didn't run away. She loved us, I know she did.'

'We have to be prepared for the worst.'

It transpired that the girl had disappeared while the Merediths were attending a service at the local spiritualist church. Gussie hadn't wanted to accompany them.

'You think someone broke in and took her?'

'No, no, there was no sign of a break-in,' his voice broke.

For a few years now Gussie had questioned their beliefs, Mrs Meredith explained, even though *'all this...'* she spread her hands to encompass the room, the house, their comfortable lifestyle, their livelihood *'depends on our faith.'* In order to heal his patients, Thomas Meredith called upon the spirits of the dead to aid his healing hands. He extended his hands towards Archie and invited his visitor to examine palms that were large, fleshy and pink. They appeared to tremble. 'Feel them. Go on.'

Gingerly, Archie pressed the soft flesh and drew back in shock. Meredith's hands were burning hot.

'That is the healing power,' said the spiritualist. 'Do you have any aches or pains? I'll show you.'

'No, actually, I'm feeling decidedly chipper,' said Archie quickly. Somehow he couldn't bear the idea of the man's sweaty hands on any part of his person.

'My patients don't have to believe at all.' He shook his head in emphasis. 'Whatever they think, even if they are the biggest sceptics in the world, it doesn't matter. I believe I can heal them and I do, with help from the Other Side. Spiritual influence is so, so strong, you would not believe.'

No, indeed, thought Archie. Everyone was entitled to their own beliefs, he supposed, but what Frank Tyrell would have made of these people he could only imagine. Frank was an out and out atheist. He didn't trust in anything that couldn't be proved logically or scientifically and had had a little more truck with the Catholic Church since it had come out against spiritualist ideas some years before, citing their so-called 'manifestations' as fraudulent. Still, it takes all sorts, he owned. There were respected and educated people, like this couple, like the author, Sir Arthur Conan Doyle, who remained unshakeable.

All Archie knew of the cult he'd divined from another keen member of the local spiritualist congregation, one Bertha Reeves, less respected and hardly educated at all. She claimed she was often singled out during the evening service to receive a message from 'the Other Side' – *Me old mum come through again, last night, Arch. Reckons it's time I cleaned me upstairs winders, inside and out. I told her to mind her own business. Blooming sauce!* She had sweetly smiling pictures of angels and others of hands steepled in prayer pinned up behind the bar at the Horse and Groom, alongside Archie's portraits of the landlord and his missus.

Archie, himself, was not a churchgoer though he had respect for what Jesus taught, and so he told the Merediths. Working with the police he felt he knew something of men's baser natures, recognising an innate selfishness in the need to survive. And having suffered the deaths of his beloved wife and their stillborn infant, he had yet to be convinced of a loving God. And what about war and poverty, ignorance and the infirmities that came with age and disability? What about gender prejudice and racial discrimination? Were they divinely ordained, or what?

'Oh, Mister Price,' said Mrs Meredith, 'that's a very sad outlook. Perhaps if you were to come along to a séance we are holding next week, your dear wife would come through and you would know that she and the little one are happy in the Spirit World. You might also find peace.'

'Never!' Archie was aghast. 'Sorry, but no-no-no-no-no-o-o…'

Polly was curious. 'I've never been to a séance, Archie. I'd be quite interested to know what goes on there. I'll bring my Kodak.'

'You will not!'

Was she serious? She stood in her shop doorway, wiping hands that were blue with developing fluid, on her overalls. He'd disturbed her in the darkroom, that magical place where she turned captured light into negatives and then into black and white photographs.

'Polly, you surely don't believe..?'

'You know I don't,' she said. 'Dear me, when I think of the ghosts who would haunt *me* ... and the messages they would bring! But I'd like to take photos of any manifestations that might appear.'

'They wouldn't let you.'

'We could do the old hidden camera thing again.'

'Polly, these people are desperate to know if their daughter is alive or dead. That's what it's for, this séance. They think if anyone knows whether their girl has passed over, the dead will. They're hoping they might get to speak to her, if she's there, find out who killed her and where her body is. It's that serious.'

'Time?' she demanded.

It was all very cosy – too damned cosy on a warm night at the end of August – in the Merediths' jam-packed and highly polished parlour. Sweat stood out on Archie's forehead and he shuddered inwardly at the folly of this enterprise as he and Polly were introduced to the other participants in their shiny suits and 'best' dresses. These were ordinary men and women, most of them, reluctant to accept that death was the end of them and their loved ones. That was the trouble: they were too simple, too open, too ready to believe anything they were told. They weren't looking to be hoodwinked. There were the Merediths themselves and their next-door neighbours, a Mr and Mrs Turner, whose second-hand clothes shop, they informed him, was in nearby Wood Street. From the reek of moth-balls he suspected they were wearing their stock.

'You'll know Ida, then – Mrs Fitzell?' he said, quickly running out of small talk. 'Her uncle runs the bicycle shop at number twenty-three.'

Indeed, Mrs Turner did know Ida Fitzell, by sight and reputation, and expressed surprise that a respectable artist like Archie Price should be acquainted with a woman of *that* sort. Ida had married into money – tainted money, by all accounts – and she was no better than she should be, in their opinion.

'Ida is one of Archie's favourite models,' Polly put in serenely. 'The last painting he did of her is hanging in the Portrait Gallery. It had very good reviews in *La Nouvelle Mode.*'

'Tch,' said Mrs Turner, 'just so…'

Sitting opposite, bejewelled and overdressed, were *Councillor* Nightingale, as he insisted on being addressed, and his wife. There was an empty chair between them, which no one was permitted to sit in as that was Gussie's chair. Nightingale volunteered the information that he was a banker, by profession, and long-standing Treasurer of the Town Council. And, oh, good Lord, who was this up at the end of the table, highly delighted to catch his eye. 'Fancy seeing you 'ere, ducks! And your young lady!'

He closed his eyes – this was the last straw. Even if he had half hoped that Lizzie would haunt him he knew, for certain, she'd have more sense than to appear before Bertha Reeves of all people. He rose to leave, only to be dragged back to his seat by a small, blue-stained hand.

'Mrs Reeves –' Polly oiled, 'how nice to see you!' Archie blinked at the ease with which his friend soft-soaped her neighbour. She knew her for a muck-raking gossip and disliked her intensely but you would never have guessed. He gritted his teeth, summoning patience.

A sallow-skinned, cadaverous young man lowered himself into the chair next to Archie and introduced himself as Edward Pike. Even allowing for the aptness of the name – Archie immediately thought of cold fish – the only remarkable thing about his face was a series of freshly-scabbed scratches across it, as if made by tines of some sort. A sharp fork? He was lucky: half an inch higher and he'd have lost one of his dead-fish eyes. Archie thought better of asking him how he'd acquired such a strange wound.

'Are you hoping to contact someone, Mister Pike?' he asked him instead.

'What was that?' The man deigned to turn chilly eyes on him. A predatory fish, thought Archie, for although he couldn't, physically, look down on Archie and a false smile lifted the corners of his thin lips, he appeared aloof, as if such small fry as Archie were hardly worth talking to. He revealed that he was researching the paranormal for his next story.

'You write ghost stories?'

'Sometimes,' he said shortly, and then, with a sigh, for the sake of politeness and to show off, perhaps, deigned to add, 'I also write detective stories, adventure stories, short stories for the *Chelmsford Chronicle*.'

'Oh really? I have a friend on the *Chronicle*. Bartholomew Spratt?'

But their paths hadn't crossed. Pike revealed that he rarely went up to Chelmsford. He generally sent his submissions by post. But he was aware of Spratt's column, now he came to think about it. Not that he espoused the paper's political leanings; all that nonsense about women's rights…

'Oh.' There wasn't much more to say when that thin eyebrow was quirking with disdain. Not here, anyway. 'Oh, I see. Well,' he cleared his throat, 'I must say I generally enjoy the short stories. Do you write under your own name?' Because he couldn't, for the life of him, recall any story by an Edward Pike.

Pike admitted to being Edgar Logan and Archie's heart sank. Logan's stories were always so derivative, so predictable. He managed to maintain his air of polite interest, however, not wishing to upset a fellow seeker-after-truth, and changed the subject.

'So, Mister Pike, do you actually believe in all this *Ouija board* stuff?'

'I come with an open mind.'

Archie searched the man's chalky face for a hint of sarcasm but there was nothing, not a twitch or a wink. The fish eyes were unreadable. 'Well,' he said, 'I'm afraid I'll take some convincing.'

'Doubting Thomas, eh?'

'I don't believe in fairies, either,' he smiled.

'Ah,' said the man, thinning his own lips in an approximation of humour. 'So, what do you do, Mister Price?'

'I'm an artist.'

'Should I have heard of you?'

'Probably not.'

'You're not starving in a garret, I can tell.'

'I get by.'

'He's got pictures in the galleries up the West End,' piped up Mrs Reeves. 'An' 'e does drawrins for the cops around 'ere, an' all. Like if someone gets beat up they can tell 'im what the geezer looked like and he can draw 'im.'

'Well, thanks, Bertha. That's blown my cover!'

And the bloody woman beamed, probably thinking she'd done him a favour – didn't want any friend of hers hiding his light.

Thankfully the medium had just arrived. A florid-faced female, in black lace with matching spidery hair was ushered into the parlour on a cloud of stale perfume, cigarettes and a clatter of jet beads. She was introduced as Mrs Araminta Laing, a lady who came with impeccable references, all the way from Stoke Newington. She nodded her head regally and began the charade by calling for the curtains to be drawn, the gas lights to be extinguished and single candles to be placed at strategic points around the room to remind them of the Great Spirit who oversees all. They were invited to hold hands, to close their eyes in order to focus their energies and warned not to disturb or startle the medium in any way whatsoever.

Archie couldn't help but sigh as, when everything was prepared to her satisfaction, Mrs Laing sank down comfortably into her chair, took some deep breaths and quavered, in time-honoured fashion, 'Is there anybody there?' He felt a slight pressure against his right shoe: Polly sharing his dismay. Now the medium's eyes would roll up, he predicted, and her head would fall back as if she were in a trance, her voice sounding hoarse and strangled. Now someone would jiggle the table...like that. Polly clutched his hand, her nails digging into his flesh. Oops! Now a picture, a study of sailing boats, would slide from its moorings on the wall to hang lopsided ... like that ... and, see, the candles would all flicker in an unearthly draught, and now Mrs Laing would go off into some well-rehearsed rigmarole, calling on her spirit guide to intercede between the quick and the dead. She was the only one still to have her eyes closed as her audience strained to see what she could see. Finally, they were served the dish they were all hungry for when she asked, 'Do you have a message for anyone here?'

He couldn't get out of there fast enough.

'Calm down, Archie, for goodness' sake!' She propelled him to a low garden wall abutting the Merediths' front hedge. 'Sit down, before you do something you'll regret.'

'God, Polly!' He freed himself from her grasp. 'What utter bollocks!' He was shaking with rage. 'Surely no one in their right mind believes all that claptrap, all that—?'

He was lost for words, staring at her without seeing, breathing like a bull through his nose. He sat down obediently, only to spring up again immediately, his fists balling. 'How *dare* she pretend to be my Lizzie? Jesus H. Christ!'

'Oh, Archie, what did you expect? I mean, did it even sound like her?'

'Not in the least, as I believe I may have said! Lizzie had a sweet voice, smooth as honey, nothing like that old dame's squawking.'

'She explained that. The poor ghosts must take what they can get in order to communicate with the living. Mrs Laing, unfortunately, smokes like a chimney and her vocal cords are shot. The voice is necessarily distorted. It's the words you have to focus on.'

'Crap.'

'Well, of course.'

'I mean, Lizzie would never have any truck with a séance when she was alive, so why would she now?'

'Forget it, Archie. It's just silly nonsense. Put it right out of your mind.'

'Bertha shouldn't have asked about the baby, she really shouldn't.'

'No, that was wrong. That was below the belt. I'm so sorry, Archie.'

He was silent for a moment, thinking about the sheer impossibility of little Iris growing up happily on the Other Side. He shook his head. Mawkish rubbish. But Bertha Reeves's smiles and happy clucks showed that at least someone believed it. 'But the poor Merediths – I mean, that was quite shocking – that voice out of the blue. How did they do that? Mrs Laing looked as startled as the rest of us. I caught her looking under the table, during the commotion, like she was expecting to see a fraudster lurking there? Or a phonograph or something. And the way she was glaring at each of us, as if we were playing tricks on her! No, she wasn't expecting that voice at all. It really shook her.'

'It shook me. Perhaps it *was* Augustine. Perhaps she was hiding somewhere.'

'It would've sounded muffled, Polly, surely? But a voice came through, clear as a bell. That was no recording. I mean, it sounded like a pantomime dame but she could have been there at the table with us and answering questions as if it were teatime and someone had asked her if she wanted more cake. That was an extremely clever trick.'

He could remember the cold trickle of ice-water down his back as the dreadful falsetto voice had said, *'Mother, Father, I'm here!'*

The parents had sprung from their seats, Mrs Meredith giving a little scream for, if Augustine was 'coming through', it could only mean one thing, that her worst fears were realised. She crumpled, but everyone else was too stunned to go to her aid, their eyes and ears drawn to the empty chair between the Nightingales, where the voice had come from. As if stung, the councillor and his wife had moved their chairs sharply back to leave space for 'the visitor'. Though there was nothing to see, just an empty chair, her father had asked, 'Is it really you, Gussie?'

'It really is…' And, of course, he knew the drill, that you had to listen to the content and make allowances for the transmission.

'O-o-h…' He'd sat down again, heavily, as though his knees had given up.

Now those nearest their fallen hostess attempted to administer what comfort they could – smelling salts, a cushion for her head, a glass of water, patted hands. Nigh on a minute ticked by as Mrs Meredith came to herself, pale cheeks wet with tears. Mister Meredith swallowed and, gathering his strength at last, asked, 'Are you still here, Gussie?'

'I am. I'm sorry for the shock, Father. Is Mother all right?'

'Yes, yes,' came her mother's tremulous answer. 'Don't worry about us, dear. Just tell us how – how it happened that you came to be – to have – passed over.'

'Woke up … dark … no one home … thumping headache … took a powder…' The disembodied voice, still oily, now sounded vague and dreamy.

'A powder? Oh, my heavens, what sort of a powder?'

'Mmmm?' She clearly didn't understand the question. *'Can't breathe! Too hot … must get out … walk … fresh air.'*

'Oh, heavens. Where did you find the powder, Gussie? What was it? Aspirin? Or, or something from my desk drawer?'

'Where did you go, dear?'

'… Down the hill … down, down the hill … go, Gussie, walk down to the river.'

116

'River! Not the River Lea? Goodness, Gussie, that was a long way to—'

'Miles... and miles... and miles and...'

'In the dark? At night? Good God, Gussie, what were you thinking? You know you can't swim!'

It was surreal, this distracted father upbraiding shadows.

'Don't scold her, Thomas. Don't, please...'

'Cool water ... sweet water ... lapping round my feet...'

'Oh, I can't listen!'

'Quiet, Bella! You didn't go in? Gussie, say you didn't go in.'

'... so heavy, so hot and tired ... water so good ... over my feet, up to my knees ... my chest...'

'Oh, my sweet child.'

'You weren't well.'

'You drowned, then.'

'...over my head...'

'Oh Gussie.'

'Gussie? Augustine, are you still there?'

'She's gone, Thomas, she's gone.'

'She's the girl they found in the river, Bella.'

'What utter bilge! The girl in the river drowned over a year ago!' Archie had flung out of his chair and made for the door, closely followed by Polly. 'Do your research properly!' he flung at the medium.

'Perhaps Augustine's there, too, and they just haven't found her yet.'

'Polly, you don't believe in all that mumbo-jumbo? It's a put-up job if ever there was one. Someone's trying to pull the wool over our eyes.'

'Yes, but who? It wasn't the Merediths – they weren't faking, I'm sure of it. They were convinced their daughter's voice was coming through from the Other Side. Nor could it have been anyone round that table working a phonograph – they all had their hands in plain view. Even Mrs Laing looked shaken.'

'Mmm, funny, that.'

'Someone wants us to believe she's dead, for some reason.'

'Could be Augustine, herself.'

'What, you mean she's running away with the circus – and all *that*,' she indicated the house over the hedge, 'all that eyewash was to put everyone off the scent?'

'Will we ever know?'

Nine

Walter Blackett

Sweat stung their eyes and trickled over their grubby faces as they picked the red fruit, as fast as their little fingers could fly, filling their baskets, as he'd shown them, queuing at the scales to have them weighed and what was owed recorded against their names.

At least, with the children released from school for the summer months, labour was plentiful. The regular work crew could never have managed to gather the fruit in the dozen giant greenhouses and do all the other work as well: the pruning and watering, the spraying and feeding, the packing and loading of crates onto the barges to be taken up to Covent Garden overnight. Besides, little fingers were light and nimble and their families were grateful for the extra money, pittance that it was.

He glanced down at his own hands, gnarled and stiff among the lithe green plants, the fingernails black and sticky from nipping out new growth in the elbows and squeezing aphids. Outside was hot enough – blazing shirtsleeves weather – in the glasshouses the barometer needles tipped a hundred and ten, despite the whitewash screening the glass against the full sun. And watering only made it muggy.

Some of the punier children flaked out, the starvelings and the unfit, but give them their due, after a hose down outside they usually came back ready for more. Woe betide the child who arrived home at suppertime with money docked for fainting or for eating the sweet ripe fruit. 'You short *again*, young Bobby? How many times I 'ave to tell you. Eat 'em, pocket 'em, if you must, but don't let 'em catch you at it.'

Whatever punishment the children got, at least they were finished for the day at six. While it was still light, the regular gardeners had then to spray against cutworms and flea beetle and any other marauders and feed the plants a goodly dose of fertiliser. 'Witches' brew', young Albert, the apprentice called it, almost gagging on the stink of it. But it was good stuff, say so himself who made it: a well-rotted mix of horse hair and manure from the stables, tea leaves, wood ash, egg shells, compost and alfalfa. 'All mixed up with a dead dog's eye!' Albert winced, as he stirred water into the slop. 'Bejesus, me girl won't come near us, the night.'

Walter mopped his brow and neck with his handkerchief and filled his tin cup, twice over, from old Gregory's water bucket. It was thirsty work, in the stifling heat, dodging in and out of the pickers, up and down the long length of a great glasshouse, one row then the next, from dawn 'til dusk. Bent almost double, tending the plants, it gave him jip. Much as he could do to straighten up these days. Secrets weighed heavy on old shoulders.

He almost envied the vegetables, in the prime of their lives. Short and sweet. The cucumbers, two houses down, were over a foot long already, green and lovely, and the tomato plants had shot up this last week, taller than a man, with strong trusses to the very top and the fruit turning red as you watched. Barring blight, they'd have a bumper crop and the master might even crack a smile.

'That'll be the day,' said Gregory, eyebrows a-waggling like two fluffy white caterpillars. 'Mister Redfern en't had 'appy 'alf hour since his girl run off. He been in a black melancholy this twelvemonth or more.'

So had Walter. But he held his tongue as he always did, remembering that day when Elsie had told him the truth of it, that fateful morning over breakfast.

'See young Nellie Redfern run off from that school.'

His cup had hit the saucer with a clatter, spilling the tea. 'Did she, by crikey?'

'More fool them, tryin' to turn that one into a lady,' she'd said, sawing doggedly at the loaf tucked into her breast. She might have been slitting its throat. 'A-larnin' all they dappy lah-di-dah ways. Got her down, it did.'

'Allus were a wild young thing.' He remembered Nellie, the child, a pretty little girl with dancing eyes and hair like a burnished conker, playing in the yard with their Gil. They'd been great pals, her and him. Like Jack and Jill. The friendship had ended when Redfern had sent the child away to school. She'd come home, year after year, for the summer's length, before returning, in the autumn, to her studies, prettier than ever. Glowing. But Gil had never mentioned her again.

A thought had struck him then. 'Where d'you get this, Else?' She weren't one to gossip.

She, focusing deliberately on her task, had muttered, 'Off our Gil, last night, arter you turned in.'

Gil had come down, on a rare visit, seeking his father's advice, he said. Some problem with the tomato crop at Ardmore, easily remedied – he could have looked it up in the gardening almanac or asked one o' the other gardeners. They all knew it was a pretext. He was a good-hearted lad and had simply wanted to check up on the old folks. Or so Walter had thought.

'Our Gil? Where 'e got that from?'

She'd taken a deep breath then and, holding onto the bread for dear life, swallowed against a rising vomit of words. 'Gil do reckon 'tis time I told ye.'

He frowned. 'Telled I what?'

She cleared her throat to let it come out. 'They bin seein' each other, off an' on, these past four year, Walter.'

He started up then, ''Oo 'ave?'

'Him and Nellie. Sit down, sit down afore your eyes pop out

your 'ead.' And she'd told him then what Gil, with a child's innocence, had told her years ago, of his burning love for the Redfern girl. Told him that he had gone on loving her, had been courting her, in secret, ever since, sending letters to her at school, keeping the embers alight.

'Why di'n' ye tell us?'

'Knew ye'd put a stop to it, Walter.'

'Damn right.'

'I reckoned t'were puppy love an' t'would fizzle out. An' ye 'ad trouble enough wi' that there black spot and mildew. See no reason to pile on more agony if none else knew. But he'm still full of 'er, after all these years…'

'No-o!' He couldn't take this in. ''E'm 'ad plenny o' lasses, at dances an' that, football matches … an' that there Maureen he were sweet on, lived over Romford way…' He faltered, noticing her head was wagging in denial.

'There weren' no Maureen,' he'd told himself bleakly and sagged with a despairing breath. The fools, the mad young fools. How had they managed to get away with it? Eleanor Redfern, with her looks, her inheritance, her expensive education, was a rich prize, the jewel in Redfern's crown, a bargaining tool he could use in business deals. One whiff of anything improper between his lovely daughter and a lowly under-gardener with patched trousers and Redfern's rage would know no bounds. The girl would be packed off to relatives and, as for Gil, if he'd lived, word would spread, his name blackened and he'd never find employment again.

And that was why Elsie had never told him, of course. She'd thought he'd let the cat out the bag and she was probably right. He'd have to say summat. And if it had got back to Redfern they'd all be for it. Walter would be out of a job. Him and Else'd be out of their cottage. Nothing left for them, at their age, but the workhouse. And he'd see to it that Gil was finished at Ardmore's, an' all.

'He'm bound to find out, Else. 'Ow long we got? When she run off?'

'A week last Sunday after church. Took 'er this long to get here, walkin', 'e said.'

'Straight to his door, I don' doubt. No doublin' back or misleads, the stupid little bitch! On'y a matter of time afore the police track 'em down.'

'He'd never turn her away, Walter. She'm in 'is blood, allus was and allus will be. An' likewise, he'm the only one for her. That's what he come to tell us last night. Reckons he'm tekkin' her down Cornwall, changin' their names, gettin' wed.'

It was too much. 'By crikey, I'll swing for the lad!' He'd thumped the table, sending the plates jumping, the spoons and forks tinkling. 'I bent Heaven and earth to get him placed at Ardmore's an' this is…' He'd jammed his fist into his trembling lips to block the tears. 'Oh, Else…' he said as he stared into a hopeless future. 'They'm gold dust,' he mourned, 'jobs like that on they big estates.'

'Well,' she said, looking down rather than watch her husband be wrecked by grief. She paused and then came the big news. 'Gil reckons she wen' home first and Redfern slung 'er out.'

He'd sniffed then, puzzled. 'Why'd e do that?'

She frowned, then, and pulled the drawstrings of her mouth tight.

'What?'

'She'm in the family way, Walter. She went to ask the ol' man for help.'

He might have sworn then but all he could remember was his head filling with foggy despair. In silence, lips pursed on unsaid words, she'd served him his slice on the flat of the knife, butter spread thin as pity. She had a good system. So good she could give her mind to worry and not spoil the job she was doing. She scraped butter on the bread again then cut another slice.

'What you thinking?' she said after a while, looking down at his stunned face, her starch-water eyes behind their specs a challenge.

He'd shaken his head as he'd taken the bread and slapped his rasher of bacon on it, folding it into a wad before taking a bite which he didn't remember swallowing. It didn't bear thinking of – their Gil and Nellie Redfern? A baby? Suppose the police tracked them down and did Gil for kidnapping an heiress or rape?

But that were a twelvemonth since and nothing of the sort had happened. Gil had covered his tracks well. Walter and Elsie had kept their mouths firmly shut, Gil and Nellie likewise. Not a word, not a letter. They had no idea whether the young couple had gone to Cornwall and found happiness. Or not. No idea. They hoped for the best, of course…

As for Nellie, when the master had them all out combing the estate for her, Walter had joined in as was expected of him giving no hint that he knew she was alive and well and living with his son, either in sin or in holy wedlock, who knew?

His employer must have repented his actions because he appeared to be a broken man, searching for her high and low, at first. Clearly he didn't know about Gil's part in Nellie's disappearance and Walter wasn't about to put him wise. As winter came on he seemed to come to himself, losing himself in matters of business, reconciled, at last, it seemed, to the probability that Nellie would never forgive him for turning her away and that he would never see her or his grandchild again.

That's what Elsie said, anyway.

Ten

'Will there be a reply, Sir?'

Scarcely able to see through his tears, Archie shook his head and the boy faded from view. The shock of it, the loss, could not be put into words, concise and pithy, with stops, at four pence a word. But they'd expect a reply. He raised his hand and croaked, cleared his throat and cried, 'Wait!'

He somehow found himself sitting on the third stair up, trying to get his thoughts together, when the telegraph boy, who must have propped his bicycle against the wall, reappeared, solidly framed in the doorway. 'Sir?'

He couldn't take it in. The news. The unbelievably dreadful news. All he could see were images that were burned into his memory: Da, wrapped in a blanket, having been caught in a downpour, out on the hills, his feet in a mustard bath beside the kitchen range, the dog's head on his knee. Da in his striped butcher's apron, straw boater on his head, cleaver in hand, flanked by meat, by the leg, by the flank, by the trayful. He recalled the proud stance of the big-boned body that he had inherited, the kind eyes, the generous mouth. And there was Da on the beach at Llantwit, paddling, his trousers rolled up to his knees, his chin raised in the bliss of sun worship. That lovely smile. Oh, Da.

He began to dictate. '*So sorry Stop what a shock Stop I simply cannot take it in …* No, scrub that. Um, *It never occurred to me that Da would ever um, could ever…*' And there was Da outside in his beloved garden, in the deckchair, with his glasses perched on his forehead, newspaper put aside as he pulled little Clara onto his knee, to tell her a story about the hedgehog they'd found or singing nursery rhymes to her in that rich baritone of his. Archie choked on a sob. 'Oh, bloody hell! No, no, don't put that.' He tried to gather his thoughts. 'Where was I?'

'Archie!' her voice floated down the stairs. Lord, he'd forgotten about her. *'I need your help – do come!'*

He couldn't…

The boy read it back.

'… *that Da would* … No, forget all that. Make that, *This is the worst news in the world…'* but immediately buried his head in his arms, muttering, 'Shit, shit, shit!'

'Archie!'

'Oh, shut up!' he muttered.

Now here was Polly. She had been trying to make sense of the situation from across the street without success. 'Archie, Archie, whatever's the matter?' but receiving no reply asked the boy, 'What's happened?'

The boy shrugged. 'Bad news, ma'am. I think someone's died.'

She snatched the telegram from Archie's grasp and quickly read the contents.

'Oh my God, oh, my poor boy.' She sat on the stair below the one he'd retreated to and tried to rub comfort into his leg. He looked up with tears wetting his cheeks, grabbed her hand hard, and clung on as if he were drowning.

'Now what are you waiting around for?' she asked the boy. 'A reply? Oh, just say, *"Coming right away Stop Archie,"'* she said. 'How much is that? Oh, keep the change, do. No, wait…' She turned to her grieving friend. 'Now what about Clara? She can't take time off school.'

'I … oh, I don't…'

She patted his hand. 'Don't worry. It'd be best coming from you but …' she was talking to herself. 'See, if the funeral's tomorrow, and it takes all day Saturday to get back … do you think you'll be up to going over there on Sunday? No, I don't suppose … Eh? Archie? Oh, never mind. I'll do it.'

She dictated another message to the boy, gave him the address in Camden and half a crown, plus sixpence for his trouble and told him to hurry. 'All right? Now Archie,' she said, closing the door, 'upstairs with you.'

'Archie, what are you doing? I need you! I've put too much red in the mix!'

'God, *she's* not here again!'

She stepped over him and stormed up the stairs like a tornado. 'Out!' he could hear her yelling. 'Go on, clear off out of it! Haven't you got somewhere to be, school or something? He can't be doing with you now. He needs a friend, not a leech!'

There were squeaks from the studio. *'Archie, tell her!'*

'He's in no state to teach you skin tones. He's had some tragic news! You'd best pack up your paints and bugger off.'

Sophie was already cleaning her brushes when he came in, and protesting that Polly had no right to order her about, that she was Archie's student and was halfway through an important lesson on portraits.

'What, that? That's supposed to be him, is it? Jesus Christ, I could do better than that, blindfold. And you teach children how to paint? You're a fake, woman. Get your coat on, take that, that strawberry blancmange and make yourself scarce. They're waiting for you up the road.'

'Archie…' Sophie implored, unbuttoning her painting smock.

'Go, Sophie,' he said. 'Just do as she says. Please.'

Within minutes, it seemed, Polly had him sitting down in the armchair, with a neat whisky, for shock. She had unearthed his suitcase from a jumble of boxes, picture frames and still-life props and was fast filling it from his underwear drawer, his shirt drawer, from clothes hangers and the trouser press.

'Good, that should see you right for a few days. You can travel in what you've got on. Just have a shave and run a comb through your hair while I pop across the road. I'm expecting a delivery today, but Mrs Reeves can take it in. I'll sling a few things in a bag and lock up.'

'You're coming, too?'

'I'd better, don't you think? You'd never find your way to the railway station in this state, let alone to south Wales.'

'No, Polly, please, you don't have to. What about your shop? Your customers?'

'I'll leave a note on the door. Bertha will do the necessary – she'll enjoy that. And it's half-day closing anyway. I'll let Bob know – I can hear him opening up now – he can mind the mule while we're gone. Now come along, the kettle's boiled. Or do you want me to get the razor to you?'

'Let me help,' offered Sophie, sensible now to the crisis, head down, fastening her hat.

'You still here? Best you can do, ducks, is get off to school. Leave him to me. You done? Right, off you go then. I'll be just behind you.'

He was aware, at the periphery of his brain, of Sophie's indignant clatter down the stairs and Polly seeing her off, arms akimbo. The front door opened and there was the sound of heels on cobbles, two pairs, one set plodding up the street and one crossing it and her shop bell pinging. Time must have passed before he heard her talking to his landlord, downstairs, but he wasn't aware of it.

Da was dead. It was unthinkable.

And suddenly, she was back in the room, urging him to action.

'Polly Porter, you're a – you're a –'

'You'd do the same for me and don't try denying it.'

'I was going to say *bully*.'

'Well, at least I've made you smile.'

Polly assiduously avoided any mention of Sophie on the long journey to Wales. Whenever Archie began a sentence with 'Poor

Sophie didn't deserve…' or 'You didn't have to be so…' or 'Percy's painting was going so much quicker with two of us…' her lips would clamp into a thin rigid line and those pale eyes would freeze over, glacial blue. Or she would simply turn her head away and study the speeding countryside. He gave up. She clearly disapproved of his arrangement with the schoolmistress and preferred to pretend she didn't exist. He couldn't make her out. Not so long ago she was urging him to take a mistress or a wife, to look elsewhere. Sophie was a mere student. Maybe, in time, their relationship would have blossomed but there was small chance of that now.

To while away the miles, she encouraged him to grieve, to talk about his father, to evoke sweet memories of growing up in coastal Wales. 'That's right,' she said, 'let it out,' as he wept and sighed for days gone by. She smiled to hear of them, having had no such happy childhood, herself.

There was the time they'd had to make do with lamb chops for their Christmas dinner – the only meat left in the shop after the Christmas rush. Mam had suggested Robert kill one of her laying hens but he couldn't bring himself to do it. He knew them all by name. He was an anomaly, a butcher who couldn't do the actual killing. It was always one of Archie's brothers or uncles who had to cut the throats of the local pigs and string them up for the blood to drain. Once, Mam had had to do it. Da could hack, saw, chop and slice but the taking of life was beyond him.

'Me, neither,' Archie said. 'Just as well I was good at painting. I'd have made a wretched butcher.'

'Don't tell me you faint at the sight of blood.'

'Not always,' he joked and paused to enjoy her astonishment. 'No, I've had to draw some really gruesome things for Tyrell and I don't mind the sight of my own or anyone else's blood. It's animals I can't kill.'

'You've never killed a person?'

'Not directly.' But he didn't enlighten her further.

He told her how Mam had come to the village as a teacher, only to fall in love with Da and be required to give up the job when they married. For the rest of her life, when she wasn't caring for her boys, she had to assist in the shop. 'Keeping the books, mostly.'

'What a waste of talent!'

'Not really. She taught me and my brothers – and others, on the quiet. And Da learned a lot from her. He learned to love Shakespeare and poetry. But yes, the school really missed her.' He brooded, for a moment, on the trap that barred married women from teaching, Sophie being another caught in it. He said, by way of an afterthought, 'Mam taught painting among other things.'

'You get it from *her*, then?'

'Well, I don't get it from Da, that's for sure. He could sing, though, and play the piano as can Mam. I can't play a note, though they both tried to teach me. I get other things from Da – my clumsiness, my big feet, my bouts of melancholy, my scruffiness…'

'All the good stuff…'

'My gentle nature?'

Polly spluttered with mirth.

'My good looks?'

She hit him.

Somewhere along the route the weather changed. Archie shut the train window when the rain came in and only then, slapped in the face with wind and spray, did he force himself to think objectively about the coming ordeal.

By the time the train reached Llantwit, the temperature had dropped sharply and the rain was sideways on. They set out from the station, leaning into Polly's umbrella, fighting to keep it from blowing inside out and only finding their way by Archie's familiarity with the waist-high drystone walls that fringed the fields and front gardens. There was Evans Dairy's herd of cows, all folded down in the wet grass and looking miserable. There were the sheep, huddled like tufts of black mattress stuffing under the single tree near Jenkins's mill.

The shop was closed, of course – *'due to Robert's passing,'* as a note pinned to the door, in his mother's writing, told the customers, its blue ink dribbling with rain. *'Price Butcher'* was in black lettering over the door, with *'And Sons'* squeezed underneath, some thirty-odd years before, when Hywel was born, the *'s'* being added two years later, with Dafydd's birth. Tears sprang to Archie's eyes, blurring his view of empty, white-china display dishes in the bow window, the parsley wilting in between. The chopping block was scrubbed spotless and the cash machine had its cover on. Oh hell. There was no mistake then; it was true.

'We're here,' he said, suddenly reluctant to intrude on his mother's grief. 'This is us.' An oil lamp lit the window. She was in, of course. Where else would she be?

'You live next to the shop, do you?' said Polly.

He explained that the shop and the house were two adjoining cottages originally, that Da had knocked doors through to make them one, and that the room above the shop used to be Archie's. 'Nice view over the fields,' he added, 'and a good light for painting.'

Polly looked about her, bright with interest, and he had to admit that even in the rain, Llantwit Major was a pretty village, with bedraggled sunflowers, delphiniums and hollyhocks in the gardens and wild valerian painting the grey stone of every front wall and cottage with splashes of red and pink. Some roofs, too.

At the front door they gave up the fight with the umbrella and, turning the shiny brass door handle, fell, almost sprawling, into the warm.

'Shut the door, cariad!' yelled his sister-in-law, Dilys, and even louder, 'Mam! Mam! Come quick! Archie's here!'

'And his young lady,' cried someone else.

'Better late than never!' said Dafydd, his brother. But to what he was referring was anyone's guess – was it Archie's tardy arrival or the fact that they assumed that Archie and Polly were more than friends?

There they were, most of his family, crammed into the tiny front parlour, his two brothers and their wives, bobbing up and down at the table in welcome, rattling tea cups and saucers and half a dozen children emerging from around their feet to stare. One was just puckering up to howl, having bumped his head on the table in his eagerness to see what was going on.

'You never brought a *girl*?' came the accusation.

'You're a dark horse, Archie Price.'

'Mam, Mam! Leave it, what you're doing! You'll never guess who's here!'

'Now then, Evan, give over do – it's only a bump.' Eurwen, Hywel's wife, was seeing to her youngest. 'I told you to be careful.'

'You got my wire, then?'

'Just this morning.'

'Look at you both, soaked to the skin. Let me take your coats.'

'Oh, put your bags down, cariad. Duw, what you got in there, it's heavy as hell? Just leave it by the door. It'll be all right.'

'Have a seat, have a seat, Miss … um?'

'This is Polly.'

'Polly, is it – the girl over the road? Oh, we've heard all about you, love.'

'Where we going to put you, then?' said Dilys, busily. 'You'll probably have to go on the sofa 'cause Dafydd and I are in your old room, Archie, and the children are in the boys' room.' It took the newcomers a little time to work out that she was talking sleeping arrangements. 'Archie can bed down with Hywel and Eurwen up the road, now the girls are off hand.'

'That's all right. I can sleep down here. Polly can go up the road.'

'Oh, stop your cryin', man. It's your Uncle Archie, you've seen him before. Yes, you have. And don't do that, it's rude!'

'How long you stoppin'?'

'Mam! Get in here, will you!'

Flustered, she emerged at last from the scullery, wiping her hands on her apron, tall and gaunt, wisps of fading red hair escaping the heavy braid around her head, her eyes tired and red-rimmed but opening wide to take in the full glory of her youngest.

'Better late than never!' Dafydd seemed to think it bore repeating.

'Archie, you came! Oh, my dear boy! Thank God!'

Immediately, his arms were filled with her fragile bones, her fragrant smell of cooking, her kisses, her tears wetting his neck and her crooning, 'You're home, you're home...'

'Mam ... Mam. There now...' he mumbled into her hair.

'Dear boy,' she whispered. 'Let me look at you.' She leaned away and touched his cheek. 'You're so pale, lovey, and these lines are new. Living in that smoky old place – it can't be good. And look how thin you are. You're not eating properly. Have some cake...'

'I never knew he was ill, even. Nobody said.' Somehow his voice had developed a Welsh lilt that he'd almost lost in London.

'It was very quick,' Dafydd tried to excuse them all. 'We didn't want to bother you with what looked like an ordinary dose of flu. We didn't know he was going to *die,* man.'

Archie bunched his lips. Best say nothing. He knew they all thought he should have been here, that he should never have left. Him and his big ideas – gallivanting off to London to paint pictures when his duty clearly lay in the butcher's shop with the family. They'd been proud of the skills that got him into art college but expected him to come back to Llantwit, after, and earn a proper living. Painting was for Sunday afternoons, after church – like Dafydd's cornet playing and Hywel's whittling. There had been times when he'd been tempted to chuck it all in, mind. Bad times...

Polly nudged him discreetly and gently cleared her throat.

'Oh, Mam, this is Polly. I'd never have got here without her. You've heard me speak of her...'

Now it was Polly's turn for Mam's hug. 'Oh, but you're freezing, dearie, come and warm yourself at the fire. It's good to meet you at last. I just wish it could have been in happier circumstances. This is the lady doctor he wrote about,' she broadcast to the room. 'Did you have to take time off from your work at the hospital?'

Oh Lord.

'Mam, this is Polly.'

'She lives over the road from Archie, Mam!'

'The schoolmarm?'

'The photographer! Even I know that!'

'So, it's a camera over there by the door, is it? Said it was heavy, didn't I?'

'Not much use for a camera this weather.'

'It goes everywhere with her,' he explained.

Polly, bless her, rose to the occasion, offering her condolences for their loss, wishing she could have met Archie's father who sounded like a lovely old gentleman.

'He'd have been sorry to have missed you, love…'

Archie rescued her. 'Poor old Da. When did he go? Last night, was it?'

Somebody fetched the big brown teapot, roasting hot, and a plate of still-warm Welsh cakes, while Archie sat across from his mother at the table, clasping her hands while her thumb stroked his knuckles to the rhythm of her words.

'We didn't know, we didn't know. It came on him so suddenly. It was the flu to start with but he seemed to be getting over that, Archie. Quite chatty he was after his dinner – a nice bit of pig's liver we had, with bacon and thick gravy, just how he likes it. Well, he was sitting down just there, where you are now, telling me he was going in to work, Saturday. I wasn't sorry – it gets so busy with everyone buying their joints and the old ladies, they do like him to serve them. Well, all that talking had made him tired and I said why didn't he go up and lie on the bed for an hour, out of the way? I had a bit of ironing to do before supper. So up he went. I'd hardly started when I heard this almighty crash, like he'd fallen out of bed.

Well, I scooted up the stairs, Archie, and sure enough, he was lying on the floor with his eyes shut, and I thought to myself, you don't fall out of bed and stay fast asleep, do you? And, of course, he wasn't.' Her voice broke. 'He was dead!'

They were all quiet as fresh tears were shed, even by the small children, who must have heard the story repeated a few times now, about how she'd sent for the doctor and there was nothing to be done. 'Then I went and told the boys.'

And Hywel, living two doors along and quick off the mark, had sent the telegram to Archie. 'Just got it off before the Post Office shut,' he said. 'Better late than…'

'Do you want to go up and see him, Archie? Before they bring the coffin round. Bessie Jones is coming to lay him out shortly.'

Archie nodded and got to his feet, remembering to duck to avoid cracking his skull on the ceiling. He was the tallest of the brothers and the joke was that he had left home sooner than turn into a hunchback. Polly silently agreed to stay with the family until the old man was brought downstairs.

'They's putting Grandpa in a box!' piped up young Evan, his bump on the head forgotten.

'And they're digging a hole in the ceiling to fetch him down here,' Archie's small niece Bethan announced, her eyes popping at the prospect of a show.

Archie looked up. It was the custom in these old terraced cottages, with their narrow staircases that turned a corner or two on the way down, to take out the 'coffin boards' in the bedroom floor for ease of access.

Da was lying on the bed, in his best suit – fresh out of mothballs, a clean white shirt, collar and tie and highly polished shoes. Were it not for the clothes Archie would have found it hard to believe that his father was not quietly sleeping. He almost expected the pale lips to part on a whistling out-breath or for him to suddenly snore.

Without thinking, he took his father's hand in his and was

shocked to find the thick fingers cold and unresponsive, the skin papery dry. Da had been such a vibrant man, a dedicated carnivore, ruddy and robust and now… Tenderly, he stroked the dear cheek, cross-hatched with thread veins, and blinked away a smear of tears.

'He looks very peaceful, Mam, despite the fall.'

'Doctor Pritchard helped me lift him back on the bed. Said he may have had a bad dream going to bed after the liver and that he died of a heart attack. He wouldn't have suffered long, if at all, he said.'

'That's something, I suppose.'

'I know, but it was so unexpected…' she swallowed. 'I'm never going to be able to eat liver again. Oh, what am I going to do without him, Archie?'

'Mam…'

They sat for a while, sharing the bed with the dear dead man and grieving for him, until a hubbub below told them that Bessie Jones and the coffin had arrived.

Hywel came up with some ropes. The two of them lifted out the floorboards and took up the coffin while Mam sat stroking her husband's hand. Of all the faces gazing up through the gap in the floor, Polly's was the one he sought. The others were trying to lighten the mood, recalling the time the boards were removed to hoist Granny's wardrobe into their parents' room when she passed on. So, yes, Evan, my love, Grandpa would be reunited with her, and Auntie Blod and Uncle Huw.

He shivered, remembering the séance at the Merediths. Suppose, just suppose there really was an Other Side, was Da's spirit there now in the company of other grey transparencies? Had he met up with Granny and Grandpa, and if so, how had he found them among the trillions of souls who had passed over since time began?

As if in sympathy, it rained continually all night and the next day, as the villagers scurried down the lanes, under shawls and bonnets and caps and umbrellas, to Price's house, ostensibly to pay their last respects to the corpse but also to give Archie and his young lady the once-over. His two older brothers had opened the shop early, both for something to do until the funeral that afternoon and in order to supply the demand for fresh meat. The weekend was coming and how would anyone manage, otherwise, for their Saturday night stew and their Sunday roast? Da, balanced in his coffin on the bare sideboard, was privy to the sounds of sawing, chopping and mincing through the dividing wall and continued to smile stiffly. His youngest son was greasy with bacon fat and fried tomatoes, wondering what Clara would have made of seeing her dead grandfather in his coffin, his dear face surrounded by carnations and valerian. Would it have been too much for her?

He said as much to his mother and discovered that she had been saddened by the girl's absence.

'No, it's all right, Archie, really, she's had enough tragedy in her young life. And you said she had school…'

'There wasn't really time to fetch her, Mam.'

'I know, Archie. And your father would have understood. All I'm saying is, it would have been nice. He loved that child, like she was his own.'

'The feeling was mutual, Mam. She thought of him as her friend.' Archie wondered, with a pang, just how he was going to break it to the girl that her lovely Welsh Grandpa had gone. Poor child.

'He never forgot her birthday. What is she now? Thirteen? Growing up fast…' She paused as a thought struck her. 'Now you must take his pocket watch with you and give it her to remember him by.' She was already up and relieving her husband of his timepiece. 'Here.' She slid it into Archie's hand. It was a pleasure to hold, worn smooth with handling. Clara would treasure it, picturing the old man slipping it in and out of his pocket. *Time for you to go to sleep now, young Clara. We'll finish the book tomorrow night.'* He had consulted it on getting up, and all day long to the time he rewound it on going to bed. 'It'll be no use to him where he's going. No, put it away – no ifs or buts. He'd have wanted her to have it.'

Archie couldn't help feeling guilty. As she sat down again he found himself trying to count her freckles as he had when he was a boy and she'd taken a moment to ponder the punishment she'd mete out to him for swearing, for fighting his brothers, for climbing out of his bedroom window to go to the village dance, for smoking, drinking, for climbing back through the window. Generally, she'd stop his pocket money or confiscate his paints (that was a hard one) or give him extra chores like chopping wood or polishing boots. She tried to keep his misdemeanours between themselves. If his father had found out it would have been six of the best.

'Thirteen, eh? Goodness, she's growing up. She'll be noticing changes, you know. And with no Lizzie to tell her what's going on, poor little thing, she won't know what to expect. That grandmother of hers won't tell her – far too strait-laced – and I doubt you should, Archie. It's not something a man can – not without embarrassment on both sides.' She frowned, lowered her voice. 'I don't know how close *she* is to Clara…' she tilted her head towards the house, two doors along, where Polly was getting ready for the funeral. 'Could she, d'you suppose, you know, speak to the girl?'

'Well I'm sure she would, if I asked her, but it's my place really. I've been worrying about it, too. I've actually been leaving this medical book out for her to read – she reads a lot – or she might get it from a friend.'

'Friends of that age aren't reliable, Archie. They have all sorts of weird notions.' She frowned. 'Oh dear, the poor child needs a mother…' She sighed and scratched her nose. He knew what was coming. 'So, tell me, Archie – is she the one? Polly? She seems very nice and fond of you to come all this way.'

'She's the best, Mam. I'd marry her tomorrow if she'd have me – but she won't.'

'She *won't?*' Her hackles were up. 'What's the matter with the girl? You're earning good money these days, aren't you?'

There was nothing for it but to tell his mother that bad things happening to her had not only made her, well, unable to participate in lovemaking; they had also put paid to Polly being able to have children –

('Who said? Has she been properly examined?')

– And that being the case she didn't think it would be fair to marry him.

'Poppycock!' said his mother. 'You never struck me as one to take no for an answer. If she's the one you've set your heart on you must keep on trying, son. You're getting on, you know – thirty-seven next birthday.' She shook her head at his rolling eyes, his desperate face, and busily brushed breadcrumbs from the tablecloth into her palm. 'Faint heart never won fair lady, Archie. Anyway,' as though that matter was already settled, 'about Clara, son, would you – would you like me to? I mean I could come for a visit and take her to one side–'

'Mam, you know you're always welcome, but you'd better make it snappy. She'll be ahead of you before long.'

'I will then. And try a different approach with Polly, is my advice. You'd be surprised, Archie. Love can work miracles.'

They came at him from all angles, the neighbours, who thought they had a right.

'*Your brothers will be needing help in the shop now, boyo…*'

'*If you take my advice, Archie, you'll leave off your London life. Your mother needs you at home, look you…*'

'*Your poor father was always full of you … worried to death, he was. His youngest in that den of iniquity – all those loose women…*'

Polly suffered, too, though she covered it with a polite smile. '*So, you're Archie's young lady, are you, cariad? Polly, is it? He always did*

*have an eye for a pretty face. It was Angharad Jenkins once, and her a
beauty queen. He was all of fourteen.'*

Archie decided to brave the weather and take Polly down to the
beach since she had never seen the 'real sea' as she called it – only
the estuary at Southend – and was determined.

Going by way of the fields would have been quicker but Polly
had no galoshes and her long skirts would have been soaked, so
they went the long way, via the mile or so of winding lanes.

The beach was deserted in the rain though there were little boats
out to sea, and the long pavements of black stone gleamed wet.
Polly stood stock still, breathing in the salt air, her eyes closed, her
face wet with spray and rain.

Oh dear. 'Not very pretty, is it?' he apologised.

She clutched his arm, her cheeks pink with excitement. 'It's
magnificent, Archie! I love it!' She gazed around at the towering
cliffs, the boulders all piled up, the clinkering pebbles, the
deposits of seaweed and shells, and smiled, utterly spellbound.
'How could you bear to leave all this – the wildness of it? And
look at the sea!'

The sea? It was doing its usual thing, seething away, back and
forth, moody and cold, smacking in with furious foam-furling
waves, smoothing out the slabs of rock, clattering the stones, then
sneaking back furtively, gathering strength for the next onslaught.
But she was entranced and stood for ages drinking it all in, before
setting off, shawl over her head, across the boulders to take
pictures. Slipping once too often, she sat down to take off her shoes
and stockings and he took over the porterage of camera and tripod.
Gingerly, she continued picking her way down to the water's edge,
exclaiming over rock pools, with their small crabs and transparent
shrimps, to set up her camera on a shelf of stone.

Frame followed frame of sea and sky and cliff and boats, of
Archie standing manfully, one foot on a rock, staring out at the
horizon, of Archie shading his eyes against a mighty squall, his coat
pulled up round his ears.

'Let's go and stand by the cliffs then,' she suggested, 'it'll be more sheltered there.'

'No,' he said, 'too dangerous, Polly. People have been killed by falling rocks. In rough seas the waves pound away at the cliffs and loosen the structure. Erosion,' he explained. As if to demonstrate, there came a loud and echoing clatter as something dislodged and fell, hitting the shelf of rock below, bouncing and clunking several times before coming to rest among the trillions of other stones that formed the beach.

'Goodness!'

'When we were boys,' he said, as they made their way back up over the boulders, 'we used to come and play cricket against the cliff face, would you believe? One day Hywel was wicket keeper when a shower of rocks came down. Broke his arm. He was lucky, we all were. It could have been so much worse.'

She looked up, with a frown, from fastening her boots. 'So that's what all these cobbles are? Bits of the cliff face that have come off over the years.'

He nodded. 'Many of them contain fossils – ammonites and belemnites. This was all under the sea at one time. Funny to think of it. Clara loves hitting them with a hammer when she's here, exposing the fossils and ... Oh hell!'

'What?'

'Clara!'

'What about her?'

'She'll be expecting us over to lunch on Sunday and we won't be...'

'No, no, she won't. I sent that telegram to Vic, didn't I?'

'Did you?'

'Archie! You were there! Don't you remember I asked him to break the news gently to Clara, that we were going to the funeral and not to expect us for lunch on Sunday? I *told* you!'

'Did you? Oh God, you're an angel, Polly. What would I do without you?'

'Muddle along,' she grinned, 'same as always.'

'That's my fate, is it?'

'You could marry that teacher and let her look after you.'

'Why would I want to marry that little sycophant?' he made a face. 'I'm under no illusions about her, Polly. She's a user. As soon as she's sucked me dry she'll throw me out with the peelings. Anyway, I doubt she'd have me now she's seen what a harridan I have as a best friend.'

'Who, me?'

'I mean, hounding her out of my studio like that. Bullying her. She had as much right as you to come to Wales, you know.'

She frowned. 'No, she didn't. She wouldn't have been any help at all.'

'Unlike you?'

'Well, yes.'

'I happen to agree with you. You're the best person for the job. Until such time as I meet the woman who will become my wife.'

'You haven't met her yet?'

'I might have. She might be here, in Wales.'

'Oh?' Her face was a study.

'Oh yes, my mother has someone in mind, she tells me.'

'She has?'

He nodded. 'But it's not on, is it?'

'Why not?'

'Because you wouldn't stand for it, Polly. You'd come hurtling up the stairs and pitch her out into the street, just as you did poor Sophie. You're a jealous little cat, Polly, and bossy, to boot.'

'I – I'm *not!*'

'You are.'

'Well, maybe a bit…'

'So, what's to be done?'

'Archie…' She had opened her eyes wide, blinking away the rain.

'What?'

'You know I love you.'

'But you can't keep me in mind when I make love to you...'

She bit her lips together, closed her eyes. 'I suppose I could try...'

His heart leapt. 'You could? One more time? Oh, Polly.' He reached for her hand. 'I'll kiss you very nicely and gently and you keep your eyes open and look at me, at my crooked nose, at my whisky-brown eyes, my beetle brows, and say to yourself, over and over, this is Archie, Archie, Archie, who loves me passionately, who would never hurt me in a million years. I can trust him.'

And there, standing on a wet slab of rock, he did and so did she. But she closed her eyes in the end, even though the rain came down in sheets and they couldn't tell what was rain and what were tears.

They broke into Brenda's Tea Rooms for shelter. The door wasn't locked. Everyone would be up in the village for the funeral. That was where he kissed her again, not quite so gently, just inside the door, there being not much room for anything else. The counters were bare, the tea urns cold; the chairs were all upside down on the tables; there were no matches to light the oil lamps and the flowers in the vases had gone over. Brenda had obviously decided she had better things to do on a dark wet Friday lunchtime than wait in the cold for stray customers.

This kiss was a narrative, a story of his long love for her and of hers for him, of wounds healing and bad memories fading. Nor did she, when they finally came up for air, scrub her lips with the back of her hand and break away as he'd feared. Instead she stayed with her head up-tilted, her eyes closed and her lips asking for more. 'Oh Polly!' His heart was beating so hard he was sure she could feel it as he wrapped his arms around her and kissed her eyes, her cheeks, her neck, murmuring endearments into her wet hair, her hot skin, not entirely believing that she was kissing him back. But kissing was only the start of it. They'd been here before. How would she take the rest of it?

He leaned back to peer into her mysterious eyes through the

gloom and saw his own worried reflection. He couldn't tell what she was thinking.

'Oh,' she breathed. Her cheeks were flushed and her breath was hot on his neck. 'Oh, Archie, I love you so much.' She'd said that before. And back then, when push came to shove, as it were, he'd had to withdraw quickly, tail between his legs. He waited. And it was what her eager fingers were attempting to do with his fly buttons that put his mind at rest.

'Glory be!' he cried, and with one gigantic sweep of his arm sent four spindly chairs clattering to the floor.

'I didn't know,' she wept. 'I didn't know it could be like this.'

'You liked that?'

'So much! Do it again.'

'Give me a moment.'

But a moment was too long for her and she roused him with a kiss. This time she set the pace, called the tune. And their lovemaking was an altogether less hurried, less anxious affair, with more sensual and arousing variations on a theme. Apart from the climax, which had them crying out as they tipped over the edge together.

'Thank you, God,' said Archie.

'Thank you, Archie,' said Polly. 'Wonderful man.'

'Wake up, beautiful.'

'What? Oh, heavens, was I asleep?'

'We both were. Better hurry, or we'll miss the funeral.'

They stopped off at home to make themselves tidy, and then the three Price brothers (one with a new spring in his step), and the friends – Morgan Bread, Colin the Fish and Dai Wheeler – bore Price Butcher in the now sealed coffin, down through the puddles to the little church. And it seemed to Archie that the entire village trudged behind, carrying flowers and umbrellas.

It was a simple service: a few hymns sung with Welsh gusto and harmony, and appropriate gospel readings. Hywel, as firstborn son, gave the eulogy, unscripted, and the Reverend Brynmor Llewellyn, who had known Robert all his life, followed up the second hymn with his memories of a popular schoolboy who had grown up to play hooker for the local rugby team, to inherit, from his father, the running of Llantwit's butcher's shop, and to meet, at a local dance, the captivating red-headed teacher from London who later became his wife and the mother of three lovely boys; later still, the grandmother of five. Even with his nose buried in his handkerchief, Archie was conscious of a warm hand squeezing his, speaking without words.

His mother, on his other side had, of course, noticed their bright eyes, their heightened colour, and gave him a watery smile of approval. He reminded himself that some forty years before she had been a bride in this very church. He put away his hanky and put his free arm around her thin shoulders.

That's all that's left of us, eventually, he thought. Memories. And they would fade and die as those who remembered faded and died. It was one reason for making paintings, he supposed. Paintings and photographs. They were something tangible to leave to the world.

Babies were the other thing. He knew he would never now father a child. He'd marry Polly; he wanted no other, and they'd provide a home and family for Clara. The Grants were getting too old to look after her. But there was no immediate hurry.

Despite the rain the graveside was well attended and, as the village band played 'Abide with Me', heavy drops spattered their caps, rolled down a shield wall of brollies and pelted the coffin as ropes lowered it into its final resting place. The grave already contained several inches of water.

'Please don't stay around to get drenched,' the widow begged her neighbours, but they hung on gamely until the vicar said the final Amen and the band finished playing.

'Dear me,' Dilys said to Dafydd, throwing in her single rose to join Mam's and Eurwen's, 'your poor Da will be washed away!'

145

Spades of squelchy mud were flung in to flump on the lid, there were final blessings and farewells, and the cortège made its way more quickly up the lane than it had come down, to the house where Mam and 'the girls' had prepared tea and sandwiches.

Later that night when the last visitor had left, Archie and his exhausted mother were coming to the end of the washing-up.

'It's still raining,' said Polly, coming in from the midden and making for the sink to rinse her hands. 'It hasn't let up since we arrived. Why do we have summers like this? Hot as hot for months and then torrential rain, swilling everything away.'

'Let's hope it's not a repeat of last year.'

'They were flooded out round your way, weren't they, Archie?'

'Yep. The river overflowed. The marshes got it worst, of course, but apart from a few shacks no one had built on the floodplain. People don't.'

'Didn't you say Tottenham had it particularly bad last year?' Tottenham was where his mother had been born and raised. 'That'll be the Mosel bursting its banks. About time they did something about it – flood defences or something.'

'They're trying,' said Polly.

'Not fast enough.'

Crockery clattered as Archie piled it into the cupboards. Polly hung her sopping tea towel over the line strung across the scullery and sighed. In the silence that followed a squall of rain beat against the window.

'What a day it's been,' Mam said, 'especially for you two. A beautiful thing, really, a new love springing up just as my old love goes into the ground.'

Archie made a rueful face. 'Don't say that, Mam. Makes me feel as if we're cheating somehow, me and her.'

'Don't be silly. I'm so glad for you, and Da would have been, too. He was worried you'd never find the happiness that we had.

And I already love Polly.' Her voice caught as she swilled the dirty water down into the slop bucket. 'Life goes on,' she murmured.

'Mam…' He put his hands on her shoulders.

She reached up and patted one of them. 'Do you think, with all the water in the grave, the body will rot more quickly?'

'Lord, where did that come from?'

'I keep thinking – he's all alone out there in the churchyard, buried under all that wet mud. My poor Robert – he'll be cold and – oh, dear…'

'Mam – Mrs Price,' cried Polly, '*he's* not there. Just his body.'

'Da's not been around since Thursday when he died, with a nice liver and bacon dinner inside him.'

'I know, I know. I'm a silly old woman who's had too much sherry. All the same…'

'Mam, why don't you go to bed? And Polly, Eurwen will be waiting up for you. Go on, I'll see you in the morning.'

'She won't expect you to turn out in this weather,' said his mother. 'You'd better come in with me, Polly.'

Polly looked dismayed, as well she might, at the thought of sleeping on the deathbed but Eliza was already halfway up the stairs with the lighted candle and Polly meekly followed.

Archie was smiling as he tidied the scullery, turned down the lamp and took it into the darkened parlour, where he lay down on the sofa, listening to the ceaseless flurry of rain outside and the soft female voices upstairs give way to the creaking of bedsprings and then silence. Despite what he'd said to his mother his thoughts now went out to his poor father alone in his watery grave. Out of nowhere came his sister-in-law's remembered cry, *'Your poor Da will be washed away!'*

Just then a floorboard creaked overhead. He waited. The door to the stairs was dimly outlined as someone with a candle crept down. At its brightest the door swung open to reveal Polly in her shift.

'She's fast asleep,' she said. 'Budge up.'

It came to him, when she murmured his name in her sleep some hours later, just how Jane Doe's bones might have washed up at the Pride of Lea, minus the right foot. His arm tightened around his love.

Eleven

1902: Gilbert

This was no ordinary downpour. More like they monsoons in India Missus talked about, or the deluge in the Bible when Noah took in the animals, two by two. T'was dark as night, darker, with sheets of rain sweeping across the gardens like the bellied sails of a ship, made visible by blinding lightning that bore into the ground like taproots, casting sooty black shadows. Deafening thunderclaps shook the greenhouses, loosening the panes – you could hear them smashing, one after the other, on the gravel paths. All along the walls of the shed pots and trays and tools were rattling off shelves and hooks, making everyone who had made it to shelter look up and, listening to the rain hammering on the tarry roof, picture the havoc being wrought outside. Poor plants!

The lawns were awash in minutes. After the dry summer, the baked ground couldn't cope with all that water at once and a muddy broth crept slowly up the garden, boiling and bubbling.

When they cried out that fence palings were floating on the flood, Gilbert's heart sank to his boots. The river, that had been so low and sluggish last evening, must have filled right up, overflowed the towpath and flooded the land. Soon it would find where he'd dug his hole and scour it out, like gruel from a pot, showing the world what was down there.

No chance to make it good now. He had to save himself.

He chewed his lip and waited his chance.

Them as had been working near the house when the storm broke, would be waiting it out in the servants' hall, drying their socks and coats round the range, drinking tea or sparking with the maids. Down this end of the garden it was a different story. Down this end was bloody dangerous. Putting a brave face on it, some of the lads, them that didn't have their noses pressed to the streaming windows, tried to make the best of it by keeping busy: potting up by lantern light and labelling cuttings, cleaning and sharpening tools, mending an old lawnmower, folding sacks, hoping to God the flood wouldn't come up this far.

Filing, that's what he was doing, should anyone ask. Sorting through the dozens of drawers in the wooden cabinet and putting the precious seed packets in alphabetical order. Making sure they contained what they were supposed to, and hadn't been spilled or spoiled, and were sealed up securely.

For these were special plants from the other side of the world. Kew Gardens would be itching to get their hands on some of these. He'd already done the A's and B's; now it was the turn of the C's: *Calendrina umbellate, Calendula officinalis, Callistephus chinensis* … each precious brown paper packet labelled in Miss Ardmore's own hand, describing the mother plant, saying where she'd found it and what it needed in the way of sun and soil. Broxbourne wasn't quite India or China but the greenhouses were rigged out to mimic the conditions they'd come from – acid soil, warmth and humidity. Not much chance of that now though. There went another pane of glass letting in the banshee screaming of the wind and a fatal drop in temperature.

As he took out each packet he tipped a few seeds into his palm, just to check they were what the packet said they were. He memorised their type and the instructions for each, repeating them under his breath until he had them pat, and slipped them into his pocket – curly, dried-up caterpillar seeds, wizened-skull pea-types, wafer-thin discs, pellets and pips. He'd never stolen anything in his life before and felt bad doing so now but told himself the Missus could spare them. She'd collected far more seeds than she could ever grow. She wouldn't miss them.

He'd started taking them on Wednesday, the day after Nellie turned up on his doorstep, getting him out of bed. The night his life had taken a sharp turn for the worse.

He'd never been so glad to see anyone in all his life but she shouldn't have been there. He shushed her crying. Couldn't have anyone knowing he had a woman in his room. Lord love her, she was in a shocking state. She'd lost her hat, her hair was straggled down her back, her dress all torn and muddy, as though she'd waded through quagmires and been caught up in thorns; her shoes and stockings were fouled, one buckle gone and a sole flapping. She looked done in: her poor face all smirched with sweat and grime and so pale. Too weak to smile.

She'd fallen into his arms. The poor darling was faint from exhaustion. He almost wept to see her. Gently he helped her inside, pulled up a chair, made her sit.

'I'm – I'm all right, Gil, I'm all right!' she said through parched lips.

He'd never seen anyone less all right. 'What's happened, Nell?' he whispered. 'What have you done?'

'Could I –,' she gasped. 'Gil, a drink of water?'

She could hardly wait for him to fill his tin mug from the jug before she snatched it from his hand and drank it down in one go, never mind ladylike sips. She coughed and spluttered and wanted more. He refilled the mug quickly, shocked at her need. How long since she'd had anything to drink? In this hot weather, too.

'Do you – do you have anything to eat?' she said between swallows. He found her some bread and cheese and it was some time before he could get any sense out of her. She'd run away, of course. Jesus! The school was in Ipswich! Could she have come all this way on foot?

151

When she was able she told him. 'I'm never, ever, going back to that awful place. What Mrs Pankhurst would have made of it, I dread to think. Crooked little fingers to drink your tea! Knees together, ankles crossed. And *glide* across the room, ladies, as if you're on wheels! And that stupid uniform! D'you know, they locked me in my room because I wouldn't wear stays for church, refused to let me out if I didn't put them on. But, you see, Gil, I just *couldn't* ... I didn't want to hurt it.' She bit her lips and lowered her eyes to her belly. When she raised them again, he knew...

'Nell!' Oh fuck. He'd tried to be careful, that last time he'd seen her, when the field was wild with flowers – cowslips and campions, cornflowers and lady's smocks. And she had spread herself out before him, her hair bright among the blooms, her cheeks rosy with desire. He hadn't been able to stop himself.

'Nellie, don't say you're...'

Her smile was both sad and glad. 'I am,' she said. 'We are...'

'Oh, to blazes...!' This was the worst news. His head whirled. God, he loved her, but Christ, not yet, not yet! 'You sure?'

'Of course.' She brought his hand to her belly and he felt the roundness. And a pulse ticking. This was it, then, their mistake. Their creation. Their little one, their baby.

'Well,' he said, 'that settles it.'

'It does rather,' she agreed.

'Does anyone else know?'

'At school? No one. That's one of the reasons I ran away. To see a doctor. Not that I had money for one, but I couldn't ask Matron for my allowance, could I? I thought Father could get Doctor Fergusson in. I mean,' she grinned, 'it might have been too many pies. But it wasn't. I mean, I knew that really...' She shrugged.

'I'll take care of you, Nellie.'

'I know, and – and I would've come straight to you, Gil, but – I thought he'd help us. Father, I mean. I knew you wouldn't have any money.'

'So how did you get to Tottenham?'

'Walked. Not along the main road, of course – they'd've had people out looking for me. It took me ages through the byways – five days.'

'Nellie! Oh, my poor girl! What did you do for food?'

'Pinched stuff from the fields. Carrots, peas, strawberries. Salad stuff. I didn't starve. I wasn't bothered about living like a tramp, having no money. I felt sure when I got home Father would make everything all—.' But she couldn't finish the sentence for the sob that overtook her. She bit her lips as she re-enacted the scene in her head, staring at her twisting hands in disbelief. 'It didn't occur to me he would be so – so – oh Gil, what a fool I was to think he loved me.'

'He did, he does.'

Her pretty mouth turned down. 'Until I told him about the baby. Before that he wasn't too bad, cross that I'd run away from school when he'd paid so much money but happy to see me safe, I think. They'd told him I'd run away and he'd been out looking for me, he said. He was so worried, he said. He cared, he said and I almost believed him. He sat me down and had food brought up. Got Maria to run me a bath and find me a change of clothes. Said if I hated the school that much he'd take me out. There was plenty I could be doing at home. I could help him with the business, book-keeping and stuff, just – just until I married. In fact, he had someone in mind, he said. I told him not to bother. I had you.'

He blinked. Shit. Redfern must have been beside himself. And she was so naïve, so used to money, privilege, having everything she wanted. She must have just assumed she could have this, too.

'And that's when I told him about the baby coming and – and, oh, Gil, he hit me! Clumped me round the head, dragged me to the door and threw me out, Gil! Can you believe it? I mean fathers are supposed to cherish their daughters, not – not push them down the steps as though they were some gypsy woman come begging at the door! Look!' she lifted up her skirts to show him her knee, the stocking torn, the skin scabbed over a deep graze. Gil cradled her leg and kissed the sore place. She sighed, 'It was horrible –,' she sagged again and shut her eyes. 'I mean, his face, Gil!' Her lip trembled. 'He hated me! 'You're no daughter of mine,' he said.' She couldn't contain a sob that rose to the surface and, for a few moments, tears overtook her. He comforted her as best he could, holding her in his arms and kissing the top of her head and the rest of her words were a mumble into his shoulder. 'Don't you ever, *ever* come back here again,' he said. 'D'you hear? You're a disgrace, a slut, and I can't bear to look at you!' And then he slammed the door.'

'Oh, Nell…' Gil breathed. That foul old man. How could he? He smeared the tears from her cheeks and she took a deep breath, forced herself to continue.

'I was stunned, Gil,' she sniffed, 'I – I couldn't believe what had just happened, that he'd actually cast me off. My mind was in a whirl. I just gazed at the shut door, waiting for it to open again, for him to come out and say he'd made a mistake; that I was still his Eleanor when all was said and done. I was in shock, I suppose. It felt like drowning must feel, like he'd thrown me in the sea and left me to sink or swim and I couldn't breathe, couldn't see any hope. Where else could I go, what could I do? It was already dark – I couldn't go around banging on doors, pestering people.'

'You should have gone to ours,' Gil said. 'It's their grandchild you're carrying.'

'Gil, dear, your people would hate me, too! Like everyone else on the estate they'd be too frightened of Father and of losing their jobs to risk taking me in. So, I set off up the road to town. I thought if I could get to the market I'd maybe beg a lift on a cart or something and come here.'

This was awful. She made out she was strong, with her head screwed on straight and nobody's fool, but she'd been brought up so soft, she bruised easy. Her old man had beaten her before, mostly because of him, but *this* – this rejection must have been a

154

knife in her heart, and then to have to slog round Tottenham, all alone, at night, begging lifts. She must have been desperate.

'Anyway, Gil, I was walking down the main street when I saw there was to be this meeting at the Guild Hall, you know, Woman's Suffrage, the very next evening, and the main speaker was to be Emily Perkins, no less! It was the answer to a prayer, Gil. You remember I've spoken to you about Miss Perkins.' He frowned ignorance. '*You* know, she taught French at our school, but she left last year after a row with the headmistress. She wanted to start a Debating Society but the head wouldn't have it. Girls shouldn't have opinions of their own. Yes, I did, I *told* you!' She sighed. 'Anyway, I thought she might help.'

He almost wept as, in her refined, cut-glass accent, she revealed that she'd bought a platform ticket with her last penny and slept on a bench in the waiting room on the railway station. It was a warm night, so that was a blessing. In the morning she'd washed her face in the 'Ladies' and tidied her hair and killed time looking in the shops, sitting in the park, drinking at the water fountain and eating stale bread someone had put out for the birds. At five o'clock she'd made her way to the Guild Hall. There she'd met up with this Emily Perkins who'd set her to work putting out chairs, ushering people to them and giving out leaflets. Taking pity on her, her old French teacher had paid her five bob which was a sight more than the job was worth, and said that if she'd come back with her that night, she could probably get her work at their London office.

'But London was out of my way, Gil, right then. It was more important to get to you. I just had to follow the river.' She'd spent the money on food.

And what were they to do now?

'I'll go and get that job with Emily, Gil. We could both go to London. There'll be openings for you, I'm sure. Kew or – or...' she put her pretty head on one side to think. 'Or the Chelsea Physic Garden,' she said triumphantly, 'or one of the big houses in

Kensington. When the baby's here I can find someone to mind it while I work in the office. I'm good with numbers. Or I can be a filing clerk while I learn how to type.'

He raised his eyes to heaven and swore under his breath, knowing that neither God nor Lucifer could help them now. 'Sweetheart, no one's going to take on a bloke halfway through an apprenticeship. And for all their talk I doubt the suffragists will take on a married woman – a married woman with a *child* on the way.'

'Oh…' and her eyes salted with more tears. 'Don't you think so? I'm sorry, I had it all worked out and now I'm … Oh, I've made things so much worse for you.' She blinked and frowned until the sun broke through again. 'I know – I'll teach piano! Or if the worst comes to the worst I can do needlework – or cleaning.'

Some hopes! Nellie had never worked in her life. He thought of his mother and all her cronies, slaving away, scrubbing floors, doing the washing, ironing, cooking, cleaning, scrimping and scraping. And her needlework was rubbish, if those samplers she'd showed him were anything to go by. As for cleaning, dear God, she'd die of shame. The drudgery, the chapped hands, the backache, the housemaid's knee! She'd hate the women who did it. Their backbiting, their complaints, their crude jokes. And they'd hate her, with her fine manners and her way of talking. Blooming suffragists and their talk of equality … Women weren't even equal to each other!

He let her sleep while he stewed, the bedsprings twanging as each new difficulty came into his head. Her father was probably sorry by now. His precious girl was all he had, after all. He might even be out looking for her now. He might even have roped in the police, told them about the apprentice gardener lodging up in Broxbourne! Bloody hell – if they traced her here they'd have him banged up in no time. How long do you get for rape, for kidnapping? The baby would be born a bastard, for sure, and would die from starvation. As would she if she didn't go on the streets.

It was too soon. A few years more and they'd have managed. As a master gardener he'd've been pulling down a decent wage.

Why hadn't he taken more care? Oh God, he did love her; he couldn't abandon her. But there was no denying it – an apprentice's wages were not enough for two – let alone three – to live on. There was nothing for it, they'd have to get away, start a new life someplace else, and soon.

She was breathing softly now, fagged out after running about the countryside; she had a better colour, and the worry had gone from her face. How lovely she looked; how lucky he was to have been the one to win her heart. He lay down beside her on the narrow bed, took a loose curl and wound it round his finger like a wedding ring. Soon, soon. For better, for worse, for richer, for poorer … mostly for poorer, my love … unless he could come up with some workable scheme.

He turned away, face to the wall, the better to think.

Where would they go? They'd have to change their names, of course. Make out they were older (he'd grow a beard), that he'd lost his papers or had them stolen. Where was far enough away that they could pretend they were a master gardener and his little family? Wales? Yorkshire? Cornwall?

It was supposed to be lovely down there. It never snowed, they said, something to do with warm currents in the sea. At any rate it was good growing country, with acid soil and loads of big estates where he could find work. Yes, they'd go down there. He was a good enough gardener to convince anyone, surely? Pa had taught him everything he knew even before he'd signed up for Ardmore's. The Missus said he had green fingers. She set great store by him, said he'd go far. Just farther than she'd thought, eh? He might have to spin a few more yarns. Like he could say he'd been abroad with his employer sourcing rare plants and seeds and decided to set up on his own. But then they'd come to Miss Ardmore asking for a testimonial. Perhaps Nellie could forge one if they could find paper and pen. Or he could say his employer had died of yellow fever or been killed by tribesmen. It happened all the time, she reckoned. He frowned. Would they believe him?

The candle sputtered and went out and, in the dwindling light of that hot and desperate night, staring at that leprous wall, he'd seen rhododendrons and azaleas bursting into bloom, handkerchief trees, magnolias, camellias, redbuds, Judas trees, wisteria and slowly, slowly his idea had taken shape.

'It makes sense, Gil,' she'd agreed, next morning. 'They'll be bound to give you a job if it means they can get their hands on rare seeds. And if you're sure Miss Ardmore can spare them? She's been so good to you. We don't want her going short. Do be careful, sweetheart. You really mustn't get caught.'

That night, after work, he'd got a lift downriver on a barge and called in to see his folks. As he had hoped, Pa was tired out after work and had gone to bed soon after his supper, leaving Ma alone to hear his news.

True to form, she'd flown into an ugly rage, calling him all the names under the sun. It was a wonder Pa had been able to sleep through the rumpus. When she'd calmed down a bit she'd said, 'Best get it sorted, Gil. You don't want no kiddie now. Far too soon. Get her seen to and then send her back, Gil, back to that school. En't too late. She can say she were hevin' a lark, an' thought better of it. Tell her to come back when you're twenny-one. You got indentures to work off…' She turned away and he could hear her muttering, 'Bit o' luck she'll have married some Lord Toffee-Nose, by then, and have forgotten all about her bit o' rough.'

But in the end she'd seen he was right. Agreed they'd get married and go down south. It had been hard saying goodbye, not knowing when or if they'd ever see each other again. He'd left her to explain to the old man, coward that he was.

He was late getting back to his room at the Fish and Eels – he'd had to walk the last four miles, for want of a lift. The barges were low in the water with the lack of rain, the boat people curled up in their bunks, dreaming of lochs and weirs, their horses out to pasture for the night.

He'd known, soon as he'd put the key in the lock, that something wasn't right. She'd said she'd wait up for him to bring some supper for them both, up from the bar, but the room was dark and stuffy with the shutters closed and no candles lit. He put the covered dishes down on the side table and went over to the bed. Holding his lantern high he could see she was there, all tucked up nice. He didn't trouble her but sat and ate his supper alone as he usually did.

It wasn't until he went to bed that he realised she hadn't stirred, poor love, exhausted, lying there like a china doll, all white and, and – he touched her cheek and drew back in horror – *cold!* Stone cold. He pulled back the covers and saw she was fully dressed – shoes and all.

What? Was she playing? Was this some silly game, like the one they'd played as kids, pretending to be blind, stumbling around with their eyes shut? He kissed her. No response. He shook her gently, calling her name, hoping for some sudden deep breath or a smile, or a fluttering of her eyelids, a moan, anything. His heart stopped.

'No-no-no, Nellie, please don't be dead. Don't be.' But she was. Somehow, unbelievably, she was. 'No-o-o-o!' he wailed, and his heart splintered into jagged pieces.

When he came to himself he was lying beside her on the bed, curled into a soggy ball of loss. She was dead. She had left him. Questions began to percolate through the fog of his misery. What had happened? Had she felt ill and thrown herself on the bed to recover? Was it some germ she'd picked up on her travels? At the communal water fountain in Tottenham? The stale bread she'd eaten, the raw turnips?

Perhaps there was some clue on her body? The grazed knee! Was it infected? Had some awful insect bitten or stung her? A rabid dog? But as he turned her onto her back, he saw that her right eye that had been buried in the pillow was just a slit, all puffed up, black and blue. He winced, feeling the pain himself. Had she walked into a wall in the dark? What had she done? Her poor face! He couldn't bear to think of her suffering. Look at her chin, all misshapen and bloody and, there, on her neck – *on her neck!* – finger-shaped bruises. Someone had done this to her. Someone had killed her. Strangled her.

Almost blind with tears and with limbs that shook with horror and disbelief he'd mourned her. 'Nellie, my Nellie,' he repeated, as though she might answer him, explain what had happened. Who had done this to her? Why?

Had she shown her face downstairs? Had some drunken lowlife followed her up? Tried it on with her and been repulsed? Had he hit out at her, and when she'd cried out, struggled, had he hit her harder, strangled her to death, put her to bed and made his escape? Oh, Nellie, he sobbed, didn't I tell ye to let no one in but me?

It must have been a man, he thought. Her jaw had been broken by a hefty punch and dried blood and spittle crusted on her chin and there was the missing tooth on the floor, in its own small puddle of blood. He listened at her belly but there was no tick of life, no tiny movement. Nothing. He swiped at the tears that veiled his eyes, scuffed his sleeve along the drool from his nose because that ten-fingered signature darkening around her white neck said it all. Two big hands. As big as his own.

They'd say it was him, he realised with a sudden jolt of clarity, pin it on him, the father of the child, unwilling to take on the responsibilities of a family at this stage in his young life. They'd find any excuse and it wasn't so, it wasn't so. He would never … And he wasn't even here. The landlord, downstairs, had seen him go out this morning, seen him come back in, just now, spoken to him as he'd collected his supper, hadn't he? And any number of customers would say he'd greeted them. Wouldn't they? His mother would attest to his visit tonight. Wouldn't she? The bargee, Harry Stone, would remember their trip down the river to

Tottenham. Enough proof, surely, that he couldn't have done this. Unless – unless they could be persuaded *not* to testify or lie. Hefty bribes were nothing to *him*.

Because it could only have been Redfern, couldn't it? Her father's voice outside the door, demanding entry, was the only one besides his own she would have unlocked for. And gladly. She'd have thought he'd repented his actions, his violence and welcomed him in.

Instead, he'd come to finish the job.

He must have guessed she'd come to him, the Blackett boy, the father of his grandchild and, making enquiries up at the house, had tracked him to the Fish and Eels. Perhaps he hadn't intended to kill her but simply to talk her round (give him the benefit) but, standing firm, as she could, as Gil well knew, she'd have pushed him over the edge into violence. Because surely he loved and treasured her above all his possessions?

He frowned. That was it, of course. That's all she was. He owned her and she was no longer useful. No longer marriageable. She was damaged goods and so, like any old piece of furniture, he'd destroyed her.

Why had no one stopped him, though? They must have heard the struggle from downstairs, the screaming and shouting, the banging about, though Friday night at the Fish and Eels was noisy, with a ceilidh band and Irish dancing. Perhaps the skirl of pipes and bodhran had drowned out everything else.

He'd beaten her badly – there were bruises all over her chest and arms, and big red fist marks where the baby had been growing. And then, when she was dead, he'd put her to bed, hoping that suspicion would fall on Gil. He was probably sipping brandy up at his mansion, right now, waiting for Gil to summon the police, waiting for them to knock at *his* massive front door. Then he would strike. He would deny she had ever come home that night begging for help. He might even say he'd been out searching for her. His alibi. He would feign horror and grief when they told him she was dead and ask where they'd found her. 'Broxbourne?' he'd repeat, all innocent. 'We don't know anyone up in Broxbourne.' Then he'd think a bit, frown and say, 'Hold on, though…' and, with difficulty, remember Gil, the gardener, apprenticed to a Miss Ardmore. 'She was found dead in his lodgings, you say?' And that would be it. Gil might protest his innocence, his abiding love for Nellie, 'til he was blue in the face but he didn't stand a chance. They'd come back at him with the story Redfern would have planted in their minds, that Gil had taken fright at the idea of having a wife and a baby hanging round his neck like an albatross, spoiling his hopes of becoming a master gardener. And because Redfern was a rich businessman who paid his taxes promptly, who employed a vast workforce, who was a well-respected member of the town council and a freemason, to boot, and who was clearly devastated by the death of his only child, Gil would hang.

It was this belief, inbred from birth, that money was power, that mere underlings were helpless, cap-in-hand pawns in a game they couldn't hope to win, that prompted him to wrap his dearest love in sacking, like a tree or shrub for transplanting, and carry her over his shoulder, in the dead of night, down the back lane and along the towpath to Ardmore's perimeter fence, to heave her over it into the brambles ready for him to bury when he had a chance. The bloodied sheets and pillowcase went with her.

A crack of thunder and lightning splitting the skies broke in on his thoughts. Joe Carter spun away from the window, alarm widening his eyes. 'See that? Blimmin' water's coming in the door any minute! Dunno bout you lot – I'm tekkin me chances and goin' up to the 'ouse. Give us one o' they empty trays, Gil, mate.'

He did so and, fascinated, watched Joe crack open the door and, after taking a breath as if he were plunging into deep water, disappear at the gallop through the dark wall of rain, with a wooden seed tray over his head. Others followed suit, until there were just three of them left in the shed.

'Better get going, lads. I'll lock up be'ind ye.' Clem, his boss in this section of the garden, was hanging up tools, trying to leave the place as tidy as he did every night.

'Ain't gonna be much use locking up if the water gets in,' the new boy, William, pointed out.

'What about these, Clem?' Someone had left a load of trays, prepared and seeded, on the workbench.

'Top shelf, Gil, high as you like.'

'And the rest? The seed packets in the cabinet? Can't just leave 'em here to get wet.'

'Jesus, I dunno – you're right, though, there'll be hell to pay, any o' they get damaged. What we got that's waterproof?'

Between them, with the rain clattering on the roof and dripping through the slats, they transferred the remaining seed packets from the wooden cabinet to old biscuit tins, scraps of oilskin, even a pair of waders Clem wore when he cleared out the lily-ponds. They slung everything into sacks, hoisted them on their shoulders and fled, splashing through the flood that swirled around their feet when they opened the door and made shutting it nigh impossible.

Twelve

1903

On the train home, when they managed to remain awake for ten minutes at a time, they'd decided that Archie would continue to lodge at Bob's for the painting (Polly's shop was dark and cramped, upstairs and down) but that they would share each other's beds as the fancy took them. Neither could bear to be apart from the other for long.

'We could open up the tunnel again,' suggested Archie. 'That would fool the gossips.'

'Ugh! I never liked that tunnel. Too spooky. And it smelled of wee. A real passion-killer.'

'Don't you think it would add a certain *frisson* to our liaisons?'

She made a face. 'Any more *frisson,* my boy, and we'll go up in smoke!' Nevertheless, Archie thought a tunnel might bear looking into.

But neither the shop nor the studio was suitable for a couple, even less a threesome should Clara decide she wanted to live with them. She should have the choice – Camden or Walthamstow. Then they could start looking for a suitable home. But there was no rush, as Polly pointed out. It wasn't as if they were love's young dream in a hurry to start a family.

This morning, as he woke in her bed, carefully removing her hair from his mouth, he felt that he had come home. This was where he was meant to be. The ring of hooves and metal-rimmed wheels over cobbles, the twitter of sparrows and the competing peal of church bells, sounded different on this side of the road and though he missed the peppery smell of his own unwashed sheets he wouldn't have swopped this for all the tea in China. This beautiful little creature curled into his side. His own Polly.

And this was Sunday morning, traditional 'lie-in' day! Wonderful. Just as well she had wired Clara not to expect him today. He really couldn't face one of Vic and Ivy's *bon vivant* Sunday dinners after the highs and lows of the last few days. He felt guilty about leaving the poor girl to cope with the news of her grandfather's death without him, but Vic and Ivy would provide solid support, and he'd go over tomorrow to talk to his darling girl – his *other* darling girl – give her the watch and tell her his and Polly's news. He hoped it wouldn't be too much for her, all these changes coming at once.

It was almost too much for *him*. There was a scooped-out hollow in his chest that Da had once filled, and a heavy sorrow for Mam's loss but, with Polly wearing his ring, the sun had begun to shine again.

Mam had been wearing it on her little finger when she drove them, in the butcher's wagon, to the station. When they stopped she'd eased it past her arthritic knuckles and given it to him.

'I'm sorry, Archie, I have no pretty velvet-lined box to put it in. It was your grandmother's. When she died Da gave it to me and I'm giving it to you to give to Polly. If you want it…'

'Mam – we can't take your ring!'

'Look, Archie,' she held out her hands for inspection, the long fingers knobbed and swollen. ' My *wedding* ring's going to the grave with me. Far better you have this now.'

'I suppose I'll have to ask her then, won't I?'

'With my blessing,' she smiled.

'And I'll have to accept,' said Polly, from behind.

He'd leapt off the wagon and gone down on his knees then and there, never mind the puddles. He'd never forget her incredible eyes – dark as dark could be – as she said, 'With all my heart.'

165

He was smiling still. His arm tightened round her and she snuggled in closer, making happy little grunts. Then suddenly she was struggling to sit up, consternation in her eyes.

'Archie, Archie, what's the time?'

'It's early, and it's Sunday. Go back to sleep.'

'No, no! I must get up. I'm seeing Effie this morning.'

'What! Oh, for the love of...'

Effie had left a message at the pub while they were away and Mrs Reeves had brought it round last night: the young doctor had a day off and had invited them both over there, she said. Bart was coming down from Chelmsford. 'I phoned her back saying I'd come but I didn't know about you. I didn't tell her our news. What with you whisking me off to bed – *and everything* –' she kissed him, '– I quite forgot to tell you.'

His heart sank. He'd had such different plans for the day. 'Oh, Polly! Oh, darling, do we have to? Phone her back and say we can't make it.'

'She's bringing a picnic, Archie. I don't want to let her down.'

He sighed. Polly couldn't wait to share the good news with their friends, he understood that. But so soon after the funeral he really couldn't face a lot of well-intentioned ribaldry and wedding chit-chat. If he went anywhere it ought to be Camden, but since they weren't expecting him now... 'But you must go, of course,' he said. 'Take the trap – Jessie could do with some exercise – and have a good time. Give them my love. And hurry back.'

So, for once in his life, he found himself with Sunday all to himself. He could, he supposed, stay in and paint, read the newspapers, which he'd forgotten to cancel, and brood on his lot – and what a lot it was – or he could ransack her pantry for a picnic of his own. He stuffed a heel of bread, a corner of cheese, an apple and a bottle of water into his work bag and set off at a brisk pace, down the High Street.

He headed for the river. Some things needed checking out. For starters there was the unlikely story that Augustine's 'ghost' had spun about her drowning in the river. Tyrell had dismissed it as a hoax. The girl was very much alive to the detective's way of thinking.

He'd pointed his pipe stem at Archie, 'Take my word for it, boyo, her and her accomplice, whoever he is – probably some fly-by-night the Merediths wouldn't approve of – want them to think she's dead, for some reason. They've 'eard about the skellington in the river and are cashing in on it – turnin' the tables, like, using their own beliefs against 'em. Just a pity they didn't check out the facts. Can't really blame the girl. Gawd, if I was in 'er shoes,' he'd said, 'I'd do a runner, an' all. They're a rum pair if you like, them Merediths. Fillin' people's 'eads wiv all that spiritual hokum.'

If he was right, and Archie wasn't convinced, the hoaxers must have been there in the house, listening to the séance with a glass to the wall, to a ceiling or a floor. As for the voice, her parents swore it was their daughter's but gullible people (vulnerable, grieving people) will believe anything. She'd probably been in the cellar, come to think of it, with a megaphone aimed up through a crack in the floorboards – some such device. They might even have used a phonograph, though it hadn't sounded like a recording. However, the story she told didn't hold water at all. There was no gently sloping gradation anywhere along the riverbank where you might walk into the water, as she had described, gradually wetting your feet, then your knees and so on. The Pride of Lea was on the man-made canalised part of the river, deep-cut to take barges. You jumped off the bank straight into deep water. So yes, she'd got her facts completely wrong. Or someone else had. Archie couldn't help feeling that Augustine was in peril. And it wouldn't hurt, just to have a bit of a look round.

The water was even deeper after three wet days and the towpath was treacherous, rutted and uneven from the plodding hooves of heavy horses and sticky, with mud sucking at his boots as he stepped from the bank into the rocky boat. He paid the hire people for the day, promising to bring the craft back by five o'clock. He hadn't been rowing in years but after the funeral, Mam's cooking and hours of travelling he was desperate for exercise. And it would be good to think about something other than funerals and weddings.

Slipping the oars into the rowlocks, he braced his feet against the wooden plate and the attendant cast him adrift. It took a few strokes to get into the swing of it, 'catching crabs' while the boat-keeper threw up his arms in despair and yelled instructions – 'Left 'and, matey! No, no, *left*' 'And pull on your right! *Right*, I said!' Then, 'Bring 'er in! Bring 'er in, for Gawd's sake!'

But Archie, trying to work the boat out into the middle of the river, and narrowly avoiding grounding it on the opposite bank, recovered his oar and his dignity, and suddenly finding his rhythm, commenced rowing upstream, pulling against the flow. The dwindling boat-keeper gave him a thumbs up and went back to his shed.

Archie grinned. Anybody watching would think that he, Archie Price, gentleman painter and sometime police artist, had nothing better to do on a sunny Sunday morning than scull up the river for the hell of it, but he had his reasons.

He wiped his brow on the back of his hand as the oar came up and he found himself humming contentedly, something from the funeral. He recognised the tune as one the village band had played. 'The Ash Grove' – Da's favourite. Archie could hear his rich baritone soaring above all the rest as they gathered round the piano for a sing-song at Christmas.

'Sing up, Archie, man! Call yourself a Welshman? Let it out, boy! Whispering away back there. Are you singing the song or is it singing you?'

Well, there was no one to hear now – the factories fronting the reservoirs were deserted on Sundays, the pumps still and silent, the sky above the great chimneys free of smoke for once – so he threw back his head and sang – for Da and for Polly, always in his thoughts now – in time with the oar strokes, gasping for breath at the end of each line.

Keeping to midstream so he wouldn't get swiped by the willow fronds, or caught up in the weeds or fishing lines, he pulled hard. He had a long way to go.

'Twas there while the blackbird was joyfully singing, I first met my dear one, the joy of my heart; Around us for gladness the bluebells were ringing, Ah! then little thought I how soon … we … should … part…'

He found he was only mouthing the last words. Couldn't give voice to them. Out of breath, that's what it was.

Instead he gave himself up to the twittering in the trees, to the ducks and coots marshalling their little families into the reeds out of harm's way, to the cool water's gurgle and splash as he heaved on the oars, to the bright ripples. He saw them in paint; saw himself rolling a 'round' brush, laying on a continuous thread of paint, knitting the moving highlights and shadows with the transparencies, the translucencies and, out of the sun, the densities. Smiles and frowns. Canaletto had denied himself the pleasure of making the Venetian waterways come to life. Most likely he'd left all those stylised ticks, as a tedious task, to a student. And yet that was the thing you noticed – well, Archie did. Never mind the wonderful buildings along Venice's waterways, look at the terrible water. His mind flew to his own student. Would Polly mind awfully, he wondered, if he kept her on? He cringed as the weight of her imagined disapproval came down on his head. But it wasn't fair to Sophie to give her the sack. She'd be devastated.

As the flashing pinks and purples of ragged robin, thistles and vetch went by on the bank, he saw Kitty Flanagan's lilac gown that he'd asked Sophie to finish with broad brushstrokes. She wasn't a natural but she was so eager to learn and could do it when he showed her how. And she certainly saved him time. He should be paying her, not she him.

He'd ask Polly.

A child shouted and waved to him, distracting him from the problems of paint: a little boy, too near the edge, his big sister holding on tight to his collar to stop him falling in the water. He nodded, shouted, 'Hello, there!' but didn't break his stroke. 'Lovely day!' cried their father, coming up behind them.

Clara would have loved a brother or a sister, a little person to care for, teach, take for walks and so would he. Ah well, he couldn't have it all. And just suppose Polly had been able to bear children, if the same thing happened to her as had happened to Lizzie – oh God, he couldn't have borne it. Polly was so tiny… He sighed. No, better this way. Just be thankful for small mercies, he told himself, and grinned ruefully.

Round the next bend he began to hear the faint and unmistakable cries of football practice, the shrill whistle of the trainer. On the Tottenham side it would be Hotspur F.C., no doubt – the enemy – going from strength to strength since their cup victory two years before. His own team, the recently formed 'A's', Walthamstow Avenue, played them from time to time and, invariably, lost. He thought how his father had taken him and his brothers to football matches in Bridgend, how he'd have liked to have taken a small boy of his own to see the A's play. Clara had never shown the slightest interest in the game.

Couldn't be far now.

Aha, this looked like the place: Elias Redfern's vast market-gardening empire, glass roofs glittering in the sunshine as far as the eye could see. His own Crystal Palace. He was rich and powerful, supplying all the big wholesale markets in the south east with fruit and veg, in and out of season. But Redfern wanted to be able to print the curling red fern emblem on goods trains from here to Newcastle to Aberystwyth and put even more of Middlesex under glass.

And what he most regretted about his daughter's death seemed to be that he had nothing now to bargain with and could say goodbye to doing a deal with some railway mogul. According to Tyrell, this put him above suspicion. You don't kill the goose that lays the golden eggs.

Nevertheless, the man gave Archie the creeps. It wasn't just his aloof and strutting manner, the way he couldn't quite hold your gaze – new money did that to some people, he'd found, almost as if they were suspicious of less fortunate mortals, fearing they might spot their weaknesses, try to bring them down. But this was something different: the man was hiding something, no doubt about it. He had been so sure they'd come to tell him his daughter was dead, as if he'd known all along. Unlike the Merediths, who'd thought he'd come to give them good news.

Compared with other commercial enterprises Archie had passed on either side of the river – the closed doors and windows, the smokeless chimneys – Redfern's was buzzing with activity. Looked like a full workforce was loading wagons, wheeling crates of vegetables, tending plants in the greenhouses. No evidence of Sunday observance here, even though the owner had just found out his daughter was dead. Archie supposed the workers got overtime rates, time and a half, maybe. Maybe not.

There was a barge drawn up alongside the wharf, and a couple of men loading crates of tomatoes, one the bargee and an old man, in Redfern's service presumably. Curious, he pulled his boat over to the landing stage and tied up, ostensibly to eat his bread and cheese.

'Didn't expect anyone to be working today,' he observed, casually.

The bargee turned and tipped his cap. ''Ave to get these 'ere up to Lunnon tonight, sir, or I needn't bother.'

'I see.' He hadn't thought. Purveyors of fresh food had a duty to the customer from which only fishmongers were exempt. His landlord, Bob Cheshire's veggies were piled as high on Mondays, as on Tuesdays, as on every other morning except the Sabbath. Woe betide him if he had no ripe tomatoes or salad greens in this hot weather. His customers would quickly go elsewhere. And, he supposed, wryly, commerce couldn't stop for bereavement, either. Take the case of the butcher of Llantwit. Archie's brothers had a duty to keep the customers supplied with meat, no matter what.

171

'This Redfern's business?'

''Oo's asking?'

Even the bargee looked surprised at the old man's rudeness. Gnarled and bent, he wore the loose smock of a gardener, with worn and patched trousers and rubber boots. A real character. Archie itched to draw him: the eyes squeezed almost shut by sun and suspicion, the wispy grey hair, the shapeless hat.

'Sorry?'

'Ye en't from the papers?'

Goodness, he was jumpy. 'The papers?' he asked innocently.

'Newspaperman – on a story.'

'Why, is there one? A story, I mean.'

'No, there b'en't no bliddy story!'

'Well, no, I'm not – I'm just out for the day and trying to place where I am. I, em, I thought Redfern's was hereabouts but I didn't see any signboard.'

'Sign's up there aways.' His long, blackened thumbnail pointed upstream. 'Ye comes on it from t'other direction.'

The bargee simply pointed to the curling red fern emblem on the crates. It didn't need words.

'Right you are – em, thanks.' His smile contained unashamed cunning. 'They look very good, your tomatoes. Go nicely with a bit of bread and cheese. I suppose I couldn't, em beg…'

'Cost yer,' the bargee snapped, quick as a whippet. 'Penny each.'

Well, they looked beefy and fresh so Archie handed over his penny and augmented his lunch, eavesdropping as he ate. Bigger money changed hands as the bargee paid for a score or so crates of vegetables and the gardener pocketed some pound notes and recorded the transaction on his clipboard.

Having put away his billfold, the boatman was keen to verify some hearsay with the horse's mouth, as it were. 'See they reckon that body in the river were your Redfern's lass.'

'Oh-ah?' The old man's reply was noncommittal. 'Might be, then again it mightn't.'

Travelling daily up and down the river to London, the bargees picked up more gossip than cargo, sometimes. 'Bit of a shock,' the visitor continued and waited for a response. Getting none, he tried again. 'Some varmint done her in, they reckon.'

'I 'ad 'eard.'

'They 'ent found 'er killer yet, then?'

The old man jutted his lip and shook his head slowly. Despite his mean attire and his calloused hands, he seemed to be in a position of trust here, acting for his boss in money matters and protecting his privacy. Probably the foreman or head gardener. And here he was scowling and beating a tattoo on his long boots with the clipboard, clearly reluctant to add to the gossip.

'They got posters up all over, askin' did anyone know the young maid? Did us see her round and about, last summertime, like? Don' know 'ow they reckon the likes of us'll 'member that far back?'

Archie fancied he saw the stooped old shoulders straighten. He realised he was staring and hastily attended to his sandwich. Was it his imagination or did the old fellow seem worried? Of course, he would identify with his employer's troubles. It was his livelihood at stake, after all.

'They won' catch 'un,' he said now, with certainty. 'Been over a twelve month. He be well away be now.'

Was that wishful thinking? Archie washed down his food with a swig of water, bade the men goodbye and pushed away from the little wooden dock with his oar. The old man had a point. A murderer wouldn't hang around, not unless he was sure he could get away with it.

Tottenham slipped by, and Edmonton, pockets of housing, industry and commerce along both sides of the river, separated by grazing land for cows and horses, fields of wheat and beans, cabbages, buttercup meadows, unclaimed scrub with gipsy caravans, a flour mill, a lonely pub. Here a railway line crossed the river, there a footbridge. Huge reservoirs, their steep sides dotted with sheep, looked like vast green tables behind the quiet smokestacks of Ponders End's factories and mills. Through the lock at Enfield he sculled, past a terrace of workers' cottages, past Waltham Abbey, where he fancied he could hear a single bell in the tower, announcing transubstantiation.

The sun was high in the sky as he passed by Cheshunt and came within the bounds of Broxbourne. This was what he had come to see. This was where young Eleanor's foot had been found, where the river had burst its banks last year. Now properly reinforced with strong walls of sandbags and piles of rocks held in place by chicken wire ('better late than never', as Dafydd might say) the bankside was severe and formal, with just the occasional tough weed growing through, for a mile or more. The worst of the damage had been made good, the detritus tidied away. What he could see of the towpath had been repaired and resurfaced by a prosperous town council, and the occasional horse clopped along unhampered by puddles and mudslides, dragging its barge behind. Where habitation began, new fences and walls separated private from public land, against which uprooted trees, some neatly sawn, some lopped and left as edging and seating, invited walkers to rest awhile. Even so it looked as though great swathes of private land had suffered from the flood: lawns were sparse from fresh seeding and the planting was new.

Where a few sturdy-looking willow trees still hugged the bank, Archie rowed across and butted the boat end against an exposed root. It held against the tug of water and Archie shipped his oars and tied on. Half-hidden by the trees, a swarthy handyman turned from his task of creosoting the garden fence to tip his cap and bid him 'Ar'ernoon…'

Making a show of mopping his brow and drinking thirstily from his now warm water bottle, Archie remarked, 'Not much in the way of shade along this stretch!'

'Ah,' said the man, equally glad of a break, 'trees come down wi' the flood, sir, nigh on a twelvemonth since.'

'Bad, was it?'

'Oh-ah. Lost our fence an' all, sir. This'un's the new un. Needs proofin' agin the weather now. Gatepost were the on'y thing left, like a spoon upstandin' in thick broth.'

'Really?'

'Oh-ah.' The man put down his brush to show Archie the high-water stain on the gatepost. 'Last July it were, river come right up to 'ere, afore 'er flattened everything in sight – fence, gate, the lot – and took'n God knows where.'

'Goodness!' said Archie.

His informant's nod was rueful. 'Berberis us 'ad, all along by here, inside the fence, keepin' out yon trespassers, but 'tis all gone. Washed clean away.'

'Must've taken years to grow,' offered Archie.

'Right enough, sir. Thorns like needles. Get them buggers in your backside, you'll know it. I telled next door's lad the same, 'cause 'e were diggin' *their* brambles *out!* Right down in the mouth he were, an' all. 'Cause it were 'er idea, the missus, and he knowed it were bliddy madness. Well, anyone'll tell ye, but there ain't no tellin' *them*.' His raised chin and eyebrows meant employers in general. 'Rob ye blind, they gyppos, get they over your fence. They be arter your lucky white 'eather, see, what us calls *Veronica*, an' anything else they can lay their mitts on. Reg'lar tea leaves, they boat people. She were askin' for trouble, his missus! But he daresn't say nowt, an' 'im on'y a 'prentice. Mind you, yon river made a proper job on it. Swelled right up and washed everything out.'

'You were working here when the floods came?'

'Not then, sir, not 'ere, sir. First sign o' rain, I'm indoors, me. A soakin's good for ducks an' they'm welcome, I say. Plenny more jobs to do in the dry. An' when 'er flooded...' he shook his head at the memory, 'well – 'twere like a whirlpool, mester, tekkin' out everything in 'er path – our berberis, both fences and their brambles.' He chuckled, 'Saved 'im the bother, the lad! Reckon 'e give up in disgust. Like, what's the use o' trying to tame nature? Slung his 'ook, dinne? En't seed 'ide nor 'air on'n since. No one hev.'

That was interesting. A disappearing lad. A gardener's apprentice. Where had he heard about one of them recently?

'Never forget'n,' the man was saying. 'Summat to tell us grandkids, eh?' Archie realised he was referring to the flood, not to the lad. Apparently the water had swirled around with such force it had carried away wooden benches, pergolas, plants, even tree stumps and young saplings, miles downriver, dashing them against any obstacles and depositing the wreckage here, there and everywhere. Tool sheds were smashed to smithereens, spades and rakes and trowels tossed about like twigs.

Into his mind, then, swam the vision he had had the night before last, of Da's grave filling with water and the coffin floating free. Transfer that vision to the River Lea, swollen by heavy rain in the middle of last July when, coincidentally, Eleanor Redfern vanished. Imagine a huge weight of water, a deluge, flattening fences (close to where this now absent apprentice had been digging holes), sending them floating downriver like rafts, uprooting and swilling out any plants or trees or any – *any-thing buried* – and bearing it away.

Minus a foot, Archie reminded himself – if, indeed, that was how our girl had found her way to Walthamstow – minus a foot, gnawed off by a hungry family of foxes, the remains of whose meal had been found less than a mile away. He frowned deeply and stroked his Sunday bristles to concentrate his mind. Suppose the apprentice had buried Eleanor's corpse in this very garden bordering the river and suppose a hungry family of foxes had sniffed her out, that night? Suppose they had dug in the loose earth, as foxes are wont to do, until they had uncovered a foot? Sweet and tasty. They'd have worried at it, wouldn't they? They'd probably have ripped it off, maybe by gnawing at it, or by tugging at it between them. And suppose the winner had dragged that tasty morsel off to higher ground, to an estate Tyrell called '*High Chimleys*', to consume at his leisure?

That might explain how the bones had been found up there, out of reach of the flood.

'Oh well, better be making tracks – can't keep you from your work. Um, I wonder – can you direct me, perhaps – I'm looking for the Bellinghams' house. *High Chimneys*, is it?'

He'd passed it, the man said. He could either go back down the river or tie up his boat here and continue his journey on foot. *High Chimneys* backed on to Ardmore's.

Really? 'Ardmore's? That's this next house, is it?'

'Ardmore's, aye,' the man nodded and, with a little encouragement, also revealed that Agatha Ardmore, who owned the property, was a 'real good grower.' She had letters after her name and 'wrote for the papers' about gardening. She was a judge at all the local fetes and shows and had roses and day lilies named after her. She and her assistants travelled the world picking up rare seeds and bulbs and cuttings. 'Poor ole girl lost 'undreds o' plants in the flood – water got in her green'ouses, see, floated away all 'er shelvin', pots an' all, broke the glass… They saved some of 'em but a lot was washed away. Priceless, they was.'

'You'd have thought,' posited Archie, 'we'd have had rare plants growing along the riverbank, by now.'

'Well, aye, if they'd had the right soil and growing conditions, but 't'en't likely, what with last winter's snow and this boiling 'ot summer.'

Perhaps he wouldn't visit *High Chimneys* today. The police had already dug up the garden, looking for a body without its right foot. Perhaps, instead, he'd call in at this Ardmore's and see what anyone could tell him about a young gardener who had been digging up brambles, a year ago, just before the storms, and who had subsequently disappeared.

Letting the current carry him, he drifted downriver and tied up by a newly built garden wall. Let any flood try to undercut that!

There was a freshly painted blue door and a notice heralding *'Riverbanks'* and instructions for visitors to call at *'Main Entrance in Vesey Street'*. No bell pull or letterbox, just a keyhole. So, he set out along the towpath and seemed to have been following the wall for a hundred yards or more before he came, at last, to a sharp corner with a copse and a footpath to one side.

The woman who answered the iron-studded front door wasn't Miss Ardmore, he discovered, but a Mrs Ross, the housekeeper, as she took pains to point out, and she couldn't say for sure when Miss Ardmore would be back. Her employer was in China, collecting seeds to replace those she'd lost in last year's floods. Nor could Mrs Ross oblige with the name of any particular gardener working for the Missus. This time last July? Heavens above, there were masses of them, scores, as Archie would know if he had any idea how large an estate *Riverbanks* was. And they weren't her business anyway. Mister Grace might know. He was the head gardener, living in a cottage down in the village, the prettiest one, of course, with roses and honeysuckle. If Mister Price would like to leave a note Mrs Ross would make sure that he got it in the morning. She really couldn't disturb the man on his day of rest.

But Archie had no such qualms.

Mr Grace, a rangy, stooped fellow in his sixties, was intrigued that a gentleman calling himself an artist should come to his door on a Sunday afternoon, one who produced a sketchbook for credentials, showing people and events, a coffin being lowered into a grave, a child sitting under a table, weeping, a woman drying her hands on a tea towel. There were outlandish names scrawled beneath each and Friday's date was underscored. 'My father's funeral last week,' he explained. He was an artist all right and he filled the doorway. So, what did he want with Will Grace who, besides having no money, made it his business never to buy anything at the door?

Attentive to the face that loomed over him, Grace watched for catchpenny slyness, but the man seemed honest enough. He began to relax. It turned out this man, Price, was looking for one of the apprentices. Seemingly, he'd painted him at Ardmore's last year, in a scene that had included roses and delphiniums. The painting had, lately, sold for a hefty profit and, out of gratitude and hoping for more of the same, he had come to give the youngster a share of the spoils. He'd been to *Riverbanks* and Mrs Ross had sent him over here.

Mister Grace licked his lips. 'You got a name for the lad?'

Archie shook his head with a grimace.

'Well, show us this picture and I'll see if I can fetch him to mind.'

The artist scratched his head, 'Unfortunately, I can't do that. As I said, I sold the painting. Sorry, it was a bit of a long shot coming here at all. All I know of the lad is that he planned to leave Miss Ardmore's employ last summer.'

Grace's frown deepened. 'An apprentice, you say?' He shook his head slowly, and the muscles of certainty bulged around his mouth. 'Can't help you there, I'm afraid – apprentices mayn't change 'orses midstream. I do know a couple of the *men* left after the floods. Lost 'eart, didn't they? Went to find work inland aways.'

'No, this was definitely a young lad. Oh, well, I'll just have to keep looking. Sorry to have bothered you, and on your day off, too.' As he went to leave he assumed a sudden hesitation, and, turning back, mentioned that he happened to be in these parts looking for more 'interesting faces' to sketch for his new painting to be called *Village Life*.

Mister Grace invited him in.

Using a soft pencil, Archie swiftly drew his face, furrowed and brown as a walnut after a lifetime of gardening and smoking, and that of his wife, a wizening crab apple of a dame. He also drew their visiting son, Clem, who happened also to be a gardener at Ardmore's.

'You ever hear of an apprentice going off without finishing his indentures, eh, Clem?' his father asked from the corner of his mouth – Archie had requested that he keep very still.

'Not 'til last year, Pa.' (Archie's ears pricked like a squirrel's.) 'You remember the fuss? Oh dear…' He heaved a heavy sigh, rolling his eyeballs at their visitor to signify that his father's failing memory was getting worse. 'Promising lad, he were, an' all. Missus were right cut up.'

'Oh?' They both spoke at once.

'Blackie, us called him. He just disappeared. Left his lodgings at the Fish and Eels, up the road, with an 'alf-eaten pie on the side, a change o' work clothes and his rent unpaid. *An'* he stole a pillowcase and the sheet offa the bed. Must've 'ad a funny turn, or bad news or summat. Still 'ad two year left on his apprenticeship. He would never've gone off for no good reason.'

'A girl?' suggested Archie, now cross-hatching for a darker tone beside the younger man's long nose. Blackie, eh?

'Nah, not him. He weren't stepping out wi' no lass. Too busy a-larnin' the ropes for lasses. Though they did say at the Fish and Eels that a young maid come askin' for'n. They reckoned t'were 'is sister.'

'You made enquiries then?'

''Course. First I thought he were sick, so I had to ask, like. 'Twere a shame to lose'n. He 'ad the makings of a real plantsman – see 'im 'andlin' they seedlings, real gentle – potted 'em nice, fed 'em, coaxed 'em along, talked to 'em… Not a rough bone in 'is body. Well, if he's the one you're after, the one you painted, like, you'da found the same…'

Archie nodded, keeping his eyes on his sketch. 'Where does his family live? I'd best go and call on them.'

They wagged their heads sadly. 'En't from round these parts, that I do know.'

Then the mists in Grace's memory parted. 'I mind, now, when I took'n on, young Blackie. Good gardening stock, his folks. Walter Blackett's his pa – head gardener at Redfern's, down river.'

180

Archie feigned sudden recollection. 'Blackett, of course! Tch, what was his first name, now? Thomas? Richard?'

'Albert, weren't it, Clem? Us allus called him Blackie, though.'

'Gilbert.'

Into Archie's mind came the image of a clipboard beating secrets against a wellie boot. Was Walter Blackett the old man on the quayside? He suspected he was. And no doubt this young Gilbert was the reason for his anxiety! And hadn't Redfern mentioned the name Blackett as being someone off the estate who'd moved here? Oho – suppose Gilbert and Eleanor had had some sort of a relationship? Perhaps Redfern wasn't the murderer, after all. Perhaps, as Tyrell said, he wouldn't have wanted to kill the goose that laid the golden egg. Perhaps this Gilbert…

He quickly made copies of his sketches and gave them to the three Graces. He really would use them in a painting, he felt. A country scene like a Breughel. Nothing went to waste in Archie's sketchbook. 'And if the painting sells, who knows? I might be back here with a share for you!'

As his boat slid past the sign he argued against tying up again, at Redfern's. If that old man was Walter Blackett, he was a wily old so-and-so and was bound to remember him from this morning. He would never believe the story he'd told the Graces. Much as he wanted to draw the old tortoise it would be better to let the police question him. He had no doubt that Walter knew why and where Gilbert had gone.

Thirteen

'But he *always* comes on Sunday!'

'Now you know that's not true, Claribelle,' Granddad said reasonably. 'He comes if he can, if he's not too busy. There's been plenty of times he's been stuck in Walthamstow finishing pictures, or he's been away on police business. He does have his own life to live.'

'Yes, but he always tells me when he's not coming, makes sure I know. He never just stays away for no reason.'

'He did have a reason, I told you, he had to go to Wales.'

'Why? Why did he suddenly have to go to Wales, out of the blue? Why did he have to go without *me*? He never goes to Wales without me! He knows I like to see them over there. They're my *family!*'

This was meant to hurt and Granddad sighed forbearance. 'Something came up, I told you. He thought you'd understand. He said he'll see you in the week. He has something to tell you, I believe. All will be made plain.'

She wrinkled her nose. 'I can't wait 'til Wednesday!' What did he want to talk to her about? Something was going on and Granddad knew what it was. 'What has he got to tell me? Some secret? I hate secrets! Jeepers!' She had a sudden insight. 'He's going to marry Miss Hudson, isn't he? That's why he's got to go to Wales – to break the news. She's hooked him! But she's a gold digger, Lilian told me before she went missing! I told him to watch out for her but he went and took her on as a student, all the same. She's been working on him. She doesn't love him – she only wants him for what he can do for her.'

'Oh, for goodness' sake, Clara, I'm almost sure this visit has nothing to do with his love life. Good Lord, your stepfather takes time off from you for one day and you jump to all these silly conclusions.'

'*Time off!* What am I, some horrid Sunday chore he has to do?'

Nana Ivy stepped in, 'Come and sit down, Clara, your dinner's getting cold. Leave your grandfather in peace. Everyone's waiting.'

She knew she was behaving like a spoiled brat as she made her way to the crowded dinner table, knew she was scowling, that her cheeks were red, that stamping your feet was unladylike. Knew it but couldn't stop. There was something they were keeping from her. Pops would have given a reason in that telegram he sent that they wouldn't let her see. (*'Telegrams are for grown-ups.'*) Jeepers! You wouldn't get Pops saying that. He always gave reasons, Pops did, explained things. Unlike Granddad, who treated her like a child, kept things from her. Like the time Nana had to go to hospital. He never had told her why, fobbed her off with, 'Just a minor ailment. Woman's trouble. She'll be right as ninepence in a few days.'

And if Pops was marrying Sophie Hudson she should be the *first* to know. She was his *daughter.* She had to have a say. The future Mrs Archie Price would be her stepmother, after all. He'd promised and Pops always kept his promises.

'All right now?' Nana mouthed the words over the spinach she was passing to her. Clara pressed her lips tight and shook her head. She hated spinach and she needed answers. She'd been overlooked, treated appallingly. She looked at the roast gammon, fragrant with cloves and peppercorns and bay leaves and found she had no appetite. Oh Pops, why aren't you here?

'What's up with young Claribelle?'

Pesky Henry Waddington, sitting too close again. He was always getting her into trouble.

'Don't *call* me that!' she muttered through bared teeth.

'Ignore her, Waddington.' *Don't take his part, Granddad, don't!* But Granddad was feeling sore. 'She's in a foul mood today, because Archie isn't gracing us with his presence.'

'Don't talk about my Pops like that!'

'Your Pops!' said Granddad, his eyes glittering. 'Hah!'

'What do you mean – *Hah?*'

'He adopted you when he married your mother, but you have *our* blood in your veins, not his. We provide for you, not him. I suppose he would if he could but he never has any money. I don't know what he does with it all. Well, I do, he spends it on women –' he glanced at Nana Ivy who was shaking her head and frowning a warning, '– to sit for him – models, I mean. Now please, can we stop all this nonsense? You're putting everyone off their dinner.' He turned back to Nana, who was fanning herself with her serviette, looking very unhappy. 'Very nicely cooked gammon if I might say so, my dear!'

Clara couldn't stop herself. She flung down her knife and pushed her plate away. 'I hate my dinner! And I hate you, too! *You're* not my father, either, so you can't tell me what to do!'

'I'm your grandfather, *in loco parentis* and you are a rude little girl!'

'Not so little,' murmured Henry Waddington with a greasy smirk.

'Shut up!' she yelled, flipping his plate so that the potatoes and cabbage slipped off and the gravy soaked into the tablecloth. 'You're a parasite and a toady! So shut the hell up!'

'Language…' Ivy pleaded without much hope.

'GO TO YOUR ROOM!' her grandfather boomed, lurching to his feet and pointing to the ceiling. 'AND STAY THERE!'

Battling tears, she went, grateful to escape, flouncing out of the crowded room, stair rod straight, without another word. She hated these people who took over the house once a week. Sundays were always the same: stuffy and stale. People round about went on picnics to Vicky Park or even charabanc trips to Southend. As for the other day girls at school, they did something different every Sunday – trips to the Zoo, to cricket matches, to funfairs and gymkhanas, not to mention exciting automobile rides to the country or to aunts and uncles – one outing after another. (Granddad was afraid of automobiles – 'noisy, smelly contraptions!') But the Grants never went anywhere, and all because it was 'tradition' that the Head of Fine Arts entertain a dozen or more students and single teachers – hangers-on in her view – on Sundays. Nana said it was charity – they were 'giving something back' – but Clara knew it was because they were old and stuck in their ways and nothing would change. Ever. Nana and Cook would always be up 'til all hours on Saturday nights, peeling mounds of vegetables, making custards and jellies for these freeloaders, these scroungers to gobble down, every single Sunday dinnertime. No wonder she was exhausted and fell over, poor old thing. And she, Clara was expected to be nice to them all, even when they pinched her bottom and touched her budding breasts while looking the other way.

Having stomped up the stairs and along the landing as loudly as she could, she flung open the door of her bedroom making it bounce against the wall, and slammed it shut so vehemently that a couple of her ceramics fell off the shelf. She picked one up from the floor and examined it. Oh, Lilian. The porcelain towel around her shoulders had snapped in two and several bedraggled curls and fingers had broken off. Suffering catfish, did this mean she wasn't going to win the Olympics, after all? Perhaps if she stuck it with glue? What the hell – she could always do another one and, with that thought in mind, Clara flung the figurine at the door. Now the head came off – irreparably – bringing tears to her eyes and ratcheting her temper up a notch, so that she had no hesitation in throwing her fishing boy next – her beloved Huckleberry Finn! 'Errrgh!' she growled as she yanked out her top drawer, tipped out all her unfired birds and animals and stamped them into crumbs

185

and shards and baked clay dust. She was only hurting herself; she knew it. No one else cared about her creations. Banging her head on the wall, or sticking pins in her arm might have been more satisfying. But no, she wanted Granddad to see the destruction and be sorry. She wanted Pops to be sorry, too, for treating her so shabbily, and for ignoring her warnings about the gold-digging schoolteacher. Perhaps they were going to be married now, in Wales! She sat on her bed frowning, and, coming to a sudden decision, flung a bag onto the bed and began to pack. Mustn't forget the parasol. The last thing she threw on the floor was her piggy bank.

Fourteen

By the time Archie was trudging back up the High Street, with thoughts of a bangers and mash supper with Polly, the bells of Marsh Street Congregational were tolling for Evensong. As he wove through the faithful in their Sunday best, dodging bombazine skirts and small children, he was puzzled to see a small throng gathered outside the shuttered greengrocer's shop, among them Polly, sitting up on the trap, just back from seeing Effie and talking down to – could that be Vic Grant? What was he doing over this way? When he spotted Archie he started towards him, his limp more pronounced than ever, his spectacles glinting against a dazzle of evening sun.

'Do you have her, Archie? Oh, say you have her!'

What? Oh, dear God, don't let it be … 'Have who?' His heart was missing beats in anticipation of the reply.

'Clara, of course. Do you have Clara?'

'Vic, you've just watched me trudging up the street, alone. Where would I put her? I've been out all day on the river. Haven't seen hide nor hair of her.'

'I – I thought she might have come to you. We had a falling out – about you, in fact. She was upset that you didn't come over to dinner as you usually do.'

'Polly sent a telegram. About my father…'

'I…' he paused, looking down at his feet. 'No,' he sighed, 'I mean yes, we got the telegram but I couldn't bring myself to tell the girl.'

'*What?*'

'Think about it – such sad news. It would be far better coming from you. You said, you'd be seeing her later in the week…'

'*Vic!* So, what did you tell her?'

'I just said you'd gone to Wales.'

'*What!* My God, she must think well of me, not telling her.'

'She was in a bit of a state – she could only think you were marrying some schoolteacher and that you and she had gone off to ask for your parents' blessing.'

'What! Where did she get that idea?'

Polly's mouth twisted. 'Oh Clara…' she murmured, her look of pain cutting Archie to the quick. 'I hope she didn't misconstrue anything I may have said.'

It wasn't her fault, whatever it was. He could imagine her acid remarks. Polly had never been known to mince her words about people she disliked. Oh Lord, he'd upset everyone he cared for. He wished he'd never met Sophie Hudson. He should have been more open with Polly and Clara, making it clear that he'd no more think of marrying Sophie than… But Polly was quizzing Vic. 'So, tell us slowly – she was upset…' she prompted.

'Yes, we had a bit of a shouting match, I'm afraid and, in the end –' he sighed heavily, looking rather shamefaced, 'in the end, she became quite rude, in front of our dinner guests, so I sent her to her room and we finished the meal without her. When Ivy went up about – I suppose an hour or two later, when everyone had gone – she wasn't – she'd gone!' His voice caught. 'She'd gone,' he repeated, 'smashed all her pottery and disappeared. We didn't hear her leave the house. She must have climbed out of the window – the apple tree, you know, is within easy reach. I assumed she'd come here, on the bus.'

'She could be indoors, I suppose. She has a key.'

But she wasn't.

'Where is the blessed child?' the old man muttered through bared teeth as they came down the stairs again.

Weariness forgotten, Archie's first thought was to dash over to Percy's bar to use their telephone, but found the pub closed. Then he remembered that Bertha, in her new zest for spiritualism, had probably gone to church, while Percy was working flat out to try and get the Palace open before the New Year. It had already been put back from October to December, with a pantomime, hopefully, and then the people providing the marble slabs for the stairway were having trouble importing from Pisa, and then Marie Lloyd was pre-booked and refused to do panto anyway. Something had to be sacrificed and that was Sunday night at the Horse and Groom.

Where else had a 'phone? The post office was shut. All the shops were shut. And very few of the High Street residents, those living above the shops, possessed such a luxury. In the end he went down to the Salvation Army Citadel and rang the doorbell.

Ivy answered at the first ring. No, no, Clara hadn't come home. She'd taken a bag, and, as far as she could surmise, her nightdress and toothbrush. Clearly she intended staying overnight wherever she had gone.

'Well, she's not here, Ivy. She wouldn't be. Vic told her I was in Wales.'

'Yes, but she has a key to your lodgings. If she was running away from us yours would be the obvious place to go. She was incensed, Archie. She's really against this marriage.'

'I'm not marrying Sophie Hudson, Ivy. No question of it.'

'Well, somehow she got it into her head you were. Maybe she was hoping to see you when you got back and talk you out of it.'

He groaned. 'And no mention of my father dying?'

'No.'

He sighed. 'Perhaps she's gone to a friend's house. Have you tried them?'

'One or two that live around here but, you know, Archie, they come from all over. It's not like a county school where they all live on top of each other. And they don't all have telephones.'

'What about Henry Waddington?' It was, he thought, an

inspired guess. Suppose Henry had decided to imitate his idol, Paul Gauguin, and seduce a thirteen-year-old…

'Good God, Archie, what are you suggesting?'

'I – I don't know.' He was distracted – he had to pull himself together and think.

'Henry's been riding round the streets on his bicycle, looking for her. It came as rather a surprise, I must say. I thought he was completely obsessed with himself. In any case, she wouldn't have anything to do with Henry. She, more or less, tipped his dinner into his lap today after one of his sneering remarks.'

'Good for her! Well, let's think. Have you checked the 'bus station? Someone in Camden may remember seeing her boarding a 'bus.'

But neither she nor his father-in-law had got around to doing that. After advising her to carry on 'phoning round, checking with their dinner guests, he hung up.

'Have you told the police, Vic?'

'I was waiting for *you!* Where the hell have you been all day, anyway?'

'I – oh…' He shook his head, it didn't matter. 'Look, I'm going to the police.'

At the section house they were down to a Sunday skeleton staff, but those on duty were genuine in their concern. They were fond of Archie's little girl, they said.

'She's thirteen, Jimmy, fully grown. Physically, if nothing else.' Archie showed the desk sergeant the photograph he'd brought – one he'd taken the day of the aborted swimming spree – of Clara in a white dress, as tall as Polly, her long black hair tidied into a pigtail. 'Going on thirty, Polly says.' And stabbed, suddenly, with the thought that he might never see her grow any older, he had to shield his eyes from the fellow.

'She'll be back when she's hungry,' said Jimmy, 'you'll see. Me, I ran away from home times without number! Got to the end of our street and come over all 'omesick, thinking of Ma's lamb stew.'

'She went without her dinner. The worms will have been biting long before this.'

'What's that, then, four hours? Five?'

'Long enough. Best get up a search party, I reckon.'

Vic was at last persuaded to return home to support Ivy, who was beside herself with loss and guilt. She'd let Lizzie down, she wailed; she'd failed in her duty of care; she should have gone straight upstairs after the girl instead of staying to serve everyone rhubarb crumble. They agreed to wait for news while Archie scoured the 'bus depot in Chingford Road for drivers and conductors who may have seen a dark-haired girl in a white dress. But they shook their heads over the photograph. Pretty little thing – they surely would have noticed her, travelling alone. As several pointed out, there was a reduced service on a Sunday. And no direct route to Walthamstow from Camden. She would have had to change buses or even take a tram or a train for part of the journey. Or a cab, if she'd had the fare – her piggy bank was broken. Or maybe she cadged a lift...

Oh, please God, not that. She wouldn't have, surely? Not after all his warnings, all the missing girls, Lilian and Augustine and poor Eleanor Redfern. But she was easily influenced and young enough to be taken in by a plausible story like *'Your father asked me to keep an eye out for you...'* He felt sick.

Everyone racked their brains – where could she be? Neighbours and schoolfriends had nothing to offer. No one had seen her leaving the house, walking along the street in either direction. It was hopeless. She had vanished into thin air.

Hours stretched into a night without sleep, though Polly tried to comfort him. 'She could have heard from Lilian and gone to her ... Have you tried other swimming clubs? She's probably just doing a Huckleberry Finn. Hiding out somewhere, making everyone feel sorry they were unkind to her. Give her a few days of 'roughing it' and she'll come home longing for a bath and a hot meal.'

He considered each suggestion, but nothing made sense. She'd have left word. She wouldn't have left him in ignorance, frantic with worry, blaming himself. She was better than that.

Eventually, he fell asleep, only to startle himself awake at two o'clock in the morning, thinking, 'Wales! She'll have gone to Wales, to catch me before it was too late!' He was sure of it. But how could he contact his mother in the backwater that was Llantwit? Telephone cables didn't extend beyond Cardiff. In Llantwit they still thought the telegraph magical. That was it, then, tomorrow he'd send a telegram to his mother. Ask her to put his mind at rest.

But in the morning when he put it to Polly she reminded him that the fare was prohibitive. Ivy hadn't mentioned missing any money and Clara would never have had enough threepenny bits in her piggy bank for a ticket to Wales. In any case, they would never sell a ticket to a child.

So, another day went by, and another day of tearing his hair, biting his knuckles, going over and over her known movements, snatching at hope, followed by another broken night and another. He couldn't eat, couldn't rest.

Polly shut the shop and joined him trudging the streets, searching, asking about, catching glimpses of a white dress or a biscuit-coloured coat, a black pigtail flying around a corner, swinging in the park, cycling into the forest.

It was never her.

The police conducted systematic house-to-house enquiries, checked pubs and shops, train stations, searched parks, hedgerows and ditches, yard by yard, inch by meticulous inch. Even the obnoxious Henry Waddington took a day out from college to hunt for her around Camden, in the market and along by the Lock, the canal, Regent's Park. He helped pin posters to telegraph poles and trees. And then he began a dotty painting of kites flying on Hampstead Heath in the pointillist style of Seurat and that was the end of his interest in Gaugin and thirteen-year-old girls.

In the forest, in that first week, among the ancient beeches and elms, they thought they'd found her – a wild-eyed, dark-haired waif in a dirty shift, which she held by the hem and moved slowly but rhythmically from one side to the other. As they circled closer – the police and the various good folk who'd joined in the search – they heard her humming some tuneless dirge and saw that her straggly hair wasn't exactly black as answered the police description, but dirty and tangled with dried holly leaves and bits of twig. Her bare feet, as she stepped to her song, were scratched and bloody; around her mouth were the streaks and stains of blackberry juice, mud and vomit, they thought. She was clearly off her head.

'Clara?'

She slid them an empty look without interrupting her dance. She didn't seem frightened or timid, just preoccupied.

One of the women helpers produced sweets from her pocket – soft jujubes – and held them out to her, as you would to a wild animal. Letting go her flimsy skirt she pounced, snatched at them and stuffed them quickly between her sore and starving lips. Too quickly, for she immediately choked, retched and brought them back up. How long had she been like this, without food, wandering wild? Her state of emaciation and general deterioration didn't tie in, at all, with the few days that Clara had been missing. Was it she? Was this Archie's missing girl?

By giving her sips of water and more sweets, they managed to tame her enough to allow them to put a blanket around her thin shoulders and to lead her back, silent now, chewing slowly, along the footpaths to the lane where transport was waiting. They took her to the cottage hospital in nearby Buckhurst Hill and sent word to Walthamstow.

Archie and Tyrell arrived within the hour, having driven the horses at full pelt through roads cutting through the forest.

He took the stairs three at a time and pushed aside the policeman on duty.

'Sir, sir, you cannot go in there!'

It wasn't Clara, nor was it Lilian, and he didn't know whether to be glad or sorry but he did recognise her from his pencil drawing. The girl lying in the hospital cot was Augustine Meredith. She looked the worse for wear, ragged and dirty, wild-eyed and white-faced. Soup or vomit had stained the sheet and pillow.

'Augustine – Gussie!' he shook her arm, forced her to look at him. 'Who took you? Was Clara with you? Where do they have her? Is she still there? Or Lilian? Was there a girl called Lilian? Where is Clara now? You must tell me!'

The girl frowned and slow tears spilled down her cheeks. She closed her eyes and began humming again, twisting her head this way and that.

'No, Gussie, please look at me. Listen, I'm not going to hurt you, I just need to know where Clara is. She's only young. If you know anything about her, or – or Lilian, you must…'

The humming became moaning, then wailing. She thrashed about, tearing at the sheets, dragging at the handcuff that anchored her to the cot, screaming, screaming…

'Archie!' Tyrell was suddenly there, having followed him at his own plodding pace. 'Come away! For God's sake, man, leave the girl alone. She can't tell you anything.'

'But Clara's out there, where she's been, I'm sure of it. There can't be that many predators about playing that game, surely? This girl might be able to tell us!'

'You don't know that. Clara's disappearance need have nothing to do with her. Lilian's, neither.'

'Oh Christ, she has to –.' He scuffed his wet face. It should have been Clara they'd found. Where was she? Was she being as badly treated as Gussie had been?

A doctor rushed into the room followed by a couple of nurses and the officer on duty, who helped Archie to his feet and escorted him, kindly enough, out into the corridor. 'Don't you worry, Mister Price, sir – ain't your fault. She's been like that, off and on, all afternoon anyone tries to touch her or talk to her.'

'They're sedating her now, Arch. We might get a bit more sense out of her when she wakes up. Come and sit down, boyo. The constable will get you a cup o' Rosy. Eh, constable? Make that two cups, milk, three sugars and none.'

When the doctor came out, he said that as far as they could tell without examining her properly, Gussie had been bound – there were deep scars on her wrists and marks on her neck that hadn't faded with time. She'd been starved and probably sexually abused. She'd laid into the nurses, shrieking and scratching when they'd tried to give her soup, wouldn't let them anywhere near her to remove her rags for a clean-up and a proper examination. She'd only just begun to calm down when Archie had burst in.

It would be some hours now, he said, before the chloroform wore off. Whether she would then be able to answer questions was another matter. She had clearly taken refuge from fear and pain by absenting her mind. Regarding her lack of speech there was some difference of opinion. The resident psychoanalyst thought it symptomatic of deep-lying hurt, something unspeakable. He called it 'elective mutism.' But a contributory factor might have been actual physical damage to her vocal chords. *Something* had caused that chafing around her neck.

Now that Archie had identified her as the missing girl, Augustine Meredith, they would send for her parents. Perhaps seeing them would help bring her to her senses.

In the meantime, while she was unconscious, they would clean her up, carry out the necessary examinations and let the police know what they found.

By the time Mr and Mrs Meredith arrived their daughter was washed and brushed and, again, handcuffed to the cot's railings. She was wearing a crisp hospital nightdress and lying between

195

clean sheets, absent-mindedly twirling a length of her still-damp hair into a ringlet.

She looked right through them.

'Gussie, darling!' They tried thawing the ice with good humour. 'Hello, sweetheart, what have you been up to, eh? They told us you were on the Other Side! Must've been a case of mistaken identity, eh? Because here you are, large as life!'

'You're safe, baby girl. No one's going to hurt you now.'

And when she failed to respond, the mother's tears began to flow. 'Don't you know me, Gussie? It's me, your Mother. Oh Gussie, please…'

But Augustine paid them no mind, fastening her attention on the chain that held her to the bed, more from curiosity than from any wish to be free from restraint.

In the doctors' consulting room Archie and Tyrell learned that the girl had *not* been sexually assaulted.

'*Not?*'

'No, she is still intact. A virgin.' They raised their eyebrows. 'I know. But there is no evidence of penetration whatsoever, even though her torso is covered in bruises, which she's probably acquired since her escape.'

'Poor kid!'

'She's desperately thin. Whether they starved her or it's a result of her living wild in the forest for weeks – not much to eat, I shouldn't think, except mushrooms and berries –' he made a face, '– beetles and worms.'

'Hedgehogs, rabbits?' suggested Archie hopefully.

The doctor shrugged. 'God knows how she's survived this long.' He took a deep breath. 'So, whoever it was had her captive – they abused her, kept her bound, but they held off rape. What do you make of that?'

'They were women?' offered Tyrell.

'They preferred men?'

'Or,' offered the Doctor, 'they wanted her kept intact for some dreadful ritual where virgins are the preferred currency. Don't Druids and devil worshippers believe in virgin sacrifices?'

'Not Druids. That was myth put about by the Romans to discredit them. We have our own sect in Walthamstow, don't we, Frank?' Tyrell rolled up his eyes to heaven. 'They're harmless enough, though I've heard of dogs choking on their discarded chicken bones the morning after the solstice.'

Tyrell's agreement was dismissive. 'They use a large rock near the Waterworks as an altar stone,' he explained to the doctor. 'I mean, they don't welcome spectators but everyone has a pretty shrewd idea what goes on. Drunken orgies and that.'

'But no human sacrifices?' asked the Doctor.

'Human sacrifices!' Archie felt faint. 'Oh, Clara,' he choked, 'where the hell are you?'

Tyrell said quickly, 'No, no, nothing like that. People are entitled to their beliefs. Live and let live so long as they don't hurt anyone or scare the horses, I say.'

'Scare the…? Oh I see. No, quite.'

'I mean, yes, we have our own share of cranks, like them in there,' he tipped his head sideways, 'spiritualists and that, but we don't have no black magic or demon worshippers round our way.'

'You reckon?' said Archie, grimly. 'They're not likely to advertise themselves, Frank! If people like that have got Clara…' He blinked at the horrific visions that sprang to mind and knuckled his lips against crying out in protest. Oh God, my poor dear girl. He cleared his throat. 'Can we – can't we get Gussie to tell us where she's been – if she's seen Clara?'

'Not yet we can't. We'll just have to wait until she finds her voice.'

'And her wits, more to the point,' added Tyrell.

'Can she write? Have you tried? Let's give her a pencil and paper. Ask her what happened.'

But when they did so she merely scribbled. A long unbroken line of meaningless loops and squiggles, backwards and forwards

197

across the page becoming, it seemed, more and more angry, stabbing at the paper until the lead broke.

And when they asked again, about Clara, she moaned, 'No-o-o...' banging her head from side to side against the pillow. 'No one else ... Not, not...' she seemed so sure. 'Not any Clara, just me.'

So where was his daughter?

Fifteen

When the runaway left her grandparents' house, via the apple tree outside her window, she made straight for the canal, her intention being to take the towpath route to Paddington. She'd known it since birth, apparently, according to Nana. As a last resort, Mama used to take her for long walks along the towpath to get her to sleep. It was nigh on impossible to get the perambulator down the steps from the bridge and up again, so Mama had bound the bundle of squalling ferocity to her with a shawl and carried her down. Here, she felt, the howling of a young baby would disturb the least people. Clara had been told the story countless times and thought she could remember the impact of the sudden, deep amplification of her hullabaloo as she was carried under a bridge, so startling that she had shut up, momentarily, in shock, and then screamed more in order to hear it again. She'd taken her earliest steps along the towpath, on jingling reins, still shouting under the bridges, with Mama and Papa John Kington. Later she'd fed the ducks with Pops, sailed toy boats with the Grants and watched lost balls and hoops and boats go floating off down to Limehouse and beyond. As a young larky girl, she'd jumped in – been hauled out; fallen in – been hauled out; been pushed in – climbed out. Lately, she had rowed boats and fished off the bank or some barge or other, with rod and line.

She'd learned to ride her bicycle on this path with Pops loping along behind to catch her if she fell. It was a shame she couldn't take it where she was going today, it would have eaten up the miles, but a girl on a bike is memorable and too many people would have been able to tell Granddad when he asked. That was the trouble – they all knew her along here. And today, Sunday, they'd all be out, taking the sun, stretching their legs on the towpath.

Which accounted for her disguise – even Pops wouldn't know her in Nana Grant's summer frock. Once she'd made up her mind to leave, she'd raided the old lady's wardrobe. There was nothing that fitted the demands of modern fashion (bustles are so passé, Nana!) but eventually she'd found a dress that would do. It was long enough and the old lady had never worn it. She was too stout and her fingers too stiff to do up the thousands of buttons. She wouldn't miss it. Cinched in at the waist with a wide belt, and pouched over, blouson fashion, you'd never know it wasn't made to measure. She'd wound up her plaits and pinned them like Effie did, over her ears. Turning her head this way and that she had to admit she looked years older. She plonked Nana's biggest hat on top and fixed it at a jaunty angle with half a dozen hat pins, pulling the creamy net veil down over her eyes. Quite a dish, if she said so herself. She hadn't bothered with Nana's shoes; they were all misshapen and lumpy. Besides, the new boots that Pops had bought her, with their little kitten heels, were just the thing. She'd been a little wobbly at first but she was getting used to them. She shortened her steps and held her head high.

As she emerged from the first bridge she saw the houseboat *Saucy Sue*, moored further along the bank, and, wouldn't you know, Peg and Pete were out on deck, he in a striped blazer, she in a frilly blouse and skirt. Oh, how she wanted to stop and chat, tell them all about her mission, but instead she put up the parasol and sailed on, head up, trying to make light of her overnight bag and looking straight ahead towards the Lock. Oh glory, how did one manage a bag and a sunshade, walk like a lady *and* lift one's skirts to negotiate the mud?

Walking as quickly as her heels would allow, she passed the lock-keeper's cottage and the stables, unnoticed. Everyone was too busy shouting instructions to a young woman trying to work the lock gates while her husband manned the tiller of a narrow boat. A passer-by was hanging on to the horse. There was no sign of Mister Dickinson, of course, it being Sunday – lock-keepers' day off. If anyone had looked across they'd only have seen some anonymous young woman in a cream dress, carrying a bag, with her parasol up and her head down, watching where she put her dainty feet.

Two more bridges and the character of the canal changed markedly, becoming more neglected. The towpath was worn to a muddy channel by heavy hooves and the sidings were overgrown and strewn with rubbish – broken bedsprings, greasy armchairs, broken pots and oil lamps, burnt pans, used gas mantles. No one walked here for pleasure, only to get from A to B as quickly as possible, minding weeds and puddles and piles of ash. There were a few boys fishing for eels, and a bargee leading his horse up the slope to the street. She followed, there being no towpath through this long, narrow tunnel. They both rejoined the canal on the other side of the road while the boat's crew 'footed' the boat through, lying on their backs in the dark, and pushing their feet against the curving, echoing walls until they reached daylight again.

Back on the towpath she followed the canal around the fenced-off northern edge of Regent's Park. Here the canal was different again, cleaner, with smart dustbins and painted wooden benches placed at strategic intervals along a gravelled pathway. Trees provided shade but you caught the occasional whiff of the Zoo's stinky big cat house and the sound of trumpeting elephants and squawking parrots. Now the gardens of the stately Nash mansions descended, in steep gradients, down to the water and Clara consciously straightened as she went past, balancing imaginary books on her head so as not to look out of place among the ladies and gentlemen who lived here. In their summer whites and boaters, they were preparing to partake of an afternoon's picnic, the hampers being carried up to the grassy banks by liveried footmen. They looked straight through her.

There were more people about now: singles, couples and families, sampling the colour and life of the London waterways. She could lose herself among these strangers, who were unlikely to remember a lone girl in a hurry. Just the hurdy-gurdy man to negotiate and the tea rooms and the weekend stalls that had sprung up along this popular part of the canal.

She kept her head down, recognising Giuseppe, the balloon man and the Punch and Judy man, out to entertain the Sunday strollers, who wouldn't think twice about telling Granddad he'd seen her, dolled up to the nines. She scurried past and, turning off the main Regent's Canal, took the Paddington Arm. As she left the Basin, she found she was trying to think of a name. That American who'd painted the place? Pops thought the world of him. He was better known for that picture of his mother... She sighed and shook her head. Well, anyway – he may have painted his *Little Venice* all misty and romantic but on a sunny Sunday afternoon it was anything but. In between the horses towing their barges, negotiating the poles of the lagoon, children pulled their toy boats on lengths of string, while their parents paused to watch a flotilla of ducks or racing boats speeding past, crewed by sweaty young men in vests and coxes shouting instructions. A butcher boy speeded past on his bicycle, whistling. And that was the name – of course.

The sun angled hot and she let the parasol rest on her shoulder to shade her back. It meant her face was exposed but she doubted anyone coming towards her would know her.

But there was something happening behind: crunching gravel, keeping pace with her own footsteps. Whoever it was slowed when she slowed, picked up when she picked up. Her heart beat faster. Was this a thug following her, keeping her in their sights before choosing a suitable place to strike?

Warehouses, on the far bank, loomed over their reflections. Pulleys and cranes, inactive on a Sunday, were brought to life by the current, pointing and gesturing and the grimy windows gleamed upside-down in the ripples, warning her of danger. Goose pimples prickled her arms. She quickened her step, her bag bumping against her legs, the handle numbing her fingers. But she couldn't stop to change hands.

Oh Lord, who was it? A pickpocket? Pops was always warning her about the bad people at work in London crowds. Opportunists. Robbers. You had to be careful. Hide your purse. Or he might just snatch your bag and run ... Oh help. But no one would rob her on a busy towpath, surely? They'd wait for her to be alone. Like under this next bridge with its dark underpass yawning to gobble her up. It might even be a kidnapper who would make off with her. Or a madman, who would stick her with a knife just for the fun of seeing blood spreading across her nice cream blouse. Then he'd shove her in the canal, another Jane Doe.

Or it might be bloody Henry Waddington. Of course, that's who it was. He'd followed her from the house and was waiting his moment to pounce. She often encountered him on walks, on the way to school, in the library, like he'd happened there by accident. Him and his silly ideas. According to him, artists didn't have to obey the rules of ordinary society. They were passionate creatures who went with their instincts. They could seduce thirteen-year-old girls. All for the sake of their art, of course. He had talked loudly over dinner about free love, brazenly winking at her and evoking much laughter. Horrid boy. He wasn't normal. His loud braying voice, lacking in any nuance; his obsession with particular artists; his little-boy tantrums when things weren't exactly as he liked them; the way he couldn't meet her eyes; his rudeness. It was a wonder her grandparents hadn't thrown him out.

Oh Lord, what was he playing at? Idiot. What had he in mind? Juggling her parasol, she managed to free one of Nana's enormous hat pins. That should curb his passion, she thought. Then she'd drop everything and run.

Sixteen

Augustine

'*Please, please…*'
Awake and cognisant at last, Augustine relived her worst moments while one of the policemen wrote them down in shorthand. The other was waiting for a description, she knew, but didn't want to disturb her flow. In any case, she hadn't seen her attacker as he'd come up behind her and shoved a sack over her head. He must have been hiding behind a tree near the house. She'd just managed a squeak of fright when a large hand clamped the sack tight over her nose and mouth. She couldn't breathe! She'd struggled and he'd grabbed her arm and muttered in her ear, 'Shut it, girlie – I'll do for you, else – no skin off my nose. Right?' He was expecting an answer. She nodded and he unhanded her. As she drew in a life-saving breath the pressure on her arm became sharper, stinging. 'Feel that? It's a blade, right? One peep out of you, girlie…' And then he was whispering in her ear and she was petrified; she really couldn't move from fear. She may have sobbed; she may have wet her drawers. He said if she struggled he'd stab her to death and leave her in a heap by the side of the road with her entrails spread out for the dogs to share. He said he was Jack the Ripper come out of retirement, thirsting for blood, but if she was good he'd be kind. Then he twisted her arms behind her back and snapped handcuffs around her wrists. She was a prisoner! In broad daylight!

'Please, please!' she'd whispered, feeling a bead of sweat or a tear crawling down her cheek and, suddenly, her arm was stinging. He'd cut her! Drawn blood!

'I *said* no talking!' he hissed. 'You keep that up, my girl, and I'll slit your throat, I swear. No loss to me. Plenty more where you came from!' Then he'd grabbed her elbow hard and half shoved, half pulled her along, and, when she tried to wriggle free, she felt a quick movement and hard pressure against her throat – the flat of a blade. 'I'll do it, bitch … I'll slit your…'

'Now, now, Ned…' came another, pacifying, voice at her back! She hadn't realised there were two of them! *'Take it easy, mate,'* said this other, this oily voice, then, in her ear, a whispering. *'I'd come along quietly, if I were you, duckie…'* And then, to his companion, a loud reprimand, *'Ned, behave!'*

There was a moment's hesitation and the pressure at her throat went away. *'Tch. We discussed this, Ned. Have a care – you'll defeat the object. And be warned, Missy – he'll slice you soon as look at you. And don't you go thinking I'm a soft touch. I have a gun and I'll use it.'*

She gasped; she staggered, almost swooning into blessed blackness, only to be jerked upright. She truly believed they'd kill her. They didn't care. 'What d'you want?' she whimpered.

'Shut the fuck up!'

The sack was lifted a little; large hands forced something between her teeth – a piece of smelly rag – and tied it tightly behind. The sack came down again.

But where was everyone – the neighbours? All those twitching curtains in The Drive, why did nobody see what was going on and challenge them? Why did nobody interfere?

Her captors didn't speak another word. Her ears strained to pick up clues of any sort but there was nothing, just the clump and scuff of boots on fallen leaves, an occasional huff or grunt. Light and shade flickered through the coarse weave and now and again, looking down, she caught a glimpse of a black boot or a hand holding a knife – and then a cartwheel. No sooner had it registered than one of her captors picked her up bodily and threw her onto the vehicle like a sack of potatoes, banging her shoulder and scraping her knee. Never mind that she was hurt and probably bleeding – they simply didn't care. The cart bounced as the men took their seats in front, there was a 'Giddup', a jerk and a jingling of harness, wheels began to creak, and the cart moved off, juddering over the rough ground. Where were they taking her? Was that a left turn or a right at the bottom of the road? By the second turn to the right she'd completely lost track, fear making her more than stupid.

After a while they reached a metalled road – she could hear the spit and crunch of stones under the heavy wheels – Forest Road? Wood Street? And then another. And another. The steady clip clop of hooves went on for miles it seemed to her, before turning off onto a track of ruts and potholes. A bit of a wobble and then they stopped. Where was this?

The tailboard was let down and rough hands pulled her towards them, lifted her, set her on her feet and gave her a push to start her walking.

It was a big house – of that she was sure. She'd tripped up at least three steps. As the front door opened and she was shoved, stumbling, into the hallway, a sickening smell filtered through the hessian. Smoked haddock took days to disperse.

She was too concerned with staying upright to object and, in any case, the gag would only make a gurgle of it. In fact, she'd stopped hoping they'd take any notice, long ago. Despite her dread and her addled brain, she did try to think.

She'd thought at first her captors might be the louts who'd hung round the school gates the other day, talking dirty and making rude gestures as her class filed out. But this was far from a prank, a lark. This was deadly serious and these were grown men. They had clearly made a mistake, taken her for someone who might be exchanged for a ransom. Mother and Father were comfortably off, like most of the families who lived in The Drive but they weren't what you'd call wealthy, not really. Or – her heart flipped – maybe these were the 'nasty men' she'd been warned about her whole life long and this would be the 'fate worse than death' that awaited girls who fell into their clutches.

Her arm still smarted where the man called Ned had cut her. Now his knife was prodding her in the back. Thank God she was wearing her bony stays, her protective armour, or she'd be pouring blood by now. There came the rattle of a latch lifting, a door scraping open, and a draught, coming up from underground, which burned like ice. They pushed her ahead of them down some stairs, never bothering to warn her or help her when she collided with some jutting piece of brickwork, lost her balance and fell, like a log, onto the cold dirt floor, fear and pain screaming through the gag.

They didn't give a jot. She'd banged her nose and the thick sacking over her head made filling her lungs doubly difficult. Tears and dribble didn't help. Then, suddenly, the sacking was snatched away and she blinked, her breath juddering in terror. It was a cellar, shadowy-dark, with a dirty plank ceiling, strung with cobwebs. The edge that had floored her was part of a brick-built wash tub.

Adjusting slowly to the phenomenon of sight, she saw that one of her captors had remained upstairs, and this, the one who had pushed her downstairs, was not the rough-looking thug she'd expected to see but a respectably tailored and groomed gentleman, tall and thin. He wore a peaked cap and a large white handkerchief, folded into a triangle, across his nose and side whiskers, beneath eyes that glittered.

'Shut it!' he snarled at her mewling fear. He spun her round and untied the gag. Now she spotted a straw mattress, a thin blanket and a lidded wooded bucket, prisoners for the use of. Never! When he turned her back she lunged at him, her teeth bared to bite. He drew back his fist and hit her.

'Uh!' she gasped, hardly believing what he'd done. 'You – you brute…'

'*Ned, Ned, gently, please!*' She spun around the better to see the speaker. '*Best not rile him, duckie. My friend has a temper on him, I'm afraid.*' There were only dark shadows. Where was the voice coming from? She frowned. She and this Ned were alone.

'Where..?'

'Never you mind!' said Ned.

So, the other one was keeping out of sight for some reason? Perhaps she knew him and he didn't want her to recognise him. She certainly didn't know that slick, sludgy voice, like he had a bubble in his throat and needed to swallow. But he was there somewhere, spying.

Augustine blinked fiercely, to clear her eyes, as the tall man removed her handcuffs. It was almost wonderful to be free again, to be able to bring her hands to the front, to take one up to examine her poor nose. It came away with blood on it. Just as she was about to explore again, Ned grabbed her wrist and clicked a different sort of fetter round it – a medieval iron manacle! 'Dear God!' she protested, struggling to pull free, 'What are you doing!' But he grabbed her other hand and imprisoned that, too. As she pulled, she realised, with a sinking heart, that the manacles were attached to heavy clanking chains embedded in the wall and, though her wrists were narrow, they wouldn't pull through these bracelets.

'You've got the wrong person!' She held out her hands, pleading as a street beggar might, at the same time cringing against the next blow. But it didn't come. This time his hand fastened on her throat. Her arms were too heavy to put up a fight and she choked on her puny protests. Pushing her against the wall, he picked up a larger bracelet from the floor, opened it on a hinge and locked it about her neck. A barbaric iron collar! Its thick chain was also attached to the brick wall. 'Don't do this, Ned!' she begged. Raised her eyes to the dirty ceiling, 'Tell him, whoever you are up there. My parents aren't rich. You've made a mistake, both of you. I'm not who you think I am.'

She needn't have spoken. Ned simply picked up his lantern and turned to leave.

She tried again. 'Don't leave me here in the dark, *please!* You've got the wrong girl!'

Her chains reached as far as the bottom step. Hopelessly, she watched the lantern disappear through the door at the top of the staircase. Then everything went dark and she heard a key turn in the lock.

Fighting to keep her chattering teeth still, she tracked Ned's footsteps overhead back down the passage above her and heard a door close. That way lay their living quarters, then. When she released her breath, it was with the sobbing judder of a wretched, hopeless child. It was so dark. She couldn't see a thing. She would die here from cold and fright or … oh God, what would become of her?

As the minutes passed, her eyes, though sore with weeping, grew sufficiently used to the dark to make out slivers of light between the floorboards in the ceiling, and a mottled dusk coming from a grid or grille high up on the wall opposite. For ventilation, she supposed. Its original purpose was to let the steam escape from laundry boiling in the copper. As a light source it was rubbish, all crusted over with moss or rust but it was enough for her to make out heaps of coal and kindling, an old washstand, a mangle, a chopping block and shelves empty of anything but dust, all beyond reach of her chains. In despair, she went back to the wall, slithered to the floor and nursed her sore jaw. Far away she could hear them arguing, the high querulous Ned and the guttural tones of the other one, talking sense, or what passed for sense in this crazy set-up. Whatever they discussed it wasn't her freedom.

Time passed and, eventually, she heard heavy boots returning along the passage above, the sound seeming to reverberate in the very bricks at her back. When the door opened she sensed a quickening behind the wall. Was that where Ned's better half parked himself to stay out of sight? Her chains chinked as she moved sharply away. Down the steps came Ned, still with his kerchief across his face, swinging a lantern and bearing a tray which he left on the bottom step. It was as though she had something catching – her misery, perhaps – and he wanted to keep out of range. Calmer now she was able to say,

'You're making a big mistake, you know. I don't know who you think I am but…'

But it was dark again. He'd gone.

She couldn't eat. He'd left her a hunk of bread and dripping. Foul stuff. It smelled off. She sipped the water and took the mug back to the straw mattress. It looked as though they would keep her fed and watered, then. That was something. They didn't intend that she should starve to death. *They had some other purpose than simply to see her suffer.* She took another sip of water – and became aware that she was not alone.

Now rats are no one's friends, and she was well enough acquainted with the species to know that they are best left alone. They only attack when challenged, and here were at least four of them in various shades of dark, whiskers twitching in the meagre light, long tails snaking along the floor as they investigated the crusts, the ends of a loaf, spread with fat and meat jelly, that she'd left on her plate. She watched them carefully. They had their holes, their exits, perhaps they would provide clues as to how she might escape. As they devoured the bread it dawned on her that they must be accustomed to having food brought down the stairs; the excitement she'd felt in the damp wall when the door opened, had been rats *expecting* a meal of sorts at regular intervals. Perhaps not an entire meal like today, maybe just crumbs, but clearly this was a routine they were used to. Someone else had been kept prisoner down here. What had happened to them?

When the rats, having nosed around for a while for hidden extras, decided to call it a day, she tried to see where they went. If there were bricks or mortar missing it might indicate a weakness that could be worked on. She had to get out of here. But their hole, found more by touch than sight, was disappointingly made in the dirt floor. They had tunnelled *under* the all-too-solid wall. Could she do likewise?

She sat down again to weigh up the possibilities of escape. Chained up like this, she could do nothing. Could she persuade Ned and his friend to unchain her? Unlikely.

If she starved herself her hands might eventually become thin enough to slip through the manacles, but by then she'd be too weak to scratch the dirt floor with a finger nail let alone dig a tunnel. And what about the metal collar? Perhaps she could develop a cough and they'd take pity on her and remove it. Perhaps not.

Or maybe she could work the chains loose from their beds in the bricks, if she had a tool of some sort, something tough, something sharp? And supposing she succeeded? Lugging three heavy chains around with her was hardly conducive to escape.

It wasn't until she saw a rat scooting up the wall where the grating was and somehow disappearing, that a real plan began to take shape. It was too dark, from where she sat, to see how it had managed to escape but there had to be a hole around the grille that could be improved on. Oh, to be able to vanish like that with a whisk of your tail into the outside world! Her plan involved that chopping block if only she could reach it. If only she could free herself of her chains. A pity they'd taken her bag with its useful nail file and scissors, not to mention a handy little buttonhook and tweezers. And her hat with its three or four hatpins – where was that? Inside the sack that they'd taken away. Her hair was a total mess: all the pins and combs and grips coming loose. She blinked. *Surely a girl with time on her hands could work out a way to use hairgrips to her advantage.*

There was nothing for it: she had to use the bucket and discovered, on lifting the lid, that she wasn't the first to use it. The stench took her breath away. Others had wept over the need to relieve themselves in this dungeon in the presence of these awful men; others had felt the despair of privacy violated. Others had worn these shackles, had lain on this mattress and planned *their* getaway, like her. Maybe some had managed to escape. She hoped so.

She readjusted her clothes and replaced the bucket lid, quietly. She was sure she heard something. A footfall, a disturbance. Another rat, or something less savoury… Something overhead.

She looked up, trying to catch a movement. Someone was there, lying on the floor above, watching; she was sure of it. She could almost smell his breath. She shivered. What was he, her captor – a sleazy voyeur? She strained her eyes, searching for a clue among the cobwebs, but the grey light from the ventilation grille revealed no spyhole, no light or shadow between the floor boards.

'Who – who's there?' she dared to whisper.

'I have many names.'

She gasped; she was hardly expecting an answer. So, he *was* watching! Her chains rattled with fury. 'How long have you been there?'

'Long enough.'

'You – you *filthy*…' Words failed her. 'Is that what I'm here for – to, to provide some sort of sordid entertainment for you and your friend?'

'Just keeping an eye, girlie. Making sure you don't do anything silly.'

'What silliness had you in mind? Escaping? What can I do, chained up like a dog?'

'We wouldn't want you to hurt yourself.'

'Huh!' She gave a short mirthless laugh. 'All right for *you* to hurt me, though, knock me about, stick knives in me.' It occurred to her, in a sudden flash of insight, that her metal comb might make a useful sort of weapon if it were sharpened against brick or stone. Or would Peeping Tom spot her and stop her?

'You need to be careful of Ned. He can be unpredictable.'

'You don't say.'

'We need you in one piece, you see.'

'What for? A ransom?'

Silence.

'Why won't you tell me? Where's the harm?'

'You don't need to know.'

'But you've made a mistake, don't you see? I'm no heiress. No one's going to pay for my release.'

'Exactly.'

'What does that mean?'

'They will think you are dead.'

'Dead?' This wasn't an answer she could have expected, so smug, so certain, so puzzling. 'Why would you want them to think that? In any case, my parents would need to have evidence. They'd need to see my body for themselves.'

'Not necessarily.'

Silly, of course they would. They were never going to be satisfied with just a letter or a telegram or however else Ned and his mate were going to tell the lie. They'd want proof.

'Do you even know who my parents are?' It occurred to her now that they'd never asked her name or called her anything but 'girlie' or 'Missy'.

'Of course.'

They did? 'Well then, you'll know they converse with the dead.'

'Indeed.'

'Well, they'll soon find out I'm not on the Other Side, won't they? And they'll get the police to search for me.'

Silence. That gave them something to think about.

'It was them at the Merediths' séance!' Archie cried in a moment of enlightenment and Tyrell wagged his finger in triumph, 'Yesss! They must have been hiding somewhere, Ned Thingy and his mate!'

They told Augustine about her parents' attempt to contact the Other Side and how her vocal 'appearance' had caused consternation. 'They must have recorded your voice somehow – it was the device they used to replay it that distorted it – not the medium's vocal cords!'

'How? How did they do that? What am I supposed to have said?'

They told her.

'But I've never said anything like that – about rivers and drowning. I'd never have lied to Mother and Father, never have let them think I was dead.'

'But they did – they were convinced.'

'Oh, the poor things…'

Her lip began to tremble and Tyrell patted the bedcovers in the proximity of her foot, preparing to move on. 'What did he say next?' he demanded. 'The geezer in the cellar?'

She swallowed, squared her narrow shoulders. 'Nothing,' she sighed. 'They must have gone away to plan their next move.'

'And what did you do?'

'I tried to escape.'

She'd sat down on her mattress, thoroughly shaken. Not content with jailing her in this – this *dungeon*, they would tell her parents she was dead. They fed on her distress. And they *spied* on her. They were unnatural. Perverts. Especially the oily one. Why didn't he want her to see him? Was he hideously disfigured?

With the onset of night, the grating almost disappeared, coming and going like the Cheshire Cat and, as clouds went across the moon, she couldn't see a hand in front of her face. It was so quiet, too. Even the rats had stopped squeaking. Would Ned come again? She was so thirsty. But he didn't. She supposed he and his sleazy mate had gone to bed. Even kidnappers need sleep.

She lay down on the prickly mattress and covered herself with the blanket, thinking of her immediate predecessor. 'What happened to you?' she whispered. 'Was it bad? Well, my dear, I am not hanging around to find out for myself.'

One of the advantages of belonging to the spiritualist church was that you got to meet interesting fellow spiritualists. During one of Sir Arthur Conan Doyle's visits to London, he'd attended a

Convention in Westminster and witnessed Doctor Meredith performing spiritual healing. They'd got talking, afterwards, and in order to continue an interesting conversation Conan Doyle came to stay, for a few days, at the healer's house in The Drive. There it was that Sherlock Holmes's creator taught Meredith's young daughter the gentle art of lock-picking, as taught to him by his friend, Houdini.

All you needed was a bent hair clip, the sort she took from her hair now. Hopefully she could remember how to do it. She pulled the rubber knobs off with her teeth and straightened it out into a long flat ribbon of steel. Hopefully, neither Ned nor his mate was familiar with Sherlock Holmes and his lock-picking prowess. Gently, she felt for the keyhole in the cuff on her right hand and poked in her probe. She didn't need to shut her eyes to visualise the mechanism within. In the dark there were no distractions. She could almost see the metal roller with holes that housed the cylindrical locking pins. A bit like bolts that fitted into holes drilled in the wall. Ah, she could feel them with her probe: one – two – three. That was all. These manacles were so ancient, the locks were simple, basic. It shouldn't be too hard to free each pin from the barrel but for that she needed a 'key' to turn it. She found another hairgrip and bent it at the end. She poked it into the bottom part of the keyhole and wriggled it about until it found a snug mooring place. Then, not daring to breathe, she turned it anti-clockwise – *lefty-loosey* as Mother would say – to turn the barrel. Holding it firmly in place with the long middle finger of her bent right hand she took her probe and examined each pin in turn. There was the first one. Lift it up and out of the way of the hole. There was a click and she quivered with excitement. Yesss! Calm down, Gussie. Stop shaking. Deep breaths. Next one. Click. The third one stuck but, with patience and a little more pressure, it, too, behaved itself.

The manacle sprang open. One hand was free! Thank you, Sir Arthur.

Swiftly, she scanned the ceiling for light, listened for heavy breathing. Nothing!

What a burglar she would make!

The left cuff was easier and, with two hands free, she could now tackle the accursed collar. She twisted it round so that the lock was against her throat and she picked away gently, patiently, listening for clicks, feeling for stubborn pins and applying more pressure until, at last, the collar came off.

Halfway there. She lay still, listening for breathing or movement. Still nothing. She let go her own breath. Dear God. She mustn't get too cocky. She thought she could probably unpick the door lock, too; the one at the top of the stairs. But that would be courting danger. Suppose someone was sitting on the other side, on sentry duty?

Better not. Her initial plan was probably best – the one involving the grating. She tiptoed over to the chopping block – a well-seasoned tree stump, its upper side rough with blade marks – and rolled it on its edge, quietly, quietly, until it was underneath the ventilation grid. Climbing up she was able, at last, to see the sky, silver bright with moon now, and breathe in the warm scents of summer. More importantly, she could examine the grille close-to. Would she be able to squeeze through any hole she made? It was an iron grid about eighteen inches by eighteen. If she took off her dress with its leg-of-mutton sleeves, she would. Probably. She had to.

The grille was embedded in mortar, *except* where the rats had chewed it away to make their own hole. The gap they'd made exposed the straight edge of the rusty old grille and she could just get her fingers in to try and jiggle it loose. But the mortar on the other three sides still held the thing firmly in place. This was impossible. Wait, though. Rats had their teeth and claws to dig away at the mortar. She just needed something sharp.

Her thick braid swung down as she took out the metal comb. The chalky mortar was softened by half a century of damp steam and, as she scraped with the metal teeth, it came away in chips and crumbs. In half an hour she had the grille clear. With one hand she held it in place and, with the other, she wiped the comb on her blouse and stuck it back in her hair. Then she stuck her fingers into the grid holes and detached the grille from the wall. Don't drop it, don't drop it! Quietly, she hopped down and laid it on the floor. She stripped to her stays, gathered up her dress and shoes, climbed back on the stump and shoved them through the hole. No turning back now. It was now or never. Gripping the sides of the opening, using her elbows as levers and her bare feet to push against the wall, she hauled herself up and through.

Oof! The grass was wet with dew. She lay still for a moment, flat on the ground, listening. And heard a match struck overhead. The darkness brightened and, looking up, she saw a single window, alight, among the creepers on the house. They must have heard her! Oh God, no time to dress. She gathered up her things and scooted across the lawn.

She didn't make it to the garden fence.

Ned, aroused in every sense of the word, caught up with his near-naked prisoner and brought her to the ground in a rugby tackle. Though she screamed and kicked and clawed at him, her knickerbockers were soon down past her knees and he was pulling up his nightshirt.

'Ned, stop!' came the guttural voice. 'Ned, you cannot do this. You must *not damage the goods!*'

Ned blinked and froze. It was as if his conscience had spoken. Seeming to come to his senses, he moaned, 'Go away! Leave me alone!'

His momentary distraction was enough. She whipped the comb out of her hair and raked him with its teeth, once, twice…

'Wait! Wait!'

They stared at Archie scrambling back through his mind to sallow skin with a combing of wounds – it had to be… 'I know

217

who it is!' he cried. 'At the séance, that bloke sitting next to me had these strange tracks on his face! That's what they were, Gussie – the marks of your comb where you'd scratched him. Tall beanpole of a man, skin like raw dough, dead eyes? What was his name? A fish. Freshwater. Perch? Roach? Wait,' he said. 'I'll draw him. The name will come.'

After she had identified Ned, or Edward Pike, her head fell back on the pillow and she yawned widely. 'Sorry, sorry,' she said, 'I'm just…'

'No,' said Tyrell, 'we're sorry – you must be exhausted. You just sleep, now.' But she already was, breathing deeply, soundly.

They stared at each other, then at the sketch in Archie's pad.

'Bastard!' They both spoke at once.

Was that when she had got away? She certainly wasn't mad then, clawing at her would-be rapist's face with a comb. That was quick thinking; that was sane enough. So, what happened?

Seventeen

When they returned the next day, Augustine was still asleep and Mrs Meredith was by her daughter's bedside, getting ready to leave.

'Home to bed!' she announced, brightly. 'I didn't get a wink. My poor girl, thrashing about all night long! Hysterical, she was. They had to sedate her again. My husband's tried healing but the damage is all in her head: you can't cure memories or dreams. I'm off to have a word with Mrs Laing. See if she can't send angels to watch over her. Perhaps you'd like them to intercede on your daughter's behalf, too, Mister Price? If those wicked men have her there's no knowing what harm they'll do...'

Archie couldn't speak. His lips were white with suppressed fury and fear.

'Thanks, Mrs Meredith,' said Frank, hastily. 'Erm, no Mister M today?'

'He'll be along later. Just gone to the church to tell the spirits she's been found alive and in one piece.' She shrugged. 'Well, getting there. And the neighbours need to know, of course.'

'Oh, f – for goodness' sake, Mrs M!' His moustache quivered.

'What? What's the matter? Is something wrong?'

He took a calming breath. 'Well, it might have been wiser to keep quiet about it for the time being. I mean you never know who's listening.'

'But they were worried. You have to put people's minds at rest, both the living and those on the Other Side.'

'Hell's bells!' Archie exploded when she'd gone. 'What that poor girl has had to contend with! Angels! What utter bilge!' He frowned and shook his head. 'And, no doubt, those 'angels' will tell their mates and it'll be all round the church and the parish and Pike, with his ear to the ground, will find out that Gussie has been found and is recovering in Forest Hospital.'

'Let's hope he don't do a runner.'

'Rather that than come here and do her in – though she'll be going home soon, won't she?'

'Very likely. She'll still be in danger there, though, Arch. He knows where she lives. No wonder she's having bad dreams, all she went through.'

'Better out than in, according to Freud.'

'Thought that was food poisoning!'

'Well, I guess it is a form of poisoning. Poisoning of the mind. Oh, hello there, Gussie, you're awake.'

She was sitting up against the pillows. Her eyes, dark and shadowed, in a pale and sleep-starved face radiated sanity.

'Gussie! Good morning!'

'It's that voice I hear in my dreams. That's what wakes me up. Sort of guttural.' She shivered. 'Ugh! I can still hear it. It clings to the inside of your skull. Fills your mind with ugly visions from which you can't free yourself even when you're awake.'

'What did he say in your dream? Can you remember?'

'It was what he told me when they got me back in the cellar. That I was a silly girl to try to escape, that I would soon be glad they'd caught me again. That I was destined for a life of luxury. I was to be the – the p-pet of a rich foreign gentleman.'

'Oh Jesus!' said Tyrell. 'White slavery!'

Archie closed his eyes in despair.

It appeared that Pike, her would-be rapist, had only been momentarily inconvenienced by the injuries she'd inflicted with

220

her comb. He pursued her round the garden on his long legs, cornered her against the fence and quickly had her back in the cellar by punching her unconscious and slinging her over his shoulder. When she came to, with a thumping headache to add to her other injuries, she found she was once again chained up, that her hair had been raked for hairgrips and that the escape hole had been blocked off from the outside. The cellar was now in complete darkness.

She was so very cold. She was only wearing her shift. They'd taken her other clothes and all she could do was weep and shiver. That was when Pike's invisible 'other half' had informed her of her fate. Death would have been preferable. Sold off like a slave, she'd be ruined, a fallen woman. She'd never be able to go home, never be able to get married and have babies. Her life would be utterly, utterly spoiled.

'Is that supposed to make me feel better?' she'd retorted.

'All you have to do is pleasure the gentleman and he'll give you anything you ask for.'

'I can't, I just can't!'

'You can and you will.'

Whether weeks passed or months Augustine wasn't sure. In constant darkness it was impossible to tell what time it was, what day. Food arrived randomly – sometimes she woke up to find a cold stew on the bottom stair, skinned with fat, sometimes bread and jam, sometimes pie and mash from a shop, or a kipper or porridge. She ate what she could. She had to try and stay alive. Her midden was emptied from time to time but mostly she was left alone. She amused herself by exercising: walking the length of her chains and back, over and over, attempting handstands up the wall, even encumbered by fetters and chains. Then she kicked the wall until the soles of her feet were tough, and practised climbing up the bricks and along, as far as her chains allowed.

There came a day, wonder of wonders, when Ned unchained

her, twisted her arm behind her back and shoved her up the steps to the cellar door. 'God, you stink!' he said.

She screwed up her eyes against the glare of daylight. And blinked again. A woman stood in the hallway, silhouetted against the stained glass of the front door, a woman dressed in a coat of blue wool, and a hat made of the same material, such as Robin Hood might have worn, feather and all. As Gussie came within range she pressed her handkerchief to her nose and winced, turning her face away. 'My God, Ned, she smells like a goat.' Addressing Augustine once more, she said, 'The first thing you need, my girl, is a bath. Upstairs with you.'

'No, I don't…'

'Now!' She held up her hand. 'No arguments. I need you out of those dirty rags and clean. I can't breathe!'

The woman seemed to know her way about the house for she marshalled Augustine upstairs to a bathroom where a claw-legged bath stood steaming with water. It smelled scented and so inviting. There was a washstand beside it with jugs of hot and cold water and even one of shampoo. Flannels and sponges and a new bar of Pears soap lay about. And oh heavens, a toothbrush and a tin of tooth powder! White, fluffy towels hung on a rack. And for what? To make her clean enough to grace a rich man's bed. A whimper of fear was working its way up into her throat.

'I'll be back in half an hour,' said the woman, briskly. 'I'll expect to see you sparkling clean when I return. Properly now,' she stipulated, like a fond mother, 'behind your ears and in between your toes – otherwise I'll let Ned see what he can do. We'll cut your nails, too. Your hair, I believe, is an extraordinary shade of blonde when it's clean, so make sure it is. Your gentleman, from the East, I understand, has a partiality for blonde hair. So – look sharp and get to it. When you're ready we'll see about dressing you in a fitting manner. Leave your rags in the corner there and Ned will burn them. Ned? Shall we?'

With a swish of her skirts she was gone. Gussie heard the key turn in the lock and their retreating footsteps. 'Looks like a pretty one, Ned,' came the woman's voice. 'Well done. They should pay you well, my friend. How's the writing going?'

Their voices faded as they went downstairs. Only two voices, Gussie observed. Where was Mister X? Had they left him outside on keyhole duty? She hung the face flannel over the doorknob, just in case.

Better be quick. The windows seemed to be nailed shut, as she might have expected and the air vents, set in the outside wall, were ineffective judging by the mildewed grouting in the tiles. Mother would have a fit.

She emptied the hot-water jug, a metal enamelled affair, into the bath and breathed in – oh God – the scent of roses on the steam. But escape was the priority. She couldn't end her life as slave to a desert sheikh – and his court. For she was under no illusions. It was her virginity he was after. When he had used her, what then? What did he do with his cast-offs and hand-me-downs?

She was certainly not prepared to find out. She tucked her shift into the waistband of her drawers, and the toothbrush into her cleavage. Shame about the bath, but she'd rather be dirty than soiled. She draped a towel over the lower sash window to muffle any sound and heaved the jug to break the glass, snapping off any jagged pieces remaining round the edges of the frame. The other towel padded the window sill so that she could slide through backwards. As she had hoped, this outside wall was covered in ivy like the one she'd seen on her first escape attempt. There were footholds enough for a girl with tough feet and handholds among the thick vines clinging to the bricks. For once she was glad she had no long skirts to hinder her. Her drawers might be filthy but they freed her legs perfectly.

She didn't look down until her feet touched solid earth. Then she broke into a sprint. Across the lawn, up and over the back fence and into an alleyway. Now where? That way lay houses. That way there were trees –

'You chose the forest…' Archie said, his elbow denting the counterpane.

'I knew Ned would be after me in no time, I had to hide. I mean I was only wearing a shift and – and underwear. I was afraid – in town – other, other men might have, em, taken advantage of me…'

Archie suddenly understood how any man, men in general, or women for that matter, would now appear threatening to this girl, who had been through so much at their hands.

'You should have gone to the police station,' said Tyrell, but Archie frowned and gently shook his head. She'd had to give herself time to regain her trust in mankind.

'I ran and ran until I got a stitch in my side. Somewhere deep in the forest. When I came to higher ground I climbed a tree hoping to see a road or something that would give me my bearings but all I could see, in any direction, were more trees. It was getting dark by then. I did see lights coming towards me – lanterns, I thought – so I stayed put until they'd gone past.'

'Was it him?'

'I don't know. They were on a different path, whoever it was. When they were well past I came down again. I thought if I went to sleep up in the tree I might fall out and break my neck.'

'So where *did* you sleep?'

'Well, I walked on for a while, and then like Hansel or Gretel I just sat down among the branches of a fallen tree and covered myself with leaves. And I did sleep, surprisingly. I felt safer than I had for ages.'

'Despite the foxes and rats and goodness knows what?'

'I'd slept with rats before.'

'Indeed.'

'Augustine, I take my hat off to you. What a plucky girl you are!'

'I had little choice, Mister Price.'

'So, you were all alone in the forest for – how long?'

'I don't know. I lost count of the days.'

'What did you eat?'

'Anything I could find, really – birds' eggs, crab apples, dandelion leaves. Blackberries and sweet chestnuts. Rosehips and the leaves they call 'bread and butter.''

'Hawthorn,' Archie provided. 'Dear God, you must have been starving. You had no means of cooking anything.'

'No. Everything was raw. I avoided mushrooms. I don't know one from another and I know some are poisonous. I drank water from the streams and when it rained.'

The two men shook their heads in wonder. 'And you didn't meet anyone who could help you?'

'No, I avoided everyone. How would I have known whether they were friend or predator? I couldn't trust a soul.'

'Ironically, you were near a bridle path that would have led you out of the forest when the search party found you.'

Quietly she said, 'I don't remember anyone finding me.'

'Yeah, you was off your 'ead, ducks,' said Tyrell. 'Well out of it. Doing a funny little dance, they said. Musta been something you ate or bad water.'

'Don't know. I remember going a bit woozy and when I came to I was here.'

'Ri – ight, and that was the first time? I mean you don't remember feeling like that before, while you were in the cellar?'

'Arch?'

'No, never. I felt hungry, but never so that I didn't know what I was doing.'

'See, it's been bothering me how Pike got your voice on that record he played at your parents' séance. I mean they were convinced it was you, despite the distortion. They explain that away, of course, because the dead are obliged to use the medium's vocal cords to transmit their messages. We all believe what we want to believe, I suppose And you say you don't remember saying anything of the sort? Nor feeling at all, em, woozy? Like you had no control? Ever?'

225

'No, I…'

'Maybe he mimicked her voice?'

'But I was sitting next to him, Frank. I'd have heard him. And the voice was definitely coming from across the table, from Augustine's chair.'

The answer came to them, simultaneously.

'Ventriloquism!' They stared at each other, while the girl looked from one to the other, utterly perplexed.

'Of course! Lord, why didn't I think of it before? You know what a ventriloquist is, don't you, Gussie? I expect you've seen them on the stage.'

But she hadn't. She explained that her family were not theatregoers. They didn't hold with actors taking on another's persona as it interfered with their afterlife in some way.

Archie briefly considered the plight of a sad, culturally deprived child but was far too excited with his new theory to dwell on Gussie's upbringing.

Tyrell took pity on her and described how a ventriloquist could somehow speak from his belly, forming the consonants with his throat and tongue, 'throw' that voice so that it seemed to come from a dummy, or life-sized puppet sitting on his lap, or even from a box.

'Or an empty chair,' added Archie.

'And you can't even see his lips move.'

'Some are quite versatile, with a selection of dummies and voices. Girls, boys – they can do the lot, though they're all a bit – as you say – oily. I think that comes from a closed throat, somehow. Most of them are entertaining – though not all.' Archie was thinking, particularly, of Mickey Markov and Algernon. 'Yes, Pike has to be a ventriloquist.' He scratched his chin as his mind spun off at a tangent. 'In fact,' he went on, 'that explains why you never saw the other fellow, the one who supposedly shared his house. He – Pike – was probably throwing his voice, and changing it, to make you think he wasn't alone. And you say Mister X seemed to act as his 'better half' or his conscience?'

She nodded. 'He stopped Ned attacking me that time in the garden. Pulled him up sharp.'

'You see, I reckon it was Ned's own voice you heard, his 'gut' voice – Ned telling *himself* to behave. I think maybe Ned – Edward – has a split personality, and his *alter ego,* as Sigmund Freud has it, keeps him in check.'

'You mean he's up the pole?' said Tyrell. 'Barmy?'

'Dangerously so.'

'I wonder how he got himself invited to that séance.'

'They generally put a notice up at the Spiritualist Church, stating time and place,' said Gussie, 'and whoever wants to attend calls round to book a place.'

'That's how we did it – and Bertha Reeves, too, apparently,' said Archie.

'Oh, I know Mrs Reeves. She's a regular.'

'But you'd never seen Ned before he took the sack off your head in the cellar? I mean, he wasn't one of your congregation?'

'Don't think so.'

When her mother returned that afternoon they told her that she had nursed a viper in her bosom.

'You mean *that – that's* the man –' stabbing her finger at Archie's drawing, 'who held my poor Gussie prisoner – that Pike person? And we let him into our house, let him sit at our table and – and he used some jiggery-pokery to make us think our Gussie was – was lying at the bottom of the river. How could he? How *could* he!'

Her husband couldn't speak he was so angry but it was plain from the way he kicked the bedpost and punched the counterpane, just what he would like to do to his daughter's kidnapper. Gussie jumped back in fright.

Archie seethed. Years of practice at drawing villains – murderers and rapists – had trained him to draw them without prejudice so that he wouldn't influence the viewer, but it had been hard to draw Pike as a poker-faced neutral. Because suppose that bastard had Clara now? Or Lilian? His chest heaved. They had to find him soon. Wringing his hands for want of the bastard's neck, he stared, unseeing, at the window.

'Is there nothing you can tell us that might help trace him?' The detective appealed to the mother who seemed slightly more in control.

'Like what? I've told you what he told me – he was researching spiritualism for a book he was writing. I thought that was fair enough and we admit all-comers to our seances, believers and sceptics, like yourself.'

Archie turned back to the room, his hands in his hair, blinking ghastly images from his eyes – he had to stay sane, for her sake. 'It's what he told me,' he grunted. 'I think that may have been partly true.' He cast his mind back. 'Didn't Augustine say that the woman who came for her, the procuress – didn't she ask about his writing?'

'Can't be paying very well,' observed Tyrell, 'if he needs to sell girls into slavery as a sideline. You've no idea where he came from?' he asked Mrs Meredith now. 'His address?'

'You think if I had any idea where he lived I wouldn't be out of this door and round there in a flash? I can't believe how he hoodwinked me! I thought he was a decent soul. A writer. And all the time he had my poor Gussie chained up in his cellar, in the dark, with rats for company. The Great Spirit alone knows what harm he did her!'

'He didn't actually, em, interfere with her, you know.'

'Only because he was going to *sell* her – *sell* her to some filthy Arab, who wouldn't want damaged goods! Oh, my poor girl, my poor, poor girl…'

'Thing is, Mrs M, your Gussie reckons she wasn't the first girl held prisoner in that cellar, and my guess is she won't be the last. We gotta put the blighter behind bars, and soon.' Tyrell shot a glance at Archie, who was sitting beside him now, lost in thought, raking his side whiskers. 'See, he could've got another girl, already, to take Gussie's place, like. If you could 'elp us out – if you can think of something that would help us trace him…' Archie looked up, his face haggard. 'For instance, how did he get to your house that night? Did he walk or ride an 'orse or a bike? Did he have a carriage, a cart or even a motor car?'

'Let me – let me think – Thomas, can you remember? You let him in on the night of the séance. Was there a carriage waiting outside for him?'

'A cab, I believe. At least, a cabbie knocked at the door to pick him up afterwards. He shared it with the Nightingales.'

'The Nightingales?'

'On the Council,' muttered Mrs Meredith and Archie together.

'Well, we know where *they* live. They just might remember where the cabbie dropped him off.'

But the Nightingales had been so preoccupied with what had happened at the séance, voices coming out of nowhere announcing they'd drowned themselves, that they had trouble remembering that they'd shared a cab home with anyone. It was only when Archie described the tall young man, Pike, that they recalled him sitting in the corner – 'Nothing to say for himself!' – and that the cabbie had let him off at some point. Only when they reached home had it occurred to them he had loped off into the darkness without paying his share of the fare. They hadn't really noticed where he'd been dropped off.

Eighteen

Clara

Her pursuer was too close. Any minute now she'd feel Henry's hand on her shoulder and she'd skewer him with her hatpin. That'd teach him, maybe cure him of his obsession with her. She was about to break into a run, when she heard a woman call her name.

A *woman?* Now she stopped and turned.

'Effie!'

The little doctor was unnaturally flushed, the whites of her eyes pink. Her blonde hair was stuck to her forehead. It wasn't just that she'd caught the sun. It wasn't just that she'd been hurrying. It was on her breath. She'd had a drink or two, Clara thought. 'Sorry, did I scare you? I thought it was you but I couldn't be sure. It's the new get-up. You look so – different. Grown-up. Where are you off to? Meeting a boyfriend?'

'I – oh, Effie, oh, my heart's still thumping…' She puffed out her breath, put down her bag and stuck her hatpin back in Nana's hat. 'Glory be,' she said, 'I thought you were about to attack me.'

'Silly…'

'How did you know?'

'That it was you? I suppose there was something in your walk. Sort of straight and free and – and young.' *Gauche, she means, thought Clara, gloomily. Awkward.* 'And the kitten heels…' *(Can't even walk in them without turning my ankle.)* 'You showed me them the day I came over. I admired them then, if you remember.'

'Oh.' She was no better pleased. She was a failure at disguise. She explained that she was making for Paddington. 'I, em, yes, I'm meeting somebody.' *(How difficult it was telling lies. Perhaps that, too, came with age.)* 'Crikey Moses, you gave me a fright!'

'Sorry, sorry.'

'Why – what are you doing out this way?'

'Going back to work. I'm on at five and I have to change and – and sober up,' she confessed with a giggle. 'Just come from Regent's Park. Been having a picnic with Polly and Bart – our tame newspaper reporter.'

'He's down from Chelmsford?' Clara's heart skipped a little. When she was younger she'd had a bit of a crush on her father's friend. Not now, of course. She was thirteen, after all, and he was ever so old. Nearly thirty.

'Came down specially. We were toasting the happy couple in champagne.'

'She was all right?' she said anxiously, 'Polly, I mean.' Poor Polly. She'd be so upset when she heard about Pops and the gorgeous Miss Hudson.

'Never better. Wonderful news, isn't it? Them getting married at last?'

'No, it's not, Effie – she's only after his money and connections.'

She threw back her head and laughed, in a most unladylike fashion. 'You're joking! Oh, Clara, grow up, do. She's an independent woman. And your father deserves to be happy. I'd rather have liked it if he'd chosen me, but he didn't. I know he loved your mother fiercely and he always will. But these two, you must admit, they're made for each other.'

'No, no, they're not! It's disastrous!'

'Oh dear, you are out of sorts today. Well, I can't stand around arguing with you. You'll excuse me if I dash.' She ran ahead a few yards and stopped. 'Don't worry, dear,' she said, smiling, 'it'll be fine. It's the best news ever.'

Out of sorts? Yes, she supposed she was. She was rubbish at

acting the lady, and there was this persistent dull ache in the pit of her belly of which she was becoming more and more aware as the day progressed.

Effie would have been the very person to ask but she couldn't call her back and Effie must be fed up with people telling her about their symptoms. Clara watched her out of sight, trudging slowly along now, thoughtfully kicking the odd stone, the odd tuft of grass. So, Polly was putting a brave face on it? Bully for her! But it would put an end to their outings together, and Pops would want to bring his new wife round to Camden on Sundays, instead of Polly. That would be horrible. Even more horrible was the thought of Miss Hudson as Clara's new mother! No, no, she'd die rather than let that happen.

She began to hurry.

The little photographer must be broken-hearted really. She had always been adamant that she was perfectly happy to live as a spinster, that she preferred it, didn't want any man horning in on her business, interfering, but that was because her best friend, Archie, was just across the road. She could call on him every day. Wait until Sophie Hudson got that ring on her finger. They'd move away, bound to. Sophie wouldn't put up with living above a greengrocer's shop in one room, albeit a large one. They'd go somewhere more fashionable and Polly would be left all alone, with no one to talk to.

Now, here she was at Paddington. The huge building reared up before her, black with soot but she wasn't in the least intimidated. She loved the busy station: the crowds, the bustle and excitement, the porters and their baggage carts, the squeal and clang of heavy metal, the banging doors, the guards' shouts and whistles, the smell of steam and smoke and the oil they put on the wheels. She breathed it in for grit and energy. Shoulders back! This was her mission. She had to be strong, stop this marriage. Lives depended on it.

But she couldn't afford a ticket.

She went into the Ladies' lavatory and, in a cubicle, exchanged her outer clothes for those she was wearing earlier in the day. At the sink, she let down her plaits, scrubbed her face, hopefully losing about five or six years. She squashed the hat and dress and the kitten heels into her travelling bag and slipped on her school shoes.

Now for the hard bit.

She found the right platform and hung back by the tea stall until she saw a family showing their tickets to the guard. She let them get some way up the platform and then charged at the turnstile. It stood firm.

'Mama, Mama!' she cried. 'Wait for me!'

'Ticket, love?' demanded the guard.

'I – I don't have a ticket. My Mama has it. I was just looking at the cakes and she went off without me. Look, there she is now, the lady in the blue coat, getting on the train. She thinks I'm following her. Oh, they'll all go off without me and then what shall I do-o-o?' Her heart was beating in true panic.

Suddenly she wasn't acting any more. She remembered the grief of a child parted cruelly from her mother, the utter misery as the thief bore her away on his horse and Mama running after her with outstretched arms. 'Mama-a-a!' she sobbed now as though her heart would break.

A crowd was building up behind her. 'Let her through, mate, poor little blighter!'

'I'm going to miss my train, young man.'

No policeman came to arrest her, no one challenged her right to travel. The only people who entered the Ladies Only compartment were women returning from Sunday trips to the city. She took a deep breath as the soot-black buildings sliding by the train window gave way to fields of cows and sheep and felt herself relax. She struck up a conversation with a young seamstress on her way to stay with her sister in Newport. All went well until Clara's companion began searching in her handbag for something. She'd heard, she said, the guard arrive in the next compartment to check passengers' tickets.

Oh, help! She'd thought she was out of danger. Now images flashed through her mind of being put out at the next station, or worse, being sent back to London, under guard, to be prosecuted and jailed for cheating the authorities. Her eyes filled and her hands grew damp and she needed the lavatory. Oh, indeed, she did. She excused herself and hurried along the corridor to the Ladies at the end of the carriage.

'Tickets, please,' came too soon, with an officious rap on the door.

'Oh, *really*!' she said in her poshest, most affronted, grown-up voice, 'Just a moment, young man – oh, how embarrassing. I can't – em… Look, I'm feeling quite unwell,' which, all of a sudden, was perfectly true. Fear or bellyache was making her all hot and clammy, her eyes swim. If only the train would stop moving around. She couldn't think straight. 'I'll have to – em – what? I'll have to – push it under the door. Yes, I'll just… Now where..?' As she made the pretence of looking in a non-existent handbag for a non-existent ticket she made the mistake of glancing down into the lavatory bowl and seeing the railway track rushing past at the bottom, in a blur. On other trips to Wales with her father, she'd found it fascinating to think of defecating directly onto the rails. Now, though… 'Oh,' she wailed, 'I'm going to be… Oh, God…' and ohhhh – nausea overtook her.

'Young man?' she croaked feebly as she surfaced, 'Are you still there? Listen, I've left my ticket in my coat pocket on my seat. I can't come now. I'm going to be… ohhhhh!' And she was.

'Madam, are you all right?'

The train lurched. 'No, I'm not. Oh, God… Please go away. I'll – I'll come and find you.'

She heard him sigh, took another look at the track and threw up again.

This time, she heard him step smartly away from the door, shuffle his feet uncertainly and then hurry off about his business. She almost smiled. Gosh, she thought. Perfect.

After a minute, she called, 'Is anybody there?' And when there was no answer, ventured out, wobbly but triumphant and wove her way back to the compartment.

The seamstress was all concern. 'Goodness, dear, you look terrible! Perhaps if you were to close your eyes for a bit...'

Thankfully, the woman woke her before she got off at Newport, otherwise Clara might have slept through Bridgend and ended up in the back of beyond. As it was she caught the little shuttle and stepped off the train onto the deserted platform at Llantwit, wide awake and feeling hungry, pleased with herself for fooling the guard and making this long journey all by herself.

Now for the final deception. She'd practised a sob story about losing her ticket but by the time she emerged from the Waiting Room, the station was deserted. No ticket collector in sight.

She still had to find Grandpa and Granny's house. She'd been there so many times with Pops but she'd left it to him, not really noticing which fork in the road he took. If only she had a lantern. As she set off up the unlit road her bag got heavier and heavier and she stepped in one puddle and then another. No, this wouldn't do. This was horrible. Her lip quivered.

'Are you all right, Miss?'

A policeman.

Oh Lord ... Come on, Clara, you can do it – you've got this far. Policemen are your friends.

They walked along to the main street, with him holding his lantern high in one hand and her bag in the other. He asked about her journey and said how lucky she was to get the shuttle on a Sunday, asked about the weather in London and the rain they'd had here over the past few days. 'Coming down in buckets, it was, and all through the funeral, too. Everyone was drenched and the coffin floating like it was in a pond.'

She frowned. What was she supposed to say to that? What had a funeral to do with her? She put it down to village mentality, everyone knowing everyone else's business and assuming visitors knew it, too. 'Oh, that's a shame,' she said, politely.

'At school last week, I dare say.'

Was it a question? 'Who, me? Yes, that's right.'

'So, you've come down today, instead.'

'Yes.'

'By yourself.'

'Yes.'

'You're the granddaughter, aren't you? I recognised you straight off.'

She said she was and edged around a muddy cart track with grass coming up through a puddle.

'Come to pay your respects,' he nodded sagely.

The Welsh had a funny way of putting things. Perhaps he meant had she come to offer her congratulations to the couple on their betrothal? She skipped over another wet place and answered with a non-committal, 'Mmm.' She wasn't telling a stranger how she felt about Sophie Hudson.

'Must have been a shock for you,' he said, and shook his head sadly. 'So sudden.'

What a very understanding man or perhaps he was just digging for gossip. Thank goodness they were nearly there. She recognised the shops: the butcher's, the baker's, the sweet shop… 'It was,' she said.

'Well, well, here we are, then!' And he knocked on Granny's door for her. When it opened, he said to Granny. 'Look who I found in the street, Mrs Price.'

'Clara?' Her hand flew to her throat in surprise. 'What in heaven's name…?'

She was bustled in and hugged and the policeman dismissed with a penny for his trouble. The kettle was put on and she found out that Pops's hasty trip to Wales had nothing to do with any forthcoming marriage – well, not at the outset it hadn't. Granny had never met any Sophie Hudson and a good thing too, from the sound of her. Not Archie's type at all. No, *Polly* had kept Archie company and *she* was the one who had won his heart. They went back yesterday morning. Clara had missed them.

'Polly and Pops are getting married? Oh … oh!' she could hardly breathe. 'That's so lovely!'

When she found out they'd come up for Grandpa's funeral, that he'd *died*, the shimmery feeling came back, and the hot sweat, and Granny's voice seemed to fade and she just had to put her head down on the table, spilling her tea…

'Oh, my poor love,' Granny's voice came through a fog. 'Oh, it was the shock. I'm so sorry, I thought you knew. Oh, dear girl, can you manage a sip of water?'

Clara looked about her. She was lying on the sofa and Granny was kneeling on the floor beside her, passing smelling salts under her nose, and had put something on her forehead. A cold wet flannel, she discovered.

'You passed out, you poor mite. You've gone quite green. Oh, dear … oh, Archie will never forgive me for springing it on you like that, but I thought you knew, that you'd come here to offer me your condolences or something. Do you want to be sick? Shall I bring you a bowl?'

'No, I don't think so. I was sick as I could be on the train. I've got this horrible ache in my belly, see. I don't think I'm very well.'

'Well, sweetheart, I'll tell you what that is. I'm afraid your dress, at the back, is all bloody.'

'What! What's happened? Have I cut myself? Am I ill?'

'Has nobody explained? Tch. I told Archie he should make sure you were told. Oh, don't look so worried, it's all perfectly normal. In fact, I must congratulate you, dear. You've become a woman.'

That was how she learned that she was starting her periods, and why women have them.

'But I don't want babies. I'm only thirteen.'

'You will, one day, I think. Now let's get you tidy.'

Granny brought her a bowl of hot water, soap, flannel and towels and retired, discreetly, to the scullery so she could clean up and pad herself with bits of Granny's old sheet that the old lady tore up specially. 'Having boys, I never had to do this for them, only for me.'

Clara put on a clean pair of drawers from her bag, and her nightdress, and left her clothes, as Granny had instructed, in a pile for washing.

The old lady told her how she would steep the bloody clothes in cold water overnight before rinsing them out in the morning and only then plunging them into the suds. 'Because hot water sets any stains. Many's the time I've ruined a pair of drawers by not steeping them first.'

Many's the time … only me..? Suffering catfish! 'So how often do you get these bleeds, Granny?'

'Every month. Don't gape, child! It stops eventually, when you're my age.'

'Bloody hell!'

'Clar-a-a!'

'But it is! That's what it sounds like.'

'That's life for you.' She smiled sadly and broke into song. *'It's the man wot gets the pleasure and his wife wot gets the pain.'*

'Lan'-sakes, Granny, that's not fair!'

Granny shrugged. 'They call it a woman's lot, sweetheart, and it *is* a lot. There's pain every month, pain on the marriage-bed, pain in childbirth and, just to add to our woes, we have no rights, no say in what happens to us. Men have it all their own way and that, certainly, isn't fair. Women are just as clever, just as able as them, and don't you forget it.'

'And prettier.'

'Oh, that's just so men will find us attractive. Like a flower. But what's more important, the flower or the bee?'

'Well…' she thought about it, 'They need each other.'

238

'Exactly.'

'Yeah, Pops said that's what you taught him. He's a suffragist, you know.'

'Well, I'm glad something went in. Now then, it's washday tomorrow – so there's no need for you to worry about a thing. But I'm afraid your clothes won't be ready to wear for days in this damp weather. Did you bring something to change into?'

But when they looked, Nana's dress was stained as well.

'Never mind, I'll put it in the tub, too. Oh, come on, cheer up. I'm sure we'll find something to fit you. I'll go and see.'

Her inclusive 'we' meant Auntie Eurwen down the road. In the ten minutes she was gone, all the news was exchanged and Eurwen sent to find a decent frock for Clara to put on in the morning. She brought it round. 'Got the curse, then, love, have you? Ah well, it had to happen. No looking back now. Archie never said nothing, did he? No, that's what mothers are for.'

'Or grandmothers,' said Granny, sharply, and buttoned her lip tight. She meant that Nana Grant hadn't said anything either.

'Anyway,' said Auntie Eurwen, 'you know what to do from now on?'

'I'll get in trouble tearing up sheets,' said Clara.

That seemed to tickle them and their laughter went on and on. It seemed a release of some sort. Perhaps they hadn't laughed since Grandpa died. Granny explained that you reused your rags, washing them out after each soiling, just as you would the rags you used as hankies.

'And that's something you'll probably want to do yourself. You wouldn't want your Nana's maid to have that job, perhaps … Though once they're clean they can go in the boiler.'

Clara sighed. Oh, for a mother.

'Well, you're all taken care of here,' said Auntie Eurwen. 'Make the most of it.' She made for the door and turned. 'You'll miss your old Grandpa, won't you? Oh. Oh now, cariad, don't take on. I shouldn't have said. It's all new to you, isn't it? Here, use my hanky, it's clean. I expect Archie was going to break it to you when he saw you next. Better coming from him than anyone else. We'll take you over the graveyard tomorrow and you can say your goodbyes, like. It was very quick, I expect Mam's told you. He wouldn't have felt any pain. Best way to go if you ask me.'

Even so, she cried herself to sleep that night in Pops's old bed, with a hot-water bottle on her belly and a powder mixed in hot milk. In the morning she woke to the smell of laundry boiling in Granny's copper mixed with an enticing scent of fresh griddle cakes. The old lady must have got up early. When she poked her head into the steamy scullery, Granny said, as though she'd been thinking about it all night, 'They do know where you are, your people?'

When she explained that she'd left in a huff, she thought Granny might hit her with the copper stick, she gripped it so tight. 'Oh, Clara, how could you? Silly girl! They'll be worried sick! And what about Archie? He'll be going out of his mind! All those young girls going missing over your way – he'll think you've been taken or – or worse! Here, mind the washing – just give it a poke now and then, while I go round to the post office. See if it's not too late to send a message.'

It was roasting in Granny's scullery and sweat mixed with tears trickled down her cheeks. She'd thought, of course, when she'd set out, that Pops would be here to greet her when she arrived, that he could send a telegram to Granddad to set his mind at rest. And last night self-pity and grief had so occupied her that telling the Grants where she was had gone completely out of her head.

Granny came back and said she'd sent a telegram to the pub, the Horse and Groom, the one across the road from Pops. She expected they'd give it to him. You have to, don't you? Telegrams are urgent.

'Why didn't you send it straight to him?'

'Well, Clara,' she cleared her throat and her cheeks went red, 'I don't, somehow, think he'll be at home for a day or two, especially if he's worried about you. He'll want to be with Polly and I don't know her surname *or* her address.'

'Oh, she lives…' she paused as what Granny had said sunk in. 'Oh, never mind. Mrs Reeves will pass it on.'

'I said you'd be here three or four days. It'll take that long for your dress to dry.'

It was raining again.

Nineteen

'Effie said she was dressed up like a dog's dinner, Polly, going to meet a boyfriend. I don't know who that could be. She's never shown any interest in boys. Only boy I can think of is Young Waddington – you know Henry – I think he might have taken a shine to her but, Christ, Polly, she's only thirteen. Thirteen! What does she know about – about that sort of thing? And she wouldn't dress up for him, wouldn't give him the time of day! So, who *was* she going to meet? Pike, do you think? Or maybe there's some other predator on the prowl. I mean, how many of these monsters are there? She was walking into a trap, I know it. He'll have her down in some secret room, tied up and helpless. Oh Polly, I must do something…'

When Archie failed to show up for his usual pint on Monday night, Bertha went across with the telegram, knocked on his door, found he'd gone out and Bob Cheshire, lowering his shutters, told her that his lodger was out on police business, hunting for some missing girl. Over Camden way, he thought.

Bertha tried again on Tuesday and again Archie was out. Bob hadn't seen him all day. He thought he might be staying over with his in-laws.

Well, Bertha had more important things to do than worry about Archie Price. She pinned the brown envelope, curled and grubby with her thumbprints, to the noticeboard above the pub telephone. She'd steamed it open, of course. Just in case it was anything important.

'CLARA HERE STOP UPSET ABOUT DA STOP I WILL BRING HER BACK ON WEDNESDAY STOP YOUR LOVING MAM STOP'.

So that was all right.

On Wednesday afternoon, Bertha saw the studio window open for a change and decided to give it another go. The midweek market was in full swing but she heard the hullabaloo from Archie's lodgings before she was halfway across the road, his voice and Clara's and another which seemed to be that of a more mature woman.

'Oh, don't keep on, Archie. She's said she's sorry, what more can she say? She thought she was doing the right thing in coming to warn you about this gold-digging schoolmarm. I mean she came all that way on her own. No money. Doesn't that tell you how important she thought it was? She expected you to be there. Her grandfather Grant told her that much – that you'd gone to Wales. Didn't tell her what for, stupid man, and she jumped to conclusions.'

Bertha didn't quite catch what Archie said in reply.

'Yes, you did, you gave her plenty of reason. The woman was practically living in your pocket, Clara says.' There was a pause, a rumble of protest, and then she continued. 'Well, she was certainly getting her money's worth, student or no. And young Lilian had warned her about Miss Hudson's intentions. Of course, she was worried.'

Clara chimed in. 'Effie told me you were getting married. Didn't tell me who to. Assumed I knew. I mean, most parents *would* tell their child first if they were thinking of getting married again.'

'I DIDN'T TELL YOU BECAUSE YOU WEREN'T BLOODY HERE! YOU'D RUN OFF!' Bertha heard this bellow loud and clear. 'I FULLY INTENDED!'

'Granny sent you a telegram, Pops, on Monday morning, care

of Bertha at the pub. We thought you'd got it and everything was all right. What more could we have done?'

There was a deep bass accusation, a girl's wailing protest … 'No, I couldn't have come home straightaway! I – I wasn't very well and I bled onto my clothes. Granny had to wash them. I mean I had nothing to wear. But we weren't worried. We thought you'd got the telegram.'

Another thunderous roar.

'It's not Clara's fault you never got it, Archie! You'd expect this silly Reeves woman to put it through the door, wouldn't you? But if she's as nosy as you say she probably wanted to hand it to you in person and find out all the ins and outs. Didn't she know you were missing Clara, by then, and were out of your mind with worry?'

Bertha slunk away to keep watch through the public bar window which she had to spit on and clean with her apron before she could see clearly. Pretty soon her efforts were rewarded. The trio emerged through Archie's front door, wreathed in smiles. Thank the Great Spirit for that. All was forgiven and forgotten.

Oh. Oh. Not quite, perhaps. They were coming here! She scuttled behind the bar and busied herself washing and polishing glasses, until she realised they had all trooped next door to the photographer's shop.

Through the wall she heard shrieks of delight and excited cries. What was all that about? Quickly, she tried to think of credible reasons to call at the photographer's shop – the telegram, of course. Showing willing. But customers came in, wanting pies as well as beers. And where was Perce when you needed him? Down at the blooming Palace, overseeing the stocking of the vestibule bar, that's where. There was always some reason he couldn't be here of a Wednesday, one of the busiest days of the week: first, it was overseeing the seating in the stalls then fixing the taps in the Ladies' Washrooms and seeing to the carpets. Today, he was interviewing for cleaners and usherettes and taking his time about it, an' all. Come five o'clock the market traders'd be in to wet their whistles after a day shouting the odds, then the rush hour bringing home the businessmen and only old Sam and young Dotty, the barmaid, to handle the drunks. Still, according to Perce, everything was near enough ready to roll at his *Aunty Alice* as soon as blooming Archie Price got his blooming act together and finished his blooming picture. Well, having got his daughter back he'd hopefully get a wiggle on now and Perce could have his blessed opening night before he pegged it, and play the grand impresario and then maybe pay his wife some attention for a change.

Ah, now, here was Archie pushing through the swing doors, looking very pleased with himself and wanting to use the 'phone. He saw the telegram and ripped it off the wall with a 'Bertha! What's this!' She ducked down and when she dared to put her nose over the bar a few moments later, he was talking to the operator. If she could quickly serve these two old geezers, parked here by their wives while they went shopping, she might be able to catch something of what he said.

'Vic? It's me, Archie. We've got her! Yes, she's fine. She arrived with my mother about half an hour ago. Yes. That's where she's been since Sunday night. Eh? Yes, Wales. Yes, on her own. What's that? Well, she'd got it into her head that I was going to get married to some floozy and came out to stop me. No, I'm not. No, Vic, I'm not! No, she got it wrong. I'm marrying Polly!' He grinned and held the phone away from his ear while Vic yipped and cheered.

Well, fancy that! Despite her air of busy preoccupation Bertha couldn't help her sparse eyebrows rising to her hairline and her lips pursing like spiders' legs. Who'da thunk it? So, Polly Porter had netted her fish, after all. Overlooking all Archie Price's faults and foibles, his womanising, his lack of money, she'd agreed to take him on. Well, sooner you than me, ducks, she thought.

Clara's granddad seemed to be thinking along similar lines. And, no doubt, the operator had her eyebrows raised.

'Well, you know how I feel about her,' Archie was saying, 'and you always counselled patience, didn't you? Anyway, she finally said she would and we're getting married as soon as the banns can be read. And Clara's agreed to be a bridesmaid. You'll come, won't you?' He paused and winked at Bertha. She was forgiven. 'Eh? Yes, very happy. Well, better late than never as my brother always says. Clara? Yes, she is – a dog with two tails. Right. Yes. I'll bring her over on Sunday, but Vic … No, wait … What?' Bertha watched as the prospective groom's face darkened. 'Mmm, well, we'll discuss all that when I come over. Yes, I'll bring Polly. Eh? Oh thanks, Vic. I'll tell her. Give my best to Ivy.' He hung up. Then he called the operator back.

'Hello there, Maggie, I need another number. Yes, the police station, please.'

As far as she could make out from this second conversation someone, some mother or father, had taken their sick child home that morning from hospital, and Archie was urging that a careful watch be kept on them. 'See, Clara's back with me now. Chummy didn't take her, after all. No, she's been with her grandmother in Wales since Sunday. I know. I *know*. Well, she had her reasons. Bit of a misunderstanding. The thing is, Frank, this plan of yours – Chummy's bound to want to get his goods back, if you get my meaning.'

Aha, thought Bertha, she knew from Archie's past use of the telephone that *'Chummy'* meant the current villain. She inclined her head, not to miss a word and Archie's eyes, sliding her way, caught her listening.

'Uh-oh. Wait a minute, Frank.'

He adjusted the bar stool so his back was turned to her and lowered his voice. Sauce!

'Yeah,' he murmured, 'exactly. As you say, very interested. Anyway, as I was saying, it seems to me he'll be watching and waiting his chance to get his, erm, his 'property' back so he can sell it on, if you get my meaning… Yes, exactly. Well, I was there this morning and they say she's well enough to go home today… Yes, this afternoon and … Well, I was thinking, can we really take the risk? He's a clever bugger… I *know* it's our only chance of catching him, but … Well, if you're sure … Mmm, I agree, round-the-clock … All right, then…

'Me? Well, I've got my mother and daughter here. I'd like to spend some time … What? *Another* drawing? … Oh, I see… Yes, no problem. How many would you …? Right… Oh, about an hour. I'll see you up there. I'll leave the girls to talk weddings. Oh, didn't I tell you, I'm getting married? No, well, I thought I'd tell Clara first… Oh, she is, over the moon, mate… Lucky lady? Don't know about that – *I'm* the lucky one… No, it's not *her*, not in a thousand years… Not her either. Good God, man, give me some credit… Of course, it's Polly! … Oh, you were joking? Thanks, mate!'

Twenty

Archie strode up the hill from the High Street, past the red-brick school where Sophie worked, where Lilian used to play hockey. Where was that girl? Surely someone would have heard something by now? He doubted she had been sold into slavery or prostitution or become the thirty-fifth wife of the Sultan of Baghdad – it didn't seem likely somehow. Not our Lil. She was no oil painting and that carroty hair … *Had* someone whisked her off to the United States to be trained up for the 1908 Olympics? Or had she simply taken herself off on a whim, packed up a few essentials in a red-spotted handkerchief and gone into service somewhere? Perhaps she would come home soon, like Clara, unharmed, having spent the last month or two with loving relatives. Not that he held out much hope of that. All her family, aunties, uncles, cousins twice removed, were here in Walthamstow, just doors away from each other, all at their wits' end.

He was so lucky. No words could express his relief at having Clara back. He'd been imagining all sorts: murder and torture, slavery, the poor child begging on the streets – and the nights drawing in, too!

Even now the lamps were blossoming, one by one, as the lamplighter released the gas and reached his lighted wick up to the mantle where, with a gentle pop, it ignited and a soft glow spread, silvering the surrounding pavement and trees.

Virginia creeper, swarming like flames over the new school

walls, already hinted at the purple of evening and the long windows of the art room, up there on the first floor, suddenly brightened. Maybe Sophie had been the one to light the lamps so she could see to mount the best of the girls' offerings for display or to prepare materials for Monday's classes. What would she have in mind for her pupils, he wondered? Autumn in the style of Cezanne, angling your brushstrokes and outlining in dark blue, or painting London through fog as Monet had done? He had suggested that she, herself, try painting impressions of scenes in order to break free from her pernickety, tightly-laced style and was not at all surprised to learn that her School Certificate girls had followed suit. They'd already produced variations on Turner's steamboats in a snowstorm and Van Gogh's swirling skies. Yes, she'd picked his brains but he had used her, too. The Palace's vestibule painting was almost finished, thanks to her work on the drapes and chandeliers. Officially she was his student for a year. Would she be happy to continue in that role knowing Polly was his true love, his intended? Or was it as Lilian had told Clara – that she wanted to copy his style, use his connections, trade on his name, in order to further her own career?

He hated the idea that he was being used but, he supposed, female artists, no matter how good, had to battle with centuries of misogyny. There were women in the London galleries now, the likes of Mary Cassat in the National, Gwen John in the Tate, Alma-Tadema's daughter, Anna, in the V and A, but most of them had ridden on the shoulders of the talented men in their lives. However, Polly had been adamant – the lovely Miss Hudson had better look elsewhere for a leg up. He should pop into the school and tell her – perhaps on the way back. This business wouldn't wait. He stopped to light his lantern as he turned into the darkening Drive.

The big detached houses and the overhanging branches, their leaves sadly dwindling, cut out most of the twilit sky and hid the moon. The Merediths' house lay around the corner from the L-bend, out of sight. Plane trees had been planted, half a century ago, at intervals on either side of the dirt road, creating a pleasant, elitist sort of avenue, though a hazardous one, the residents being too posh for pavements, too select for streetlights. In order to avoid tripping on tree roots hidden by great drifts of fallen leaves, and stepping into mud, Archie had to walk in the grassy middle of the road between parallel wheel ruts.

Another lantern was bobbing along towards him on the same track and, as it drew nearer, he realised it belonged to Tyrell, coming to look for him with a dark scowl on his face.

'There you are! Glad someone's got time to wander along like love's young dream! We was wondering where you got to, boyo…'

Six likenesses he'd had to draw! Frank had no idea – he just clicked his fingers and expected them to appear.

Everyone was in position, the inspector said, waiting for him to issue each with his personal drawing of Ned Pike. The Merediths had done as Tyrell suggested and locked all the outer doors and windows, despite the convalescent's objections. She said she was sick and tired of prisons. 'He won't strike again,' she was sure, 'he's not that brave.'

But it was necessary, Tyrell insisted: Edward Pike was mentally ill. People with split personalities could become fixated, obsessed, he'd been reading up about it. Pike wouldn't be able to rid his mind of her, or more specifically, of the money he would get for her when he sold her to the Sheikh of Araby or whoever the devil was with a preference for blondes. When he was safely behind bars, *then* they could unlock the doors.

There were five men on the first watch. A pony and trap were in position a few doors away from the Meredith premises; in the driver's seat was DC Mackenzie, watching for anyone coming up the road. His lamps were lit, his pony whiling away the time in a nosebag of oats. Inside the house, with a view of the back garden from his perch on the landing, DS Beckett kept company with PC Ince, the only uniformed officer, on a chair outside Gussie's room.

And across the road DC Clark, wearing a cloak and top hat, played cabbie in a borrowed hansom, facing away from Mackenzie, towards the sharp bend in the road and the tennis courts. Tyrell joined Clark in the cab.

They waited.

Archie visited them all, distributing his drawings, making sure they memorised Pike's long thin face before, reluctantly, leaving them to do their task without him. He wasn't on the payroll, or only in his capacity as an artist. If he chose to involve himself in the excitement of the chase, as he had on a few occasions, it was understood he did so at his own risk. Another time, maybe. Right now, he couldn't wait to hurry back to his family: mother, daughter and wife-to-be, and spend what was left of the night with them.

Smiling at the prospect of a four-handed game of *Whist* or *Newmarket*, he became aware of a horse and cart trundling towards him and, as he stepped out of its path, made out 'Ned' Pike's long body hunched over the reins, his grim visage lit by a lantern. Aha – so Tyrell's hunch was correct. The obsessive had come to pick up where he had left off. Well, he was in for a surprise.

He bawled a greeting loud enough to alert any law officer within earshot. 'Mister Pike! Fancy seeing you!'

Unable to avoid him, Pike reined in his horse and lifted his hat. Archie was almost surprised to see limp, thinning hair exposed rather than devil's horns. 'Good evening!' said the fiend. 'Mister Price, isn't it, from the séance the other week? You left in a bit of a state, as I recollect.'

Archie's protest was heartfelt. 'D'you blame me?' Tears still pricked his eyes at the memory. 'It was a cruel trick, that medium attempting to impersonate my wife's voice.'

'So why were you there, if you didn't believe?'

'I – I…' The challenge was unexpected, especially from this creature. 'I wanted to be convinced, I suppose, but it was so obviously a hoax.'

'Was it, though?'

251

'Of course, it was.' *And you know it,* he wanted to say. Instead he asked, 'What about you? Did you get enough material for that story you were writing?'

'I did. And it's a good one, if I say so myself. Haven't quite finished it, but I will, I will.'

It was as much as Archie could do to keep a smile pasted to his face. Even now, like a hungry animal, the evil bastard was intent on recapturing his prey and carrying her off to his lair. Was this the theme of his new story? 'I look forward to reading it,' he lied. Little did Pike know that, at best, he would be writing it in jail while he waited for justice to be meted out. 'The *Chronicle* you said?'

'You've a good memory, Mister Price.'

Clamping his jaw on a venomous reply, he tipped his hat to take his leave but, as the cart drew away he couldn't help wondering if he shouldn't have just wrestled the man to the ground, made a citizen's arrest. Augustine would have had the satisfaction of picking him out of a line-up and justice would have been served, just the same. But Tyrell would have his way. He had his heart set on catching the villain red-handed. Though his heart wasn't in it, Archie's lips thinned in anticipation of this horrible specimen, this purveyor of innocent young girls, falling into the trap the police had set for him just around the corner.

Archie walked on a few yards, his steps slowing as he tried to imagine the scene. He stopped and cocked an ear to a twitter of sleepy birds, someone playing a piano somewhere, a clatter of supper dishes. He walked on again, dragging his feet in the fallen leaves. Stopped, waited before turning into the main road. And there it was, out of nowhere, a cacophony of police whistles and yells piercing the night, followed shortly by a rattle of wheels, the crack of whips, and horses' hooves pounding the bare earth. A hue and cry? It wasn't quite what he had expected to hear. Had the bugger got away? Dammit. He turned on his heel and broke into a run. But, by the time he reached the dogleg, the stretch of road ahead was empty but for Beckett and Ince heading back, on foot, to the house, casting long looks over their shoulders. Where was everybody else?

Gussie's parents stood by the front gate, distraught and wringing their hands.

'He's got her, Mister Price!' wailed Mrs Meredith, when they met up.

'What! How the hell did that happen?'

'God knows! But she's gone!'

They described how Gussie, still weak and exhausted after her experiences, had gone to bed early, leaving her parents in the sitting room, the mother knitting, the father writing notes to spiritualist friends about his daughter's ordeal and recovery. When Archie left, the bodyguards had settled in for a long night's surveillance.

Beckett took up the story, telling how they'd only been at their posts a few minutes, five, maybe ten when they heard Tyrell's hoarse whisper up the stairs, *'Get down here, you two. Quietly! Careful now, he might be armed.'*

By the time the two of them had tiptoed down the stairs to the hallway, Tyrell was nowhere to be seen. The front door was open and they assumed he'd wanted them to follow.

They'd heard their inspector's urgent cry, *'Quick, men, he's getting away!'* and a whistle blown in emphasis.

Out they ran onto the front path in time to see Mackenzie's pony and trap charging down the road and Clark's horse wheeling to follow, with Tyrell aboard blowing his whistle like a crazy man, stopping only to yell as he passed the two bodyguards, ''E's twigged us.' And as the cab drove off his voice floated back. *'Yous two check down to the end of the road, 'case he's ducked in someone's front yard!'* So, like fools, Beckett said, they'd jogged off down the road, leaving the Merediths' house completely unguarded.

The healer and his wife, thoroughly alarmed, had gone up to their daughter's room to find it empty save for the sweet smell of ether. The window was wide open. Broken glass lay everywhere.

Beckett and Ince, back from their fools' errand, swore Augustine had been in bed, sleeping soundly when Tyrell had called them away.

Clearly Pike was already in the house when 'Tyrell' had called up the stairs to Beckett and Ince. It hadn't been the inspector at all but Pike impersonating him, in a successful attempt to leave the way clear for himself. Once Ince and Beckett were out of the house he had driven the rest of the police into a hue and cry by throwing his voice, imitating Tyrell and others, and when they were all out chasing shadows, had come back inside and helped himself to the prize.

'The devil!' said Archie. 'How could you fall for a trick like that?' And then realisation dawned. 'It was my fault! My stupid fault!'

'What do you mean?'

'Soon as I saw him coming I should have ducked out of sight. Lord knows it was dark enough. Seeing me up this way he must have guessed it was a trap. He knows I draw for the police. Lord, and I thought I was being so clever keeping him talking so you'd have a bit of time to get ready.'

'Clark was on the dog-leg,' said Beckett, 'and he heard your voices. He passed the word along, like, and so we waited. But no cart ever came around that corner. He must have parked it and gone ahead on foot.'

'No cart in the Drive,' said Archie. 'He probably took it round by the tennis courts, out of sight.'

'Ready for off when he come out with poor little Gussie. He had it all figured out.'

The vehicles returned from their wild goose chase, their drivers and passengers looking mortified when told they'd been duped.

'I told you he was clever,' said Archie. 'He's a ventriloquist.'

'We've been had.'

'Good and proper.'

'Poor little Gussie. How we gonna find her now?'

'Don't ask me!' said Archie, who was kicking himself for underestimating Pike, arousing his suspicions. 'I'm the last person…'

'Oh, give over, man … It was a simple…'

'No, hold on!' Archie was looking around wildly. Why hadn't he thought of it before? 'A telephone! Quick, who's got a telephone? Meredith?'

Twenty-one

Bartholomew Spratt said he'd drop everything and get over there straightaway. Give him half an hour, he'd phone Archie back from the *Chronicle's* offices.

'I'll wait.'

Archie had to ask Mrs Meredith twice for her telephone number. The poor woman was almost too traumatised to know what he was asking. Her hands were shaking as she held them to her head to focus her mind.

'*'Coppermill 401,'* Bart confirmed. 'Back in a mo'. We can't let the bastard get away with it, Arch. Jesus, that poor girl, what she's going through. Hogan, you say?'

'Hogan, Morgan, Bacon, something like that. Two syllables. Oh Lord. Come on, Arch,' he scolded himself, 'where's your bloody memory when you need it? I can see the story in front of me – *The Missing Link,* I think it was called – absolute drivel.'

'Could it be Logan? He writes tripe.'

'Yes, yes! Logan, that's it. Go, Bart! I'm hanging up.'

The officers clustered around the table, planning their strategy while the Merediths' cook served them tea and biscuits. Every shoe tapped with nerves; every timepiece was consulted every few minutes. Every second counted. That poor girl was in a madman's clutches. They had to save her. Archie couldn't help thinking of the last time he'd been sitting around this table, between Ned Pike and Polly. Spectres of a different sort stalked his imagination now.

At last the phone rang and Archie sprang away from the table, knocking over his chair. The others looked up, hardly daring to breathe.

Spratt had an address for an Edgar Logan aka Edward Pike and could he please run the story?

'Not yet, Bart, not yet! We don't want him getting the wind up. He might do her real harm. I mean – you know…'

'Absolutely, mate. Trust me, I won't breathe a word until you say so. You will remember? Archie…? Anyone…?'

But the receiver was lying on the shelf and his voice spilling out to an empty room.

Number fifteen Forest Edge was a large detached house just up from Chingford Station – the posh part of town. On such an evening the well-to-do residents could look out and see the skyline of trees dark against the grey dusk, a half-moon bright against scudding clouds and animal eyes glowing in the night.

The police had whipped along the intervening roads, their horses' hooves striking sparks from the stones, their wheels clattering, ringing their bell, yelling to other vehicles to clear out of the way! Through the forest, down the lanes to the great grassy clearing of Chingford Plain, where fairs came in the summer, circuses in winter and glossy horses were exercised, where raptors flew and pretty children sailed their kites.

They were in luck. The wagon was out in the road under a streetlamp, the nag removed to some stable at the back of the house. PC Ince, being unarmed but for his truncheon, was left to mind their horses and transport up the road, out of sight of the house, while his companions ducked along by the privet hedges to the detached property. One or two of the windows showed lights but there was no movement within that they could see.

Silently, Tyrell gestured that Mackenzie and Beckett should go around the sides of the house to the back, get in if they could, without being seen, and cut off any escape that way. Clark hid behind a rhododendron bush in the front, ready to stop the villain if he got past them. Tyrell crept up the front steps with Archie but flattened himself against the wall, his pistol cocked ready.

Archie was the decoy. He pulled the doorbell and waited. His job was to get a foot in the door and keep Pike talking while Beckett and Mackintosh moved in behind him. Feeling rather foolish he shuffled his feet. There wasn't a sound from inside. Or … perhaps … was that the yowl of a cat, or someone in pain?

He hung onto the bell pull for longer, listening to its clang fading away. Gussie had told them that no servant was employed here – Pike fended for himself – so where was he, to take so long – in the cellar with his prisoner? He couldn't pretend to be out with lights on and the cart outside.

Ah, here, at last, came worn soles scuffing down the hallway; the doorknob turned and the door cracked open an inch. A lantern was raised high.

'Who is it?'

If Archie was right, Pike knew he was with the police. He had to be careful.

'Archie Price for Edward Pike.'

The crack widened, revealing an oil lamp burning in the hallway and Augustine's abductor with his long bony face and bad skin. His cold, unsmiling eyes levelled with Archie's.

'You?' he scowled. 'What do *you* want?'

'Hello, again,' Archie smiled. 'I've come with a proposition.'

'What?' Pike looked thoroughly annoyed. He frowned, 'How did you know where to find me?'

'I have a friend at the *Chronicle*.'

He looked taken aback. It was so obviously the truth. 'Well, what do you want, Price?' he said impatiently.

'Oh, right, well –,' Archie cleared his throat, praying for inspiration, '– after I saw you this evening I had to walk back past the girls' school – you know the one in Church Hill? Red-brick building went up a year or two back? You must have passed it.'

258

'Ye-es?' he said, suspicion darkening the pasty face as he scanned the road and garden for signs of an accomplice.

(Beckett, get a move on!) 'Well, it occurred to me, having just left you, you see – it occurred to me that I might be able to put some work your way.' Pike did a double take, trying to make the connection. Archie explained. 'A few weeks back they – the school – asked me to give a talk to the girls about my work as a police artist.'

'Really?' He stretched his mouth in a discouraging smile. 'And what has this to do with me?'

'Long story short – they asked me – when it was all over – if I knew of any other interesting people who might talk to the girls.'

'And you thought of me.'

'I did.'

'Presuming on our short acquaintance...'

The man was clearly making fun of him and Archie bristled. Nevertheless, he forced a smile – pressed on, regardless. 'Indeed. I thought you could talk about your writing, your short stories, or advise them how to go about getting a foot on the ladder, so to speak.'

A spark of interest flickered in the cold eyes. 'What do they pay?'

'Well, it wouldn't be much. But if you have any anthologies printed you could sell them and—'

'Girls, though.' He made a face. 'No future for girls in writing.'

(*Where was Beckett?*) 'I beg to differ, Mister Pike, there are lady journalists on the *Chronicle* – and not only writing about fashion and bringing up children. There's a Miss Emmerson writes an interesting financial column and a Miss Pettifer who is a news reporter. As for lady novelists, well, just think of Mrs Humphry Ward and Mrs Annie Ritchie, Thackeray's daughter. My daughter used to love her fairy tales.'

Pike made no attempt to conceal a wide yawn. 'Uh-huh...?'

'So, you're not interested?' Ah, thank heavens, there was

movement in the dark corridor behind the writer. But a swish of silk told him it wasn't a detective.

'I wouldn't say that…'

'Who is it, Ned?'

'Oh, Nora – just an acquaintance offering me a speaking engagement.'

Archie could see 'Nora' was dressed in the latest fashion, looking rather like a pretty, rosy-cheeked Renoir painting, her head tilted, fetchingly, on one side. Damn, they should have known there were two of them, one to look after the girl and one the horse. This must be the accomplice Augustine had spoken of.

And here, at long last, came Beckett, with a drawn pistol.

'Police!' the detective barked, and both Pike and the woman turned their heads sharply. 'Put your hands in the air, both of you.'

Prettiness abandoned, she snarled. 'You led them to us, Ned, you – you – blithering idiot.'

Pike started forward just as Archie heard the scrape of boots on the step behind him and Frank's commanding voice. 'As you were, Pike, as you were. You'd better come quietly, the two of you. This gun is loaded.'

'Like hell!' said Pike and, to Archie's dismay he found himself caught by the wrist and pulled round towards Pike in a half nelson, a buffer against any bullet. They were of a height and Archie smelled the abductor's sour breath as he saw the glint of a blade level with his throat. Pike smiled nastily. 'Your weapons, gentlemen – drop them *now* or I'll slit Price's lying throat.'

'Don't be a fool, man,' said Frank, 'there are more of us outside – you're asking to get hurt…'

In response, Ned Pike pulled Archie's head back tighter against his shoulder. There was a tickle as the blade touched his skin. Jesus, his heart stopped beating. He would bloom like a flower, Archie thought distractedly. *Do you like butter, Pops?* flashed through his mind.

'Damn and blast,' muttered Tyrell, his gun clattering on the tiles. 'Beckett – do as he says.'

'No, don't!' cried Archie. *Don't give up your advantage. Don't let them win.*

'Shut it!' growled Pike, and the knife bit into his skin.

Damn and blast, this couldn't be it. This couldn't be how he would die.

Beckett threw *his* pistol to the ground and there was the rustle of silk petticoats as the woman picked it up. She disappeared from Archie's view as she bent to retrieve the other one, too. The tables were well and truly turned.

'I see you have brought your handcuffs, gentlemen. Were you expecting to arrest someone? Sorry to disappoint you. Perhaps you'd be kind enough to give them to Ned.'

How could they refuse when she was waving a police pistol first at Tyrell, then at Beckett? They did as they were told and Pike had to take the knife from Archie's throat in order to take the cuffs from them. Archie sagged and his hand went to his neck. It was wet and sore.

'Put your hands where I can see them, handsome,' said this 'Nora'. 'In the air, up, up!'

With tears in his eyes, he was forced to watch as the kidnapper, a sneer curling his lip, handcuffed Detective Inspector Francis Tyrell to a stair spindle. The policeman growled, 'Let the girl go, you evil bastard! She's been through enough.' Pike punched him in the kidneys and Frank crumpled.

'Now then, Ned,' came a disembodied voice, somewhere near his left ear, a guttural voice that raised goose pimples on Archie's arms. *'No need to kill him. You'll hang if you do.'*

'Tch!' The woman, 'Nora', rolled her eyes in scorn.

'Right,' Pike replied and, because his alter ego had warned against murder, he disabled Tyrell by thumping his forehead on the jutting base-rail of the stairs. With a grunt he collapsed.

Beckett was still struggling to get his breath as he was chained up next to his unconscious superior. 'Don't do this,' he pleaded in turn.

'Shut it.'

Now. Archie cast around for some way of stopping this. He must act *now.* But even as he shifted his weight, 'Nora' raised a shapely eyebrow and her eyes glittered.

'Oh no, you don't, darling…' she menaced.

He found he was looking down the barrel of a gun, listening to the slow click, click, click of the hammer cocking.

She wouldn't, would she? Kill him in cold blood? He had no illusions about a softer, tender-hearted breed – any woman would kill if she were pushed hard enough. He could still knock the gun out of her hand if he were to—

'Keep your hands up!' she rapped.

Damn. He'd missed his chance.

Where were the others? Mackenzie and Clark? Why hadn't they turned up?

'We must go, Ned,' she said as he stepped away from the hapless detectives. 'You get the girl. Go on, I've got these.'

As Pike sloped off down the hallway to the cellar door the woman stood back, behind him, covering them all. 'Think you're so clever – you, coppers. Just look at you…' she gave a derisive laugh. 'Pathetic. And it's no use looking for your friends. They can't help you now.'

His stomach clenched. The bitch had killed them – probably while he was holding Pike in conversation at the door. He was their only chance. The gun's nozzle was pressed hard against his spine. That was one gun – in her left hand. The other, he guessed – he hoped – was trained on the detectives, though she's clipped their wings… Tyrell groaned as he started to come to. So *now*, while she was momentarily distracted…

Where was her head – his shoulder height? Lord, he'd never lifted his hand to a woman in his life. But she was evil, a child trafficker.

Sod it!

He balled his fists and twisted round, flinging out his left arm

262

to bat her squarely on the side of her head. Down she went and off went the pistols, simultaneously, one bullet – the one meant for him – grazing his right cheek and shattering the lovely red glass in the front door, the other firing into her foot. She wasn't dead, she wasn't even unconscious: she was screaming in agony and swearing like a sailor. His follow-up right to the jaw put paid to her suffering, at least for a while.

He kicked the guns away, just in case, and turned to free the prisoners. Dammit, Pike had the keys to both sets of handcuffs. And now he was coming back up the cellar stairs. The cellar door was opening. He'd heard the shots.

'My pocket, man.' It was Beckett's voice. *'Quick.'*

There *was* a spare set, then. Archie fished around in one of Beckett's coat pockets. 'No, Arch!'

Pencil, notebook, baby's dummy, small change. No keys. He tried the other one. 'Archie, man!'

'You sure about this, Stan…?'

'Weren't me, Arch, I'm telling you, I never said nothing.' Beckett's voice was low and urgent as he twisted his head to look at Archie. 'It's him, ventriloquising!' Suddenly his focus switched. 'Behind you! Look out!'

He spun round to find Edward Pike rearing up at him, like one of Poe's madmen, more shark than pike now, with pointy teeth bared and eyes red with rage, his knife raised for a killing strike, his other hand fastening on Archie's right arm, fingernails boring into his flesh. With his free hand Archie grabbed the bony wrist and tried to shake the knife from his grasp but the man had a grip of steel. Archie held him off and held him off but couldn't gain any ground. It was his left hand, his weaker palette hand, and his muscles were beginning to tremble. Jesus, for a thin man Pike was strong. Even mustering every ounce of strength to push upwards, Archie knew he couldn't win. The knife was bearing down, inexorably lower, inches from his eye. Face to face with death again, twice in a matter of minutes, he thought of his responsibilities, of

Polly and Clara, his mother, Gussie, the detectives ... Percy's picture ... but, before his entire life could flash before his eyes, Augustine was there. He saw flailing arms, heard the impact of metal on cloth and bone, a cry of surprise and pain – and a girlish wail of disappointment as the gun she'd picked up to use as a club was knocked from her hand and bounced along the floor. She'd been aiming for Pike's lowered head, but even jumping up, couldn't reach. She'd caused a distraction rather than a solution but that was enough. As Pike swung round, slashing the air just over her head, Archie, instinctively, put out his foot and the man fell sprawling, giving Archie time to go for the gun.

'Don't!' he roared, turning back, revolver in hand. Pike had scrambled up, seized Gussie as hostage, his knife at *her* throat, now; he was sidling along the wall towards the door. 'Drop it!' yelled Archie, 'Let her go!' and, when Pike ignored him, pulled the trigger. He'd hoped to hit Pike sideways on but he was no marksman. Lumps of plaster fell to the floor, just enough to startle the kidnapper and cause him to duck, but not enough to stop him in his crab-like retreat along the passage wall, dragging a struggling Augustine along with him and crunching over the debris.

Dear Christ, that was close. Enough with the shooting, thought Archie. I could have killed her.

Who should choose this moment to appear in the open front doorway but DC Clark, his white face all bloody in the lamplight? Seemingly too dazed to take in the situation he began moving aside to avoid collision with the tall man coming at him, sideways on but, his injuries catching up with him, he fell against the opposite wall and slid to the floor, unconscious. Pike, still intent on keeping Archie in his sights, stumbled over Clark's legs, threw up his arms releasing Gussie, who scuttled out of harm's way. With no other choice, Pike turned and ran, with Archie hard on his heels.

PC Ince, waiting up the road, high on the driver's seat at the back of the cab, saw the men erupt from number fifteen, swing round the streetlamp and come pounding towards him. In the dark he couldn't make out who was who. What to do? What to do? He was facing the wrong way to give chase. He geed up the mare and started turning his vehicle. The cab was still sideways on across the lane when the front-runner was upon him, swarming up the back of the cab and knocking him off his perch. It was the man in Archie's drawing – that damned Pike – he'd caught hold of the leg-rest and was hanging on grimly with one hand, despite being swept off his feet as the wheel turned this way and that with the mare's skittish backing and prancing. He let fly with his truncheon at Pike, catching him across the chops, but Pike shook off the blow like it was an annoying insect and continued climbing up and bashing at his legs. He kicked out sideways, while simultaneously tugging on the reins to try and bring the mare under control. She was, by now, rearing up in fright and Archie Price, in close pursuit of the kidnapper, narrowly avoided being decked by flying hooves.

As Archie ducked out of the way, he saw Ince fall backwards into the road and the cab turning towards the forest.

He couldn't leave Ince, who was in a bad way, and it would take too long to go back for the pony and trap. His one hope was to shoot Pike in the back, and he ran after the cab, firing wildly as it drew away. It was way too dark to see his target clearly and, knowing there wasn't a hope in hell of his bullets striking home, he turned back to help Ince. They had rescued Gussie – that was the main thing. Pike would have to be hunted down and arrested another day.

He helped Ince into the trap and drove him to the hospital, calling in at the police station on the way there to report the incident.

On his return, he found the Chingford police standing over Mackenzie's body, in the back garden. He was inexplicably dead, poor man. At first they thought it was a heart attack. There were no obvious wounds apart from the tiniest trickle of blood from the tiniest hole in the back of his neck.

'Hatpin,' said their superintendent, knowledgeably. He'd seen something like it before.

'Nora' had stabbed him, the bitch, at an angle to penetrate his brain. How often had she performed this murderous operation, Archie wondered? It seemed a practised skill. Mackenzie wouldn't have known much about it, the super said, but how were they going to break the news to his widow and children?

Clark had apparently regained consciousness to find Augustine relieving him of his keys. 'Oi, oi!' he'd protested weakly. The girl had apologised, smiled sweetly and promptly set about freeing the detectives and helping DS Beckett, then, to fasten his restraints around Nora's dainty wrists, none too gently at that. When the Chingford police arrived, they found Gussie with a bowl and water, bathing Clark's head. He, still woozy and weak from loss of blood, enquired of her, 'Guv, what have I missed?' before they escorted him to the waiting ambulance.

From somewhere in the front garden the police recovered a garden shovel, wet with Clark's blood. While Archie had been doorstepping Pike, 'Nora'– more Hieronymus Bosch she-devil than sweet Renoir painting – had circled the house, seeing off the enemy. Still refusing to give her full name, she, too, was led, dazed and limping, though cursing loudly, from the house. They took her to Connaught Hospital, in Walthamstow, to have her wound dressed. Next stop, the Forest Road police cells, to await transference to Holloway Prison.

Augustine was taken into protective custody – a cosy, spare bedroom in the section house, carefully tended by Tyrell's wife, Emma and Mrs Meredith – to catch up on some sleep. It was unlikely that 'Nora' would do likewise. She had killed one policeman and assaulted another with a heavy spade and she had been party to at least one child abduction with a view to selling said children into slavery. She would be hanged, sure as eggs.

So why wouldn't she reveal her name? What harm could it do now?

Tyrell had a headache and a large bump on his forehead but he couldn't rest, he said; not while Pikey was free and some miserable A-rab geezer was still at large, still free to buy up little English girls for his harem. Suppose Lilian Steggles was one of his victims? Suppose young Lilian was now in some kasbah in Istanbul or Timbuktu or somewhere, eating camel stew and learning the 'Dance of the Seven Veils'? Poor kid.

Twenty-two

'You reckon she might have been the other girl?'

'What 'other' girl's that, Arch?' Frank regarded Archie with one eye closed in pain. When Pike had slammed his head against the stairs he'd seen stars. Now his brain was fuddled and here was Archie wanting action.

'The one before Gussie in the cellar. Remember she had a strong impression that she wasn't the first to be shackled down there. The bucket had been used before and the straw pallet. Was it Lilian? If not, who?'

He didn't remember anything. 'Ah,' he said.

The cellar was rank, the stench clearing Tyrell's head wonderfully. The bucket had never been emptied and the men gagged as they pounded down the draughty steps, sending rats scuttling and cobwebs fluttering.

'Phew! You should get the night-soil man down here, Frank.'

'Can't disturb the evidence, Stanley.'

'Jesus Christ, Frank. You aren't intending to examine it, are you?'

'No, I bloody ain't. I meant the night-soil man might disturb vital clues.'

'Rat droppings and the like?'

'Less of your cheek, boyo. You're only 'ere on sufferance. Now bring your lamps over 'ere, you both, then put on your gloves and we'll see what's what.'

Chingford police had issued them with paper bags, sacks and envelopes and, as their breath steamed before them, they began filling them with hair grips, scraps of bloody rag, the straw mattress in its entirety. Anything that needed to be thoroughly looked at, said Tyrell, thinking of needles in haystacks, no doubt. Their collection included the sole of a shoe, a tin mug, a dish with the dried-on remains of Gussie's last meal here.

'Look at this,' said Beckett, holding up his lamp. 'Looks like somebody's scratched something on the wall, initials or something.'

'JW,' Archie read. 'Wonder if it's recent. Anyone on your Missing List with the initials JW?'

Tyrell couldn't remember. Beckett made a note. ''Course,' he said, 'Gussie wouldn't have seen it in the dark. And JW, herself, would only have been able to feel her way. Wonder what she used to write with?'

'Hairpin? Though it's quite deep. Archie can you do a rubbing, just for records, like?'

It wasn't exactly a rubbing: he didn't have the requisite ball of wax, but he did have a soft pencil. As he scribbled over a piece of sketching paper held firmly over the marks on the wall, he thought of a young girl imprisoned down here in this dark dungeon, determined to record her presence. JW, though. Not LS. Who could it be? Was she still alive; was she a slave, or was she dead? His mind teemed with questions. Was she a Walthamstow girl? Why hadn't she been reported missing? Who was the devil buying these girls? Could they get 'Nora' to spill the beans?

Beckett and Tyrell were examining a bent six-inch nail they had found, originally hammered into a dirty wooden shelf along the back wall of the cellar. There were several that may have been put there as a hook for tools, long ago, or jugs or dead rabbits. But this one had been worked loose and now hung upside down. Quite possibly they had found JW's tool. Pike would never have noticed it, but somebody feeling their way blindly along a wall for something, anything that might help, would have been sure to come across it. A thing that sharp might have made a good weapon and that surely would have crossed her mind, but, of course, like Augustine, she'd probably thought there were two captors, one spying, who spoke in a slippery guttural voice. If she'd killed or injured Ned, the other one would have punished her.

It was with a feeling of relief that they shut the cellar door behind them and proceeded to sift through the other large but sparsely furnished rooms in the house. Of these the most fruitful was the study, lined with sagging bookshelves, containing the dusty tomes from which Edward Pike had lifted his short stories. They were arranged, meticulously, in alphabetical order: Austen, Alcott and all the A's, then Balfour, Ballantyne, Bennett, Blackmore, the Brontës and so on. A pity he couldn't have realised, from his reading, that he would never match them. If he'd set his sights lower, say as a librarian or a secretary, he might never have had to resort to trafficking children to make ends meet.

There were no pictures on the walls, no telephone, no family portraits. Taking up most of his office were a large swivel chair and a desk, honeycombed with holes for handwritten, rolled-up manuscripts and small drawers for stamps and paper clips. But there were no files, no account books, no bank statements, no diaries, just a muddle of scraps, half-written stories, letters from publishers, cuttings from newspapers. There were bills for horse feed and stabling, for overnight stays in hotels, and 'bus and rail tickets, claims for postage and packing. Some of these were fastened together in bundles with bulldog clips and labelled variously.

Beckett looked through them. '*Evening Standard?*' he said over his shoulder to the others. '*Daily Mirror? Morning Post?*'

'Probably sent his stories there,' Archie confirmed. 'Yes, look, there's a list of titles. I guess the ticks are where he struck gold, and R stands for Rejected. Well, I never – twenty pounds for '*Clementine's Secret!*' That was a direct steal from a penny dreadful.'

270

'*Chelmsford?*'

'That'll be the *Chronicle*.' And, so it proved, with invoices for various expenses, as well as handwritten drafts of stories sent and returned. 'It would help if he was consistent.' But Pike's filing followed no rhyme or reason. It was as if he enjoyed a jumble and the appearance of being busier than he was. Of course, he had the two businesses to keep track of – his writing and the dreadful trade that paid for it. And the two personalities to placate. Perhaps – and Archie allowed his fancy to roam – one side of Pike's split personality was responsible for his creative drive and one the destructive. Pity neither one of them was tidy.

'*Leads?*'

'Leeds? No idea what he was doing up there. But I suppose northerners read tripe too…'

'Not Leeds, Yorkshire. *L-E-A-D-S.*' The DS spelled it out, 'Like business opportunities.'

Despite his cracked head, Tyrell almost bounded from the bookcase. 'Now you're talking. Let's 'ave a gander.'

They all crowded round to see the list, written in a backward-slanting hand, where the short stories had a right-leaning cursive flow. So, Pike even had two styles of handwriting, one for each of his pursuits.

'Can't see Lilian Steggles,' Archie frowned. 'Is that a good thing?'

Tyrell's lugubrious moustache twitched with doubt.

But there, eighth down the list was Augustine Meredith, her address, her age, her school. Her colouring. Blonde, with an asterisk. Fair maidens were in demand, then.

'No JW, that I can see. So, whoever wrote on the wall must have been incarcerated in the cellar way before this list was compiled.'

'He's been at it for years,' murmured Beckett. 'I mean look at them all, pages of young girls – boys, too, looks like.' He was clearly sickened. 'There must be dozens of clients.'

They all paused for a moment to consider the enormity of the man's crimes.

'Unbelievable.' Archie shook his head in pity for children who, unlike Augustine, had never come home again.

They were all west Essex girls and boys from Walthamstow, Chingford, Woodford and outlying villages, all within easy reach of a man with a horse and cart. Perhaps there were men like him in other neighbourhoods, creaming off youngsters to sell abroad. How had he compiled his list? Had he taken them from old church registers, those dating back thirteen, fourteen, fifteen years? That would have been easy enough. Or perhaps that was someone else's job? Gussie had said the woman who had come to prepare her for 'her *gentleman*' had spoken as if there were some sort of managing body – '*they* should pay you well,' she'd said to Pike.

And here, in a folder marked *Orders* were other lists – all typewritten, this time – names and addresses of men, plain Esquires and Sirs and Doctors sprinkled among more foreign-sounding names, some unpronounceable, from addresses as close by as Bloomsbury in London, and as far afield as Lagos, Montreal, Marrakesh, New York, Melbourne. And their preferences. Pike possessed neither typewriter nor the means to travel abroad and acquire details of foreigners willing to pay for a '*blonde virgin*', a '*prepubescent male*', a '*well-developed female adolescent.*' These details must have been supplied by some central agency or organisation. There were no letters, though they searched high and low, nothing that could be traced back to any crucible of evil. Just lists of lustful men who paid well, very well. Pike must have destroyed any correspondence.

'Pity there are no bank statements.'

'You're jokin', ain't you, boyo? This sort of operation's cash in hand. They avoid banks and official channels like the plague. Don't wanna leave any traces, do they? Or pay tax? They probably have to go and collect any money they're owed, from HQ.'

A search of Pike's wastepaper basket was more fruitful. Among crumpled sheets of handwritten manuscript (*Rebecca's Folly* and *One Night in Soho*), several rejection slips, grocery and hardware bills, they found a curt note signed 'Nora', announcing her impending visit, torn across, together with a used envelope bearing the postmark *Shoreditch*.

'Result!' crowed Tyrell.

'Shoreditch is a big place,' Beckett felt obliged to point out. 'And who's to say she wasn't just passing through when she posted it?'

'Yes, Stanley,' Tyrell said through his teeth, 'and the sky might fall tomorrow! It's all we got, mate. Make the most of it.'

Archie swallowed. It wasn't much, as Beckett said. They covered their tracks well, the organisers of this vile trade. Perhaps 'Nora' could be persuaded to spill the beans. Wouldn't it be marvellous if she would give them the names of the movers and shakers and they'd be able to stamp them out, at least here in Walthamstow? Though that was, perhaps, a vain hope when she wouldn't even divulge her own surname. And Shoreditch must be home to a thousand Noras.

Back at the station the detectives matched the type on Pike's list of clients to a Remington 6.

'Well, that narrows it down, Guv!' said Beckett with undisguised sarcasm. 'There's how many Remingtons in Britain?'

'Not many with a wonky *t*,' he said. 'Look, here…' He pointed to someone's preference for a *white female*. 'See, the tail of the *t* don't quite print. Nor there, nor there, not ever. The key must be bent.'

'Gotcha!' Beckett fisted his palm in triumph.

'Well, it's a start.'

They compared their list of missing girls with Pike's list of targets and discovered, to their horror, that there were three, besides Augustine Meredith, on both. But it was too late: according to Pike's large ticks against their names, these poor wretches had already been paired off with men in Persia, Borneo and Brazil.

'What will you tell the parents?'

Tyrell's mouth muscled into a thin line. 'You tell 'em their girl has ended up the plaything of some rich Maharajah and you might just as well tell 'em they're dead. They stand just as much chance of getting 'em back. I suppose we'll have to try, poor little girls, but it's anyone's guess what state they'll be in. Left to me, I'd say let the mums and dads go on hoping – no news is good news.'

'But, surely they'd sooner—'

'No, they wouldn't, Arch, believe me.'

It was hoped that the names on Pike's list, after Gussie's, hadn't yet been taken and, quickly, the police paid visits to the families concerned, checking that their girls were safe and warning them not to let their daughters go out alone.

Word soon spread that there was a gang of evil men preying on adolescent girls.

'Is Your Daughter Safe?' was a poster that went up on every notice and billboard. It portrayed an Alice in Wonderland lookalike standing cupped in a pair of beautifully manicured parental hands. It was the title of a pamphlet, the headline in the local paper and was listed as a public meeting in the Town Hall where Tyrell addressed four hundred or so worried parents and teachers.

Young Pauline Appleby looked to have been the next intended victim after Gussie but, thankfully, she was found safe and sound at home and completely mystified by the fuss her parents made of her after the policeman left. She was the only pupil at the High School to have been targeted by the child traffickers: Lilian Steggles wasn't on Pike's list.

Miss Hubbard, the headmistress, told Inspector Tyrell that, besides Lilian, she was rather concerned about a Jean Williams, one of the 'poor unwashed'.

Tyrell's eyes may have widened a fraction; he may have puffed a little more ferociously on his pipe, but otherwise, he told Archie afterwards, he was proud of his composure. 'JW!' he'd inwardly crowed. 'The writing on the wall!'

Miss Hubbard had checked and rechecked the class registers. All the other three hundred and fifty-three children were accounted for, having either consistently shown up at school to get their red 'mark' since term began, or had the occasional black-inked nought, usually explained by a note from the doctor. Only Jean Williams in the third year had an uninterrupted row of black marks beside her name. Her new class teacher had never even seen her. They were well on the way to Christmas now, girls practising carols and rehearsing nativity plays. Twelve weeks was a long time to be ill, if that's what the problem was. It was well known that ringworm was rife down that end of town. Many a girl had come to school with her head shaved and painted with iodine. Not to mention all the other unmentionables: scabies, scurvy, impetigo. But at least the sufferers had come to school, eventually. Education was their only means of escape from a life of penury. The School Board Man reported that the Williamses were out every time he called. Miss Hubbard suspected he hadn't stuck around long enough to find out. School Board Men were not the most popular of the Council's employees and were regularly barracked and spat upon.

DC Beckett and PC Ince were assigned the task. The sight of a constable's helmet, they thought, might gain them entry.

The smell hit them as the front door creaked open – the smell of poverty, dirt and decay, unwashed bodies and clothes, stale cooking smells, cats and dogs.

'Whatdja want?' A woman, probably far younger than she looked, nervously owned up to being Jean's mother, but Jeannie wasn't there, she said. Jeannie had buggered off some time ago.

'And you never reported her missing?'

'She's a wild one, Jeannie, always in trouble, always running off. Gone to seek her fortune she said, or some such nonsense. She'll come back when she's good and ready.'

'May we come in?'

'Best not. We got scarlet fever here.'

'S'all right,' said Beckett. 'I've had it.'

'You can get it twice,' warned Ince.

Beckett winked at him. Oh. Stanley didn't believe her story.

Nevertheless, they both put handkerchiefs over their mouths before they barged their way in. For the stink, more than anything. They found Jeannie, of course, upstairs in the communal bedroom, with a customer.

Father, it seemed, was the one who had 'buggered off' and had left it to Jeannie and her mother to put bread on the table for the rest of them. Six kids under ten. So, Jeannie, aged thirteen, hadn't had time for school. Nor no shoes, neither, she explained, tearfully, when, eventually, they'd got her and her siblings to Doctor Barnardo's. 'And Miss Hubbard sends you 'ome if you ain't dressed proper.'

Mrs Williams was arrested, along with the punter. 'Six months if you're lucky,' Tyrell told the weeping mother at the station, 'and if you've any sense, you'll leave the kids where they are. They'll be well looked after and they've fitted Jeannie out with some shoes so's she can go back to school. Her teachers reckon she's got a good head on her shoulders and will go far. They'll put it about you was ill and she had to look after the kids.'

'So,' Beckett said to him when they were alone, 'whoever JW was in that cellar it wasn't Jeannie Williams. She's living another sort of hell.'

'Oh, she'll be all right now. Them Barnardo's are saints. But you're right – there's gotta be a Jenny West or a Janet Watson or even a John or a Joe, who's been missing from home for ages. We'll try round the other schools. Public and council. At least we stand a chance of stopping it now we got that she-wolf behind bars. An' there was that sighting of old Pikey over Hackney last week. Shouldn't be long before he puts a foot wrong.'

'Christ,' said Ince, 'who'd be a kiddie, this day and age?'

'Don't think he's listening,' said Becket, 'Christ, I mean.'

Twenty-three

'Nora' sat in her cell with her foot in bandage, her lips sealed tight. She wasn't spilling anything. Meanwhile Tyrell seemed content to play the waiting game. With the procuress in custody, waiting for her hearing, with a permanent police presence at Forest Edge and her contact, Edward Pike, Essex's most wanted man, unable to operate without her, it was hoped the vile trade had been halted for a while at least.

Archie suspected his friend was hatching some plan. Otherwise why insist that 'Nora' remain in Walthamstow until her foot healed? She should have been transferred immediately to Holloway prison pending her trial for murder among other things.

The corner of his dustsheet lifted high one afternoon, with a *Tara-a-ah!* to rival any stage magician's act. Archie peered beneath the scaffolding board to see Tyrell's familiar face beaming up.

'You done here, boyo?'

'Looks like I might be,' he said, heavy sarcasm weighing his words as he slung his brushes, resignedly, into the pot of thinner. In fact, he was glad to see the man: any distraction. Sophie had packed up her overalls and left the moment she heard of Archie's impending marriage, leaving him to finish up on his own. It was now just a matter of titivating but it was this part that made or marred a painting and you could go on forever.

'What is it, Frank?'

'You reckon that storm done it?

'Sorry?'

'Eleanor Redfern.'

Archie put his finger to his lips and indicated listening ears out beyond the dustsheet.

Tyrell lowered his voice. 'You reckon last year's storm washed her body out of some grave somewhere into the river?'

A police artist's work is never done, thought Archie.

Tyrell wagged his head and hissed, 'If it had washed her out and left her stranded in some field or someone's back yard, she'd a made things a lot easier for us. She'd a been found straight off – maybe within days of her death. People's memories would be fresher.'

'Indeed.' He wiped his hands on his trousers and came down the ladder to floor level. 'Better take this outside, Frank.'

They were halfway to his lodgings when he spoke again. Polly had taken his mother and Clara up to South Kensington for a treat. Mam had never seen the V and A. It would be safe to talk in his studio, if that was what Tyrell wanted. 'So, you agree with the shallow grave idea? And that that young gardener, Blackett, could have buried her?'

'I do, mate. Good work.'

'The question is, Frank, did he kill her? Or was it someone else? I mean she may have killed herself.'

'What, and then he found the body and thought it looked like *he'd* done it so he got rid of the evidence, like, and run off?'

'Or someone else strangled her and tried to frame him…'

'Mmm … Possible … Though running away like that says *'guilty'* in my book, no two ways about it. Any old how, first things first – how we gonna find the bloke, whatisname, Blackett? His old boss give you any clue where he might have gone?'

'Somewhere with an acid soil and a warm climate.'

'Eh?'

'Don't you think he might have helped himself to some of those rare seeds before he left – bit of bargaining power with a new employer? Daft not to. I would.'

'Would you, indeed?' Tyrell looked askance and then his eyes narrowed in thought. He stroked down his moustache, slowly, methodically. 'Yeah, knowing you, I suppose you would.'

'And those kinds of seeds won't grow just anywhere.'

'Says the man who's killed more aspidistras than I've had hot dinners.'

'Two, Frank, just two,' he protested. 'I told you I'm no good with plants. I can never remember to water the damn things.'

'So how come you're such an expert on rare seeds.'

'Mam likes gardening. I asked her.'

'An acid soil, eh? She got anywhere in mind?'

'Cornwall, she says.'

'You just wanna go down there with your easel and paints.'

'Well, yes, there is that. I could take Polly.'

'It's a big place, Cornwall, and he's bound to've changed his name. I'll bet there's 'undreds a places taking on new gardeners every day. How the hell are you gonna find the bugger? Any case, if he is down there it's out of our 'ands, now. The Cornish police won't thank you for interfering.'

'Frank, *Frank!* I was joking! It's a long way to go on a whim.'

'This time of year, any old how. You say his dad works at Redfern's?' Archie nodded. 'How's about we go and have a word with old man Blackett?'

'*That's* what this is about, is it? Give us a minute to wash up and change.'

'Be quick about it.'

'Winter seascapes are out then?'

'For the moment.'

They found Walter Blackett up a ladder in an empty glasshouse, cleaning whitewash off the panes with a mop and hose. This was one of the last, explained the young lad who'd taken them to him.

Only another two left. It was a job that had to be done before spring when the new crop would be started. He seemed very proud of his knowledge and Archie gave him a penny for his trouble.

He shouted up, 'Mister Blackett, sir, can you spare a minute? These 'ere coppers want a word!'

They watched Blackett stiffen and slowly descend the ladder on bowed legs, holding on for dear life, feeling for the unseen next rung with the toe of an ancient rubber boot. His face, when he reached the path, was pink with exertion. He mopped his brow and pushed back his hat, revealing straggles of dirty white hair. It must have been hot work, all that stretching and scraping, even though the glasshouse was relatively cool at this end of the year. He jerked his chin, acknowledging Tyrell's proffered identification documents and held up a finger. 'Be wi' ye shortly.' He carefully propped his mop against some shelving and shuffled slowly to the end of the row with the still-running hose, where he turned off the water at a standpipe. He wound the flaccid rubber between finger and thumb and elbow, and set it down carefully, like a coiled snake, beside the tap.

He returned, taking his time, not lifting his head until he met up with them again. 'Now, sirs,' he said, 'wha's all this?'

'It's about your son Gilbert.'

'Oh ah? Wha's 'e been up to, then?'

'Could be nothing, Mister Blackett. Need to ask him though.'

'En't seen 'im in a while. En't 'eard from 'im neither.'

'Do you know where he is, how we could reach him?'

'Nope. Up and left us last summer twelvemonth wi' nary a word.'

'September?'

'Afore that. June, mebbes? Tomatoes was jest settin'.'

They raised their eyebrows. 'Why did he leave, do you know?'

Wrinkled eyelids twitched with cunning. 'Never said. 'Tis a puzzle. He were getting on all right 'til that flood. 'Prentice up at Ardmore's over Broxbourne way. On'y 'ad a year or so left afore he went journeyman.'

'You think the flood might have had something to do with it?'

'Oh ah. Stands to reason, seein' all 'is good work swilled down the river.'

'True,' said Archie, looking up from his sketchpad. The lines and furrows in this old man's face were fascinating, wrought by weathering and a hard life, the crows' feet caused more by squinting at the sun than laughter.

'Or,' said Tyrell, slowly, 'Eleanor Redfern's death might have had the same effect.'

'Whassat!' He flinched, physically shrank, and could hardly bring himself to look Tyrell in the eye. 'Why, who's sayin' 'e 'ad any truck wi' that one?'

'No one. Just seems a coincidence, her death and his disappearance.'

'S'all it be, then, a coinc-*ide*-nce.'

'He didn't know her, then?'

'Course 'e knowed 'er. At school wi' 'er, weren' 'e, when they was nippers – Miss Prescott's school up in the village? But when her Pa sent 'er packin' to some big school up Ipswich way 'er become a stranger, too good for the likes of us. Young Gil kep' well clear of 'er and 'er fancy ways.'

'He's a good-looking lad, from all accounts. Did he have a girlfriend?'

'Don' know as he did, don' know as he didn't. Elsie'd know, mebbes.'

'That'll be Mrs Blackett – his mother?'

'Oh ah. They was close, 'er and Gil.'

'Perhaps it's her we should be talking to.' Clearly they'd get nothing out of him. Yet Archie couldn't forget how shifty the man had been that Sunday on the river, at the mention of Eleanor Redfern. He had secrets, this old man. 'Mind if we talk to her?'

He shrugged. 'She'll tell ye same as me.'

She did. Exactly the same, almost word for word, almost as if the pair had rehearsed what to say when the police came a-calling.

They'd interrupted her preparing a stew for her man's supper and they talked to her in the scullery over the scraping of carrots and turnips; watched as she added them to the pot on the stove.

'Nor 'ide nor 'air – not since June last year.'

'Your husband said. About the time of the flood.'

She was as surly as he, a bony little woman with wispy hair scragged back from her face and knotted; it was still black though she would never see sixty again. Her clothes were a non-colour, a no-shape, from hundreds of washes, and Archie counted four knitted cardigans, most of them out at the elbows. On her sharp little nose, she wore a pair of thick-lensed wire-framed glasses over which she had to peer in order to address them.

'Why ye askin'?' Her mouth pursed tightly and her faded blue eyes beaded as she scrutinised them, head on one side.

'We're enquiring into the death of Eleanor Redfern and wondered if he could help us with our enquiries.'

The knife clattered into the enamel bowl.

'She *en't* dead!' she protested, her eyes big behind the glasses, her face sharp. 'She en't! Never in the world!'

They assured her that remains found in the river were, undeniably, those of Eleanor Redfern.

She threw her apron over her head. 'No, no, no! 'Tis a mistake! I telled my Walter the same – 'tis a wicked, wicked lie!' But one look at their sorry faces told her it wasn't and she burst into hysterical tears, 'Not 'er! Oh Lord love us, not 'er, please God!' She sank to the floor in despair. Gently, they raised her up and helped her to a chair; gave her water to drink and a towel for her tears. Heavens, she really was fond of her master's daughter. Wasn't that strange?

Tyrell patted her shoulder as she twisted the towel, a wringing action. She seemed to find more comfort in that. 'Oh, poor Nellie. We 'eard they found a skellington but we didn't, for a moment, think it could be 'er.' She turned to Archie at the table as she wiped her eyes again. 'She really dead?'

282

'I'm afraid so.'

'And ye wanna know if my Gil done it, I dare say? Well, it weren't him! He'd never hurt a fly, wouldn't our Gil, specially not her!'

They glanced at each other. They'd done right to question the mother, thought Archie. There's none so forthcoming as a woman in defence of her child. 'That so?' said Tyrell. 'He admired her, did he?'

'Admired her! He worshipped the ground she walked on – an' she were soft on 'im, an' all!' Tyrell stood straighter, writing it all down.

Having extracted promises that they wouldn't tell her husband, she revealed that Gil and Nellie, as she called Eleanor, had been friends as children. '*Too* friendly for his lordship's liking,' she added darkly, cocking her head towards the window. She didn't mean her Walter but his employer, Elias Redfern, who had flared like fat on an ember when he'd discovered his girl's best friend was Gil Blackett, a common labourer. Elsie and Walter had feared for their lives at the time, well, their livelihood at any rate. It amounted to the same thing. 'Lucky there weren't no complications,' she said ominously. 'Well, they was just young uns, thirteen, fourteen – hardly knowed nothing, did they? But be on the safe side, Master packed Nellie off to Ipswich, quicker'n a wink, to turn her into a lady that a gentleman be glad to marry and poor old Gil were left to moon about with his heart broke.'

'Did they keep in touch?'

'Well, between you, me an' the doorpost – but don' let on t'were me as told ye – they met up whenever she come 'ome for the 'olidays, like. S'posed to be out riding or up to Lunnon on the train, she'd go up Broxbourne to see our Gil.'

'Broxbourne…' Tyrell's pencil scratched the word into his notebook.

'Bound apprentice up there. Not as far as Ipswich but far enough.'

'They kept in touch?'

'I told him and told him no good'd come of it but would 'e listen? 'Ardly surprising what happened next.'

'What?' they chorused, agog.

'Got 'er in the family way, din' 'e?'

'What!'

'When was this?'

'Gil come and told us the night afore they left. Said 'er come a-runnin' to his door from the school.'

So, it was confirmed. Gilbert Blackett *had* met up with Eleanor Redfern just before she died, and the motive for murder was there. It wasn't unheard of for a young man to go to the gallows rather than face up to his responsibilities.

Eleanor's skeleton hadn't told them about any pregnancy. The girl couldn't have been far gone if she'd managed to get away with it at school – perhaps only a month or two into it. Any foetus would have decomposed along with the rest of her, washed away, food for the fishes. Had the skeleton been whole when it was found, they might have seen the changes the body makes at such a time, but a pile of muddy bones hadn't told them anything, even when pieced together on the mortuary slab.

Elsie Blackett recalled her son's farewell visit last summer. 'He were a-setting where you are now, young sir, glassy-white like that there mistletoe.' She glanced over to the door where a bunch was hanging. They hadn't noticed. 'Last thing he wanted, leaving that job at Ardmore's. He'd worked hard for it, loved it. But needs must an' he'm a good lad, standing by his Nellie, an' all. He said they was gettin' wed and going down Cornwall to make a new life for theirselves.'

'Cornwall, eh?' Tyrell said with a meaningful glance at Archie. 'You gave them your blessing?'

'No choice,' she said shortly, her lips snapping shut then, to hold back all her untold complaints and regrets. Knowing how badly his own parents had taken the news that he, still in his teens, was leaving for London, Archie could imagine how the Blacketts must have felt that night, knowing there was little likelihood of ever seeing their son again. He had paid regular visits to his parents but Gilbert Blackett wouldn't have dared.

'Your husband knows all of this?'

'Some. I told him about them gettin' wed and goin' off. I never mentioned the babby. No need to go upsetting him even more.'

'So, when you heard that Eleanor Redfern had disappeared, you both thought she was with Gilbert in Cornwall.'

'S'right. Never give it another thought. Couldn't say nothing, though. Promised, didn't we?' That accounted for the old man's shiftiness that Sunday. He *had* been nursing a secret, one he'd promised not to divulge.

'And, just to be sure, Mrs Blackett, when they found the body in the river and said it was Eleanor Redfern you thought it was a mistake.'

''Course.'

'You haven't heard from Gilbert at all?'

'Never a word. *He* could be dead an' all for all I know.'

'But, if he's not, he'll be down there somewhere – Cornwall…'

'Reckon so, if he had money for the train. Tek 'im months, else. Time he got there, walking, he'm be all wore out and raggedy. Never get a job looking like a tramp.' She put her head on one side, and her glasses glinted with light. ''Course,' she said, at last, 'he could'a fetched up somewhere else altogether. Never know.'

'And he never got in touch with you?'

She rocked her old head from side to side. 'What the eye don' see and the ear don't 'ear, the tongue can' wag, innit?'

Tyrell frowned and stroked his moustache. 'Do you have a photo of your son?'

No, she had never had no call for any o' they fancy do-dabs. So, Archie put together a likeness of Gilbert Blackett from her description, which seemed to overwhelm her. He gave her a copy of the drawing and Tyrell another for his files. They would send a third copy to the *Chronicle*.

'But cross my 'eart, Mister, he would never a killed Nellie. Never in the world. You take my word for it. She meant the world to him.'

Twenty-four

Spring, 1903

Gilbert found work along the way by knocking on cottage doors.

'Morning, missus,' he would say, putting on a friendly smile. (He'd learned to hide his tears, live with the pain of loss. Nobody would ever know.) 'I were just passing and couldn't help noticin' your hedge'm gettin' away from ye. Could ye do wi' a bit of help? I'm a journeyman gardener on me way to a new job. Gi' us a pair a shears and I'll do ye a tuppenny trim.'

Invariably this led to other jobs like picking plums or mowing lawns, deadheading dahlias, pruning roses, pulling weeds, for a bite to eat and a beer and payment in small change. Sometimes he was invited to come back next day and the next, as more jobs were found for him – tree-lopping or mending a thatch or building a bonfire to burn the waste.

If they didn't have a standpipe or well where he could draw off a bowl of water for a clean up, he washed in streams. He slept in hedges and barns, grew a beard, told them he was twenty-one and that his name was Gilbert Button. He avoided the bigger houses as they'd ask to see his papers but old maids, widows and widowers never thought to question what he told them. He had an honest face, and they told him so. Sad eyes, but an honest face. He'd done a good job for old Mrs Batts down the road and that was good enough for them. Some wanted to make it a regular thing, this tidying of straggly gardens that made their old backs ache but he never stayed longer than a month, tending maybe four or five gardens in a village, flitting backwards and forwards between them, like a bee.

He felt bad about leaving a village where there were good people who appreciated his work, but he was afraid the police would be on his trail sooner or later and he couldn't bear the thought of being shut away from the fresh air and plants, or indeed, of being hung for something he didn't do.

As the summer ended and the cold settled in, he took lodgings where he could and offered himself as an odd-job-man-come-gardener: laying paths, cleaning wells and gutters, rebuilding garden sheds, mending carts and barrows, outdoor work if possible. Bit by bit, job by job, he worked his way from Hatfield to Sawbridgeworth, up through the Rodings to Felsted and Braintree, avoiding the centre of any town, and skirting Colchester altogether. He didn't spend much, except on lodgings and boot repairs and a bit of food to keep body and soul together. By the second week of March he'd reached East Bergholt and was back to touting for gardening work. Having smartened up a long cottage garden to his and the customer's satisfaction, he collected his shilling and set out to find an inn for the night. It was a pleasant evening, not too cold, and this was the sort of country lane he loved, with a mix of deciduous trees and bushes across the road, in bud or blossom, wildflowers on the verges, in the ditches...

And then his breath caught on the scent of blossom. What a beauty, what a sight! It made his heart leap for the first time since Nellie passed... Oh, just look at it, though! Growing outdoors, an' all, strong and sturdy, and silver-stemmed, like it was surely meant to be. Summat he'd only ever see at Miss Ardmore's. Not very tall. On'y a young un, three- or four-year-old, at most, but it was in full flower, with pinkish purple blooms like praying hands pointing up to God.

He leaned on the garden wall to drink it in, careful not to disturb the rock plants.

'Magnolia,' a man's voice informed him. He hadn't seen him, on his knees a few feet away, attending to a clump of wallflowers, a silver-haired and ruddy-cheeked gent in overalls. 'All the way from China.'

'Oh ah,' he knew that. 'But,' he couldn't help asking, 'how'd ye get it to grow out here in the open? Only seen 'em in heated glasshouses. And the soil? Ent it too limey and that?'

The man unwound, dusting his hands. He was taller than Gil and slim built and he examined his visitor closely. 'You're a gardener?' He might have known from his visitor's black fingernails, his patched and muddy trousers. 'You know the tree?'

'Used to grow 'em, uh, further south – we called them 'tulip trees' but we had to protect 'em from the frost an' that. They'm that delicate.'

'Well, you see, we're close to the sea here, warmed by the Gulf Stream and –.'

'Gulf Stream, right up here?'

'Indeed, all the way from Mexico, washes past Norway and comes by here.'

'Mexico?' He tried to remember that map in school. Mexico was half a world away.

'And the forest, of course is a great windbreak. Between them they make for a warm climate, in this part of Suffolk, warmer than you'd get elsewhere.'

'Excepting Cornwall. They got the proper ericaceous soil down there.'

'We have it, too – now. Spread sulphur and peat over your land and – *voilà!*'

He didn't understand that last remark. 'That a fact? Vinegar did for us.'

'Vinegar can get expensive over twenty acres. Sulphur stinks but it does the trick. Anything they can grow in Cornwall I can grow here now. And all the spring bulbs.'

Gil couldn't help smiling, as he feasted his eyes and nose on primroses coming into flower, daffodils, pink and green hellebores. And what was that with its pink blossom growing out of the bark? 'Never seen a real Judas tree,' he confessed, 'only from a drawing the Missus made. It's beautiful.'

The man, who introduced himself as Richard Burns, the owner of this place, said he'd had it, as a cutting, from a friend in Cornwall who'd brought a small tree back from abroad many years before. It was now twenty years old and thriving, he was pleased to say.

Before he could stop himself, Gil found he was telling the man all about Miss Ardmore, not by name, of course, but saying how she used to go on hunting trips to the Orient and bring back plants and seeds for him and the rest of them to grow.

'So, you're familiar with rare plants?'

'Aye,' he said, fingering the paper packets that were burning holes in his pockets and holding his tongue with difficulty. This man was a high-up. The only other high-up he'd known, albeit a self-made one, had killed his own daughter. You couldn't trust them.

But it didn't stop him asking questions. What other delights had the man managed to grow? Had there been any casualties?

It wasn't long before Mister Burns was showing him around the estate, uphill and down dale, past a freshly dug lake, through immature groves and plantations, dizzying him with the exotic names of trees and shrubs, climbers and bulbs.

'Cornwall in Suffolk,' the man said with a smile.

'An' all on your tod, too.' Gil was impressed.

'Not quite,' Burns hastened to explain. 'I had to hire half a dozen labourers from farms round about and a few ploughs and harrows to do the landscaping, and my friend in Cornwall came up to help us with the planting. I'm not formally trained, you see. I'm actually an architect but when my father died he left me rather well off.' He looked uncomfortable, pressing his lips together as though it had occurred to him that Gil was nowhere near as fortunate. 'Anyway,' he went on, 'Fred let me pick his brains and I read everything I could on the subject. Had lots of plants brought over and, I'm pleased to say, most things took. There was this Japanese maple that didn't do so well, quite sickly it was, losing colour, leaves dropping, so I dug it up and put it in a more sheltered spot and now it's fine, in among the other acers. That oriental plane tree over there isn't doing too well, though. It's only three years old.'

'Pot-bound, I reckon. They grow enormous, them. You'll have to plant 'er out soon as you can and shift them rowan saplings – they'm gonna choke each other else.'

'I think you might be right. Weather permitting, I'll probably tackle that on Monday when my gardener comes in. I'm down to two part-time gardeners, now – Sam and Harold. Just to keep the garden ticking over, you see. We manage it between us.'

'Oh.' He couldn't help sounding disappointed. Truth be told he was envious of Sam and Harold. He'd have given everything to work here.

Burns gave him a sideways look but said nothing. Yes, thought Gil, as they walked under a pink camellia that, in four years, had grown taller than a man, everything was doing very well. When it matured this would be a show garden.

'Come and see the greenhouses.'

He led the way downhill to a level area given over to immature plants, some in pots, hardening off, some indoors still. This was a world that Gil knew intimately. Tray upon tray of seedlings filled the greenhouse shelves, many of which he recognised by their shoots.

'*Callistephus chinensis*… China aster. Reckon 'tis the purple one you got there.'

Burns scratched his head. He confessed he didn't know there were any other colours.

'Oh aye,' said Gil. He had pink, white and yellow varieties in

291

his pocket, from a bit of cross-fertilisation he'd done when he was first apprenticed. 'Ready to go outside, these.'

'To be honest, this is the first time I've grown them. I only had half a dozen seeds and I'm reluctant to put them out in case they don't make it. I'd like them to flower, of course, so I can collect more seeds.'

'They'll do just fine – ye could try a rocky wall or a big pot, bit a sand and grit to 'elp – an' seeing it's nice a warm they'll do well, two or three planted up together, like.' He took a deep breath and dug into his pocket. Now or never. 'And – and if they don' make it I – I got a few here I can let ye have.' He pulled out his twists of paper, flicked through them and opened one, carefully. Burns watched, goggle-eyed, as Gil tapped a few seeds into his palm: pill-like, feathered and crinkled. He sorted the purslane from the rest and transferred them to Burns's palm.

'But – but these are…! Dear God, these are gold dust! How did you come by them?'

'The Missus down at Broxbourne. She had loads, an' to spare.' That was the truth, at least. 'Let me help meself.' That wasn't.

'I must pay you for them.' Gil waved away his offer. 'Really? Well, thank you so much, and – and what were those others, if you don't mind me asking – the crinkly ones, look like beetroot seeds?'

'They're related,' he said cagily.

Burns sucked on a tooth as covetousness entered his soul.

By the time they came to the end of the tour it was all settled. Full-time and no questions asked. He'd even put him up until Gil could find somewhere suitable in East Bergholt. As for references, Gil suggested a tour of the neighbouring villages. Burns drove the barouche, while Gil pointed out the work he had done on the cottage gardens, most of them still trim thanks to the advice he had given their owners.

For six months it worked well. Gil got to sow his seeds and plant out the seedlings in Burns's beautiful garden. The bees and his employer were delighted. They didn't ask too many questions about the plants' true provenance, just went about their business. Burns and his new gardener rubbed along fine and Harold and Sam found other work easily enough.

And then, one morning in late October, reading the *Chronicle* over his bacon and eggs in the *Blue Lion* inn, Gil found himself looking at a face he knew. Two faces. He'd seen the drawing of Nellie a week or two back – did anyone recognise this young girl? – had cut it out and popped it in his jacket pocket, next to his heart. But there she was again, a photograph of her in school uniform, this time. His knife and fork fell with a clatter. 'Oh, darlin',' he breathed.

It had taken this long, over a year, for her remains to turn up in the river. She was little more than bones when they'd found her, the paper said, but somehow they'd discovered who she was and how she'd got there. And now things had taken a new turn, a turn for the worse, and his heart was pounding, the newspaper trembling. It was like looking in a mirror!

Underneath a remarkably accurate drawing of *himself* was the caption *Wanted in connection with the murder of heiress, Eleanor Redfern.* He blinked, shook out the paper and hid behind it, though there was no one else in the room. He read on. Eleanor was known to have visited a drinking establishment in Broxbourne just before she died and was thought to have been romantically linked to one Gilbert Blackett, a gardener in the area.

Romantically linked? Dear God. She was his life, his dearest love, and he was the father of their dead baby.

Would anyone knowing the whereabouts of said Gilbert Blackett please get in touch with the Walthamstow police, as they need to eliminate him from their enquiries.

Not true. What they wanted was to nail him for Nellie's murder and they'd get him, too, with this picture. It was so like. He wondered how they'd come by it. *Artist's impression of the suspect.* Ah, there it was – *suspect.* Damn.

Back at Burns Gardens (his employer had recently put a brass plate up on the gate), Gil showed him the newspaper and explained his part in the disappearance of Nellie Redfern. Burns said he'd always known Gil was in trouble of some sort. Gardeners like him didn't just drop from heaven. Something awful must have happened to drive him out of Broxbourne where he had been so happy.

'You loved her?'

He sighed.

'Yes, I see you did. And you didn't do it?'

He closed his eyes.

'So, what do you want to do, as if I didn't know?'

'I must clear my name, Mister Burns.'

'Yes, indeed. Well, I'll expect you back shortly, then...' He couldn't continue for the lump in his throat.

He gave Gil money for the return train fare to Walthamstow and an overnight stay, crossing his fingers for luck. Gilbert secreted away his remaining seeds. Not that he didn't trust Richard Burns but, as the man said, they were gold dust and he didn't want to put temptation in his way.

Twenty-five

A cowherd, hunting a lost heifer he'd been grazing by common right, in the forest up by the waterworks, found what was left of Lilian Steggles. The poor girl had climbed high into an oak tree, shimmied out to tie her dressing gown cord firmly to a stout branch (the other end was looped around her neck) and jumped. Because she was so high up, nobody passing along the track beneath the tree, with cart, or dog or girlfriend, had seen her. But now that the branches were bare…

From the state of her Tyrell reckoned she'd been there for weeks, if not months. When they cut her down they found, inside her skirt pocket, an explanatory note.

> *I do not want to swim in the Olympics*
> *I do not want to be a swimming champ*
> *I do not want Smithy doing dirty stuff to me.*
> *I do not want to be fat.*
> *I do not want to have carroty hair and freckles.*
> *I do not want to be me no more.*

'Fat?' Archie was incredulous. 'There was nothing of her.'

'Even less now. Not much more'n a skellington.'

'Frank!' His beer slopped onto the table as he set down the tankard and buried his head in his hands. He was devastated. He'd been so wrong about the girl.

'Sorry, mate, I've had one hell of a day.' Tyrell leaned back in his chair and stretched his neck to ease out the stress. 'Oh God …

Fetching her down, telling the parents ... Then the Doc had to examine her, like. It ain't been a bed a roses.'

Archie lowered his voice, though the nearest possible eavesdroppers were either engrossed in a game of dominoes or gossip. 'So, this Smithy, would that be…'

'Oh yeah, that evil bitch Miss Smith at the pool. She'd been interfering with the girl.'

'Really?' Archie was shocked. He'd let her teach Clara!

'It happens. When we went round 'er 'ouse we found all sorts of nasty stuff, photos, gadgets…'

'But she's a woman!'

'Oh, Archie mate, you got a lot to learn about the world. I wouldn't mind betting she's been at it for years.'

'Oh Lord, what about Clarrie?'

'You best ask her. She'll tell you, like as not.'

'She did say Smithy was creepy. Giving her favourites little squeezes and cuddles, that sort of thing, but I never thought anything of it. I mean, some women are a bit – you know, over-*demonstrative* – well, that's all right. But that dirty business – child molesting? Corrupting young minds? That's just horrible. It goes against nature!'

Tyrell sighed, 'Yeah, well…'

'I should have known. I mean I knew she was, you know, mannish, but I thought, well, each to his own – *her* own… But Clara did say Lilian was getting fed up with all the attention. Didn't like spending time alone with Smithy.' He pulled at his earlobe, feeling utterly wretched. 'I should have suspected something was wrong. Stopped it.'

'Archie, Archie, for God's sake – how could you have known what she was up to? How could anyone?' He ran his hand over his moustache in despair. 'God,' he said, quietly, 'sometimes I 'ate this job.'

Archie mashed his lips together, saying nothing. Frank hated child molesters more than any thieves and swindlers. In their own way, they destroyed lives as effectively as murderers.

'How are Wilf and Izzy taking it?' he said at last.

'How do you think? They're beside themselves. As for identifying the body, Izzy couldn't bring herself to look – I mean her girl was strung up there for months, bits of her was dropping off like…'

'Frank!'

'Poor old Wilf passed out. Izzy's out to do murders.'

'She knows what Smithy did?'

'She does now. We arrested the bitch soon as we found the note. Shrieking and carrying on, she was. Making out she was so shocked by the news. Her great white hope killed herself. Like, how dare she? When we said she was nicked for child-molesting you should have heard her. Cursing like a trooper. Jesus, she's a nasty piece of work…'

Archie frowned. 'You don't think she could have been the one – you know – strung her up?'

'No. Though she might as well've. Far as he could tell, the Doc put the time of death, give or take, round about the beginning of August. Smithy and her Aged P's was down in Southend round about then. They go every year for a fortnight.' His eyes narrowed against the smoke as he puffed on his pipe. ''Sides,' he said, 'I can't see how anyone can force a young girl to climb a tree and hang herself. And if she's dead, already, how's she gonna get her up there – slung over her back?'

'And there was the note. It's her handwriting, is it?'

'It is.'

'Fat, though? What was she thinking? Poor, poor girl.'

'I know. And then, just to make my day, who should waltz into the nick this afternoon but Gilbert Blackett himself.'

'What! He came of his own accord?'

'Saw your drawrin' in the paper.'

'Blimey. All the way from Cornwall…'

'Not quite. East Bergholt. Come down by train. Says he never done it, of course. Admits to burying Eleanor Redfern in

Ardmore's garden but he never topped her, he says. She hopped the wag to tell 'im he was gonna be a daddy, about which he was not exactly overjoyed but it couldn't be helped, like. They made plans to get married and go down south. Start a new life.'

'Just what he told Elsie.'

'Right. But, when he come back from seeing his mum he found poor Nellie done over, dead in his bed, so knowing he'd be chief suspect…'

'Not wrong there…'

'He got rid of the body or so he thought and done a bunk. The rest is 'istory.'

'Right, so – so how – who –?'

'He reckons her old man done it.'

'Wouldn't be surprised. I mean you can't sell your daughter to a railway baron if she's with child.'

'Sell?' Frank raised a bushy eyebrow.

'It's what it amounts to.'

Tyrell nodded ruefully. He sighed. 'Yeah, like, what's the difference between what he had in mind and what Pikey and co are up to?'

'Not much, except they're taking kids off the street, and Redfern's transaction was perfectly legal and above board 'cause she was his own. His property.'

The detective sniffed with distaste. 'One rule for them, innit?' They stared gloomily into their beers. Archie was the first to look up.

'Do you believe him? Blackett, I mean.'

Tyrell screwed up his face. 'I'd like to. Be honest I ain't that partial to old Redfern…' he took a long breath and blew it out thoughtfully, 'but that's just my prejudice against pompous rich bastards. You got to keep an open mind, in this game. Proof is what we need. What I think is,' he said, from behind another puff of smoke, 'you and me's gonna 'ave to take another trip up Tottenham.'

'Now?'

'Soft ha'porth! In the morning. You got nothing else planned, 'ave you?'

'Only touching up my painting at the Palace. Percy wants it finished yesterday, in time for Christmas.' He shrugged. His life was a juggling act. 'So, what's happening to Gilbert Blackett? Have you charged him?'

'Nope. Offered to put him up in the cells tonight, free of charge. But he preferred to book into the *Bell* for the night. Couldn't face being in a cell between them two harpies, I reckon, Smithy and our "Nora".'

'You trust him?'

'Look, he come in outa nowhere, off 'is own bat. An' I forgot to say, he handed in a loada seeds, all labelled up and dated, in twists of brown paper. Oh, and her tooth – Nellie's missing tooth, I mean! Says he picked it up off the floor, washed it and kep' it in his breast pocket ever since. I mean you'd only do that if you really loved a girl. I think he wants to do what's right. Why would he run off again?'

'Just thinking...'

'What?'

'Well, if I thought my girl had been killed by her old man I might want to go and sort him out while I had the chance.'

'He's not the violent type, Arch. He's a bloody gardener for God's sake. Loves all God's creatures...' He thought about it for a moment or two. 'Nah!' he decided. 'No way.'

'Nah!' agreed Archie and drained his glass.

Redfern was out when they arrived. Some function up in town. The butler said he wouldn't be back until around midnight but they could come in and wait. So, Tyrell took it upon himself to summon the household staff; woke up anyone already in bed, sent for those few living out and, when they were all assembled in the drawing room, questioned them *en masse*. Did they see or hear anything of Eleanor Redfern after she ran away from school last summer? Did she come to the house? Speak with her father?

While Tyrell was addressing them, Archie and Beckett, watching for reactions from different sides of the room, both saw the butler catch the housekeeper's eye and look away quickly.

'You don't have to say nothing now. I'll call you in, one at a time, and you can tell us your side of things. But I want you to think about this very carefully. If she did come home and you've been pressured to keep quiet about events that night or subsequent nights, if you think you may be putting yourself out of a job by coming forward, let me just say that by not speaking out you could be condemning an innocent young man to the gallows. Ask yourselves what Eleanor would have wanted.'

It was nine o'clock when he made this speech.

By nine-twenty he had his answer. They all had it off pat. Eleanor Redfern had *not* come home when she ran away from school. The first they heard about her absconding was when the Master had had them all downing tools to go out looking for her, all over the grounds, high and low, to no avail. The last they had seen of the girl had been the Easter before last. Some recalled that she'd sat up in her room blowing and prettily decorating chicken eggs, one for every single member of staff. She always remembered them at Christmas, too, like they were part of her family. Poor lonely girl. She was sorely missed.

And did they know anything about a relationship between Miss Eleanor and young Gilbert Blackett?

This question clearly found them unprepared and sparked off fidgets and shifty looks as if they needed to confer with someone else in order to know what answer to give.

Most gave a glowing account of their friend 'Blackie,' describing him as a likeable young chap who loved all growing things and wouldn't hurt a fly, except for blackfly on the broad beans and cabbage whites on the brassicas. Oh, and slugs. Miss Eleanor had took to him real strong and they were always together when they were small, talking, laughing, walking in the woods, feeding the birds and the squirrels, playing hide-and-seek and such, building dams in the streams. Mrs Redfern, she didn't seem to mind. She liked Blackie and had him over to little tea parties with Eleanor, and that, but when she died, Redfern, when the friendship was drawn to his attention, like, thought it best to separate them.

The upstairs maid, Maria, had attended the village school with them both, in the days when the Master wasn't so particular about his daughter's manners. She said that Blackie and Miss Eleanor had been great pals and they'd let Maria and Seth Turnbull, who'd since gone for a soldier in the Crimea, play with them sometimes. They'd play lords and ladies with much romping and prancing about and building dens and climbing trees and somehow it had developed into a sort of kiss-chase with the girls being captured and imprisoned. But it had all been very innocent, nothing to worry about.

She knew that Blackie and Miss Eleanor helped each other with their schoolwork – they sat next to each other in class as the top two and as such had occupied the front desk. She'd sat behind, envying the two heads close together. Blackie was a handsome boy and all the girls were sweet on him; he was clever, too, even cleverer than Nellie. Sadly, the two of them were caught sparking under a haycart and the master straightway sent Eleanor packing – off to that posh school for safety. Maria was Miss Eleanor's maid when she was home for the holidays and knew that the two of them still met up with each other, sneaky, like. She'd never split on them.

'Do you think there might have been a romantic attachment still?'

'Don't see why not? You'd find it hard not to love Blackie. You'd never be rich, if you married him but you'd be happy.'

She was the last. The rest had all gone to bed, whether to sleep soundly, knowing they had told the truth or to lie awake wrestling with their consciences. Only the Higginses, the butler and housekeeper, were up when the Master came home. The two detectives were snoring by the fire and the artist was stretched out on the settle, his pencil and drawing pad having fallen to the floor beside him.

A disturbance in the hall, shouts and thumps, startled them all into action. Flinging open the door they found Redfern rolling about on the marbled floor, his homburg, bag and cane scattered, as he vainly tried to ward off the blows that Gilbert Blackett, astride the fat belly, was directing into his blubber. 'I'll swing for ye, y'old devil!' he yelled, waking any left sleeping, upstairs and down. '*That's* for Nellie, you murdering bastard, and *that's* for our babby! That's for me job at Ardmore's and that's for mekking us into a thief and a coward runaway!'

The butler was standing off, a grim smile on his lips, not making any attempt to pull the intruder off and save his master. That he left to the police who, to be on the safe side, took them both in for questioning.

'Blackie' hadn't even checked into the *Bell*, he said, but had used his cash to take the 'bus into Tottenham. He had dropped into his parents' cottage to say goodbye, thinking this might be his last chance to embrace them before the scaffold, and then he made his way up to the mansion, in time to see the police arrive and to hear Higgins announce that the Master was out. Never mind, he thought, it was tonight or never. He'd bide his time and wait until Redfern came home.

The rest of his statement detailed the short time he'd spent with Eleanor the previous summer. She'd come to his door on the evening of the twenty-fourth of June to tell him she was pregnant. She'd said she'd been home and asked her father for help but he'd thrown her out. She'd had torn stockings and scabby knees from falling down the front steps. And Redfern's staff were lying. They'd looked after her well enough until that moment. No one had come to her aid when she was lying in the drive sobbing in shock and pain. She'd earned a little money ushering at the Guild Hall and then set out for Broxbourne on foot. It had taken her four or five days to reach him. Yes, he said, in answer to Beckett's question, he had been surprised, not to say dismayed at her news, but it was his baby. His little boy or girl. And he'd never let Nellie down. He described how they'd decided to run away together, get married and start a new life far away from Tottenham.

The next day he'd gone off to work as usual. He wouldn't be paid until the end of the week and they needed all the money they could get. After making her promise to stay in his room until he came home – he wasn't allowed women visitors – he showed her where bread and cheese and apples were to be found in the little cupboard beside the bed and water in the enamel jug. There were books to read and a pack of cards for solo *Whist*. He'd bring supper. He showed her how to lock the latch and unlatch it for him when he returned. 'Be very quiet, darlin', and don't ye open the door to nobody else but me. Promise?' And she'd promised. That was the morning of the twenty-fifth. When he'd returned, full of joy at the thought of seeing his beloved again, he'd found the door unlocked and Nellie lying in the bed, fully clothed, beaten up and bloody, her poor belly fisted and red where the baby had been battered, too. A terrible sight.

He was unable to speak for minutes on end, weeping at the memory. 'But it was the stranglin' that done for her,' he sobbed.

He knew – he just knew, he said, that Redfern had done it. She wouldn't have unlatched the door for anyone else. She'd probably thought her father had taken his time thinking about his only daughter and his unborn grandchild, losing sleep as he replayed the events of that night, weeping over his gross behaviour. It was what she wanted most in the world, that he'd find out where Gil was lodged and knock on the door, desperate to make it up to her. Instead of which he'd made quite sure that the shame of a bastard would not besmirch the great name of Redfern and that Gil would be hanged for the deed.

They turned their attention to Redfern who, sore and irascible, had passed a fitful night in the cell between Smith, the nonce, and some chilly murderess waiting for her turn in court. He insisted his daughter's death was nothing to do with him. He suspected but had no proof that she had run to Gilbert Blackett in her flight from school. He'd certainly had no idea the bastard had impregnated her. Had she come to him first he would have made her stay, made provision for her and his grandchild, bringing the wedding to Mortimer forward. Let the railway owner think their firstborn was premature. All's fair in love and commerce.

Of course, Blackett would deny killing her. Making out they were going to get married! On an apprentice's wages? Poppycock! Top and bottom of it was he didn't want to be saddled with a wife and child. He was ambitious, as guilty as hell and trying to make her loving father out to be the guilty one. Why on earth would he, of all people, have wanted his lovely daughter dead?

'Just for the record, Mr Redfern, I'd be grateful if you would give us an account of *your* movements on the twenty-fifth of June last year.'

'What!' he spluttered. 'You don't seriously think…?'

'If you wouldn't mind, sir.'

'Well, off hand, I don't think I … hmm…' He huffed and frowned, seeing that he might have a problem, after all. 'What day of the week would that have been?'

'It was a Wednesday, Mister Redfern.'

'Ah, now, Wednesdays I'm up in town on business. I have an office there.'

'All day?'

'I tend to make a night of it. Stop over at my club.'

'I see.'

'My secretary will have all the details. You can talk to him in the morning.'

But that clearly wouldn't do. Tyrell was waiting patiently, tapping his pencil on his notebook. Redfern gave a rapid shake of his head and sucked his teeth.

'Look, I really can't remember what I did over a year ago. I'd probably have met my accountant, my solicitor, people like that – buyers, salesmen. London's more accessible for my associates, you see, more central. And I can kill a few birds with one stone as it were...' He paused for their polite smile. 'I might arrange a business lunch or – I don't know – have a drink or a meal with a friend, later. It varies from week to week.'

'I see,' said Tyrell, 'and then, when you've finished for the day you tend to spend the rest of the evening at this club of yours?'

'Or I might take in a show or a concert.'

'Presumably you have an appointments book or diary for last year, records to corroborate your story, addresses for these –' he consulted his notes, '– solicitors, accountants, buyers and so on.'

He looked nonplussed. 'Worse than the bloody tax man,' he muttered.

'It's just a formality, Mister Redfern, but we do need you to account for your whereabouts on the twenty-fifth of June last year. I'm afraid we'll need details of any meetings you might have had on that day, any business deals, records of expenses, fares, bills, theatre tickets, that sort of thing. And your club will vouch for your residency that night, I dare say?'

'What? You want to *look* at my books?'

'Please.'

'But I'm the injured party here...'

'No, Mister Redfern, your daughter is the injured party. This is a murder case, and I'm afraid everyone is suspect.'

'Am I under arrest then?'

'Not at this moment. You are 'helping us with our enquiries'. The sooner you can account for your movements that day, the sooner we can let you go.'

'Do I have a choice?'

'Not unless you want to be arrested on a charge of obstructing the police in the course of their enquiries.'

'You'd better take me home then.'

305

In his office, the shelves were lined with diaries going back some twenty years. The page for June the twenty-fifth, 1902, was tightly scheduled. Meetings in London all day, just as he'd said, a light tea at the Criterion and then on to see *Merrie England* at the Savoy with, of all people, Ephraim Mortimer. He had had a late supper at his club in New Cavendish Street and had spent the night there.

'And this is a true record of your movements on that day?'

'Of course, Inspector! What do you take me for?'

'You can assure me that it has not been altered or added to, in any way.'

He exploded in a bluster of affronted self-righteousness.

'I suppose there are people who can vouch for your presence at these various places, Mister Redfern.'

'Good Lord, this is over a year ago, Detective. Everyone will have to consult their own records. It'll take time.'

'See what you can come up with, sir. We need witnesses or, rather, you do.'

'Fra-ank…' Archie pondered, when Tyrell explained why he had had to release Redfern, 'did he once ask why you wanted to know about the twenty-fifth, in particular?'

'He didn't. I never told him that was the night young Blackett found her dead. You didn't. And I'm sure Beckett didn't. But somehow he accepted that the twenty-fifth of June last year is a significant date for which he must provide an alibi. All we've told him is that she was pulled out of the river this summer. We've said nothing about Blackett burying her or the flood washing her out into the river so, if Redfern really is innocent, the blameless father, if he really hadn't seen her since last Easter, he'll have no reason to suppose she didn't have all summer, all *year*, in fact, to get herself killed and dumped in the drink.'

'Interesting.'

'Telling me.'

Twenty-six

'Nora' was a hard nut to crack. She didn't know anything about a hatpin that had killed DC Mackenzie, nor about the shovel that crowned poor DC Clark. It must have been Pike did those terrible things. He was a bit weird, you know, making those voices that told him what to do. As for guns, the police were the ones who'd brought them into the house. She didn't know one end of a gun from the other, hence the accident. Frightened out of her wits she'd been with a houseful of armed policemen.

The girl in a cellar? Nothing to do with her. She'd just been calling in on Pike at the request of his poor old mother, her friend. First time she'd set eyes on that child was when Pike brought her into the house.

She was going to sue the police for her injured foot, never mind the rights and wrongs of it. She didn't know where Ned Pike had gone; he didn't confide in her. She didn't know anything about this white slave racket they were on about. Didn't rightly know what a white slave was. She thought all slaves were black and worked in American cotton plantations.

Her husband? She hardly ever saw him: he was a salesman, on the road. She believed he was presently in Manchester.

'God forgive me,' muttered Tyrell when he looked in at the *Aunty Alice*, as he had learned to call it, to share an idea with Archie. 'That's a suitable case for torture if ever there was one. I keep having to stop myself stamping on her foot. We've got to get

Pike, and whoever he works for. Augustine is quite convinced they were doing someone else's bidding. 'They'll pay you well,' she heard Nora say to Pike. And 'I understand,' when she was telling Gussie about that scumbag preferring blonde hair. I mean, like she didn't know directly. There must be someone – someone with a Remington 6 typewriter – supplying the names of clients, doing the donkey work abroad. We can't have any more girls disappearing. And we can't hold her indefinitely.'

'How *is* her foot?' asked Archie.

'Her foot? Well, she's walking on it now. Limping a bit but it wasn't that serious. Bullet shaved her bunion a bit. She did herself a favour there. Her shoe lets water though.'

'I don't understand why you're still hanging on to her. Shouldn't she be in Holloway by now?'

'Ah, now that's what I come to talk to you about…'

'Frank?'

'See I was wondering…'

'Oh Frank, can't someone else…? I'm sorry but I must finish this. I've my mother and daughter here for Christmas and I can't spare the time. Besides, she's a murderess and a procuress and she should be in Holloway. God –,' it suddenly occurred to him, 'have you even reported the case to them?'

Tyrell tapped the side of his nose in a telling way. 'Less you know the better, young Archie. Now I've got a proposition for you. I'm going to suggest that we release our "Nora" on the grounds of insufficient evidence – say we believe her story and see where she goes. She might lead us to Pike or the ringleader.'

'You what! Good God, she's not daft, Frank.'

'We'll let her think her blackmail was successful, that we want to avoid being sued for shooting her in the foot.'

'Really? You're joking! She'll guess your game straight off. She won't lead you anywhere but up the garden path. Then you'll have lost the only lead.'

'I thought *you* might do the honours.' (Archie cast his eyes up

308

to heaven.) 'You and your family could follow her in your trap.' (Archie's jaw dropped.) 'She wouldn't suspect a family out on a jolly…'

'No!' Tyrell had lost his mind. 'In the words of the song, Frank, no, no, a thousand times no – I'm not going to expose them to any sort of danger. Besides, she knows my face.'

Which was how Archie found himself leaning backwards over Polly's kitchen sink, next morning, having his hair dyed black.

'What *are* you doing?' His mother, who had been sleeping in Polly's spare room, now appeared in the doorway. He told her he was going to track a released prisoner – a police killer – around London.

'In disguise? Oh, how exciting!'

'Eliza don't encourage him! It's so dangerous!'

'I've told them I don't think black hair alone will do it,' Clara told her grandmother. She described how she had attempted to disguise herself for her big adventure and Effie had known her from behind, from her size and shape and distinctive gait. '*And* she was drunk,' she added. 'I expect Polly was, too. They'd been toasting Pops and Polly's engagement, but,' she blushed, 'I got the wrong end of the stick.'

'Effie's the lady doctor?'

'Archie, keep still!'

'You think this murderess, glancing behind, would know your Pops by his long legs and broad shoulders?'

'I do, Granny.'

'How dangerous would she be? Would she be armed?'

'Of course not. They'll have made sure of that before they let her go.'

'What do you have in mind, Mam?'

'Well, if you were driving the buggy with your elderly mother beside you, she wouldn't think you were a snoop following her, would she?'

'*Mam – No!*' Good God, what was she thinking? A snoop? She meant a stalker, didn't she? And, it was true, no one would go stalking accompanied by his mother. She and Tyrell thought alike.

'I was going to suggest the same thing except I saw *me* sitting beside him.'

'Clara!' he objected. 'No, never…'

'Well, if you're both going I'd better come, too – Archie, will you keep still! The dye's going everywhere!' Now he had to endure a cold wet flannel swilling his ear. 'No, she's right. They both are. Think about it. You need to look inconspicuous, darling, and there's nothing so normal as a family outing. I'll bring my revolver.'

'No, Polly!' he shrieked. 'I'll go alone, thanks! And certainly, no firearms!'

'Well, you'd be no good, you can't shoot straight.'

Eliza's old face was alight with excitement. She regarded him critically over her glasses. 'His eyebrows should be black, too, Polly. His lashes are dark enough, I think. And you might want to have a closer shave, Archie. Those red bristles are a real giveaway.'

When he was dry and his hair was trimmed, he looked quite presentable, he thought.

'You can't wear those trousers,' said his mother. 'They're covered in paint.'

'They'll have to do. My suit is at the cleaners. Got muddy at Mackenzie's funeral.'

'Wait a moment. Don't go anywhere,' said Eliza. She snatched up her bag and was out of the front door in a trice. Ten minutes later she was back and removing from her shopping bag a sack coat and matching waistcoat and pin-stripe trousers. 'Second-hand stall,' she crowed. 'You owe me one and ninepence.'

'Dear God, Mam, they'll be crawling!'

'No, they're not, I checked them carefully. Try them on.'

He did as he was told. It's a brave man can gainsay his mother.

'Ah, a bit short in the leg but that can't be helped. I just guessed at the waist size but it doesn't look too bad. Take them off and I'll put in a dart and let down the turn-up.'

Polly's contribution was a pair of spectacles with clear lenses that she kept in her 'props box', her resource for putting customers into character for their photographs.

'Oh, Archie, just look at you! You could almost be an intellectual!'

'Thanks, sweetheart!'

'Your own mother wouldn't know you,' said his mother. 'Shame you can't grow a moustache before tomorrow. I'll pop down and get you a false one from the Dolls' Hospital.'

'You could have a really big thick one like Uncle Frank's or a twirly one like Gramps or a spivvy one like Lilian's Dad.'

'Right,' said Archie with a frown. 'Well, thankfully the Dolls' Hospital's shut today.'

However, he caught Polly's eye and knew the time had come to tell Clara what had happened to Lilian. The news had been out for days but they'd kept it from her, knowing how devastated she would be. 'I'll just go and change.' He gave his fiancée a telling look which she answered with a nod.

'Dead?' Her hand flew to her mouth, her eyes round with horror and loss. Her face drained of colour and slices of the carrot she'd been chopping for dinner ricocheted off the floor.

'Leave it, leave it, lovey.'

'She can't be! I can still see her, hear her voice!' After the shock came the tears and then, the inevitable questions: how, why, when? They tried to spare her the full horror but, in the end, had to come clean. Her plait came over her shoulder and she dusted her top lip with the soft hair, a throwback to childhood loss.

'Why'd she go and do a thing like that?' she cried. 'She was going to swim in the Olympics in a few years' time. She had so much to look forward to.'

Archie told her about the suicide note.

'But there wasn't an ounce of fat on her, Pops!' she wailed. 'It was all in her head!'

'I know, I know, love. And Miss Smith didn't help.'

'Archie...' his mother made a forbidding face.

'Miss Smith?'

'She did things to Lilian she never should have and they've locked her up for it.'

'Gosh. What did she do?'

He sighed. It was hard bringing up girls. Polly chimed in. 'Things that made Lilian feel ashamed, though it wasn't her fault.' But Clara was still puzzled.

'Archie, pick up the carrots, son, and rinse them through. We'll go and see if there's any mint left, eh, lovey? Bring your shawl.'

'I think it's all gone over, Eliza,' said Polly.

Archie's mother scrunched up her face and shook her head violently. Mint wasn't the point.

Through the scullery window, in a private moment over a bowl of potatoes, Polly, nudging Archie's shoulder with her head, drew his attention to the old lady explaining the harder facts of life to her granddaughter. Fading red hair and black were close together over the dead herb patch. Their breath steamed white between them and they hugged their shawls close.

'Poor kid. It must be hard to learn that adults are flawed.'

'Oh, she's aware of that, Poll. She's had me as a role model.'

'I said "flawed" – I meant perverted.'

'I can do perverted,' he said with a grin, plopping his potato back in the bowl.

'Unhand me, villain!'

They came in from the garden on a blast of cold air, some ten minutes later. 'None left,' said Eliza.

'It's all right, I have a jar preserved from summer.'

Clara was still very pale and she had been weeping. 'What I

312

don't understand,' she said, 'is why can't you have dill with lamb and mint with fish? Or rosemary with beef, for goodness' sake?'

Archie let out a bark of laughter. 'I thought you were discussing Lilian's difficulties.'

'Oh, we've done all that, Pops. What a nasty piece of work Smithy is. I said she was creepy, didn't I? I hope they lock her up forever and throw away the key. I'm going to make a proper statue of Lilian and give it to Izzy. She won't be swimming, this time – I think they'd rather forget all that. She can be selling sweets off the stall. And I'll make a barrow boy to go with her. She'd like that.'

'That lovely smell is telling me the lamb is just about roasted to perfection, Polly dear. So, where's this jar of mint? In the pantry? Clara, would you mind?'

That afternoon, at Clara's request, they went for a walk in the forest.

The police cordon had been removed though trampled mud showed where they had been working. But if you looked up, there, in the milky sky, a low orange sun was trying hard to percolate the delicate lacework of twigs and branches. Holly berries and wild rose hips were brave spots of colour: birds were too busy to sing, trying to keep warm somewhere, but squirrels were up and about, busily hunting the acorns they'd put into store just a week ago.

The pilgrims spoke in hushed voices, gazing up into the tree.

'How on earth did she get up there?' murmured Polly.

'It's a mystery,' said Archie. 'Tyrell said they had to use ladders to fetch her down.'

'I'll show you,' said Clara, and before they could stop her she was tackling the trunk, fastening her fingers into invisible cracks in the bark and her strong, booted toes onto lumps and gnarls and protrusions.

'Clara, no! It'll be wet – the rain and frost...'

'You'll fall, child! Please don't.'

'Leave her, Mam,' said Archie. 'She has to do this. It's her way of connecting with Lilian.'

She got halfway up the massive trunk before she slipped. Archie was waiting to catch her as she came off.

She shook her head, fighting tears of frustration. 'The wrong shoes.'

'Absolutely,' they all agreed.

She sniffed. 'It's easy in the summer. We carved our initials up there: CP and LS. I'm glad she chose that tree to do it.'

On the way home they collected armfuls of holly to decorate Polly's parlour and spent the evening painting twigs with whitewash and fixing them in pots with pretty ribbons tied in bows as decorations. The poor girl's eyes began to close. Eliza had already gone up. Polly suggested Archie carry Clara up to the double bed and she'd take her chances over the road with him. There was something about his new black colouring that was rather attractive.

Monday dawned cold and overcast, threatening rain. So, reluctantly – though much to Archie's relief – the moustache idea was abandoned. Clara seemed to be recovered. Her eyes were returned to their normal brightness after last night's tears and Archie hoped that her spirits were as resilient.

All set for their 'mystery tour', as she called it, Archie drove his little family round to Greenleaf Road, to wait on the corner out of sight of the front entrance, for 'Nora' to be released from the police cells. He was standing watch, holding Jessie's reins, when three men, two wheeling bicycles, emerged from a side door deep in conversation. On seeing Polly, they hailed her cheerfully, and didn't understand, at all, her dismay on seeing them.

'Go away, Stanley. Go on, shoo! You don't know us.'

'Damn,' said DC Beckett, 'can you tell it's me?'

'Of course. Well, you certainly look different with a beard but…'

314

Clara made a face of disapproval and whispered hoarsely, 'We're meant to be following the murderess. She sees us talking to you she'll know what we're up to.'

'We're following her, too,' said the detective, putting on the tall hat he'd been carrying. 'She's sent for a cab and I'm the driver. And DCs Hayward and Pettigrew, here, are on bicycles. Where's Archie, then?'

'Standing right next to you, Stan.'

'Good God, is that you? You look like a funeral director.'

'Would you kindly bugger off? You're cramping our style. How are we doing for time, Clara?'

She fished her grandfather's watch from her pocket. 'Two minutes,' she said, importantly.

'You'd better hurry, officer. Where's your cab?'

'Mrs Price, is it? A real pleasure. I'm so sorry for your loss, ma'am.' Eliza gave him a tight smile and mouthed her thanks. 'It's not far. Yes, all right, I'm going, I'm going...'

They watched him lope across the road to the cab, unhitch the reins from the park railing and climb up into the driver's seat at the back. Then, taking his life in his hands, he drove across the busy main road, invoking the wrath of a grocery van and a man on horseback, to end up outside the police station. A flurry of blue wool and there was 'Nora' at the door, flanked by two uniformed men.

Archie felt slightly better now he knew there were three other policemen involved in the hunt.

The procuress, her blue hat with the Robin Hood feathers pinned securely to her head, limped to the cab and, before climbing aboard, looked right and left to ensure that no one was following. She didn't notice the mule nosing out from behind the police railings. The 'cabby', drawn up in the main road, paused a moment to tie a red-spotted handkerchief to the luggage rack.

'What's he doing?' Clara whispered to Archie, now ensconced in the driving seat, poised to snap the reins.

He turned his head briefly. 'It's so that we know which one to follow. There'll be scores of cabs on the road and it'll be easy to get them mixed up.'

Now!

The road was clear. Archie waited for the cyclists to take their place in the convoy and was about to nudge the mule into the main road when a new Mercedes automobile shot across them, doing at least ten miles an hour. Damned road hog. By the time they managed to turn into Forest Road, behind a coal truck, he knew he was way behind Beckett's cab.

Cursing his luck, he heard Clara behind muttering, 'Stick with it, Pops.' She was hanging over the side of the truck. 'They're about five in front.'

'Get back, get back, you'll have your head taken off!'

The coal truck peeled off down a side street, the motor car accelerated and overtook a *Watney, Combe & Reid* dray in front, with a wild braying of klaxons and yelled abuse from oncoming drivers. The horses skittered but the brewer's man got them under control and, after a few minutes, pulled up beside a public house to unload. Archie flicked the reins and Jessie, the mule, trotted smartly past. In front now was a milk cart and, in front of that, an omnibus which came to a stop to pick up some fares. They followed the milkman in passing it.

At the crossroads they lost sight of their cab. Damn.

'I can see it, I can see it!' yelled Clara, jumping up and down. 'The red handkerchief! Turn left, Pops. Left!'

'Sit down – sit down for Christ's sake! You'll have us over.'

'Language, Archie!'

'It's all right, sweetheart,' said Polly. 'I have hold of her.'

Archie rolled his eyes to heaven. Whose stupid idea was this?

From time to time they found either Hayward or Pettigrew astride their bicycles, waiting at the kerbside to give them directions:

'Target is five vehicles in front, Mister Price, waiting to cross Burdett Road.'

'Turn left at the Commercial Road, sir. She's directing him every which way.'

Of course, she was. Nora Whoever-she-was, was an intelligent woman. She knew she was being followed. She'd brought them this way deliberately to try and shake them off and it wouldn't be hard to do. As they neared the centre of London it became more difficult to see ahead. The sky was dark with unshed rain and the smoke from thousands of homes, factories, offices. Every building, every statue, every railway arch wore a coating of soot. And the traffic was impossible, the roads cracking under the weight of horse-driven wagons taking goods to and from the great London markets, petrol-driven automobiles – many more than Archie had seen in Walthamstow – bicycles, pedestrians. There might be the occasional policeman endeavouring to direct the traffic but they were few and far between and they seemed to make matters worse, if anything. There was a hold-up at every junction.

Without Clara's keen eye keeping track of the red handkerchief, he wouldn't have stood a chance. Every now and then they caught Beckett searching for them over the tops of carts, around omnibuses, and when he caught their eye he would give them a wave of encouragement.

Ahead of them now was a massive railway arch with trains racketing to and from the great terminus of Liverpool Street. Was that where the woman was heading? To the trains? Or not. Suddenly they saw Beckett signalling with his whip that he intended making a right turn. How, though? The traffic was chaotic. Where was this? Middlesex Street. Wasn't that an extension of the notorious Petticoat Lane? One of the cyclists looked over his shoulder in order to turn right also. But it was neither Hayward nor Pettigrew! Where had they gone? To add to the confusion, trains were thundering across the bridge in both directions. Archie moved in behind the cab, signalling right, and saw 'Nora's' pretty face framed in the cab's rear window. Jesus. He turned, making a show of speaking to his passengers. 'Now, Mam, this is the famous Petticoat Lane, so called because they'll steal your petticoat off you at this end of the street and sell it back to you at the other. Oh, come on, look interested, everyone! I'm just trying to see what's put the wind up our Nora. Oh right, she's spotted the cavalry – no, don't look round! So obviously one of Tyrell's plants!'

'Pops!' yelled Clara. 'Quick!'

He whirled around. Too late. She'd gone. The cab was empty.

'Beckett!' he called out. 'Where's your passenger?' But his voice disappeared on a puff of train smoke and a deafening clackety-clack of wheels on rails. At last they turned and found themselves in a ridiculous situation. There were market stalls on either side of the road, with carts and horses parked between them. Costermongers wheeled their barrows here and there, regardless, and heavily laden shoppers were trying to cross the road between the vehicles.

He felt an urgent tugging on his coat sleeve. Clara was pointing into the crowd where a bright blob of blue showed up in a patchwork of other colours.

'Polly, take over! I'll meet you at the train station – outside, where the carriages are drawn up.' His feet touched the ground and he was off, leaving her to take over the reins. Tall enough to see over the heads of the crowd, ducking round porters carrying three or four baskets of fruit and vegetables on their heads, he kept his eyes on the bobbing feathers, a maimed exotic bluebird, limping among the sparrows. Where was it going?

'Over there, Pops!'

Looking down he found a black-haired schoolgirl at his elbow. 'Bloody hell, Clara!' And hanging on *her* arm was Polly!

'Who's driving the bloody cart?'

'Eliza.'

He groaned at the thought of his dear mother, a stranger to these parts, still in her widow's weeds, struggling to find her way to the station. If he found this part of London daunting she'd be utterly lost. Oh glory, what a to-do!

318

'She said not to worry, she'll be fine. She'll ask the way.'

He breathed deeply. Fingers crossed, then. Because there went the blue feathers and they had to keep up. Linking arms with the girls he dragged them through the crowds, albeit with a polite 'Excuse me…' But they couldn't have come at a worse time. Buy this, buy that. Christmas is upon us.

'Oi, oi, what's yer rush?'

'Mind out, yous!'

'Looking for a Christmas tree, are you?'

''Ere y'are, lady dear, fresh oranges for the kids' stockings…'

''Ere, 'oo you shovin', mate?'

Once through the heaving crowds occupying the middle of the road and onto the pavement, it was a little easier. They could see her ahead and fell back a little.

'Even if we catch her meeting up with Ned Pike,' said Polly, 'what can we do? We can't arrest them. We need a policeman.'

'We're just here to find out where she goes and report back. We won't have to confront them – it's far too dangerous.'

A young man shouldered past, 'Sorry, mate.' Archie gave him a stiff smile. 'Nice try,' he muttered, knowing the pickpocket had been disappointed. His pockets were empty, apart from one inside that held a small sketchbook and pencil. His change was deep in his pinstripes under his coat and any paper money was tucked inside his slouch hat.

'I wish they'd stop looking at us like that.'

Archie glanced down at his stepdaughter, who was peering out from under a frown and biting her lip. 'Like what?' he said.

'Like they're sizing us up or something. Speculating.'

'Really? Are they?'

Polly nodded. 'They are, Archie, men *and* women. I wouldn't like to be down here on my own.'

'Well, you're not. Just keep hold of my arm – and you, Clara. Where's your watch, by the way?'

'Round my neck, Pops, under my blouse. No one's getting that.'

'Is your camera safe, Polly?' She rarely went anywhere without one.

'Next to my heart,' she said.

It had to be her latest purchase, a Kodak which concertinaed almost flat and slipped into her inside coat pocket almost without showing, a magical thing.

'Well,' he said. 'So far, so good. It's not so different from the High Street right now. Just hang on tight to your valuables. And your petticoats,' he added with a grin.

'It's not funny.'

The difference from the High Street, of course, was that all the vendors here were cheapjacks, many selling stolen goods. Pickpockets and cutpurses were everywhere – he'd been frisked twice to his knowledge – not to mention the fences, the opium addicts, the thugs. If someone looked a bit shady, they probably were. And the women propping up the walls, here and there, and giving him the eye – well, it was obvious what they were.

'Wasn't Jack the Ripper from round here?'

'Poll-eee…!'

'Just saying.'

'Well, keep close. Come on. Don't talk to anyone.'

He guessed that 'Nora' had come here, on purpose, to give any pursuers the slip, hoping they'd be delayed by crowds or theft or loss. They were a real danger. Nobody seemed to bother *her*, though. There she went, in her nice blue get-up, favouring her sore foot, perfectly at home.

Now she had stopped by a door in what looked like a warehouse and, by the time she'd looked to left and right to spot anyone tailing her, Polly and Clara, shawls over their heads, were deep in discussion about a piece of curtain material on a stall and Archie was tying his shoelace. When they stepped away to the stallholder's disgust, she'd gone. Damn. They'd lost her. Then Polly nudged him and pointed. She had her back to them, going up the steps of a corner cafe.

'Come on, Pops!'

'No, Clarrie. Don't follow her. That's just what she wants. Give her five minutes to check out she's not being shadowed.'

They amused themselves at a pet stall, outside, fussing over poor little scraps of puppies, taken too early from the bitch; most of them could hardly open their eyes. 'Stay there!' said Archie. 'Don't move! I'll just go and see...' Cautiously, he peered through the steamy cafe window into the dark and greasy murk of an interior. She wasn't there.

'Pops, Pops!' squealed Clara, and he jumped away just in time. 'This one, ple-ease!' Their quarry was standing on the cafe step, yards away, looking about.

'No, sweetheart, you can't have a dog for Christmas,' said Archie in his best fatherly tones. 'We don't have room for one, or time to walk it. It wouldn't be fair.' He lowered his voice. 'Now where's she gone?'

She'd crossed the road and was going back the way they'd come, on the opposite pavement, past stalls piled high with brightly coloured tins of biscuits, toys, mistletoe and holly wreaths, bonbons. They kept pace with her on their side of the street and followed at a distance – until she disappeared. They'd seen her approaching the second-hand shoe stall but failed to see her pass it. Crossing the road in a panic, they were relieved to see an alleyway leading away from the market. A flash of blue told them where to go, through endless grubby side streets until at last they emerged at the entrance to the great covered market of Spitalfields where fruit and vegetables were distributed, wholesale.

A large notice required visitors to report to an office near the entrance.

'I don't think we're allowed in here,' said Polly. 'Not ordinary shoppers.'

'Who's to say we aren't here on Bob Cheshire's behalf, buying a sack of beetroot for the shop? He can be ill and we're doing him a favour.'

'Suppose you need a special pass?'

'I'll brazen it out.'

'Hurry up or we'll lose her.' Clara was craning her neck in order to keep the blue hat in view.

He came back waving a chitty and they wandered in, otherwise ignored and unhindered. Everyone was far too busy to be bothered with them and, anyway, what harm could they do? Although they could smell fresh fruit and vegetables there weren't stalls of produce, no polished red apples on display, no trimmed cauliflowers. This was a wholesale market. Human beings were miniaturised inside a vast hall, which had vegetables in sacks as building blocks; they were lost among bulky towers of carrots, cathedrals constructed from crates of cabbages, boxes of radishes. You almost didn't need those iron girders to hold up the great roof, Clara whispered in awe; the sacks of potatoes, piled high, would do it for you.

The fresh, clean smell of fruit and vegetables mixed oddly with tobacco smoke and horse droppings. And something else – drains?

The big vegetable farmers – the ones who had cornered the market in Brussels sprouts or parsnips – stood about, in suits and spats and bowlers, doing deals involving high finance – or marriages of convenience, thought Archie – while their salesmen did the actual bargaining with buyers and their trainees. Fruiterers' carts clattered up and down the aisles over the cobbles to the loading bays. Porters in aprons and overalls balanced stacks of baskets on their heads or whizzed small-wheeled trolleys here and there and around obstacles, pausing only to light up a tab or to grab a cuppa from a tea boy. At the end of the hall, an auctioneer up on a podium, gabbled bids made on lots.

'Look, look!' said Polly, clutching Archie's sleeve. 'That pile of sacks over there. The red fern emblem!'

'That cart has it, too,' Clara noticed. 'And that one.'

'He's everywhere,' said Archie. 'Half the barges on the Lea bear his brand – and trains, soon, if he has his way.'

'That looks like his office, over there behind those barrows. I wonder if he's here today?' She looked up, momentarily, from her camera which was trained on the woman in blue. The murderess had stopped to talk to a man in a top hat and fur collar who had approached her. Was he a white slaver? Every one of her contacts was a suspect now.

'What's today, Tuesday? Hold on.' He went over to a scene of activity, where men were busy unloading sacks from a huge cart and piling them up. Polly and Clara could see him exchanging words with them. They seemed friendly. Indeed, they waved to the girls and they, bemused, waved back.

He came back to where they were waiting somewhat apprehensively. 'No, he hasn't been in all week – be here tomorrow – to doctor his diary, I shouldn't wonder. I said you were here taking photos of the market for a magazine and wanted to take theirs. The manager, over there, counting the sacks in, said they'd be delighted… Nice fella.'

Polly spluttered a feeble protest.

'Not right now, obviously. When we've got some idea what "Nora" is up to. They'll be here for ages yet. Best to come back when the pile is higher, they said.'

He glanced over at Redfern's office. 'I don't know why Frank's putting so much store by the market books. They can be cooked, same as any others. People can be bribed.'

'You think Redfern has something to hide?'

'I'm sure of it.' He explained that Redfern's alibi for Eleanor's murder was that he was here all day on the twenty-fifth of June last year, going about his business as usual. 'Tyrell's hoping that the office diary for that day says something different. It'll be well-nigh impossible to pin the murder on him otherwise. We reckon he's told us a pack of lies, but how to prove it? He's covered his tracks so well.'

'But he was so convincing as the distraught father, going around that suffragist meeting asking questions, organising searches.'

'That was when she'd run away from school and he didn't know where she was. He was desperately worried, then; he could see his merger with the railways going down the pan if she didn't show up. Then she came home, pregnant by a penniless gardener, and he threw her out. Sometime after that she turned up at Gil's lodgings, spent the night with him and the next day, the twenty-fifth, while Gil was at work, she was murdered.'

'Gil has an alibi, then?'

'Not for the evening. He was late coming back – he went to see his mother.'

'Did Redfern know that?'

'Couldn't have. Gil said it was on a whim. Frank thinks the old man must have visited Eleanor around the time Gil knocked off work that night. Nipped in quick, like. It was the only way he could do the deed and make it look like Gil had done it.'

'You think he intended to kill his daughter?'

'What – malice aforethought? Couldn't say. He might just have been hoping to change her mind. She was his most treasured possession. If she could be persuaded to leave Gil she might still have been some use to him, but if she couldn't, well…'

Polly looked up from her camera and planted a kiss on his cheek. He grinned.

'So, we're not treasured possessions?' asked Clara, innocently.

'Treasures you are but you belong to no one but yourselves,' he said.

Clara kissed his other cheek. 'Do you know you're far more handsome with black hair?' she said. 'You could be on the stage.'

'How can you be so sure of the date she died?' asked Polly.

'Gilbert Blackett told us.'

'You trust him?'

'Strangely, I do. He came forward of his own accord and confessed. Out of the blue…'

'Clever…' said the girl.

'Actually, you're right to be suspicious. All the same, while we're here, I think we should try and prove whether Redfern's lying. I mean, perhaps then, the motivation and the means will follow...'

'Uh-oh, here we go!' said Polly suddenly. 'Redfern will have to wait. "Nora's" on the move.' She was shaking the top-hatted man's hand now, taking her leave. 'Keep still, woman! Where are you going? I just need to ... Dammit, that'll be a blur.' Their quarry was limping on, around the long margins of the hall where dark-windowed offices and booths were built into the wall.

'Now!' said Clara. The woman had paused before a door without step, knocker or letter box. It did, however, have a keyhole and the murderess was fitting a key into it. The door opened and closed, swallowing her up, but not before Polly had captured her profile, three times, on film.

'Right, you stay here. I'll go and find a policeman.'

'And a telephone box.'

'Got some pennies, Archie?'

The two uniformed constables he found, bored with plodding the aisles and watching for trouble, nevertheless took some convincing that Archie was who he said he was, despite his police pass. However, they agreed to accompany him to the police telephone box (for which, as a trustee, he had a key), and talk to Tyrell, back in Walthamstow, about the case. It was one of the old-fashioned 'Glasgow-style' boxes and there was standing room only for one at a time. After giving Frank a progress report, he stood in the doorway as Tyrell filled the more senior Shoreditch policeman in on the story and told him what he wanted him to do.

'He wants to talk to you again.'

They swopped places. 'Bad news, I'm afraid, boyo. Ephraim Mortimer has just confirmed that Redfern dined with him on the evening of the twenty-fifth and that afterwards they'd taken themselves off to the Savoy to see *Merrie England.*'

'Bugger. That's put him in the clear, then. I guess Mortimer wants the contract with Redfern, with or without a bride.'

'Looks like it.'

'Right you are, then, Frank.' He put the phone down thoughtfully, leaving PC Richards to call up his own station and explain what was needed.

Ten minutes later, a dozen uniformed policemen arrived. 'Nora' was still inside the building with the unmarked door.

'These are the people we're interested in,' said Archie, showing them his drawings of Edward Pike and his lady friend.

'I'm sure I've seen him around. And her!' exclaimed Richards. 'Blimey, these are them to the life! May I?' He continued idly flipping the pages of the sketchbook. 'You're good, you know. Oh look, Albert Chevalier.' He'd come upon Archie's preliminary sketches for the Palace mural. He broke into song, '*We been together now for forty…*' breaking off suddenly to exclaim, 'Now I know *him*! Mickey Markov and his Algernon! Never goes anywhere without it. Like a baby with its dummy. Different sort of dummy, heh, heh! But they say he's good. You never see his lips move.'

Archie was doubtful. Mickey Markov might be good at his craft but he was dire as an entertainer.

'How do you know him, then?' Polly asked the policeman.

'He's local. Got a place just around the corner in Lamb Street. Loads o' players live down there. It's cheap and cheerful and close to all the music halls in London. That there,' he waved his hand in the general direction of the door 'Nora' had used, 'is the back of their house.'

Mickey Markov, eh? What a coincidence! Mickey Markov, the drunken ventriloquist! Was that the connection?

But Archie didn't have time to follow the thought as the police were positioning themselves strategically, some in the market and some in Lamb Street. Any minute now they'd strike.

'Leave it ten minutes, would you, fellas?' Archie had a plan. 'Right, follow me, ladies. I'll explain on the way.'

He pushed open the door to Redfern's glass-fronted office, and Polly followed, leaving Clara keeping watch outside. They found a lone clerk holding the fort, pinioning paid bills onto a metal spike and laboriously dipping his pen and making entries in a fat ledger.

He looked up. 'Can I help you?'

'We're here to take your photograph for the *Graphic*. We've just taken one of your manager and the crew, unloading a lorry, and he sent us over here to take one of the office.'

The clerk frowned, trying to gauge the truth behind those inscrutable amber eyes.

'Just give them a wave and they'll tell you.'

Squinting with disbelief, the young man walked to the door and yelled, 'Ay, ay, fellas! You had your photo done?' They must have given him the thumbs up because he came back in, combing his hair slickly back from his centre parting and straightening his tie. Polly walked around the office, looking purposeful, framing the clerk in an oblong made with a thumb and finger of each hand.

'Oh, here's just lovely – sorry I don't know your name – oh, John. If you would just carry on with your work, John, and look up when I tell you... Yes, yes – now look up! Wonderful! And one more... Good. Do you think we could have one outside? I'd like to get the firm's banner behind you.'

Just as soon as Archie was left alone in the shop he located the relevant ledger on a shelf and heaved it onto the clerk's desk. He could hear Polly begging for just one more and the clerk complaining.

Lord, Polly, wind the film on slowly – hold him there for a few minutes more...

Just in time, Clara came running up to draw their attention to a police raid over the way. 'You've got to get a photo of this, Polly, there's dozens of 'em bashing the door down!' And of course, the clerk was on tiptoe, trying to see over the heads of a gathering crowd, giving Archie time to find the twenty-fifth of June in the book, and to carefully tear out the page. Last year's Diary was safely back on its shelf and Archie was craning his own neck to see the action, by the time the unsuspecting young man remembered his neglected desk.

'D'you see who they got?' he asked the tall man from the *Graphic* whose perch on the doorstep gave him a perfect view.

'Some longshanks with his arm in a sling,' said Archie, quietly congratulating himself. It looked as though the bullet he'd fired at Pike had hit its target, after all. 'And there's a smaller chap with dark hair and a tash. I know his face... He's on the halls, I think. They're both looking the worse for wear, bound in handcuffs. Now they're bringing out a woman, pretty little thing but spitting tacks...'

'That'll be Mr and Mrs Marks, I reckon. He does a ventriloquist act in his spare time, under the name of Markov. Runs this domestic staff agency otherwise. Gets lots of foreigners coming in, looking for help. Wonder what they've been up to?'

Archie moved to let the young man go past and resume his seat. 'They're loading them into the Black Maria now,' he reported. 'You reckon the longshanks is one of their customers, then, do you?'

'What, has he got a face like a codfish, then?'

'You could say that.'

'Don't know his name but he's here a lot. Could be an interpreter or something.'

Or something. 'Tch, my fiancée and her scoops!' he said, proudly. 'She'll be snapping away all day and no dinner hour at this rate. Using up all her film. I'd better go. Thanks for your help, John. Merry Christmas!'

'Don't mention it!'

'Don't forget – the *Graphic*. Should be in next week's edition.' (Or the next one. They'd taken Polly's work in the past.)

They found Eliza and the mule trap drawn up, quite properly, in the station forecourt. A porter was feeding Jessie carrots. 'Oh, here they are,' she cried. 'And what's that, a Christmas tree! How lovely. Did you get what you wanted?'

'Uh-uh – yes, killed three birds with one stone.'

She smiled encouragingly, trying to read their smug faces, but she would have to wait until they were on the road for an update.

A busy railway station was not the place. Clara, however, was bursting with news with which she regaled her grandmother immediately.

'Oh Granny, they had these darling little puppy dogs in the market and there was one with really long floppy ears and...'

'No! Don't go on about it, Clara, you're not having one!'

Clara slumped in the cart, arms folded crossly, refusing to speak until they were halfway home when she simply had to join in the conversation and give her version.

'So, Pops timed it to coincide with the police raid on the house and I had to rush into the office and say, 'Quick, quick!' and the man rushed out to look while Pops ripped a page out of their last year's diary, and it proves that Mister Redfern didn't go near their flipping office that day last year. There were all these things he was meant to do all crossed out and all these arrows making new appointments. NO SHOW was written in red and signed by the clerk. So that's his alibi up the spout! The police are going to throw the book at him, Granny.'

'Well, isn't that wonderful? And what about the woman, "Nora"? Did you manage to track her down?'

'Of course. We're brilliant sleuths, we are. We found out her surname, too, Granny, she's Mrs Marks, and she's married to this creepy ventriloquist Pops knows. They're both despicable people, he says, and, anyway, we followed her to this strange little door in the market wall and Pops called out a whole squad of coppers and they broke it down – and Polly took loads of photos that she's going to send to Bart Spratt – he's this lovely newspaperman in Chelmsford that we know – and this other policeman, he had Mrs Marks in handcuffs and she spat at him, and the other coppers dragged out Mister Marks and some other creepy-looking man and they were both swearing and carrying on and they slung them in the back of the Black Maria and drove off and then we all had to go to the police station down the road and make statements. And Pops bought a Christmas tree as they were going cheap.'

Archie wasn't sure his mother needed to be told much more than this. But that evening, when Clara was in bed, Frank Tyrell came by to tell them that Shoreditch had found enough useful evidence in the house to put the Markses and Edward Pike away for years.

It transpired that Markov, as he called himself, was Secretary of the Ventriloquist Club of Great Britain – and Edward Pike, one of the members. That was how they'd got together in the first place. How they'd discovered they had child-trafficking interests in common was anybody's guess. Archie thought it might be something you'd want to keep strictly to yourself, but then, these were people unlike any he'd ever come across.

'Little love,' said Polly, 'what a sheltered life you've led!'

'We don't have child molesters in Llantwit, you see,' explained her future mother-in-law. 'We keep busy.'

Archie gave her a strangled look. 'Right,' he said.

There were other folders and files, Tyrell told them, and a Remington 6 typewriter with a wonky *t* which the police immediately confiscated.

Even if they weren't child molesters, themselves, the Markses had discovered how to turn the weaknesses of many others to their advantage. They must have made a fortune.

Hopefully, they would all be behind bars for a very long time, always supposing Mrs Marks lasted the month. Women prisoners wouldn't take kindly to having a child-trafficker in their number. She might think that hanging was preferable to the punishment they would mete out. He was hopeful they'd get a confession out of her yet.

Meanwhile their clients would be hunted down and prosecuted and their victims returned to their families, where possible. Though if this horrible practice had been going on for years, as they feared it might have, many of the girls would be women by now and might prefer to be left alone.

'Including JW, the original one, whoever she is…'

'Or he is…'

'Or was,' said Polly. 'Poor soul. Don't suppose we'll ever know now.'

Where would they go, after all? What would they do? Poor souls. They'd be – *changed* – wouldn't they? Their families would be hard pressed to recognise them, let alone love them. Perhaps they'd go up north or somewhere remote, start a new life or maybe the Sally Army would take them in. Or maybe they'd prefer to stay where they were, doing what they were doing. If they'd been taken abroad there wasn't much anybody here could do for them, anyway. God, thought Archie, they'd be better off dead.

Twenty-seven

The train pulled into Hoe Street Station and a dozen men and women stepped out, looking around the sooty little platform with interest. They handed in their tickets and asked for directions. In twos and threes they hurried down the High Street to Palmerston Road, finding their way, eventually to Forest Road.

'There it is,' said Higgins, the butler, indicating a building fronting the main road, 'with the blue lamp.' In they trooped.

'Is this where you're keeping Mister Elias Redfern?'

'Who wants to know?' demanded the desk sergeant.

'We're his household staff. We've come to set the record straight.'

Elias Redfern, in the cells down the corridor, heard the voice of his housekeeper, and, for a happy instant, thought that she'd come to bail him out.

Detective Inspector Tyrell was summoned.

'I have to warn you, you could all be prosecuted,' he said, after he'd heard that they wanted to change their stories. 'Obstructing the course of justice is an offence punishable by imprisonment.'

They were adamant. They'd brooded on this for over a year, suffered sleepless nights and pangs of conscience, been unable to look each other in the eye. Yesterday, the butler had brought the newspaper down to the kitchen and showed them the pictures and read the article aloud. The Master had been found out. The police had photographs of a page in his diary disproving his alibi. He hadn't been where he said he'd been and they were beginning to think he knew more about Miss Eleanor's death than he was letting on.

Blackie was one of their own: he'd grown up on the estate. They knew he wouldn't have hurt Miss Eleanor for the world. If they lied for Elias Redfern, as he'd asked them to – well, threatened them, really, with the sack – the boy still might hang, and they'd be responsible and that wouldn't do. So, weighing self-interest and loyalty to their employer against the truth, they'd decided to come clean.

The housekeeper stated that she had opened the door to Eleanor that evening – the nineteenth of June, that would have been – and the cook had warmed up some supper for her. Down in the kitchen they'd heated water for her bath, the footman had brought it up to the bathroom and the upstairs maid, Maria, had prepared it for her and, afterwards, found her clean clothes and towelled and brushed her hair dry. After supper, a contingent of maids and footmen had been outside the door, waiting to clear away, when Eleanor had told her father that Gil, 'Blackie' as they knew him, was the father of her unborn child. Several of them, including the housekeeper, had overheard the commotion when Master had thrown the girl out into the stony front yard, calling her a hussy or words to that effect, and told her she was no daughter of his. The door had slammed and Mister Redfern had called them all to him.

'You will forget this night,' he'd instructed them. 'This never happened. If any of you so much as breathes a word, a single word, even to each other, you will be sent packing just like her. I will not know you. I will not pay you. I will certainly not write you a character reference. Is that clear?'

Perfectly. So, they had bitten their tongues. And when, some days later, the twenty-fifth, he had ridden out alone, no one had asked where to, and when he rode back that same evening, in a right old state, trembling and white, nobody asked where he had been. When the laundry maid had had to wash his bloody clothes and handkerchief, knowing that it was either Miss Eleanor's blood

333

she was soaking off in the tub or Blackie's, she had gritted her teeth and carried on scrubbing. When the boot boy had to clean blood off the Master's boots, he tried to convince himself it was from some game bird or rabbit. The stable boy may have asked the horse about the blood on the saddle and on his heaving flanks but he didn't speak to anyone else about it.

A year had gone by. Cook stopped going to church. She couldn't live a lie, she confessed to God in her prayers every night. Maria cried into her pillow. She'd wanted to leave but the Master wouldn't allow it. She was trapped. Only the housekeeper and the butler talked about it, quietly, when everyone else had gone to bed. If Miss Eleanor was dead, nothing would bring her back, and they had their positions to think of. It would blow over eventually. When the poster had gone up showing the girl's likeness and asking for information, they feigned surprise and ignorance. They were getting good at this.

'Fancy poor Miss Eleanor turning up in the Lea like any old rubbish!' they'd remark to friends and neighbours in the village. 'How'd she fetch up there, I wonder? Oh yes, the Master's beside himself with grief.'

With each other they dared to suppose. 'D'you think the Master…?' 'What, his own flesh and blood? Don't even think about it.' 'Right you are, then.'

But yesterday's news had put a different complexion on everything. The Master had been found out; he'd be hanged and his staff now saw a chance to redeem themselves. And if they went to prison for changing their earlier statements, well, so be it.

'What do you mean – earlier statements?' said Tyrell. 'I don't recall any earlier statements, do you, Stanley?'

Tyrell let Gil go and asked Redfern, in the presence of his solicitor, whether he wanted to change his story in the light of what his staff had to say. He asked again, 'Did your daughter come and see you on the evening of the nineteenth of June last year?'

'No comment.'

'Where did you go on the twenty-fifth of June last year?'

'No comment.'

'Too bad, Mister Redfern. We're arresting you for the murder of your daughter, Eleanor Redfern. You do not have to say anything. But, it may harm your defence if you do not mention when questioned something which you later rely on in court. Anything you do say may be given in evidence.'

Later, when they questioned the bar staff at the Fish and Eels the landlord recalled the gentleman in the photograph enquiring after Gilbert Blackett early in the evening on the twenty-fifth and remembered directing him to the room upstairs. They didn't notice him leave but, by then, a ceilidh was in full swing and he could easily have crept out the back way, without being seen. He didn't buy a drink, certainly.

Ephraim Mortimer also changed his story. He remembered now. He had waited for Redfern a full ten minutes before curtain-up and had been obliged to sit through the whole of *Merrie England* on his own, joining in the singing of an ironic 'Yeomen of England' alone in his box. A sorry state of affairs. He hadn't knowingly lied to the police; he would never do such a thing. He had simply got his dates muddled up. It was some amateur production of *Die Fledermaus* they'd seen, together, at the Shoreditch Town Hall, the week before. An easy mistake to make in a busy life.

Twenty-eight

Percy had been furious. 'You can't change it *now!* We're opening Monday!'

'Do you really want a white slaver in your foyer, Perce, scrutinising your customers for a likely lass, twice-nightly?'

'Bloody hell, Archie, he's in the top row. I'll have to get the scaffolders back, and everything.'

'I can probably manage with a stepladder.'

'What, palette in one hand, brushes in the other, and nowhere to put your turps? Knowing you, you'd fall off and break your neck and make a mess all over my new carpet!' He paused for breath. 'Who you gonna put in his place?'

'Thinking I'd put you up there – Percy Reeves, impresario.'

'What!'

'Why not? You've as much right up there as anyone. You're an act in yourself, banging your gavel, holding it all together. And it is your baby, after all, this theatre – your idea, you saw it through. The architects and builders have their stone tablet, the backers have their plaques but there's no mention of you, the creative force.'

'Oh … I, er … oh…' He blinked, clearly mollified. 'If you think so.'

So now here he was, up aloft, putting the finishing touches to Percy's comb-over. He'd put the two of them there: Percy in Markov's place and Bertha where the manikin had been. She was, after all, the power behind the throne. Knowing them so well, he could almost paint them blindfold. An hour or two, that was all it took. Just a touch more rouge on Bertha's soft cheeks, a highlight on Percy's spectacles, here, and here, and a couple of dabs of white on Bertha's jet beads, and, oh yes, a bit of cream brushwork to repair the background where he'd scraped it back to eradicate Markov and … there it was. Done.

Almost.

There was something not quite right about that curtain fringe…

As he peered closer he could see letters painted in the shadows between the tightly-twisted golden cords that made up the fringe and tassels of the rich velvet drapes – the frame within a frame, painted to resemble the massive stage curtains. What had she done – the witch?

It started here with an S, then a cord, an O, another cord, a P, and so on, every space containing a letter, spelling out her name. Miss Hudson had made sure her contribution to the painting would be immortalised. The paint was quite dry. She must have done this weeks ago, when the original scaffolding was up, probably before he had signed the painting himself. Cheeky little minx! Then he found himself squinting. Surely…? The negative space between this rather crooked cord and the next formed a recognisable shape. An optical illusion. Her profile! And the next, facing inwards, his profile, the lips puckered for a kiss! Dear God! She had worked overtime to make her point!

He could see her smiling in triumph at her small revenge, her dimples coming and going, her frown of determination as she put her stamp on the massive picture. He didn't know what to call it. Vandalism? Graffiti? He supposed he could paint over it – he had the cream paint mixed up.

Though why not just leave it? She just wanted to have her part in the painting recognised. He could see the time coming when women all over the country would be doing as much, if not worse, to assert their rights. And anyway, you'd need a telescope to spot the clever signature from the ground. He left it.

'Show me, show me!' Polly was leaning over his shoulder as he folded the broadsheet into a manageable square. He pushed his plate and knife, sticky with marmalade, out of the way and, with his other hand pulled her onto his lap, loving the shape of her beneath her dressing gown, smooth and rounded.

The headlines ran, **Grand Opening of the Walthamstow Palace,** and, underneath, their friend's name, *Bartholomew Spratt,* beside Archie's etching of the now famous landmark with its twin turrets and with a flag flying from each.

'Gosh, a whole half page!' she remarked. 'When did he get time to write all this? He seemed to spend the entire evening downing pints and toadying around the big names. Effie was quite put out.'

'Really? Seemed to me she was all over that skinny young man in Fred Karno's troupe – the one they call Stanley something – Laurel, was it? And Bart didn't stay for the show – he had his train to catch. Any case, I think he'd probably written up the bones of it before he came. I mean, all this –' he ran his finger over the words, '– *English Renaissance style ... imposing elevation ...* blah, blah, blah – *iron and glass awning ... spacious vestibule ...* is what I sent him ages ago. And waxing lyrical about the cream and crimson decor, polished walnut wood, I'll wager he didn't even notice it for the stars in his eyes. Oh, here we go – Marie Lloyd, Little Tich, Hettie King – what did I tell you? He does love to drop names.'

Polly took the wadded newspaper from him. 'What does he say about your picture? My giddy aunt, a whole paragraph! Oh, Archie, he's done you proud. Listen to this...' She read aloud, '*Dominating the foyer, a truly unique and fascinating artwork by the renowned local artist, Archibald Price, in celebration of British music hall talent. I confess to knowing very little about art but I know what I like and, judging from their excitement, their delight, so did many of my fellow guests who found themselves depicted in the gigantic painting. Not only has Price caught every one of their likenesses to a T, he has avoided making it look like a company photograph by getting them to interact, hold conversations with each other. Marie Lloyd is pointing (up to the gallery, presumably); Vesta Tilly is tipping her hat to Florrie Ford and Dan Leno and Little Tich are sharing a joke, so each artiste becomes an interesting, animated part of the whole, which is, after all, what music hall is all about… To quote Miss Kitty Flanagan…'* Oh no, not blooming Kitty Flanagan! She must have her say! We all know he's painted you before, my lady. You should see *my* lovely portrait! Sorry, Archie, but she makes me cross…' she cleared her throat and concluded, *'So, if you're in the mood for a post-Christmas treat, buy yourself some tickets for one of the twice-nightly performances at the Walthamstow Palace, and be sure to allow plenty of time to spend studying this masterpiece of an attraction. It will bring pleasure to your hearts.'*

'Oh Lord, how much had he had to drink?' muttered Archie. 'Over the top, or what?'

'He loves you, Archie.' She picked up his hand, turned it over and kissed the palm. 'As do I.'

He put his lips to the back of her neck and she turned her face to him. Not so bony these days, he noticed, though she had pushed her egg away this morning, the shell still half-full. And she hadn't eaten any toast. He shook his head. He couldn't remember her drinking that much last night. She didn't look as if she was suffering from a hangover. Her cheeks were quite pink, her eyes the colour of smoke. He shifted in his chair to accommodate her, and the rest of the article, waxing lyrical about the layout of the theatre, the cutting-edge fixtures and fittings, was lost to them.

Only later, when Polly had gone to fill the tin bath, was he able to read the final paragraph, which mentioned *Jail Birds* by the Fred Karno Company, the show which all the guests (except Bart) had trooped in to see and which would be running for three more weeks.

There was a brief mention of Percy's big night in the *Stage* but nothing like so fulsome a piece as Bart's and Archie was just searching for the relevant section in the day's copy of *The Times* when Polly reappeared, scrubbed and fetching in her shift, to hurry him along. There were two funerals to attend today and they had less than two hours to get themselves over to Tottenham. How he hated funerals.

Higgins, the butler, came back to usher them to a pew towards the front of the church, where there was more room. The rest of the congregation were, perhaps, a little shy of appearing to have too close a connection with a girl who was, after all, the daughter of a murderer. The whole occasion, some felt, was – well, somehow unseemly, certainly uncomfortable. What did one say, after all? And to whom? 'Sorry for your loss' didn't quite seem to cover it.

One or two loyal friends had come from the village along with Eleanor's old schoolteacher, Miss Prescott, and Polly thought the two fashionably dressed young ladies at the back might have been from the school in Ipswich. Redfern's household staff filled a central pew and a sprinkling of the grounds staff, along with Walter Blackett and his wife, sat behind. (Gilbert's invitations, it seemed, had not included any of Redfern's business associates, and why would they?)

Sitting in the front pew, a meaty-looking chap in a shiny black suit, an *Albert* Redfern, represented what was left of the girl's family, though he turned in his seat to confess to Archie that he hadn't seen the girl since she was a toddler. He'd last visited Tottenham, he said, when his cousin, Elias, was just starting out. Just two greenhouses Elias had had, then, that was all, and a happy family life with his lovely wife, Jeannie, and their baby girl. He shook his head, sagely. 'Great oaks from little acorns...' he murmured in his soft accent, and, from the way he frowned and pressed his lips together, Archie guessed that the man was questioning what his cousin had become. Although he was the sole heir to the estate, he said, he was not planning to move from Somerset when – he lowered his voice – Redfern was no more. There was nothing for him here. He was a blacksmith by trade, specialising in wrought iron. (Archie had already noted the man's

340

large, work-worn hand lying across the back of the pew.) Maybe he would now send some of his railings and window boxes to London, but other than that…

He was putting the estate into the hands of the legal people (he nodded across the aisle to two gentlemen whose impartial manner and smart attire smacked of last wills and testaments). He was not in the least bit interested in growing salad. Presumably, thought Archie, Ephraim Mortimer was. He noticed the man sneak in just now, to sit at the back of the church and await developments. Otherwise why bring a briefcase into church?

At last an elderly vicar appeared, the organ struck up a dirge and the coffin, borne by Gilbert Blackett and his brothers, made its way to the front of the church. It handled lightly as they placed it carefully on the bier.

It was a short service, much to everyone's relief. Only the vicar spoke and he made no reference to the circumstances of Eleanor's death, keeping only to reminiscences of the girl he'd known, her attendance in church and her visits to the vicarage to take tea with his daughter. Then came the old words, the Gospel promises: *'I am the Resurrection and the Life. He that believeth in me, though he were dead, yet shall he live…'*

The words brought tears to Archie's eyes as he recalled Lizzie's funeral service some ten years earlier. She and their child were buried together. Polly squeezed his hand and offered him her handkerchief.

Blackett confessed to Archie afterwards that he was only happy he was able, at last, to bury his love and their baby in consecrated ground.

'But…' Archie began and stopped, given Polly's scowl and the smallest shake of her head. Lord, how her lovely eyes took on that luminous turquoise when she was perturbed. She was right, of course. Gilbert hadn't seen Eleanor's grisly remains. He wouldn't know that the foetus had been washed away. Though, maybe he did. The boy was no fool.

'Mister Blackett … Gilbert, I – I'm so sorry – this must be very painful for you. I know what you're … I know you've suffered a terrible loss, and I, for one, completely understand why you panicked and did what you did.'

The young man nodded, his face ravaged by tears. 'That's kind. I – I don't know what I was thinking,' he admitted, sniffing and wiping his nose. 'Sorry.' He sighed heavily. 'I suppose I imagined the brambles multiplying, blossoming, fruiting, making her and our child one with nature.'

'What a lovely thought,' Polly said with a polite smile. 'Maybe you can plant one here, or a tree…'

Archie grunted, remembering the package they'd brought. 'We – my daughter and I – and Polly here – we thought that you should have this –,' he said, handing over the box containing the replica of Eleanor's head. 'As a memento, I suppose, a poor substitute, I'm afraid. Perhaps a tree would have been better.' He told the boy what it was, how and why it had been made. 'Don't open it until you get home,' he advised. 'And make sure you're sitting down with a glass of whisky to hand. I don't know whether you'll think it like her. Whether it is or it isn't, I imagine it'll be upsetting.'

They did not stay for the wake.

The contrast with Lilian's funeral was remarkable. Marsh Street Congregational was packed to the gunnels with friends and family of the deceased. The coffin was smothered in Michaelmas daisies and holly. Never mind that she had committed suicide; she'd had good cause.

That damned woman.

Eulogies came thick and fast, praising Lilian's virtues, her good humour, her kindness, her swimming achievements.

Archie felt a stirring of movement at his elbow and, to his surprise, Clara stood up. She had begged them to be allowed to come, even if it meant leaving her new puppy dog behind. She'd called him 'Huckleberry', of course. 'Huck', for short.

She cleared her throat. 'Can I say something?'

'Yeah, go on – atta girl!' Izzy Steggles was fond of Lilian's friend.

She walked quickly to the front of the church before she lost her nerve. She had no notes.

'Um … well, like a few people have said already, I – I feel I let Lilian down badly. I should have seen what was going on. I should've. I knew the woman was weird but I…' her voice trailed off. *Go on*, urged Archie, silently. She looked up and her eyes fixed on his. She took a breath. 'But I didn't understand.' Her voice gained strength. 'And Lilian never said. I could have told my Pops. He'd have stopped it and she would still be alive today. But she didn't – she was too ashamed, though it wasn't her fault at all. Instead, she went into the forest and topped herself – stopped it in the only way she knew how.' She closed her eyes and swallowed hard.

She could see it, Archie knew. Everyone could. That tree, that dressing gown cord looping around her neck. They could feel Lilian's fear, her despair, her determination. Polly's fingers squeezed his, her nails digging in as she willed Clara to carry on. All around, mouths tightened, knuckles whitened, breaths quickened.

'I know that part of the forest,' she went on at last. 'I used to go there with Lil and – and we worked out the best way to climb the trees.' She coughed. 'Those oak trees, they're beautiful, tall and majestic. If you climb up high you can see right over the forest to the reservoirs, and then the river. I hope they don't chop them down to make ships' masts and roof beams and whatnot because it's there the squirrels have their nests. They like to eat the acorns.' She blinked and frowned, as if she was wondering what to say next. Her mouth twisted. 'I'm not going to stop going there just because…' she frowned and shook her head. 'I'll go and remember it was her favourite place. She'll always be there for me. And the squirrels, the red squirrels, have exactly the same colour hair that Lil had.' Then she dropped her head, blushing furiously, and scurried back to rejoin her family. Eliza gave her granddaughter a hug. 'Brave girl,' she whispered. 'Well done.' Someone in the pew behind patted her shoulder and Aunty Vi, in front, turned to give her a big-toothed grin. Everyone else was wiping their eyes or sobbing into their handkerchiefs.

Afterwards, the entire congregation followed the coffin, carried in a fruiterer's cart, through the High Street and up Church Hill, past the school, stopping all the other traffic, to St Mary's for burial (Marsh Street Congregational having no graveyard). A forgiving patch of un-consecrated ground on the north side, near the iron railing, had been found for Lilian, a suicide. At the wake in the *Nag's Head*, where sausage rolls and sandwiches were the order of the day, with tea or beer to wash them down, Polly came up to Archie and said, 'Look at you, the proud dad. You've not taken your eyes off her since we came out of church.'

'I didn't know – I had no idea she was going to do that. Or that she could. She has hidden depths.'

Polly raised her eyebrows over her teacup. 'I've something to tell you when we get home.'

'Tell me now.'

'No, no. It's Lilian's time now, and Clara's.'

'Poll-ee!'

'Really, you'll be glad I didn't tell you here.'

'God, woman, what is it? You're bursting with it! You've won a photographic competition? You've found a house for us?'

'Nope. You'll never guess.'

And so it was, when they were walking back down Orford Road, hand in hand, behind Eliza Price and her step-granddaughter, that Archie was suddenly moved to stop in his tracks and stare at his darling girl, whose amazing eyes were sparkling bright and whose cheeks were flushed.

'I thought you couldn't,' he said.

'Well, apparently I can.'

'Oh that's…' he began, and frowned a little, thinking of Lizzie and what had happened to her.

'Archie, stop it.' She'd read his mind. 'Lightning never strikes twice.'

'No, you're absolutely right!' he said joyfully, picking her up and swinging her round and round, while her hat tugged at its pins and her best black coat flew out, revealing a red silk petticoat.

'Put me down! Put me down, you great fool!' she shrieked, beating at him with her handbag, causing everyone to stand and gawp.

'What is it,' his mother demanded, 'or can I guess?'

'What's up, Pops?'

'Not here! Not here! I'll race you home!'

With that unfair advantage he set off at a pelt, down the hill, followed by Clara, followed by Polly.

'I knew it,' said Eliza to herself, with a hop and a skip to catch up. 'They'll have to bring the wedding forward.'

Also in the Archie Price Victorian Mystery series and available from Honno

The Colours of Corruption

Mary, a cleaner, is a witness to murder. Archie, one of the first artists to work for the police, draws the man she says she saw. Archie persuades Mary to sit for a portrait, but the man who buys the picture would rather buy Mary herself, putting them both in jeopardy and linking his wealthiest clients, the grimmest slums and dangerous secrets. Jacqueline Jacques paints an intricate, vibrant picture of the myriad layers of Victorian London.

"*The story moves fast among crimes of greed and lust… a fast-paced, colourful, well-planned story…*" The Historical Novel Society

The Illusion of Innocence

Three people on a crowded train, brought there by the same crime. Archie Price, painter and police artist, is travelling to Chelmsford to testify in a murder trial. The accused, Freddie Porter, is under police escort in the guard's van. Freddie's sister, Polly, is desperately trying to escape her brother's gang before they realise what she's done, unaware he's on the same train. Then the locomotive is derailed, Archie and Polly are injured, and Polly is driven to desperate measures.

"*Perfect amount of mystery, thrills and suspense mingled with a light romance undertone. Fantastic ending.*" Raven Haired Girl

Jacqueline Jacques was born in Anglesey, North Wales but, having a close affinity with post-war Walthamstow, East London and nearby Epping Forest, is moved to set her novels in the area she knows best.

Her working life as a teacher came to an end when the itch to write full-time became unbearable. Since then she has called herself a 'writer' though, nowadays, she finds other interests jostling for her attention, her long-suffering husband, Peter, not least among them. She busies herself, in shielded lockdown, with painting, crafting, working in the garden and on the allotment, attempting to convene the Buckhurst Hill U3A Bookclub on Zoom, and keeping their Creative Writing Group up to speed via email. Then, there are family and friends to enjoy, at a safe social distance, via WhatsApp and Zoom. Sadly, travel, holidays, theatre, concerts and art galleries are now relegated to being virtual pursuits. But the writing goes on, come heat wave or the hell of pandemic, while there's breath in her body and juice in her iPad.

ABOUT HONNO

Honno Welsh Women's Press was set up in 1986 by a group of women who felt strongly that women in Wales needed wider opportunities to see their writing in print and to become involved in the publishing process. Our aim is to develop the writing talents of women in Wales, give them new and exciting opportunities to see their work published and often to give them their first 'break' as a writer. Honno is registered as a community co-operative. Any profit that Honno makes is invested in the publishing programme. Women from Wales and around the world have expressed their support for Honno. Each supporter has a vote at the Annual General Meeting. For more information and to buy our publications, please write to Honno at the address below, or visit our website: www.honno.co.uk

Honno, D41 Hugh Owen Building, Penglais Campus,
Aberystwyth University, Aberystwyth, SY23 3DY

Honno Friends

We are very grateful for the support of all our Honno Friends.
For more information on how
you can become a Honno Friend, see:
https://www.honno.co.uk/about/support-honno/